A THREE DOG PROBLEM

S. J. Bennett wrote several award-winning books for teen-
agers before turning to adult mysteries. She lives in London
and has been a royal-watcher for years, but is keen to stress
that these are works of fiction: the Queen, to the best of her
knowledge, does not secretly solve crimes.

You can find her at SJBennettBooks.com for all things crime
and royal, on Instagram @sophiabennett_writer and on
Twitter @sophiabennett.

To receive Royal Correspondence about the Her Majesty
the Queen Investigates series – including royal family trivia
and more – sign up at bit.ly/SJBennett

Also by S. J. Bennett in the Her Majesty the
Queen Investigates series

The Windsor Knot

Her Majesty The Queen
Investigates

A THREE
DOG PROBLEM

S. J. Bennett

ZAFFRE

First published in the UK in 2021
This edition published in 2022 by
ZAFFRE
An imprint of Bonnier Books UK
4th Floor, Victoria House, Bloomsbury Square, London WC1B 4DA
Owned by Bonnier Books
Sveavägen 56, Stockholm, Sweden

A CIP catalogue record for this book is
available from the British Library.

Paperback ISBN: 978–1–83877–484–4
Hardback ISBN: 978–1–83877–482–0
Trade paperback ISBN: 978–1–83877–483–7

Also available as an ebook and an audiobook

3 5 7 9 10 8 6 4 2

Typeset by IDSUK (Data Connection) Ltd
Printed and bound in Great Britain by Clays Ltd, Elcograf S.p.A.

Zaffre is an imprint of Bonnier Books UK
www.bonnierbooks.co.uk

This book was written before the death of Prince Philip on April 9, 2021, at the age of 99. It is dedicated to him with affection and respect for a life well lived. And not a little nervousness. Would he have laughed and chucked it across the room with an exasperated grin? I hope he would.

Part 1

Sangfroid

'I will show your illustrious lordship what a woman can do.'
Artemisia Gentileschi, 1593–c.1654

OCTOBER 2016

Prologue

Sir Simon Holcroft was not a swimmer. As a trainee pilot in the Royal Navy, about a thousand years ago, the Queen's Private Secretary had endured being dunked in the water on various training exercises. He could, if necessary, escape from a sinking helicopter in the Atlantic Ocean, but ploughing up and down an indoor pool held no allure for him. However, as he approached the grand old age of fifty-four, his trouser waistline was two inches larger than it should be and the palace GP was making noises about cholesterol levels. Something needed to give, and it wasn't just the button above his flies.

Sir Simon felt tired. He felt flabby. On yesterday's long, uncomfortable car journey back from Scotland he had come to the conclusion that here was a man who had eaten too much Dundee cake and not offered to accompany the Queen on enough cross-country walks. His first thought on arriving back at his cottage in Kensington Palace was that he needed to jolt himself out of this slump.

Those last few weeks in Balmoral had been bloody. It was as if the midges had been staging a Highland Games of their own. He had been busy most mornings with Prince

Philip, discussing the details of the impending Reservicing Programme, and then up most nights on the phone, conferring with fellow courtiers about the Duke's latest suggestions and questions, as well as adding several of his own. If they hadn't done all their homework by the time they presented it to Parliament, the proverbial ordure would hit the fan like a fireworks display.

Vigour was what he needed. And freshness. Despite his lack of enthusiasm, the Buckingham Palace swimming pool seemed like the best solution. Staff tended to avoid it when the royals were in residence. The problem was, when the family were away, he tended to be so too, and vice versa. However, catching sight of himself in an ill-advised full-length mirror in the bedroom at KP that night, he made the decision to take a risk and nip in early. He prayed that, with his midge-bitten body stretching the seams of his Vilebrequin trunks, he wouldn't encounter a super-keen young equerry in peak physical condition or, worse, the Duke himself, fresh from a royal dip.

Sir Simon walked across Hyde Park and down through Green Park – one of the few forty-minute commutes you could make through central London that was entirely green – in time to arrive the Palace by 6.30 a.m. He had stupidly put his trunks on under his trousers, which made both uncomfortable. He parked his briefcase on his office desk, hung his suit jacket on a wooden hanger on a hat stand, and took off his brogues. Neatly rolling his silk tie, which today featured tiny pink koalas, he placed it safely in the left shoe. Then, shouldering the backpack containing his swimming towel, he walked the short distance to the north-west pavilion in his socks. By now it was 6.45.

The pavilion, attached to the North Wing that overlooked Green Park, had originally been designed as a conservatory by John Nash. Sir Simon always thought they should have kept it that way. His mother had been a plantswoman and he saw conservatories as paeans to the natural world, whereas heated swimming pools were a little bit naff. Nevertheless, the Queen's father had decided to convert this one in the thirties for his little princesses to swim in, so there it was, with its Grecian pillars outside, and its somewhat-the-worse-for-wear art deco tiles within, as much in need of updating as so many nooks and crannies of the Palace that the public didn't see.

The pool area was reached from inside the main building through a door papered with instructions for what to do in case of fire and reminders that nobody should swim solo, which he ignored. The corridor beyond was already uncomfortably humid. He was glad he'd left his tie behind. In the men's changing room, he divested himself of his shirt, socks and trousers and draped his towel across his arm. He noticed a cut-crystal tumbler abandoned on one of the benches. Odd, since the family had only arrived back from the Highlands last night. There must have been a homecoming celebration among the younger generation. All glass was banned in the pool area, but you didn't tell princes and princesses what they could and couldn't do in their granny's home. Sir Simon made a mental note to tell Housekeeping so they could deal with it.

He showered quickly and walked through into the pool area, with its windows overlooking the kissing plane trees in the garden, bracing himself for the shock of coolish water lapping against this too, too solid flesh.

But the shock he got was quite different.

At first his brain refused to register what it was seeing. Was it a blanket? A trick of the light? There was so much red. So much dark red against the green tiled floor. In the centre of the stain was a leg, bare to the knee, female. The image imprinted itself onto his retina. He blinked.

His breath came short and punchy as he took two steps towards it. Another two, and he was standing in the gore itself and staring down at the full horror of it.

A woman in a pale dress lay curled on her side in a puddle of darkness. Her lips were blue, her eyes open and unseeing. Her right arm reached towards her feet, palm-up. All were soaked and stained with congealed blood. Her left arm was stretched towards the water's edge, where the dark puddle finally stopped. Sir Simon felt his own blood pulse, pounding a one-two, one-two rhythm in his ears.

Gingerly, he knelt down and placed reluctant fingers against the neck. There was no pulse, and how could there be, with eyes like that? He longed to close the lids, but thought he probably shouldn't. Her hair lay fanned around her head, a halo soaked in red. She looked surprised. Or was that his imagination? And so fragile that, had she been alive, he could have easily scooped her up and carried her to safety.

Rising, he felt a sharp pain in his knee. As he tried to wipe some of the sticky blood from his skin, his fingertips encountered grit. Examining it, he could just make out small shards of thick glass. Now his own blood, freshly seeping from a cut on his leg, was mingling with hers. He saw it then – the remains of a shattered tumbler, sitting like a crystal ruin in the crimson sea.

He knew the face, knew the hair. What was she doing here, with a whisky tumbler? His body didn't want to move, but he forced it back outside to seek help. Though he knew it was too late for any help worth having.

Chapter 1

THREE MONTHS
EARLIER . . .

'Philip?'

'Yes?' The Duke of Edinburgh raised half an eyebrow from the folded *Daily Telegraph*, which was propped up against a pot of honey on the breakfast table.

'You know that painting?'

'Which painting? You have seven thousand,' he said, just to be difficult.

The Queen sighed inwardly. She had been about to explain. 'The one of *Britannia*. That used to hang outside my bedroom.'

'What, the ghastly little one by the Australian who couldn't do boats? That one?'

'Yes.'

'Yes?'

'Well, I saw it yesterday in Portsmouth, at Semaphore House. At an exhibition of maritime art.'

Philip stared pointedly at the editorial page of his paper and grunted, 'That makes sense. For a yacht.'

'You don't understand. I was launching the navy's new digital strategy and they'd put up a few paintings in the lobby.' The digital strategy was a complicated business, bringing the Royal Navy up to date with the latest technology; the art exhibition had been more straightforward. 'Mostly grey things of battleships. A J-Class yacht in full sail at Southampton, because there's always one. And next to it, our *Britannia*, from '63.'

'How d'you know it was ours?' He still didn't look up.

'Because it was *that* one,' the Queen said sharply, feeling suddenly and vertiginously sad at his lack of interest. 'I know my own paintings.'

'I'm sure you do. All seven thousand of 'em. Well, tell the staff johnnies to hand it over.'

'I have.'

'Good.'

The Queen sensed that the *Daily Telegraph* article was probably about Brexit, hence her husband's more than usually prickly mood. Cameron gone. The party in disarray. The whole thing so fiendishly botched . . . A single painting by an unremarkable artist, presented long before Britain joined the Common Market, was hardly important. She glanced up at the landscapes by Stubbs, with their wonderful horses, that adorned the walls of the private dining room at the Palace. Philip himself had depicted her here, reading the paper, many years ago. And he had done it better, one could argue, than the man who had painted *Britannia*. But that picture had once been very precious to her.

It had become a favourite in ways she had never shared with anyone. She intended to get it back.

A couple of hours later, Rozie Oshodi arrived at the Queen's study in the North Wing to collect the morning's red boxes containing Her Majesty's official papers. Rozie had joined as the Queen's Assistant Private Secretary a few months ago, after a short career in the army and then at a private bank. She was still relatively young for the role, but so far had performed admirably, including – and perhaps especially – in the more unconventional aspects of it.

'Any news?' the Queen asked, looking up from the final paper in the pile.

Yesterday, Rozie had been tasked with finding out how the painting of the ex-royal yacht had ended up where it was and organising its swift return.

'Yes, ma'am, but it's not good.'

'Oh?' This was a surprise.

'I spoke to the facilities manager at the naval base,' Rozie explained, 'and he tells me it's a case of mistaken identity. The artist must have painted more than one version of *Britannia* in Australia. This one was lent to the exhibition by the Second Sea Lord. There's no plaque on it or anything. It's from the Ministry of Defence's collection and it's been hanging in his office for years.'

The Queen eyed her APS thoughtfully through her bifocals.

'Has it? The last time I saw it was in the nineteen nineties.'

'Ma'am?'

There was a belligerent glimmer behind the royal spectacles. 'The Second Sea Lord doesn't have another version. He has *mine*. In a different frame. And he's had it for a long time, you now tell me.'

'Ah . . . yes. I see.' From the look on her face, it was clear that Rozie didn't.

'Go back and find out what's going on, would you?'

'Of course, ma'am.'

The Queen blotted her signature on the paper on her desk and put it back in its box. Her APS picked up the pile and left her to ponder.

Chapter 2

'This place is a deathtrap.'

'Oh, come on, James. You're exaggerating.'

'I am not.' The Keeper of the Privy Purse glowered at the Private Secretary across the latter's antique office desk. 'Do you know how much vulcanised rubber they've discovered?'

'I don't even know what that is.' Sir Simon's raised left eyebrow managed to convey curiosity and amusement. As Private Secretary, he was responsible for managing the Queen's official visits and relations with the Government, but he ended up taking an interest in everything that might affect her. And the deathtrap status or otherwise of Buckingham Palace most definitely fell into that category.

His visitor, Sir James Ellington, was in charge of the royal finances. He had worked with Sir Simon for years, and it wasn't unusual for him to make the brisk ten-minute walk from his desk high up in the South Wing to Sir Simon's spacious, high-ceilinged ground-floor office in the North Wing, so he could complain about the latest fiasco. Behind every stiff upper lip lies an Englishman bursting to share his withering irritation in private. Sir Simon noticed that his friend was unusually exercised about the vulcanised rubber, though. Whatever it was.

'You treat rubber with sulphur to harden it,' Sir James explained, 'and use it to make cable casings. At least, they did fifty years ago. It does the job, but over time it degrades, with exposure to air and light, and so on. It becomes brittle.'

'A bit like you, this morning,' Sir Simon observed.

'Don't. You have no idea.'

'And so . . . What's the problem with our brittle, vulcanised rubber?'

'It's falling apart. The cables should have been replaced decades ago. We knew it was bad, but when we had that leak in the attics last month, they discovered a nest of the blasted things that practically disintegrated on contact. It means the electrics around the building are being held together by a wing and a prayer. A hundred miles of them. One dodgy connection and . . . pffft.' Sir James made a gesture with his elegant right hand to suggest smoke, or a minor explosion.

Sir Simon briefly closed his eyes. It wasn't as if they didn't know the dangers of fire. The Windsor Castle disaster in '92 had taken five years and several million pounds to put right. They had opened Buckingham Palace to the public each summer to help pay for the repairs. Unfortunately, when they'd done a survey of *this* place, to be on the safe side, they discovered it was even more hazardous. Plans to fix it were under way, but they kept discovering complications.

'So what do we do?' he asked. 'Move her out?'

No need to specify who may or may not need to move.

14

'We probably should, pronto. She won't want to go, of course.'

'Naturally.'

'We ran the idea up the flagpole last year and she didn't exactly salute,' Sir James mused, glumly. 'I don't blame her. If she did go, it would have to be to Windsor, so she could keep up her schedule, and we'd clog up the M4 with ambassadors and ministers and garden party guests zipping up and down. The castle itself would need to be reconfigured to cope. She'll soldier on as is, if she possibly can. If it ain't broke . . .'

'But it *is* broke, you say,' Sir Simon pointed out.

Sir James sighed. 'It is, as you rightly remind me, broke.' He raised his eyes heavenwards. 'Buckingham Palace is broken. If it were a terraced house in Birmingham the experts would stick a notice on the front door and forbid the family to return until it was fixed. But it's a working palace, so we can't. We were just finalising the Reservicing Programme to work around her – this will add another million or two, no doubt. Oh, and I almost forgot: you know Mary, my secretary? The efficient one who always answers emails on time and knows everything in the Reservicing planning agenda and is a bit of a genius?'

'Yes?'

'She's just handed in her notice. I didn't hear all the details, but she was in floods of tears this morning. So—'

He was cut off by the arrival of Rozie with the boxes, which she placed on a marble-topped console table by the door, ready for collection by the Cabinet Office later.

'All good?' Sir Simon asked her.

15

'Mostly. How do I find out if we loaned the Ministry of Defence one of the Queen's private paintings back in the nineties?'

At this question of negligible interest, Sir James stood up and took his leave.

Rozie observed his departure with curiosity. Leaning forward, meanwhile, Sir Simon steepled his fingers and focused on the matter in hand. He was good at leaping from one problem to another – like a gymnast on the asymmetric bars, Rozie had often thought, or a squirrel on an obstacle course.

'Hmm. Talk to the Royal Collection Trust,' he suggested. 'They look after her private art as well as Crown stuff, I think. Why do we care?'

'The Boss saw it in Portsmouth,' Rozie explained. 'The MOD say it's theirs. The thing is, she says it was a personal gift from the artist. You'd think she'd know.'

'She tends to. What's the MOD's excuse?'

'They're suggesting there must be two of them.'

Sir Simon whistled to himself. 'Brave move on their part. Can you ask the artist?'

'No, he's dead, I checked. His name's Vernon Hooker. He died in 1997.'

'Did he paint a lot of boats?'

'Hundreds. If you google him, you'll see.'

Rozie waited while Sir Simon duly typed in the artist's name to Google Images on his computer and instinctively recoiled.

'By God! Did the man ever sail?'

Rozie was no expert on maritime paintings, but Sir Simon's reaction didn't surprise her. Vernon Hooker liked to depict his subjects in bright colours, with exuberant disregard for light and shade. The images featured more emerald green, electric blue and lilac than you might expect for scenes that were largely sea and sky. But then, one of the Queen's favourite artists was Terence Cuneo, whose paintings of trains and battle scenes were hardly monochrome. And to Rozie's surprise, when she looked up Hooker online yesterday, it turned out that his work generally sold for thousands. He was quite collectable.

'They're probably right, aren't they?' Sir Simon concluded, peering back at his screen. 'The Ministry, I mean. There are dozens of the bloody things. I bet this Hooker would get more money for a Day-Glo royal yacht than a bog-standard seascape. He probably did loads of them.'

'She's adamant. And actually, he didn't do any others of *Britannia* that I could find.'

'As I say, talk to Neil Hudson at the RCT. See if we loaned it. Twenty years is long enough for the MOD to hang onto it.'

'OK.' Rozie changed the subject. 'Why did Sir James look so uncomfortable just now? I hope I wasn't interrupting anything.'

'Only existential despair. It's the bloody Reservicing Programme. His secretary's leaving, and they've discovered vulcanisation or something. Dodgy electrics, anyway. The Palace is a deathtrap, apparently.'

'Good to know,' she remarked breezily, heading for the door. 'It sounds expensive.'

'It will be. The budget has sailed past three hundred and fifty million already. We need Parliament to sign it off in November, and they can't even give themselves a pay rise.'

She paused at the threshold. 'Yeah, but this is the second most famous house in the world.'

'But . . . three hundred and fifty million.' Sir Simon folded his shirtsleeved arms and stared despondently at his computer. 'When it was only three hundred it didn't sound so bad, somehow.'

'Over ten years,' she reminded him. 'And it'll come in ahead of time and under budget, like Windsor Castle did. And the bill for the Houses of Parliament refit was four billion, the last I heard.'

The Private Secretary brightened slightly. 'You're absolutely right, Rozie. Ignore me, I need a holiday. How d'you stay so chipper?'

'Fresh air and exercise,' she said decisively. 'You should try it some time.'

'Do not cheek your elders, young lady. I'm very fit for my age.'

Rozie, who was very fit regardless of age – hers happened to be thirty – threw him a friendly grin before heading back to her office next door.

He tried not to show it, but her remark rankled with Sir Simon. She was a tall, attractive young woman, with a short, precision-cut Afro, an athletic physique and a fitness level that had hardly dropped since she left the Royal Horse Artillery.

He, meanwhile, was a quarter-century older, and his knees were not what they were. Nor was his back. As a young helicopter pilot and then a diplomat at the Foreign Office, he had been reasonably athletic: an ex-college rower who was handy on the rugby pitch and a demon at the wicket. But over the years, his consumption of good claret had increased in inverse proportion to the time spent wielding an oar, a ball or a cricket bat. He really ought to do something about it.

Chapter 3

Back at her desk, Rosie clicked on a series of images stored on her laptop. She had asked the facilities manager at the naval base in Portsmouth to send her a photo of the *Britannia* painting, so she would have some idea of what she was talking about. The image he'd sent showed the royal yacht, flags fluttering, surrounded by smaller boats with a flat blob of land in the background. She wondered briefly why the Boss was so attached to it. This was a woman who owned Leonardos and Turners, and a small, very lovely Rembrandt at Windsor Castle that Rozie would have cheerfully sold her Mini for.

The facilities manager had been quite firm. The Second Sea Lord – a vice admiral in charge of all 'people' matters in the navy – had a variety of paintings in his office, all legitimately sourced from the Ministry of Defence. Any loans from other places were quite clearly recorded and always returned shipshape and Bristol fashion. This wasn't one of them. There must simply be two paintings.

And yet the Boss was equally certain there were not.

Rozie made a phone call. The artist's dealer in Mayfair wasn't aware of any other paintings of *Britannia* by his late client, but suggested she talk to the son.

'Don's the expert on his father's stuff. He's in his late sixties, sharp as a tack. He lives in Tasmania. It'll be evening there now, of course, but I'm sure he won't mind talking to you.'

Rozie considered what a generous offer that was, then remembered on whose behalf she was calling. No – the artist's son probably *wouldn't* mind talking to her about the Queen's little problem. People were usually fine with it.

Don Hooker was everything the dealer had promised.

'The royal yacht in Hobart, for the regatta? Oh yeah, I know the one. It was 1962 or '63 – something like that, and Her Majesty was on one of her tours. I remember Dad telling me the story. He was so proud of that painting! He was a big monarchist, was Dad, and there she was, this beautiful lady, travelling the world on her boat. He followed her on all the news broadcasts and made us listen too – even though, to be perfectly honest with you, Rozie, I was a callow youth at the time and I didn't really care. But Dad loved the whole thing. He had a map on the wall and he marked off where she went with little green pins. Collected postcards, mugs, the lot. He said she looked so happy on that trip, and he wanted her to have something to remember it by. "A piece of that joy", that's what he said. He copied the picture from a newspaper photo, added the colours, you know . . . And he got a proper Pommie thank you on Palace notepaper, with a big red crest. It said the Queen had never seen *Britannia* look so colourful. It was the only one he did. We've probably still got that letter in Dad's archive somewhere. I can look it out if you want . . .?'

When Rozie rang him back, the facilities man from the Ministry of Defence was much less confident about his multiple-paintings theory.

'Perhaps ours is a copy?' he suggested. 'I agree it's very unusual, but I can absolutely assure you it's not a loan from the Palace.'

Sir Simon was due to see the Queen next and, at Rozie's request, he updated the Boss while he was there.

'She says it's not a copy, it's her original,' he informed Rozie on his return. 'Find out how they got it and tell them to stop stalling. She's pretty pissed off.'

'How can she tell it's the original?' Rozie wanted to know. After all, the Queen had only seen the painting for a couple of minutes in bad light in a makeshift exhibition at a naval headquarters building on a visit about something else.

'No idea. But she's certain.'

If she was certain, Rozie would get the job done.

'Just a little closer towards the light.'

The Queen adjusted the tilt of her neck, which was getting stiff.

'Like this?'

'Lovely, ma'am. Perfect.'

She closed her eyes, briefly. It was nice and peaceful in the Yellow Drawing Room. Beyond the heavy net curtains, sun-rays gleamed off the golden statue of Winged Victory on the Victoria Memorial – or the Birthday Cake, as the guardsmen called it. Warm shafts of light fell on her left cheek. If only one didn't have to maintain this wretched pose, one could quite easily fall asleep . . .

But she *did* have to maintain it. The Queen opened her eyes sharply and rested her gaze on a Chinese pagoda in the corner, which was nine tiers high, reaching almost to the ceiling. Her third-great-grand-uncle, George IV, did not do things by halves.

'Are you getting what you need?' she asked.

'Absolutely. Won't be long. You can roll your shoulders in a couple of minutes.'

Lavinia Hawthorne-Hopwood, who stood at an easel making preparatory sketches of her, was a considerate artist. She knew what her sitters went through and tried to minimise the trouble. It was one of the reasons the Queen liked to work with her. This wasn't their first rodeo, as Harry would say. (What a marvellous expression. The Queen was delighted by rodeos. She had always thought that, under different circumstances, she might have been rather good at them.)

'Which bit are you working on now?'

'The eyes, ma'am. Always the trickiest.'

'I see.' Through the window, she watched several people posing for photographs outside the Palace gates. One seemed to be doing dance moves. Was this for one of those social media crazes Eugenie had told her about? The Queen craned slightly forward to get a better view.

'If you wouldn't mind, ma'am . . .'

'What?' The Queen was jolted out of her thoughts and realised she had changed position. Lavinia had stopped drawing. 'I'm so sorry. Is that better?'

23

'Thanks. Just another minute or so and . . . there. That one's done. Phew! Would you like a glass of water?'

'A sip of tea would help.'

A porcelain cup and saucer appeared at the Queen's elbow, proffered by Sandy Robertson, her page. After a welcome hit of Darjeeling, she stretched discreetly and rubbed her stiff knee, while the artist reviewed her sketches.

Nearby, two video cameras on tripods and a boom microphone on a stand recorded the session. A small team of three, dressed in practical T-shirts and trousers, moved softly between these and their assigned chairs against the far wall. A lanky young man in the red and navy-blue Royal Household uniform stood by to help or corral them, as appropriate. A documentary was in progress: *The Queen's Art*, or something like that – they hadn't finalised the title. Not just what one owned, but also what one contributed to.

Today they were filming the making of the latest artwork she had agreed to sit for: a bronze bust. There really should be someone recording the filming, the Queen mused, just to round the whole thing off. Or someone to write about the recording of the filming of the sketching . . . ad infinitum. She was used to being watched and used, by now; to being such a source of fascination that her watchers were watched too.

'Is it going to be life-size, the bust?' she asked Lavinia.

She knew the answer to this question, but also knew the need to make small talk for the cameras, and the need for that small talk not to be about Lavinia's recent, horrendous divorce, or her son's arrest for drug dealing at boarding school. The poor woman was entitled to some privacy.

'Yes,' Lavinia said, peering at a group of sketches spread out on a table near her easel. 'Actually, slightly larger. They want you to stand out at the Royal Society.'

'Mmm. Was the last one larger too?'

'I think it was, ma'am, from memory. Did you like it?'

'Oh, yes. I thought it was rather good. You managed to avoid making me look . . .' She puffed out her cheeks and made Lavinia laugh. 'Too much like my great-great-grandmother.' Heavy. Jowly. Old.

Lavinia went back to her easel. 'My aim is to make you shimmer. Even in bronze. Right, are you ready, ma'am? If you can turn your head to look at my hand, here. Just a bit more. That's lovely . . .'

The artist kept up a gentle patter of conversation while she worked. She got more from her subjects when they talked than when they stayed silent. The Queen's face, in particular, lit up when she was animated. At rest, it could look grimly forbidding, which gave quite the wrong impression of her.

'Have you been to any good exhibitions recently?' Lavinia asked, and then regretted it. She should have asked about racing.

But the Queen didn't seem to mind.

'We're opening one next year that I'm looking forward to,' she said. '"Canaletto in Venice". We have rather a lot of Canaletto.' By which she meant the largest collection in the world. 'Bought in bulk by George III from Joseph Smith. He was the consul to Venice at the time. A dull name for a rather interesting man, I've always thought.'

Lavinia gulped. 'Goodness.'

The Queen smiled to herself. She'd had a lively chat on the subject with her Surveyor of Pictures recently. After several decades of living with them, she knew her Canalettos very well, although she preferred her own impressions of the place. Sailing from Ancona to Venice on board *Britannia* in 1960 – or was it '61? – visiting the ancient little island of Torcello with Philip, and taking a moonlit gondola ride . . .

She thought back to those early tours on the royal yacht. Italy, Canada, the Pacific Islands . . . *Britannia* had been fitted out after the war, in another time of austerity, and its interior was practical, rather than extravagant. It suited the Queen's temperament better than the gilt and grandeur that surrounded her now. How *happy* they had been, she and Philip and the 'yotties', visiting the furthest corners of the globe together. So many marvellous memories. The 'ghastly little painting' uniquely conjured some of them in particular.

'I saw one of my personal paintings at an exhibition by the Royal Navy recently,' she said aloud. It still rankled.

'Oh, that's nice,' the artist said absently.

'It wasn't really. I hadn't lent it to them. The last time I saw it, it was hanging opposite my bedroom door.'

Lavinia's head jerked up in shock. 'Oh dear.'

'Oh dear precisely,' the Queen agreed.

'How did it get there?'

'That's a very interesting question.' A minute later she added, 'There. I think we're done.'

Her tone was friendly but firm. The artist looked up, then glanced at her watch. The hour was up, precisely, and her subject was already removing the diamond tiara she had kindly agreed to wear for the sculpture, which had looked delightfully over the top above her shirt and cardigan. The documentary team took charge of their cameras, watched over by the eagle eye of the lanky young man from the Household. The Queen's equerry was already hovering in the doorway, ready to accompany Her Majesty to her next appointment.

'Thank you very much, ma'am,' Lavinia said.

The Queen nodded. 'I look forward to seeing the shimmer.' Her tone was dry, but there was a twinkle in her eye.

Chapter 4

With her usual efficiency, Rozie took the opportunity of a cancelled meeting to visit the Royal Collection Trust, as Sir Simon had suggested. The sun was shining and it would be nice to stretch her legs and tick the problem of the Queen's little painting off her list.

She strode briskly across the dusty pink tarmac from the side gate near her office, dodging between a black cab and a couple of tourists on Boris bikes. The air was warm, the bright sky brushed with pale clouds. Nipping across the edge of Green Park, she passed Clarence House on the corner, tall and white, where Prince Charles lived when he was in London. Behind it was her destination, St James's Palace.

This collection of buildings was quite a different proposition. Tudor, squat and red-brick, they were much older than the rest. Sir Simon was a history buff who enjoyed telling her endless anecdotes about the place. Rozie's favourite was about Prince James, the younger son of Charles I, who had been imprisoned there by Oliver Cromwell. He'd escaped by playing games of hide-and-seek with his jailers. Each time, the young prince would make himself a little bit harder to find, until one day he let himself out of the garden gate with a stolen key, and was halfway across Westminster before they realised he was gone. He made it all the way to France. According to Sir Simon, who was an old romantic, Charles I had been led from here to the scaffold in Whitehall wearing three shirts so he wouldn't shiver and seem to be afraid.

Rozie walked round to the staff entrance at Stable Yard, musing on the fact that all ambassadors were still appointed 'to the Court of St James', for reasons she failed to understand. At the gate, a guardsman in a scarlet tunic and a bearskin stood impassively as she showed her pass to a security officer. She was escorted down miles of corridors to an office on the first floor. Here Neil Hudson, the current Surveyor of the Queen's Pictures, welcomed her in with a puzzled smile.

'What on earth brings you here, Captain Oshodi? I do visit, you know. No need to beard me in my den.'

Rozie looked around. It wasn't bad, as dens went. A pair of windows overlooked the wide street that led up to Piccadilly, a stone's throw from Fortnum's and the Ritz. One panelled wall was lined from floor to ceiling with small but priceless works of art; the others were lined with books. The Surveyor's walnut desk – so huge it looked like two abnormally large ones pushed together, was a riot of papers, paperweights, bronze statuettes and photographs in silver frames. There was no sign of a computer. Rozie assumed Neil Hudson hid it in a drawer when he had visitors. Surely he didn't work with a quill? His yellow waistcoat and chin-length wavy hair gave the impression of a man who would love you to believe that he did.

'I'm here to trace a painting,' she explained. 'One of Her Majesty's. We know where it is, but not how it got there. It went missing a while ago.'

'Stop!' Hudson raised his hand. 'Stop right there. I can assure you it didn't. We don't lose things in the Royal Collection.'

'I think you do,' Rozie said firmly, meeting his eye. 'Sometimes.'

'Very occasionally. Hardly ever. I resent the implication that we did.'

'Well, that's great. You'll know what happened then.'

She explained as much as she knew, and the Surveyor nodded non-committally.

'The nineties? Should be fine. The records are pretty good. But if it was . . . mislaid, shall we say, much earlier, we were still working in a fairly ad hoc way, especially for Her Majesty's private paintings. I can't really imagine her lending it, though. We lend Crown stuff all the time, if it's in a fit state to travel. But something small and private like that . . .' He wrinkled his nose. 'Apart from anything else, who would've seen it to ask? However, you're welcome to check.'

He called for an assistant, who dutifully led Rozie down several drab corridors, up half-sets of stairs and down others, past a couple of well-lit studios, through whose open doors she saw various conservators quietly at work. Eventually they arrived at a stuffy back room a couple of buildings away, with a window that wouldn't open and a ceiling light that constantly flickered. Three walls were lined with glass-fronted cabinets housing a motley collection of boxed paper records going back to 1952. A computer on a desk under the grimy window gave access to a database of everything that had been digitised.

'I'll leave you to it,' the assistant said, after she'd explained what was where. 'You don't need gloves or anything. We're not that precious about the twentieth century. Just put everything back where you found it and turn out the light. Good luck.'

Rozie thanked her, but luck was elusive. After an hour of painstaking searching among the boxes of files, all she found was a line in a yellowing ledger acknowledging receipt of '*Oil painting: HMY at the 125th anniversary of the Hobart Regatta, 1963, gilt frame, 15" by 21"*', by Vernon Hooker, received 1964'. There was no mention of it ever leaving the Palace, though she trawled through every available box and digital database up to the year 2000.

Before leaving, she decided to pull the original box file down again and take one last look at the ledger from 1964. Had she missed something? She lined up the page to take a picture of it on her phone. At this point, she noticed the positioning of a word scrawled in pencil in the margin. She had assumed it applied to the sculpture listed below, but it might just as well have been meant for the painting. It was scribbled at an angle, and hard to make out. She peered at it. *RUBBISH*.

Did it say 'Rubbish'? Really? It couldn't, surely? Although, thinking back to the photos of it that she'd seen, perhaps it did. Did record keepers write their true thoughts about acquisitions in the margins? Had they meant to rub it out?

Rozie peered again. There was a slight gap between the first few letters and the last two. Wait – they weren't letters, those last two, they were numbers. Eight something. Could it be '82'? Or '86'? And there was an 'f' or 'g' in the first word, so it couldn't be 'Rubbish'. 'Ref'-something, perhaps? She couldn't make it out.

She made sure the picture she took of it was as well-lit as possible, so she could examine it properly back at her desk.

At lunch, however, she was distracted by an earlier remark Sir Simon had made in passing.

Rozie had just loaded up her tray in the staff canteen. 'Canteen' was typical Royal Household understatement. Here, it consisted of a servery and two panelled dining rooms adorned with Old Masters from the Royal Collection and guarded by a statue of Burmese, one of the Queen's favourite horses, a gift from the Royal Canadian Mounted Police.

According to Sir Simon, until quite recently the staff here had eaten in different rooms according to hierarchy, but now they all mucked in together and that was the way Rozie liked it. You never knew who you were going to bump into. The atmosphere was generally relaxed and the food as good as you would expect from kitchens that catered for heads of state on a regular basis.

Today, it was different. At tables in the outer dining room, set as always with pristine white linen cloths and silver cutlery, people sat in twos and threes, holding desultory conversations. The restaurant-quality meal on Rozie's tray looked as appetising as ever, but the mood was tense. Was it the recent Brexit referendum that had done it? She had heard senior courtiers speculating that the vote had swirled the waters of private opinion and brought previously unspoken rivalries to the surface. Were you nationalist or European? Did you support the Commonwealth, or Germany and France? You could support all of them, Rozie thought. Until a few months ago, everybody had. Now there were sides to be taken. Whatever it was, Rozie felt the mood had shifted during her few months working in the Private Office.

Her eye was drawn to a couple in the far corner: a younger woman and an older one, heads together. She recognised the younger woman, whose flame-red hair hung, Pre-Raphaelite style, halfway down her back. This was Mary van Renen, one of the assistants to Sir James Ellington. Rozie gave her a nod of hello and went over to join her. Only when she was nearly at the table did she notice that Mary's eyes were red-rimmed, her expression bleak.

'Oh, I'm sorry. D'you want me to go elsewhere?' Rozie offered.

'No, do join us.' Mary gestured to the seat opposite. 'Please.'

The smile appeared again, but it was watery and forced. She had hardly touched the roast chicken on her plate, while her companion, prim and sharp-faced, had nearly finished hers.

'You can help me,' the older woman said, as Rozie sat down. She seemed quite unruffled by Mary's distress. 'I was just trying to tell this young lady what a silly girl she's being.'

Rozie threw her friend a questioning look. 'This is Cynthia Harris,' Mary said, dully. 'Cynthia, this is Captain Oshodi, the Queen's APS.'

'It's Rozie,' Rozie said, holding out her hand.

'I thought that's who you were,' Cynthia Harris said, flashing a set of dull, uneven teeth, busily loading her fork with carrot and potato. Rozie withdrew her hand. 'I've seen you around,' Cynthia went on. 'How exciting, Mary, having one of the bigwigs sitting with us.'

'Not that much of a bigwig,' Rozie insisted.

'Oh, but you are. You're Private Office. Top of the tree. We're honoured by your presence, aren't we, Mary?'

Rozie couldn't tell if she was being serious or not. Mary, whom she knew fairly well because she was always popping over on various errands for Sir James, was staring miserably at her plate. Then Rozie remembered what Sir Simon had said about one of the secretaries.

'Don't tell me you're leaving? Is it you who handed in your notice?'

Mary nodded without looking up. A pair of tears fell on the untouched mashed potato.

'She *says* she will,' Cynthia Harris said from the seat beside her. 'Thoughtless child. Overreacting.'

Rozie, whose instinct was to like people unless proved otherwise, gave the older woman a penetrating look. Cynthia Harris was whip-thin, with straight, almost-white hair cut in a sharp bob and dark, beady eyes that reminded Rozie of an inquisitive bird. Her uniform was that of a housekeeper: a spotless white cleaning dress worn with a dark blue cardigan. She looked fit and wiry, but older than average for such a job. She couldn't be under sixty-five, Rozie thought, though she wondered if her face made her seem older than she was. Her cheeks were gaunt. Deep lines were etched around thin

34

lips and between the eyes. Her beaky nose had a small pink bloom of broken veins. Rozie tried to interpret her expression as the housekeeper calmly forked the remaining carrots into her mouth. Was she calm? Triumphant? Disapproving? Suddenly those beady eyes were looking straight into hers. Rozie realised she was staring and shifted her gaze to Mary.

'Are you really leaving?' she asked.

The younger woman nodded. 'I have to. I can't go on.'

'Such theatrics!' Cynthia Harris said with a little laugh.

'I don't feel safe.'

'You should feel flattered, if anything.'

'Not safe? Why?' Rozie asked.

Mary looked up at last. 'I've had . . . Someone's watching me. A man. Sending things to me.'

'You don't know that,' the other woman scoffed.

'I've seen him outside my flat.'

'Do you know who he is?' Rozie asked.

'I've had messages, from a name I don't recognise. He says we met via Tinder and I brushed him off.'

'And did you? Meet, I mean.'

'I don't think so. I've gone over and over the guys I've met and there have been some weirdos, sure, but I don't think any of them would've . . .' Mary trailed off.

Rozie silently absorbed the fact that her friend was on Tinder. Mary van Renen – shy, methodical, old-fashioned – had always struck her as the sort of girl who would be happily single, or loved-up with a gentle boyfriend she'd known for years. At least she was looking for love – Rozie rarely had time even for that.

'What did he write?' she asked.

'It doesn't matter,' Mary said, looking so upset Rozie didn't want to pursue it.

'And you don't know it was him outside your flat, do you?' the housekeeper added. 'It could have been someone just pausing to have a conversation on his mobile phone.'

'He wasn't holding a phone.'

'People have earphones these days, you know,' Cynthia Harris countered. 'Or buds, or whatever they call them. Or he could have been waiting for someone.'

'He was there three times, at least.' Mary closed her eyes.

'So you say.' The housekeeper rolled her eyes and shrugged at Rozie. 'And even if he was, the police said it doesn't prove anything.'

'You went to the police?'

Mary nodded. 'But they said I need more evidence before they can do anything. They seemed to think I was imagining it. But – but afterwards there was my bicycle.'

Rozie saw how her arms trembled as she twisted her hands in her lap. Mary was deeply upset – traumatised, even – and Rozie simply couldn't understand why Cynthia Harris kept belittling her feelings, without a shred of sympathy.

'What about your bicycle?' Rozie asked.

Mary had to take a deep breath before she could get the words out. Her eyes were closed, her words spoken in a low rush.

'He left a note taped to the seat. Said he liked this was where my . . .' She looked as if she was going to be sick, and carried on. 'I can't say it. Where a part of me rested against the saddle. Where I sat. Said he liked to watch me.' She opened her eyes. 'I cycle here every day to work. I can't do it any more. Mummy says to come home and that's where I'm going, as soon as I can.'

'Oh, Mary, I'm sorry. Did you tell the police about that too?'

Mary shook her head. 'I couldn't.' More tears raced down her cheeks. 'Each time you say it you live it again. I just . . .'

Rozie reached out across the table and Mary tentatively placed a hand in hers. Rozie squeezed it in sympathy.

Cynthia Harris gave a hiss of disapproval. She was looking indignantly at Mary.

'It's *you* who'll be sorry. For a note on a bicycle! Go on, then! You just head home to *mummy* and leave Sir James in the lurch. You girls are all the same. One date gone wrong and look at you, you're a snivelling wreck. When you think what the Queen's been through in her life. Call yourself loyal?'

'I just . . . I can't . . . Excuse me.'

Mary scrabbled for her handbag, which hung on the back of her chair, and got up to make her way unsteadily for the door. 'Well.'

Rozie looked at the older woman, who had an odd smile on her face. The housekeeper gave Rozie an apologetic shrug. 'Like I say – no backbone. These look nice.'

She took a grape from a bowl beside her plate and popped it into her mouth.

Chapter 5

It was mid-July, the height of summer. Parliament was about to rise and the usual business of state was winding down. This gave the Queen the odd precious hour of unstructured time. After lunch, her next appointment was a dress fitting for a couple of evening gowns, but that wasn't for a while. And the racing wasn't on yet. What to do with this gift of freedom?

In the East Wing at the front of the Palace, overlooking the Birthday Cake and the Mall, there had recently been a leak in one of the attics. A half-century-old water tank had developed hidden cracks and deluged a couple of bedrooms in the corridor below. She had seen the damage the day it was discovered: drenched carpets and sodden furniture. The tank had since been taken away, to be replaced with something more suitable. According to the Master of the Household the bedrooms would be all right after an airing and a new coat of plaster.

Still, one liked to be certain. She thought about taking one or two of the dogs with her, but they'd had a long walk at lunchtime and seemed content to keep snoozing. She told her page where she was going and headed up on her own, happy to be alone with her thoughts for a while.

She was picturing the Highlands. The next two weeks would be dominated by the upcoming move to Balmoral for the rest of the summer, and the Palace already felt as if it was in a state of flux. Philip, who loathed all the fuss, was taking himself off to Cowes to watch the racing for a few days. For herself, she simply couldn't wait to go north. There, one could breathe good, clean, Scottish air, and be 'Lilibet' a bit more, and 'ma'am' a bit less. The great-grandchildren and the dogs could romp about without fear of breaking much. She was looking forward to watching George tear around, and getting to know baby Charlotte better.

Reaching the second floor, in the corridor leading to the damaged rooms, she felt a tingle up her spine and could have sworn she got a sudden ghostly whiff of cedar. How very odd; she had been expecting damp. Instead, she was instantly transported eighty years into the past. Was it thinking about George and Charlotte that had done it? Why this sudden, powerful feeling of being a little girl herself, and slightly naughty, and the sense that Margaret should be beside her, urging her on to be naughtier still?

She walked along further, peering into rooms either side of her and sniffing for that elusive scent. Gradually, her attention fixed on a large mahogany wardrobe half hidden in the corridor behind a pillar. One of its doors was slightly open and as she approached, she noticed the dull gold tassel hanging from its key. Ah, yes!

Memories floated through the fog of time, sharpening with each step. This was the piece of furniture that had sat outside the nursery, adopted by Mummy's chief dresser as an overflow for grown-up clothes. It was wide and solid, polished to a rich, red patina over time. She laid her hand flat against the nearest door, like greeting an old friend.

The half-open door revealed a barren space, marked with battens along each side that must have been used to hold wide shelves – to store linen, she assumed, in more recent times. But the wardrobe had been stripped of everything, shelves and all, ready to be moved, and now it was almost back to the way she remembered it.

When Uncle David abdicated as Edward VIII in the dying days of 1936, the family hadn't wanted to locate to the large, cold, shabby Palace from their comfortable home in Piccadilly, but this was where Papa worked now and Mummy said they needed to 'live above the shop'. Mostly, it was a series of endless corridors lined with tall footmen in red coats, and the feeling of being watched and needing to be a proper princess, and not being sure quite how. But it had its compensations. It was simply marvellous for hide-and-seek.

Mummy's long furs had hung on the right-hand side of the wardrobe, covered in cloth bags, and her cashmere shawls had been carefully rolled and stored in a hanging rack on the left. In the middle had been mink jackets and opera coats, and if you stepped up onto the solid floor, you could disappear among them. She remembered Margaret Rose hissing, 'Lilibet! Quick!' as she secreted herself among the protective cotton bags. And not being able to resist joining her. Her sandals were clean (she checked), their small, slim bodies both fitting neatly inside without ruining the clothes. It was lovely to be surrounded by Mummy's evening things and to catch a faint wisp of her scent mixed up with the powerful smell of the cedar lining, to keep the moths away.

She must have been about eleven and Margaret six or seven. They were hiding from Crawfie, their governess, who didn't know she was playing a game. It was terribly, terribly wrong, and that's what made their hearts pound faster. Poor Crawfie. She called and called, and Margaret's body shook with laughter.

They hid there several times and only got caught and punished once. She couldn't remember what the punishment had been – probably something to do with missed treats at teatime – but Margaret had declared it was worth it and she was right. Now that the wardrobe was empty of clothes one could probably still fit inside, even at this great age. Even with a dodgy knee.

The Queen grinned at the thought and then, to her own astonishment, found herself stepping up, just to see. She braced a hand against the closed door on the right. The wardrobe floor was only six inches above the ground. Her right knee complained, but as she brought the left one up to join it, she could feel Margaret's presence, and Mummy's too, though the velvety scent of L'Heure Bleue was gone, along with the cedar smell. She must have imagined it.

It was warm and dark inside, and peaceful. In the fifties, Anne used to hide here in her turn – just as scornful of the punishment – and she said it reminded her of Narnia. Yes, you could imagine Narnia behind the wall, a hidden world of magic, accessible only to children. The Queen half closed the door behind her and paused to breathe in that air again.

She only had to stoop very slightly. The wardrobe was capacious and there were occasional – very occasional – advantages to being a shrinking five-foot-three. She said a silent hello to her sister, who would have laughed like a drain to see her here.

Then, without warning, the image came back to her of the poor young Russian who had been found dead in a wardrobe not long ago. She suddenly needed to get out fast, but just as she was turning round to step out backwards, safely, she heard voices at the top of the distant stairs, and the footsteps of two people rapidly approaching.

What to do?

Of course, the obvious thing was to keep calm, carry on with her exit and pretend nothing out of the ordinary was happening. It wouldn't be that easy, though. Climbing down would be harder than climbing up. Could one bear the staff to have the sight of their monarch appearing clumsily from inside a piece of furniture, bottom first? No, of course not.

The pair were only a few steps away. She pulled the half-open door a little closer, leaving barely a six-inch gap. They would be able to see her if they looked, but surely nobody would ever search for a queen in a cupboard?

She waited anxiously. They stopped. They had opened a door into one of the nearby bedrooms, but lingered on the threshold, talking. Her knee was screaming, but there was nothing to do except wait.

They lowered their voices. Up to now, they had been chatting noisily about preparations for Scotland. There was a rustling. The mood changed, the tone was furtive.

'There's three here. You get her to do one in a fortnight and two after that. You know the timing?'

'Yes. Christ! You said. I'm not stupid.'

'Same method as before.'

'She's doing OK, isn't she? No complaints so far. She effing hates it, though.'

'D'you think I give a rat's arse about her feelings?'

Sulky. 'No.'

'Then kindly do as you're bloody told. If you mention *any* of this . . .' The menacing tone was followed by a pause. 'Come on – this place gives me the creeps.'

They headed back quickly the way they'd come. As soon as the Queen heard the door in the corridor close behind them, she staggered out of her hiding place and bent to rub her knee, which was puffing up in agony. Her eleven-year-old self would have shivered with delight at the adventure, but at ninety, she should have known better. She paused for a long time to let her aching body recover while she mused over what she'd heard.

Had they both been men? Or did one of those voices belong to a gruff older woman? What on earth were they cooking up? She would have to think about this some more.

Meanwhile, she hobbled back downstairs to the dogs with what dignity she could muster, which right now didn't feel like very much at all.

Chapter 6

The Queen was surprised when, at teatime, her page asked her if she would mind having a quick word with her APS. She looked a little longingly at the slice of chocolate biscuit cake, of which she had only eaten a forkful so far. It was very moreish. 'Do show her in,' she said – but she hoped she wouldn't be long.

'I thought you might want to know, ma'am,' Rozie said, 'I think I know how your painting disappeared. Or at least, when.'

This *was* worth a teatime interruption.

'How interesting. Tell me.'

Rozie explained about the morning's visit to Stable Yard and the note in the ledger. 'Looking closely, I think it says "Refurb '86". Does that mean anything to you?'

The Queen thought for a moment. 'Not exactly. I'll think about it. Go on.'

'I spoke to the Operations team and they tell me there was a minor refurbishment of your private apartments at that time. The people I talked to weren't there then – it was thirty years ago. But I'll keep on it, ma'am. I'll let you know as soon as I find something useful.'

'Thank you, Rozie.'

After Rozie had left, the Queen had another forkful of chocolate biscuit cake and turned her mind to 1986. What had been happening then? Sometimes the years merged into each other, but surely she should remember the refurbishment of her own bedroom? It would have been highly inconvenient – so they must have done it while she was up at Balmoral. It still didn't ring any bells. Unless . . . ah. Unless she wasn't there at all, but far away. Back in those days she was as likely to be in Acapulco or Oslo as in Scotland. Where did she go in '86?

She googled herself on her iPad. It was quicker than ringing anyone to ask.

Oh, of course: China. Such an important tour. It was all about preparing to hand back Hong Kong in '97. She visited the terracotta warriors and hosted the Chinese government at a banquet on board *Britannia*. Then she and Philip sailed down the Pearl River from Canton to Hong Kong in the royal yacht. So beautiful and tranquil, watching the locals practise their early-morning tai chi on the riverbanks. There had been some interesting problem-solving moments in Victoria Harbour, too. Mary Pargeter, her APS in those days, had been involved, much as Rozie was now . . .

She had been very busy, not thinking of day-to-day practicalities at home. That must have been when the Works Department refurbished the rooms. They looked more or less the same when she returned: the familiar shade of pale jade, but slightly less shabby about the skirting boards and dado rails.

And one less picture on the wall opposite her bedroom door. Yes, of course, that's when it had disappeared – half a decade earlier than she had assumed. She had temporarily replaced it with a sketch of the garden by Terence Cuneo, signed with his signature mouse. It was very nice, but not the same.

The sketch was still there. And that was thirty years ago. Time flew. It crawled. Sometimes, you didn't know how you would endure until teatime. Sometimes, half a decade was gone in the blink of an eye.

Rozie, meanwhile, had been very unsettled by her meeting with Mary van Renen and the housekeeper at lunchtime. She needed to find out more and thought she knew a good place to start.

When she had started as APS eight months ago, she'd been given temporary accommodation at the Palace while she looked for a decent flat nearby. The rooms she'd been assigned were in the West Wing, on the top floor, above the dressmaking suite. There were three of them: all very small, hot and stuffy in summer, freezing cold in winter, surrounded by pipes that chuntered and gurgled incessantly through the night. Rozie had enjoyed a bigger bathroom as a cadet at Sandhurst – which was saying something – but here the windows overlooked the gardens, with the lake among the trees, and the view was never less than magical. She had grown up in a busy, full-on household with her mum, dad and sister, and her cousins popping in and out all the time. She liked the constant bustle of this place, and the rent was low. She still hadn't moved out.

At seven forty-five that evening there was a tentative knock at the door. Rozie had carefully timed the quick visit to her rooms. Housekeeping usually came round at about this time to check who was in and might need fresh towels or bed linen. The regular housemaid for her corridor was a woman called Lulu Arantes, who was far more au fait with the backstairs gossip than poor Sir Simon.

Rozie shouted, 'Come in!' and Lulu popped her head round the door.

'Evening, Captain Oshodi.'

'How are you, Lulu? How's the shoulder?'

Lulu rubbed at her right sleeve with her left hand. 'It aches like you wouldn't believe. I'm still taking the painkillers. I can't lift it above here – look.' She raised her bent right arm until it was level with her collarbone, winced and let it fall. 'The ankle's better, though, you'll be pleased to hear. I just get the odd twinge now.'

For a woman who did such a physical job, it amazed Rozie that Lulu managed to be permanently injured in some way. A human dynamo, she didn't ever use it as an excuse not to work, but winced and limped gamely from one task to the next.

'I'm glad about the ankle,' Rozie said. 'I was wondering, actually . . . I met one of the housekeepers today and I thought you might know her. I was just a bit curious because she seemed very old to be doing the job and I—'

'Oh, you mean Cynthia Harris. Poor you.'

47

Lulu glanced into the corridor behind her and came inside, shutting the door behind her. She leaned against it, nursing her right arm in her left. Rozie had prepared a series of gentle questions to tease out whatever gossip Lulu might know, but they proved unnecessary.

'I'm surprised you haven't encountered her before,' Lulu said. 'That cow! She's been here since the year dot. She started off doing the Queen's bedroom and wormed her way in. Then she got all the plum jobs. She was supposed to retire three years ago, and we all thanked God and chipped in for a present. Except, guess what? The lady who was hired to take over from her, who we all liked, very nice woman, calm and efficient, you know . . .? She had to leave. Apparently she just couldn't do it right.'

'Do what right?'

'Prepare the Belgian Suite for heads of state, mostly. You must know how fussy the Queen is that everything should be just so, which is right and proper, no problem with that . . . Well, apparently only Cynthia Harris could do it to her standards. So anyway, the new woman was sacked and they promoted Solange Simpson. She's been here for donkey's years. Very capable, professional woman. D'you know her? So, she was in charge when the President of Mexico came to stay the following year, and *still* it wasn't right. She said she'd done everything in the handover notes, and I'm sure she had – but who says the notes were the right ones? That's what I want to know. Long story short, the poor man in HR who'd been trying to replace her gets given his marching orders and Cynthia comes back. Special request from the Master. Just for an "interim period", they told us. They knew how much we all hated her.'

'Ouch.'

'And guess what? Suddenly it's all fine again. The President of China comes to stay – big deal, obviously – and the Queen's happy and Cynthia gets a pat on the back and a year goes by and she's *still* here, and who knows how much longer she'll be around for? She's a right piece of work, that one.'

'What is it about her, exactly? What do people hate so much?'

'Well, you met her. What did you think?' Lulu folded her arms, winced, unfolded them and put her hands on her hips.

Rozie sighed. 'She was being unpleasant to someone,' she admitted.

'She always is. Was it Mary, from the Keeper's office?'

'I couldn't say.'

'I bet it was. Cynthia's always sucking up to the people at the top. The "bigwigs", she calls them. She made friends with Mary because she thought it would give her some kind of aura, knowing someone who works for Sir James Ellington. She was probably nice at first. She can be. But once she's got you in her net, she likes to watch you squirm. Poor Mary – and those messages!'

'What kind of messages?' Rozie hadn't wanted to press Mary in the canteen, but she was keen to discover more.

'Oh, didn't you know? It's amazing what the Private Office doesn't know, if you don't mind me saying. Where was I? Oh yes. First off, he left her messages on Facebook, so she blocked him, whoever he was. Then she started to find little folded-up letters in her clothes. You know, like her coat pocket. Creepy. She thought he must be putting them on her on the bus, which was how she came in, so she took to riding a bike and he *still* did it.'

'What did they say? The ones in her clothes?'

Lulu made a face and shrugged. 'Calling her a you-know-what. A slag and a slut. The usual stuff guys do, you know?' Rozie didn't, from personal experience, but Lulu seemed to assume she would. 'Saying what he wanted to do to her. Saying she deserved it. Saying he was following her.'

'How d'you know all of this? Are you friends with Mary?'

'Who? Me? Never met her,' Lulu admitted. 'But it's all over WhatsApp. Everyone knows everything around here. Well, everyone except the Keeper and the Private Secretary, obviously. You wouldn't want them finding out, or who knows what'd happen?'

She gave Rozie a friendly smile. Just two women, having a chat. It didn't seem to occur to her that Rozie might mention any of this to Sir Simon, and Rozie was glad it didn't, because it meant she didn't have to make any promises she couldn't keep.

Lulu heard a clock in the corridor chime and realised she'd better be going.

'The police didn't take Mary seriously.' The housemaid paused at the door before returning to her trolley, screwing up her mouth at the memory.

'She didn't seem very happy about the way they treated her,' Rozie agreed.

'They don't get it. Happened to my sister-in-law's cousin. He drove her mad for six years, then he killed her.'

'Oh my God!'

'Oh, yes. With a hammer. Just a few feet from her front door. Said she drove him to it. She hadn't said a word to the man in five years, had a restraining order against him. It meant nothing, of course. Right, I'll just get your towels for you. Have a good evening.'

'I think you should know,' Rozie announced to Sir Simon the next morning, 'that secretary of Sir James's . . . Mary, the one who's leaving . . . she's being stalked by a man who's sending her foul messages and, on top of that, there's an elderly housekeeper who's being a real bitch to her. No wonder she wants to resign.'

Sir Simon frowned. 'D'you mean Mrs Harris?'

'So you *do* know.'

'Yes. Horrible woman, by all accounts. She should have retired years ago.'

'She did, but came back at the Master's request, I gather,' Rozie said, unimpressed. 'Shouldn't we tell him about this?'

The Master of the Household was Mike Green. He formed a triumvirate of senior courtiers with Sir James and Sir Simon. His office was near Sir James's, in the South Wing, where he held 'stand up, no coffee' meetings with servants who had erred in their duties, known among the cognoscenti as the 'rollicking bollockings'.

Mike Green was responsible for the domestic staff at all the Queen's residences, from chefs, pages and laundry-maids to the yeoman of the cellars, the florists and French polishers. During his career in the RAF, where he had risen to Air Vice-Marshal, he had gained a reputation for knowing how to throw a good party. This was useful, because, including garden party guests, the royal family entertained nearly a hundred thousand people at the Palace each year. On top of that, the Master was required to help deliver the fateful Reservicing Programme proposal in the autumn, so it didn't surprise Rozie that Cynthia Harris might have slipped under his radar.

But she hadn't.

'Believe me, Mike knows,' Sir Simon said, stretching his arms and putting them behind his head. 'The woman is a pest. But the Queen has always had a soft spot for Mrs Harris. She never sees her mean side, of course.'

'Why doesn't somebody say?'

Sir Simon straightened and looked at Rozie sharply. 'We don't worry the Boss with this stuff. She pays us to deal with it. Well, the Master, in this case. And he *is* dealing with it, but it's tricky.'

'Why?'

'Well, the HR procedures are Byzantine, to say the least. And – I emphasise, this mustn't go any further – Mrs Harris been on the receiving end of some rather vicious letters herself. If we got rid of her, she might get the lawyers in. She's the type.'

'But she was the one victimising Mary van Renen!'

'I wouldn't be surprised. However, the attacks Mrs Harris got were particularly awful. She and Mary are not the only victims, actually. There's been a spate of poison pen stuff recently. Mike's livid about it.'

'Has he told the Queen?' Rozie was horrified.

'Absolutely not.'

Sir Simon stood up to his full height, which didn't quite meet her six-foot-two-in-heels, and gave her a firm look. 'It's our job to protect Her Majesty from unpleasantness like this, not expose her to it. Mike's launched an investigation, and no doubt he'll find the perpetrator soon and deal with it. As you know, Rozie, our job is to come up with solutions.'

'Yes, but—'

'No buts. And you categorically mustn't mention this to the Boss. I know you and she get on, but this is important, and highly confidential. I'm slightly regretting telling *you* now. Promise me.'

Rozie wasn't often on the receiving end of Formal Sir Simon and it unnerved her a little. Staff who knew dogs said his normal demeanour reminded them of a friendly beagle. Their working relationship was smooth, but if the situation demanded, he was also a man who could quell an ambassador with a look, or bring a recalcitrant minister into line with a two-minute phone call. Right now, he was radiating the same ruthless authority as the sergeant major from her officer training days at Sandhurst.

'I promise,' she said reluctantly.

'Thank you. And don't think I won't know, just because you're at the other end of the country.'

Rozie would soon be travelling to Balmoral with the Queen and the first wave of staff. Sir Simon was heading for Tuscany for a couple of weeks, after which he intended to keep an ear to the ground in Whitehall and Westminster as the new Prime Minister set about building a Cabinet and creating a response to the Brexit vote. Everything seemed quiet on the surface, but all hell would be being let loose behind the scenes. His job was to interpret what he could from the screams.

Chapter 7

A month passed happily in the Highlands. Here, the Queen felt, one could surround oneself with sensible people – the Scots were so much more down to earth than the Sassenachs – and participate fully in the life of the place. The castle might look imposing, with its granite walls and Gothic turrets, but it was surrounded by gardens and made for enjoying nature, for relaxation and for fun.

At Buckingham Palace one necessarily had to rely on servants for everything because it took a cast of thousands to make it all work. At Balmoral, she could tack up a horse or take a Land Rover for a spin. The family could all go for a picnic at a moment's notice, if the weather was good. This August, particularly, she could sit glued to the Olympics in her tartan-carpeted study, with whoever wanted to keep her company, cheering on Nick Skelton in the show jumping and Charlotte Dujardin in the dressage from her armchair until her voice was husky from the effort. It was all very jolly. The only cause for concern was Holly, a very elderly corgi in dog years, who was increasingly uninterested in food and walks. The Queen kept her close eye on her faithful companion, fed her the choicest titbits and hoped, against reason and experience, that she would recover some of her old vitality.

With September fast approaching, it wouldn't be long before the traditional visit of the Prime Minister. She had been thinking about this.

'Cameron may have messed up the country,' she said to Philip over a barbecue, 'but at least he was a joiner-inner. I have a feeling the new one won't be.'

Philip nodded his agreement through a fug of sausage smoke. 'I always liked Samantha. Very easy on the eye. Excellent manners, too. And she was always game for a laugh. What do you do with a PM whose biggest party trick is wearing leopard-print shoes?'

The Queen looked at him with a perfectly straight expression. 'Strip poker?'

He laughed so hard he had a coughing fit.

But the problem remained. The United Kingdom's second female prime minister, much like the first, did not shoot, fish or display any particular fondness for animals. She was not renowned for her sparkling repartee, nor her dancing. She was most famous for her colourful footwear, being tough on the police and saying 'Brexit means Brexit' ad nauseam – which meant nothing at all. Sir Simon had mentioned that she was fond of walking. One would simply have to take her on a lot of walks.

After four weeks at Balmoral, Rozie was replaced at the Queen's side by Sir Simon. Though single, Rozie did not live life as a hermit, and one of the royal equerries had become a friend with benefits, one of which turned out to be a family cottage in the Caribbean. She spent a happy fortnight soaking up the tropical warmth, sipping pina coladas at a beachside bar and listening to live music under the stars.

Back at work, she spent her weekends in the country houses of various political grandees, eating salmon en croute with junior ministers and going on duck shoots with government advisers, gleaning what she could about the plans for a post-Brexit world. She duly reported back her findings to Sir Simon up in Scotland, but the more she learned, the less she understood. The one thing that was clear was that nobody really knew, but everyone was happy to argue about it with anyone who could bear to raise the subject.

She spoke to various people around the Palace about the *Britannia* painting, but made little progress. Her much greater concern was the mental health of Mary van Renen, who was still working out her notice – Sir James Ellington had said he couldn't do without her – and who was a shadow of her former self. The notes in her clothes had stopped, but only, Mary thought, because she made sure she was never alone. Friends had formed a rota to travel to work with her and she rarely went out. She couldn't imagine socialising for pleasure now.

Keeping out of the way of the half a million paying visitors who trooped through the State Apartments over the summer, Rozie and Mary swam regularly in the Palace pool in the early evenings. Rozie had suggested the idea. She had seen how much her friend was suffering and this was the best way she could think of to help. The two women usually chatted for the first few lengths, doing a leisurely breaststroke together, then Mary watched from a rattan chair as

Rozie sped up and down at her normal pace, her long limbs carving through the water as she chased her personal best. Occasionally, one of the male staff members would offer to take her on in a quick competition. They usually regretted it. Rozie enjoyed it very much.

'I'm glad to see you're not in kitten heels,' Philip joked, as they piled out of the Land Rovers and started off up the hill.

Theresa May gave him a tight smile. Every politician needs a gimmick and, to start with, she had been rather proud of her footwear which, as Home Secretary, had often guaranteed a front-page picture when the contents of her speech could not. The shoes played well in the Tory heartlands, but there was more to her than a kitten heel, and the way the Duke said it led her to suspect jokes had been made on the subject of which she would not approve.

'I thought about it,' she said, game as ever. 'But they didn't go with my Barbour.'

He barked a laugh and gave her a friendlier look. They set off together up the path between the pines and larches, past a couple of cairns built of stones to honour the marriages of Queen Victoria's children. There is only so much you can say about a neatly arranged mound of stones, and the Prime Minister said it, but she was relieved to find that what they were really heading for was the view from the ridge.

This was something she could genuinely admire. Ahead of them, clouds scudded across a wide blue September sky and below, grassy slopes alternated with jagged trees all the way to the distant hills, which faded from bottle green to midnight blue against the horizon. The bright patches of soft grass nearby reminded her of Alpine meadows and, with a brief sense of being Maria in *The Sound of Music*, she was tempted to spread her arms and run through them all.

'You must love coming here,' she said to the Duke beside her. However, when she didn't get a reply she turned to find empty air. He was a few paces back, talking to a ghillie. She caught the last two words.

'Really? Bugger.'

'Is there a problem?' she called.

He gestured past her. 'Change in the weather. Rain. Coming in fast. We'd better get going.'

She looked to the east, where he was pointing – and sure enough, dark grey columns of cloud were moving in from the direction of the North Sea. The air was changing; there was an edge to it now. The Duke was impressively sprightly as he led the way back down the path towards the Land Rovers, where the Queen was waiting with the dogs. But they were not quite in time. Theresa felt one fat raindrop land on her nose, and another on her cheek, before the heavens opened.

'Oh dear! You look quite bedraggled!' the Queen said, laughing, as they finally reached her.

This was not how Mrs May had imagined spending her early days as Prime Minister, shaking herself down like a wet Labrador before climbing into the passenger seat beside the sovereign in borrowed wellies and a waxed jacket. However, none of the days so far had been what she'd imagined. Picturing this life had been quite pointless, she realised: you never knew what it would hold, and it was impossible to guess.

The Queen, meanwhile, was enjoying herself. The Mays were not the life and soul of the party, it was true, but they meant well and tried hard and, really, what more could one ask? The Prime Minister had talked through her plans for the next few months. She had a busy schedule of talks ahead with the European Union, and had ruled out a snap General Election after her appointment by the party, which was a relief. The country had had enough shocks recently. It was time for a steady hand.

They were talking about the unpleasant nature of surprises as the Land Rover pulled up outside the castle. One of the footmen was waiting for her with an umbrella.

'You might want to come upstairs, ma'am,' he said with some urgency. 'They've got the nets out.'

'Oh, have they? Where?'

'Your bedroom.'

'Goodness! Yes, of course. I'll come straight away.'

The Prime Minister asked what the problem was. The Queen grinned, then grimaced.

'Bats.'

It was as comical as it was frustrating. The poor creatures wanted to get out just as desperately as one wanted to move them from there, but their famous sonar seemed quite incapable of detecting a wide-open window. Usually they caused a nuisance in the white-walled Ballroom below, where the long-handled nets were kept on standby for the purpose of shooing them to freedom. It was rare for them to visit one's bedroom, and the Queen tried not to think about the droppings that might be accumulating on the fixtures and fittings. Charles said the guano was good for the garden. Well, let the bats do it there.

Meanwhile, from a position of safety in the corridor (the Queen was not a huge fan of squeaky, unpredictable pipistrelles close up, despite appreciating them in principle), she and the Prime Minister urged the staff on as they manipulated the nets. There were only two bats, as it turned out, and they got outside eventually. She congratulated the man and woman who had done the work. They made a comical, mismatched pair; the housekeeper, small and slim, she recognised as the stalwart Mrs Harris, who always did such wonders with the Belgian Suite. They exchanged smiles as the housekeeper curtseyed. The large, balding, broad-shouldered man in the footman's red waistcoat was not a familiar face.

'And you are . . .?' the Queen asked.

'Spike Milligan, Your Majesty.' He bowed at the neck.

'Oh, really?' She grinned, but was slightly confused. Spike Milligan was a comedian. Charles had been one of his most ardent fans as an adolescent. He was also most definitely dead.

The footman blushed slightly. 'My real name's Robert, ma'am, but with a surname like mine . . .' He shrugged. 'Some bright spark at school thought it was a good idea and it stuck.'

'Have you ever chased a bat before?'

'Indeed I haven't. It was quite the exercise. I think I've burned some calories.'

The Queen laughed, as she was meant to, but something about Spike Milligan's voice caught her attention. 'You don't normally work up here at the castle, do you?' she asked – purely to hear him talk again.

'Not at all, ma'am. It's my first time. I must say, I'm enjoying it very much.'

'I'm delighted. And thank you for your help.'

He bowed again and left. The Queen glanced at her bed. That top blanket would have to go. But she was thinking about something else. She was back in the wardrobe, listening to the furtive conversation. Had that been Spike Milligan, taking the orders, somewhat unwillingly?

It had been, she was fairly certain.

What on earth had he been asked to do?

Chapter 8

The season turned. Patches of lush green grass in the glens baked to sullen brown. Gin was now drunk at twilight, rather than in the fullness of a bright summer evening, and one needed a padded jacket to hand at all times, as well as a warm stole for after dinner. Soon it would be time to leave the peace of Balmoral and head back to the office on the roundabout.

Alongside the selection of letters from the public that she read each day, the Queen noticed her official boxes getting fuller as the new Cabinet got into its stride. There were more briefings on the US election too. In just over a month, America would be choosing its new president, but the clashes between candidates had taken on a sour note. It seemed very likely that Hillary Clinton would step into the Oval Office. And yet . . . for each story celebrating the notion of a first female president, an ex-Secretary of State with significant government experience and a big team, there was another to criticise and cast doubt on her judgement. Mr Trump, with his tiny team and diatribes on Twitter, had achieved extraordinary results. Nothing was certain. Would one really end up entertaining an ex-reality TV star at Buckingham Palace?

He certainly had some very dedicated followers, if those rallies were anything to go by.

As things stood, there might not be much of a Palace for him to visit. If the Government could be persuaded to let the Reservicing Programme go ahead, the place would be dismantled around her, many of its treasures put into storage and work done to make it more manageable for all concerned. It was ridiculous that a footman should have to walk half a mile from the kitchens to the State Dining Room, and the ceiling of that room was so dangerous it had recently been taken out of commission. The Queen only needed six rooms for her personal use, and they were all perfectly serviceable. It was the other seven hundred and seventy that needed attention.

What would they do if the Government said no? She vividly remembered the failure of the Major government to get Tony Blair's Labour Party to agree to replace *Britannia*. Thank goodness there were no elections coming up to make the thing contentious. She decided to worry about that when the time came.

Meanwhile, Holly's health did not improve. As the return to London approached, the elderly corgi deteriorated rapidly. The vet was called and she agreed that it was time to take action. The Queen felt her heart constrict, but knew what she had to do.

At a cottage in the grounds, Cynthia Harris prepared to return to the Palace. It had been a difficult summer. She knew she wasn't exactly popular with the others, but there seemed to be a real campaign against her now. Several housemaids and footmen weren't talking to her. Soon after her arrival in Balmoral, one of her uniform dresses had been 'damaged' in the wash (hardly accidental: someone had taken a Sharpie to it). She carried on regardless, keeping herself to herself. There had been three letters, all disgusting, written with such hate. One of them even called her a murderess. There was a scribbled image of what had looked like a kidney bean at first, but was obviously supposed to be some sort of foetus, almost scratched out in red ink. *That had been nearly thirty years ago.*

She had told the head housekeeper of the castle about them . . . and now, of course, everyone knew. There was no privacy in the Royal Household. Dirty linen was very much aired in public, not just in the staff rooms and canteens these days, but on Snapchat and WhatsApp and StaffList, the Household intranet that was little more than a sewer of gossip and innuendo. Who knew what they were saying about her? She was probably the subject of half their mean, illicit conversations.

But she wasn't alone. The other half would probably be about Leonie Baxter in the catering office, who was getting letters too, apparently, calling her a bitch and a whore. Nothing as . . . *imaginative* as Cynthia's own persecution. Anyway, Mrs Baxter probably deserved it. She was always causing problems, throwing her weight around, criticising the way things were done. It was no surprise to hear the woman had enemies. Recent speculation in the servants' hall had been all about her.

Cynthia tramped up the stairs to her bedroom. This summer, she had shared the cottage with three other hospitality staff. Needless to say, they treated her like a pariah. Her room was her sanctuary: transformed from dreary functionality with Indian sari fabric used as throws, and flowers begged from the chief gardener, who was one of her few abiding friends. Cynthia knew how to travel light and yet transport a sense of style. Off duty, her clothes were her glory. She wore mostly vintage, which suited her gentle bosom and slight frame. Some of her favourite pieces were by Ossie Clark and Zandra Rhodes, unusual items she'd unearthed in charity shops over the years, irreplaceable and perfect. But she also made things inspired by ideas from Instagram and Pinterest. Her dingy little plywood wardrobe concealed a riot of colourful silks and velvets, all stitched with infinite care.

She was thinking about this as she opened the bedroom door. A moment later, a piercing scream shattered the rural peace of the afternoon.

A dining room assistant, who was sharing the cottage, ran up the stairs two at a time to see what the problem was. Mrs Harris was standing just inside the doorway, trembling, incoherent, looking at the bed. It was covered in a pile of scraps of fabric, so many they took up the same amount of space as a human being. She was shaking so hard she could hardly speak.

'What is it?' the dining-room assistant asked.

'M-my clothes,' Mrs Harris managed to mutter. She pointed a bony finger in the direction of the bed. 'They've c-c-cut up all my clothes.'

Mary van Renen was packing up her belongings, ready to move out of her Fulham flat. She had a few more days left to work and then she could flee to Ludlow, where her childhood bedroom was waiting for her, there were ponies in the field to feed, and her mother had already made a freezerful of coq au vin and stroganoff to celebrate her return.

Mary had chosen this room in the flat because it had the largest wardrobe, even though it was at the back and overlooked by half a dozen nearby offices and houses. At the time, clothes had seemed more important. London clothes, city clothes . . . for her posh job at the Palace and lunches with friends at Instagrammable cafés; for dates with men at glamorous restaurants where, in between the courses you ordered, they served you courses you hadn't, where dishes arrived smoking under glass bell covers and a starter of shellfish was made to look like a beach.

They didn't have restaurants like that in Shropshire, or at least, if they did, it was a big deal. So was finding a straight single man with an interest in art and culture and settling down. But then, that had proved equally impossible in London. Not for either of her flatmates, who had sexy, devoted, rugby-and-football-playing boyfriends, one of whom was a high-flyer at the National Gallery. But for Mary . . . all she seemed to attract were nutters. One nutter, anyway. One was enough.

She glanced out of the bedroom window at the patchwork of lights outside. In the summer, people tended not to draw their curtains. She'd recently seen a couple having sex in one of the windows above a row of garages. Today, that window was dark. The one above it and to the left was dimly lit, though, with a dummy of some sort propped against it, outlined by a pale amber glow. She peered to see what it could be, exactly, and thought for a moment she saw it move. With a familiar sensation of her body plummeting through space, she stifled the scream in her throat. Was it human? Was it watching her? How long had it been there?

'Ella?'

She shouted for her nearest flatmate while trying to keep the panic from her voice. Ella had been at home half an hour ago, but now no one came. Mary closed her curtains and carried on watching through the gap, trembling as she muttered Ella's name into the silence, unable to drag herself away.

The light behind the silhouette was turned out. The shadow merged into the darkness.

At the Palace, Rozie was coming back from a run. She had permission to do a few circuits down behind the lake when the public weren't around. They had gone for good now. The place was being prepared for Her Majesty's imminent return and Rozie's thoughts were on the schedule for next year, which would be her main task in the coming weeks. She had a vast folder of requests for visits and there was not nearly enough time for the Boss to perform them all. Of course, she would want to do as many as she could.

Rozie had left her work clothes ready to change back into in the ladies' toilets near her office, which were posh and contained a shower and comfortable dressing area. No Boss didn't mean no sartorial standards, so her linen jacket was hanging on a wooden hanger behind the door and a Prada pencil skirt she'd found in the Selfridges sale was neatly laid out on a padded stool. Lifting the skirt to reach for the towel folded underneath it, she noticed a plain white envelope tucked between the two.

Strange.

It was not addressed to anyone. The toilets, like the corridor outside, were empty. With a feeling of increasing discomfort, she picked up the envelope and opened it.

Inside was a torn-off piece of paper from a child's exercise book, folded three times so it was the size of a business card. Rozie opened it slowly. It contained three childish drawings executed in blue biro, and four words written in stencilled capital letters. The effect on her was visceral, like a punch to the stomach. For a moment she was suspended in time: a confused little girl herself, watching fear and fury flick across her mother's face. Then, crumpling the note in her hand, she steadied herself while the shock tunnelled down to her core.

Part 2

The Breakages Business

Chapter 9

'Simon, you look dreadful. What's happened?'

On her first morning back at the Palace, the Queen emerged from her bedroom, dressed and coiffured, only to find her Private Secretary waiting for her in the corridor. This was hardly protocol.

'Your Majesty.' He bowed at the neck. 'I wanted to be the one to tell you. I found . . . There's been a most unfortunate accident. A terrible thing. I found . . . There's a body in the pool, ma'am. Not *in* the pool, beside it. A housekeeper. Mrs Harris. I found . . .'

She stared at him. Sir Simon was one of the most competent men in the country. Ex-Royal Navy and Foreign Office, a pilot and a diplomat. She had never seen him like this. There was a smear of red on his earlobe. His tie was askew.

'Come with me and tell me about it. Are you sure you don't need to sit down?'

They walked briskly along the corridor to her study, while Sir Simon, limping slightly, poured out details in no particular order. The housekeeper had fallen, it seemed, and hit her head. The blood was caused by broken glass. The police were here. She looked very cold. He had found her first thing this morning.

The man was grey and she sensed that any minute the shock would kick in properly, and he would hardly be able to stand.

'Get Rozie for me,' she said, once they'd reached her desk and he was starting to repeat himself. 'Then go home and don't come back until I tell you.'

'The police, ma'am . . .'

'Rozie can deal with them. And they can visit you at home. It's not far. You'll be useless to me here.' She said it sharply, not to be unkind but because she knew he wouldn't leave unless she made him, and he was in no fit state to work.

It was her APS, therefore, who got the report from the police about how the housekeeper had died.

'A thick piece of glass cut her artery just above the ankle,' Rozie explained a couple of hours later, standing in the light from the study window, one floor above where the body had been found. She, too, had an odd look about her, but at least her manner was professional. 'A freak accident. It looked as though Mrs Harris slipped and dropped a whisky tumbler she was carrying. The bottom of the broken glass had a lethally sharp edge that must have caught her as she fell. They think she was lying there all night.'

'What was she doing with a whisky tumbler by the pool?'

'Probably clearing it up, ma'am. A few had been left around recently.'

'Can you die from a cut on your ankle?'

74

'Apparently yes, if you're very unlucky. That artery bleeds a lot. It looks as though she slipped and knocked herself out, then came to and tried to stem the bleeding – her hands were covered in blood. But she was too weak to do it, or get up and call for help. She only had a couple of cuts, but that's all it takes. That's what the police inspector I spoke to thinks, anyway. He's requested an autopsy, so the pathologist will let us know for certain.'

The Queen was grateful for the way Rozie didn't pause to check she was 'OK', as people usually did. When one had grown up with dogs and horses one was used to accidents of various ghastly descriptions. Used to death. And she had read the reports of more soldiers killed in battle than she cared to recall. She pictured the poor woman trying to stem the flow of her own blood, and was desperately sad there had been nobody there to help.

'Why was she on her own?'

'The Master's not sure. There's only one CCTV camera in the area and it's been on the blink for ages. It's possible she went to clear up after a family session. She was in uniform and didn't have her costume with her. She probably only meant to be in there for five minutes.'

'Poor Mrs Harris,' the Queen said. 'She's been with us for years. I saw her only recently, at Balmoral.'

'Yes, she went up with the second wave of staff, I believe.'

The Queen nodded thoughtfully. 'And they think she slipped?'

'It seems so.'

'Let me know if they make any unfortunate discoveries.'

Rozie knew exactly what the Boss meant. 'I'm sure it's an accident this time,' she ventured. The last time a body was found at a royal residence, it turned out not to be accidental at all.

Her Majesty gave her a piercing look through her bifocals. 'Don't be too sure of anything. It pays to keep an open mind.'

'Yes, ma'am.'

'Can you find out if Mrs Harris was in any trouble?'

The piercing look was still on her. Rozie felt the Queen's concern. She had a split second to decide whether to keep her promise to Sir Simon from the summer. And if not, whether to tell the full story. She decided to keep some of her thoughts to herself. This was about Cynthia Harris; best for all concerned if it stayed that way.

'I happen to know already, ma'am. She was.'

'Oh?'

Rozie took a breath and explained. 'There's been a spate of poison pen letters. Several people didn't like her. I mean, they had reason not to like her. I don't know how all of them actually felt.'

'What reasons?'

Rozie summed up what she had learned from Lulu Arantes and Sir Simon about the retirement and return. 'There was a lot of resentment. And . . .' Rozie paused.

'And what?' The blue stare was unwavering.

'Well, ma'am, I understand several people thought Mrs Harris had undue . . . that she was quite close to you, ma'am, because she helped out with the guest suites and you're so particular about them.'

Rozie wondered whether she was being too direct, but didn't have time to find the elegant courtier's way of telling the truth. Sir Simon would have managed – if he'd been here, and not at home with his wife and a stiff brandy.

If the Queen was offended, she didn't show it. 'Thank you, Rozie.' But she pursed her lips again. 'Why wasn't I told before?'

'About what, ma'am?' Rozie asked, stalling for time.

'About all this unpleasantness. The bad feeling about Mrs Harris. The poison pen letters. I could have done something.'

'I – I don't know. Sir Simon felt . . . I mean the Master . . .' Rozie struggled to finish her sentence without implying the senior courtiers had made a terrible mistake. Which, in her opinion, they had.

The Queen nodded and waved a hand. 'They had it under control, no doubt,' she said coldly.

'Yes, ma'am.'

'They didn't mind the implication that a housekeeper had me in her power.'

Rozie was shocked at the baldness of this statement. But she couldn't deny it.

'They were unhappy about it. But there was an HR process to go through before they could ask her to retire again. The anonymous letters made it difficult.'

The Queen was thoughtful for a moment as she looked out of the study window towards Constitution Hill. When she turned back her voice was sharp. 'Is there anything else I'm being protected from?'

A million things, Rozie thought. But nothing worth sharing at this point. 'Not as far as I know, ma'am. If I think of anything, I'll tell you.'

'Thank you. That will be all.'

Once she was alone, the Queen turned her gaze back to the view. It was a crisp October day and the sky was powder blue above the trees. For London, the air was clear and bright, but after the Highlands she could make out the fug of air pollution that rendered everything slightly grey. She had been anticipating problems on her return . . . But not this.

It was true, she and Cynthia Harris had been close in a way. When you need your home to run like clockwork, you come to rely on those professionals who work to your standards. Any room prepared by Mrs Harris was always impeccable. There was never a speck of dirt or a hint of disrepair. Fraying fabrics were magically replaced; requests for specific books or flowers were always met; even the allergies of guests' staff were considered. There had been that awful time not long ago during the President of Mexico's visit, when the Orleans bedroom in the Belgian Suite had been filled with Casa Blanca lilies, which had given his chief of staff a streaming nose in minutes. That would never have happened if Mrs Harris was in charge. It must have been while she was away. Hmmm.

The woman had been friendly but not forward, practical, tireless – and unquestionably loyal. In Balmoral she would always grab a net and leap about with the best of them to catch the infernal bats. They had shared the occasional joke. Her attention to detail was obvious in the way she looked after the rooms in her care, but they were not close in the way Rozie seemed to suggest.

The Queen sighed. After sixty-three years on the throne, she was not as impressionable as some members of her Household gave her credit for. She could see that Mrs Harris was a bit of a toady. She had noticed her occasionally being sharp with junior maids, but instantly sunny as soon as she turned her attention to a VIP. It had struck her as unusual that the woman was still working beyond retirement age, and indeed she had asked the Master about it last year, but he had said 'she wanted to' and 'it was all under control'. It always was with the Master. But what control? Had he controlled who Mrs Harris made enemies of? Could he?

The Queen took off her bifocals and fiddled with her fountain pen. She felt a mix of guilt and frustration. If Cynthia Harris had been causing problems, someone should have said. One could live with the occasional poor choice of flowers in the Belgian Suite if it meant the Household as a whole was happy. Was that the sort of thing the housekeeper hadn't mentioned in her handover notes? The Queen wished people didn't always assume that obeying one's every whim was the be-all and end-all. It was more than a whim to desire the staff to get on with each other. That mattered too, surely?

Even so. Mrs Harris's reliability and flair were a rare mix and the Queen would miss her. The poor woman had been receiving poison pen letters and now she was dead.

And there was something else.

She thought hard for a moment, gazing into the middle distance. Rozie had said something she had meant to follow up on. What was it?

A spate of poison pen letters. Mrs Harris was not the only victim.

She reached swiftly for the phone on her desk and asked to be put through to the Master.

'Good morning. I'd like to see you in my study immediately. If you would be so kind.'

Chapter 10

'You *what*?'

Sir Simon, back at his desk and, it seemed, fully recovered from the shock, was incandescent.

Rozie stood her ground. 'I told her about the letters. I had to.'

'Oh, you *had to*, did you? Why, exactly?'

'She asked.'

'Asked if there were any letters, specifically? Any damaged items?'

'No. She asked if I knew whether Mrs Harris was in any trouble. What damaged items?'

'It doesn't matter. I told you about the letters in confidence. God, Rozie! The Master told *me* in confidence. Can't I trust you?'

He was standing at the carved marble mantelpiece in his office, flexing his hands into fists while she stood facing him. This was not a sit-down conversation. In fact, it was abutting the borders of a rollicking bollocking, Sir Simon-style.

'Yes, of course you can,' she said.

'How? How?'

'I can't lie to the Queen!' Rozie raised her voice to match his, which then became icy.

'I never ask you to lie, simply to let the right person tell their own story. Is that so difficult?'

Rozie stood in silence. She understood, up to a point. But since her arrival late last year, she had developed a bond with Her Majesty that Sir Simon couldn't even guess at. She had lied to *him*, when the Queen needed her to. If he even half suspected how much, she would become one of those people like Cynthia Harris who other staff hated for their privileged access to the Boss.

She kept her head held high. It was easy to know what to do: lie again. Brazenly. And as often as it took.

'Of course, Sir Simon. It won't happen again.'

She only called him 'Sir Simon' when he was shouting at her, which was rare. She saw from the tick in his cheek that he was slightly ashamed of himself. It was his tell. Breathing hard, she took advantage by withdrawing from the room and closing the door with infinite care behind her.

He wouldn't know what she was thinking. It would drive him mad. Serve him right. And thank God he didn't know what she was holding back, because if he did, he'd be even more furious with her than he already was.

When she was alone, Rozie messaged her sister in Frank-furt to let off steam. It was rare for a day to go by without an exchange of some sort between them – often accompanied by a meme, a few jokes and a selection of emojis. She didn't tell Fliss what was happening, and Fliss knew enough not to ask. It was good just to make some stupid faces and apply the

82

cheesiest filters she could find. Fliss, as usual, tried to teach her a new word in German. Today, it was *Backpfeifengesicht*: 'someone who you feel needs a slap in the face'.

Rozie's list of approving emojis went on for two lines.

The Queen spent the weekend visiting friends. On Monday morning, Sir Simon's mood plummeted from chilly to glacial. He called Rozie into his office again.

'Can I help?'

'You certainly can. We've got the Met in. A detective chief inspector is arriving this morning. You can look after him. I have things to do. You can imagine how the press are slavering for details on the body.'

Rozie, who also had a full diary, simply nodded. 'Of course. What's he—'

'He's here about the letters. Well done. You can introduce him to the Master. That'll be an interesting conversation. "We didn't trust you to take care of it. We told Her Majesty and she's called in the police".'

Rozie peered to see if she could see actual steam coming out of his ears. 'I'll introduce the man, certainly. Do you know where he's going to work?'

'I know practically nothing. She organised this from her weekend jolly, God knows how. He may come with a hundred officers, for all I know. Put them in the Ballroom. Order up some computers and a whiteboard. Let's make it an incident room.'

'Yes, Sir Simon.'

He glared at her and left.

Soon afterwards, Rozie received a phone call to say that her visitor had arrived. She went to the entrance at the front of the North Wing in time to see the policeman striding across the Palace forecourt as the last of the scarlet tunics of the Foot Guards disappeared in the direction of St James's Palace. As she approached, she was astonished to see that she recognised him.

The man nodding to the sentry at the gate was DCI David Strong, whom she'd met at Windsor Castle. He had been part of the team in charge of solving the murder there. He was short and squat, wearing a fringed woollen scarf over his suit to keep out the autumn chill. His salt-and-pepper hair had grown slightly greyer since the spring, she thought, but there was a gentle babyishness to his round, pink cheeks that made him look disarmingly cheerful. She greeted him at the door with a smile and a handshake.

'David! Good to see you again.'

'You too, Rozie. Sorry, I'd have been earlier, but I lingered to watch the Changing of the Guard. Haven't seen it since I was a kid. All those soldiers in their busbies. What d'you call them?'

'Bearskins.'

'Do they actually make them out of bearskins?'

'You don't want to know. Come on through.'

She escorted him to her office and got an assistant to make him a coffee (she still remembered Baba Samuel's slightly mind-boggled expression when she explained that, as Assistant Private Secretary she was not a secretary, and nor was the Private Secretary, but that they shared two assistants, who were). The chief inspector made himself comfortable in an antique wing-back chair between the fireplace and a tall Georgian window flanked by silk curtains and masked from the world outside by heavy netting.

'Nice place you've got here.'

'I like to think so,' she agreed.

Strong guessed the netting was blast-proof, in the sense that it was designed to catch shattered glass and protect the room's occupants in case of an explosion. Antiques and bomb threats. Swings and roundabouts. Still nice, though.

'Did Her Majesty explain why I'm here?'

'I think I got a fair idea from Sir Simon,' Rozie said. 'You've been asked to look into the poison pen letters received by one of our housekeepers, who died a few days ago.'

'That's about it. And the others too. She wasn't alone, I gather.'

Rozie nodded as she bent down to fiddle with something on her desk. 'Yes, there are a couple of others. A secretary and a catering manager. Mrs Harris wasn't very popular.'

'So I'm told.'

Rozie looked up again. 'Does this mean the Queen thinks she was killed?'

'No more than you do. Do you?'

'No,' Rozie said. Then, a little less confidently, 'No.'

'I mean, I've looked at the pathologist's report. It does happen. Grisly way to die, but everything's consistent with her having tripped and dropped the glass, then fallen onto it with the jagged edge piercing the artery as she landed. Really bad luck. You can bleed out in minutes if you're not careful. Misadventure, he says. As far as he can tell.'

Rozie tried not to look as relieved as she felt. Of course it wasn't murder.

'But Her Majesty isn't entirely happy with the internal investigation into the letters,' Strong said. 'Thank you.' He smiled up at the assistant, who was back with his coffee.

Rozie tried not to criticise the Master in front of other staff, so she changed the subject. 'I'm amazed that it's you who came, though,' she said. 'Do you work at all the royal palaces?'

Strong laughed. 'If only. No, the Queen asked for me specifically, apparently. You tell *me* why. First and last time we met was at Windsor, and I didn't exactly come out of that one smelling of roses.'

'You solved the case.'

'I didn't.' He smiled wryly and took a sip of coffee. 'Other people did it for me, and how they put all the pieces together I'll never be quite sure. But apparently I didn't blot my copybook too badly. I s'pose I know people here already, like you and Sir Simon. That helps. And I've got the support of my team in SCD11.'

'Remind me . . .?' Rozie asked. She knew that 'SCD' stood for Serious Crimes Directorate, but hadn't mastered its administrative intricacies. Sir Simon would know, of course.

'Mine's a little unit for some of the more interesting stuff,' Strong said. 'We're the SIS of the police, you might say. They like to call us the Shadowy Investigation Service. It's "Specialist" really, but I prefer "shadowy".'

86

He downed his coffee and Rozie offered to take him to the Master. A short corridor led to a set of double doors that brought them suddenly into the gilded splendour of the Marble Hall. Strong looked up and around at the moulded ceiling and neoclassical pillars, craning his neck as if he couldn't quite believe he was really here. Rozie, who was used to it by now, carried on talking.

'Are you bringing a lot of people with you?' she asked, remembering Sir Simon's tetchy comment about the Ballroom.

'Nope,' Strong said, dragging his eyes away from a priceless sculpture and striding out so as to keep up with her. 'In fact, until I see the need to operate otherwise, it's just me and my sergeant. We'll just be asking a few judicious questions, you know. Nothing too scary. Make Sir Mike Green feel I'm not stepping on his toes too much.'

Rozie grinned at him. 'Thank you for that.'

Strong gave her a sideways look. His sharp brown eyes belied those soft, rosy cheeks. 'Might I suppose it was you, then, who spilled the beans to Her Majesty about the letters?'

'I couldn't possibly comment,' Rozie said. 'And it's Mike Green, by the way, not Sir Mike.'

'Ha! I bet he loves that.'

'Knighthoods aren't automatic and he's fairly new. He'll get one eventually.'

'You'll have to talk me through the ins and outs of it one day,' Strong suggested.

'Not my speciality. That's for the Lord Chamberlain's Office.'

'And what d'you call him?'

'Lord Peel.'

Strong giggled to himself, in a way that was not entirely respectful.

Rozie maintained her pace as she guided him along more red carpet, past gilded mahogany doors and life-size portraits of the Boss's ancestors, until they reached the end of the corridor, where the gilding abruptly ended and the carpet switched from crimson to a more hard-wearing industrial brown.

She turned left, and he had to jog a little to stay alongside her.

'I hate to ask, but are we nearly there yet?'

'Almost. This is the South Wing.'

'Do you do this every day?'

'Several times, if I need to. But the Queen's private rooms are above ours in the other wing, so that makes it easier.'

He looked at her heels. 'I mean, how?'

She smiled. 'You get used to it. Here we are. Let me introduce you to the Master. I hope he's expecting us.'

The utterly sour expression on Mike Green's face as he greeted them suggested he was.

Chapter 11

It had been a full day and the Queen was grateful for a quick gin and Dubonnet before supper. This evening she was accompanied by Lady Caroline Cadwallader, one of her ladies-in-waiting. They watched the news on television with the sound down and the Queen wondered how the Master would be coping with the chief inspector's arrival.

Just as the thought was crossing her mind, the façade of Buckingham Palace appeared on the screen, alongside an aerial shot of the pavilion that contained the pool.

'Oh goodness, look!' said Lady Caroline. 'That's us! Isn't it *dreadful*? Shall I turn the sound up? By the way, the gossip in the servants' hall is that there's a policeman at work here now. Is it true?'

The Queen merely nodded and glanced at the unused remote control at her lady-in-waiting's side.

'He doesn't think there was any skulduggery, does he?'

'Not as far as I know.'

'I wouldn't put it past anyone, mind you,' Lady Caroline observed chattily. 'Mrs Harris was an absolute pill, apparently. There was such a to-do when she was brought in from retirement. Everyone was muttering about it.'

'Not to me,' the Queen said grimly.

'Oh, ma'am, of *course* not! You have much more important things to think about. I'm sure the Master was sorting
it out. He—'

She was interrupted by a knock on the door and the
appearance of the Duke of Edinburgh, who strode into the
room and said, 'Are you watching this lunacy? Did you hear
what they just said?'

'No, actually,' the Queen told him with a little sigh. 'Caroline was talking to me about it.'

'They've made up some story about Beatrice and Eugenie
leaving champagne glasses in the pool. They're speculating
the woman fell on a broken bottle of Dom Perignon.'

'What imaginations they have!' Lady Caroline said. 'You
almost have to admire them.'

'I bloody don't.'

'So is that what the policeman is investigating?' she asked.
'Broken glass?'

'Health and safety gone bloody insane,' the Duke grumbled.

'No, actually,' the Queen said in reply to her lady-in-
waiting. She told them about the poison pen campaign and
the Master's failure, so far, to make any headway with it.

Philip made a *ptcha!* noise. 'I've been wondering about
Mike Green. Promoted to the level of his incompetence.
Typical crab. Not the first balls-up on his watch.'

'Is it really so bad?' Lady Caroline asked. 'This poison
pen thing, I mean?'

The Queen ruminated on the aspects that particularly
disturbed her.

'One of the secretaries found a rather disgusting note on her bicycle seat. Some of Mrs Harris's clothes were cut up.'

Philip made a face. 'If it's all frocks and bicycles I'll leave you girls to it. And someone needs to tell the Tristrams at the BBC that we don't all sit around by the damned pool all day drinking bloody Dom Perignon in our pyjamas.'

Once they were alone again, Lady Caroline asked about the note on the bicycle seat.

The Queen explained. 'The poor young woman – Mary van Something – was distraught. I spoke to the Master about it, and he tried to reassure me that he'd discussed it with her and it was nothing more than a "date gone wrong" and some ruffled feathers. He didn't see it as relevant.'

'Oh no!'

'Exactly. The poor thing was being stalked. The man stood outside her house. Those aren't "ruffled feathers".'

'Indeed they aren't. Have you discussed it with the Duchess of Cornwall?'

The Queen had not, but she knew Camilla would be as alarmed as she was. Indeed, it was Camilla who worked with charities in the field and who had explained the extent and the dangers of domestic violence. She cared very deeply about this sort of thing. Did it count as domestic violence if the woman didn't claim to know the man? The Queen wasn't sure, and frankly didn't care. Whatever it was, it was out of the Master's purview, and he should have known it.

She sighed. The previous Master would have got it instantly. Blessed with tact and sensitivity to match his unquestioned authority, he'd been a real rock. It was why her family had always tended to go for senior officers for such positions. They generally combined an essential esprit de corps with the subtle but ruthless efficiency she required from her courtiers. Philip was right. As a man who considered the navy the Senior Service, he was never going to give an RAF officer his due, even an ex-fighter pilot like Mike Green, but in this case he had a point.

The following morning, at her desk, the Queen was reminded of the competence of senior officers who did, happily, live up to expectations. Along with the boxes was a letter from the Second Sea Lord in Portsmouth. She had written to him from Balmoral about the oil painting of *Britannia*, the 'ghastly little painting', as Philip always called it. The Duke had never quite understood why she was so attached to it.

As it happened, the Second Sea Lord, now an admiral, had been one of Philip's equerries many years ago, and the Queen knew him well enough to dictate a note. Sometimes, it took the personal touch. She had explained politely but firmly that the painting was hers and had gone missing in the mid-eighties. She knew it was not the Second Sea Lord's fault that it had ended up in his possession: he'd only been in the job since last summer, while the painting had been in his office for at least a decade. However, one would be grateful if he could facilitate its return.

His reply was apologetic. He explained that he had recently returned from holiday himself, hence the slight delay, but as soon as he had read her note he had put a very able young lieutenant on the case of establishing how on earth he could have inadvertently acquired the Queen's private property. He had also examined the painting in person, realised it was filthy (more apologies) and arranged to have it cleaned at the Royal Navy's expense.

The Queen sighed hard at this. No! Really? Was it too late to change his mind about that? She wondered what excuse she could make.

Anyway, unlike Rozie's more laissez-faire contact in facilities at the MOD, the very able young lieutenant had rapidly discovered that the painting had been personally chosen by the Second Sea Lord of ten years ago and:

I contacted him myself, living in happy retirement in the New Forest, and fortunately for us both he's not gaga yet. Daily crosswords, he tells me, and watching Pointless on the BBC. He remembered the painting well, and says he originally saw it in the MOD building in Whitehall back in the nineties, in the corner office of a procurement mandarin of some sort. Years later, when he got the 2SL posting, he asked if the painting happened to be available. He assumed it wouldn't be, but it never hurts to ask. In this case they found it languishing in central storage. He had it installed at the office in 2004. It's been on the wall opposite my desk ever since.

The MOD's records had been better kept than her own, she mused. Although that was probably a little unfair. These days there were teams of archivists and conservators who could lay their hands on a hatpin at a moment's notice, whereas early in her reign, you could lose a framed Caravaggio and be lucky to track it down in the bowels of one of the palaces. The eighties was the decade when all that had changed, in fact. It was around the time Sholto Harvie had arrived. She remembered the old Deputy Surveyor of the Queen's Pictures fondly. Such a forward-thinker and planner, after the disaster of Anthony Blunt, and such good company. He was an expert on Leonardo, and he'd taught her more about art in a week than his predecessors had in a lifetime. It was a shame he'd stayed for so short a tenure.

Anyway, the 'ghastly little painting' was on its way home at last – though she wondered what state it would be in when the navy finally let go of it. However, that still left the troubling question of how the picture had ended up in the office of a Whitehall civil servant in the first place, when it should have been rehung in its usual place in her bedroom suite in 1986, while she was on her way back from China. If six decades of reigning had taught the Queen anything, it was that it was often the small things one should worry about. Big problems were obvious, with ministers and courtiers falling over themselves to fix them. Small ones were often a sign that someone wasn't paying attention. Had that happened in this case? If so, what else had they missed?

She was musing on this thought when Sir Simon came back to retrieve the boxes and discuss the royal diary for the day.

'The President of Croatia will be accompanied by her husband.' He glanced at his notes. 'She'll meet the Prime

Minister in the afternoon, and no doubt Brexit will be on the agenda. The Prince of Wales and the Duchess of Cornwall met her seven months ago, and so I'm sure you'll want to pass on their good wishes. I have a printed copy of the briefing notes for you here.'

He opened the slim leather folder he'd been carrying, looked horrified for an instant, recovered himself and said, 'I'm so sorry, ma'am. I appear to have left them on my desk. I can just go and get them if you'd like me to—'

'Are you all right, Simon?'

'Yes, ma'am. Perfectly. Absolutely.'

'You look distracted.'

'Not at all, ma'am.' He adjusted his tie, while she watched him silently. 'If you mean the incident in the pool, I can assure you, ma'am, I'm perfectly recovered.'

He was 'ma'aming' her like mad. He often did that when something was bothering him. He had seemed to recover well after finding the body last week, as she would have expected from a former naval officer, but perhaps she was wrong. 'Are you sure?'

The piercing blue gaze made him stiffen with alarm. Sir Simon was not, it was true, feeling at his best. Normally he would have brazened it out, but he was appalled at the idea that the Boss should think he couldn't handle the sight of a dead woman in a congealed puddle of her own blood. He was terribly sorry about the whole thing, of course, but *absolutely fine*. The problem was Rozie, and though the Queen seemed to be developing quite a bond with her and this would not go down well, he might as well be honest.

95

'Just a few little wrinkles with the APS. I'm sure she'll learn, but she's created some local difficulties recently. We're sorting them out. It's all—'

Under control, the Queen thought, a microsecond before he said it. Yes, it would be.

'Oh dear,' she said. 'Nothing I can help with?'

'Nothing at all, ma'am.'

It would be the chief inspector's arrival, the Queen reflected. The Master was probably ranting in his office even as they spoke. Poor Rozie: she had merely done as requested, in explaining about the letters. Sir Simon had confused ideas about where the young woman's loyalties lay.

'I'm sure you'll deal with it,' she said with a practised smile, at which he visibly relaxed. 'Now if you can just get me the briefing notes, that would be very kind.'

While he was away, she considered what to do. Her Private Secretary was clearly still discombobulated by his discovery of the body, and even a man of his immense capability was not above taking the stress out on a more junior staff member who didn't deserve it. She felt slightly guilty for giving him such a ready target in her APS. It was she who had encouraged Rozie to spill the beans about Mrs Harris, and then undermined the Master by calling in the police.

Three women had been targeted by the poison pen campaign. The Keeper's secretary had resigned, the woman in the catering office was on sick leave with stress, and the housekeeper was dead – in the most extraordinary manner. No one else seemed unduly concerned, but the Queen made no apology whatsoever for her response. She had asked the chief inspector to be as diplomatic as possible, but no doubt it grated.

Meanwhile, Rozie was having to take the flak. It might be best if she wasn't around for a few days. Sir Simon and the Master would have a chance to settle down and it would give the girl a little break from this atmosphere.

She looked through the printout of today's engagements. After the visit from the President of Croatia, she had audiences lined up with three senior members of the Armed Forces. William was holding the day's investiture in the Ballroom. Philip was hosting dairy farmers to a meeting in the Bow Room and heart and lung researchers to lunch afterwards in the 1844 Room. There were a couple of private audiences in the afternoon, and the evening called for silk and sparkles at a reception at the Royal Academy. However, one could squeeze in a few spare minutes between walking the dogs and getting changed, if one was careful. She made a note.

At the appropriate time, Rozie arrived at Her Majesty's private sitting room for a chat. The room was cosy and comfortable, with plump cushions on upholstered chairs, family photographs on most surfaces and a series of lamps to cast a gentle glow. But the setting did nothing, it seemed, to put Rozie at her ease. The poor girl was trying to hide it, but the Queen had never seen her look so alarmed. She stood rigidly in the middle of the room, as if bracing herself for bad news. Whatever Sir Simon had been saying to her, it wasn't reassuring.

'I have a slightly unusual proposition for you, Rozie,' the Queen said from the sofa.

'Ma'am?'

'I'd like you to pay a visit to someone who used to work for me.'

'Yes?' Rozie's eyes widened. This was not what she'd been anticipating.

'A man called Sholto Harvie. He's an art historian. He used to work here in the nineteen eighties, and he might be able to shed some light on how my little painting ended up in the archives of the Ministry of Defence.'

'I understood you were getting that back.'

'I am,' the Queen acknowledged, 'but I still don't understand why I should need to. There's something not quite right.'

'I'm sorry I didn't manage to solve it for you over the summer. I tried as hard as I—'

'I'm sure you did your best. You're usually successful, and that's one of the things that strikes me as odd.'

Rozie looked confused. 'I don't . . .'

'If everything was as it should be, you would have traced it quite easily from this end. The fact that you didn't makes me uneasy. As the Surveyor at the time is no longer with us, I'm hoping Mr Harvie, his old deputy, might be able to help. He lives in the Cotswolds, I believe, and I'd like you to pay him a visit. It was all a very long time ago and it may take him a little while to remember something useful, so I suggest you offer to stay nearby and pop in a couple of days in a row.'

By now Rozie's eyes were almost perfectly round with surprise. 'You want me to go to the Cotswolds? For a couple of days?'

The Queen faked a grimace. 'Or even three.'

'I don't think I can spare the time, ma'am. There's the chief inspector, and the state visit to finalise, and your speech about peacemaking . . .'

'The chief inspector can look after himself. Are you on top of the state visit and the speech?'

'Well, yes, I am, but—'

'Can you work on them from your laptop?'

'I could, but—'

'Could you go this weekend?'

Rozie swallowed. The Queen sensed she was struggling with something. 'You're busy?'

'A friend's getting married on Saturday,' Rozie admitted.

'I'd hate you to miss a wedding. Go on Sunday. Stay until Tuesday if you need to, assuming Mr Harvie's at home.'

'But on Tuesday you have the Patriarch of Moscow and the Archbishop. The High Commissioner . . .'

'Sir Simon can brief me. They've met me before. We all know what we're doing.'

Rozie gave her a look of pure bemusement. *All this for a painting?* it said.

Well, yes. And a bit of distance from Sir Simon. The Queen agreed, privately, how odd it must seem, but she still couldn't get rid of the feeling that something was off and it would be remiss not to try and find out what it was.

Chapter 12

Sholto Harvie, Rozie discovered, lived in one of the loveliest villages in the Cotswolds, in a cottage so beautiful it had featured in two national magazines.

He sounded delighted to get her call. 'How wonderful to hear from the Palace!' He insisted that she should stay with him for a couple of nights, rather than 'shacking up at some little B & B in the middle of nowhere'. If he was amazed – astonished, even – to be approached out of the blue in this way, he gave no hint of it. Instead, he was all bonhomie, busily exchanging email addresses and sending her a detailed list of directions to his cottage and asking her to bring a couple of French cheeses from Fortnum's that he couldn't source in Wiltshire, for which he would happily reimburse her.

Rozie ended up working late on the Friday night to get through as much of her overcrowded inbox as she possibly could. On Saturday morning, upstairs in her little attic rooms, she was woken by the cheerful banging of the cleaner's trolley and the sound of Lulu Antares singing.

Rozie opened her door to say hello, to find that Lulu was nursing one arm in a sling. Rozie didn't ask why. They had the usual conversation about towels and linen and Lulu asked what Rozie was up to today. She explained about the wedding.

'Ooh, lovely! I do like a good bash. Are they having it somewhere posh?'

'Just a church in Canterbury and a local hotel.'

'Are you spending the whole weekend down there?' Lulu asked. 'Only, I've got a cousin in Whitstable and it's not very far and they do the most incredible fish and chips. It's perfect for Sunday.'

'I'd love to,' Rozie said wistfully. There was going to be a man at the wedding she would have very much liked to eat incredible fish and chips with on the Sunday. But it wasn't to be, and probably better that way. Rekindled old relationships were usually a disaster. He'd probably show up with a girlfriend and anyway, one-night stands were tacky. She lost her train of thought. 'What was I saying?'

'You'd love to, but . . .?' Lulu looked hopeful.

'I'm off to Wiltshire,' Rozie said, indulging her. Repeating her strange plans aloud made them seem more real somehow. 'I'm staying with an old member of staff, actually. He worked here back in the eighties. He has this amazing cottage in the Cotswolds, apparently.'

Lulu rested her good hand on the trolley. 'Not Mr Harvie?'

'Yes! Goodness, how did you know?'

Lulu rolled her eyes. 'I've heard all about *him*. Awful man.'

Rozie laughed. 'You said that about Cynthia Harris. They can't all be awful!'

'Really fake, if you know what I mean. Good luck with that one.'

Rozie looked again at Lulu. How could she even know? Her curly, dark brown hair was dyed, but her barely lined face suggested a woman in her forties. She would have been a teenager when he worked here, if that. 'Did you know him?' she asked, sceptically.

'Me? No. But I've heard all about him. He was the Surveyor, wasn't he?'

'The deputy.'

'Came in after all that terrible Blunt business. A Russian spy! Maybe it's not surprising. Don't say I didn't warn you. Anyway, have a nice day.'

Rozie recalled the last time Lulu had told her to have a nice day. It was just after mentioning the sister-in-law's cousin who was bludgeoned to death.

'Thanks,' she said, without much conviction. She realised she was truly late now, and disappeared back into her room to shower and climb into the extortionately expensive dress she had succumbed to on Net-a-Porter, when Mark, the ill-advised ex-boyfriend, was on her mind.

Mark didn't show up with a girlfriend. He showed up with eyes only for Rozie's extortionately expensive dress, and a look about him that suggested he'd like to know if she'd invested in equally expensive underwear. (She had.) He looked, sounded and behaved like a man who was totally lined up for incredible fish and chips on Sunday, after an equally incredible Saturday night, and Rozie had to grip the steering wheel of her Mini very hard as she remembered telling him she needed to leave at 9 p.m. to make the long drive to Wiltshire.

He'd taken a room at the wedding hotel. They could have nipped upstairs if they'd wanted to, but that *would* have been tacky. She was regretting not doing it now, but she'd thank herself in the morning.

And it was her own fault that she was driving through the dark at half past eleven at night, fully sober, rather than making herself comfortable with Mark at the hotel bar. When Sholto Harvie had said, 'Come on Saturday night, as late as you like, then you'll be all fresh for Sunday,' she could have said no. Hadn't she deliberately accepted his invitation precisely so that she'd be here, on the M4, not creating some doomed drunken fumble she would inevitably regret?

No. She'd accepted the invitation because she assumed Mark would be with someone else and she couldn't bear to watch him. But he wasn't. And Mark wasn't a fumbler. Not even close. Drunken nights with him had been some of the best.

Damn.

The Mini trilled once, twice, three times. She shook herself and clicked a button on the steering wheel to accept a hands-free call.

'Yes?'

'Rozie?'

'I'm driving.'

'I can tell,' her sister said. 'You always sound cheesed off when you're driving.'

'Just concentrating on the road,' Rozie assured her. 'What's up?'

'Nothing. I was on my way to bed. I just felt like calling. How're you doing?'

Rozie considered this. Fliss never called on a Saturday night. Why on earth would she? Oh, Mark: Fliss was distant friends with the bride. She'd have realised he would be there.

'I'm single and sober. Thanks for worrying about me.'

'I wasn't! I just . . . How'd it go?'

'It was nice. Jojo wore Amanda Wakeley. Backless. Half the older men in the church nearly had a heart attack.'

'She always did have a great back.'

'Still does. Her brother made a pass at me.'

'Again?'

'Won't take no for an answer. His wife was standing *right there*.'

'I liked your dress. It was fly-y-y. Very Iman late nineties.'

'How did you . . .? Ah.' Rozie realised. Her private Instagram account. She'd put up a selfie and a couple of pictures with friends. She'd forgotten her sister stalked her online.

'And Nick?'

Fliss meant Mark. Rozie didn't correct her. 'Nothing. He was there. Look, I'm driving up to the Cotswolds and I've still got a way to go. Can we talk tomorrow, or something? It's dark and I need to concentrate.'

'Sure,' Fliss said, but she didn't say goodbye. Instead, after a pause she asked, 'Everything OK?'

'Yes. Why wouldn't it be?'

'No reason. How's Sir Simon?'

'He's fine. Look, I can talk about him tomorrow, if you like.' There was silence. Rozie felt annoyed at her sister's prying. Her chest grew tight. It was as if a whole cauldron of annoyance was bubbling inside. Mark. This stupid journey. The note. A casual remark at the swimming pool. Maybe Lulu Arantes was right – maybe Sholto Harvie would turn out to be a sex pest. And what would Sir Simon think, with Rozie suddenly disappearing for three days? It was all very well for the Queen to ask her to do it, but Sir Simon liked to think he was in charge, even though he wasn't.

'He's being a pain, OK?' she snapped. 'I can understand it. He found a dead body a week ago.'

'I heard about that. So Sir Simon found the body, huh? Didn't they bash their head or something?'

'Yeah. It was just an accident. But he's being a bit shitty. I said something and he's not taking it well.'

'You said the whole atmosphere was a bit shit this summer.'

'It was. It is. You just feel like you have to watch your step. It wasn't like that before. It's like everyone's watching everyone else and judging. And you don't know what anyone's thinking, about Brexit, or this Trump thing. You start to say something, and people just stare at you. And . . . Oh hell. Forget I said that. It's late. I'm tired.'

In the silence that followed, she realised that had been quite a speech. She couldn't usually get a word in edgeways when her sister called. It had always struck Rozie as funny that Fliss, the chattiest, loudest, most-likely-to-interrupt-you woman in the world, had a career as a psychotherapist and counsellor. It was only when she was in work mode that she—*Damn.*

'Are you listening to me?' Rozie challenged her angrily.

'Of course I am.'

'I mean *actively* listening. Like work. Are you working on me?'

'No! Not at all. I would never—'

'Ah-ah! Don't you dare work on me!'

She always knew when her little sister was lying. Rozie was the most on-top-of-things person in the family. Always had been. If she could survive a foxhole in Helmand Province, she didn't need her sister's bloody therapy.

'I'm fine,' she said forcefully. 'Thank you for asking. Just missing a little late-night action with Mark. It's not a problem.'

'I never said it was.'

'Give Viktor my love. See you. Bye.'

Rozie ended the call with a jab, flicked on the radio, cycled through several stations and ended up with some late-night jazz that calmed her mood a little. She sped down the motorway at eighty-five, nudging ninety, until she imagined the news reports of her being arrested splashed all over the tabloids:

QUEEN'S FIRST BLACK ASSISTANT
SPEEDING SHAME

Grudgingly, she slowed down to just over the limit, which in the sporty Mini felt almost stationary. The motorway was straight and endlessly dull, and the darkness hid whatever delights the countryside might have had to offer. It gave her time to think back to how angrily she'd responded to her sister's check-in. That wasn't like her at all. She was usually grateful for a call.

What *had* prompted that cauldron of fury? Mark was a part of it, yes – but he was just a guy she used to know. It was thinking back to Sir Simon and the Palace that had done it. There was crackling tension in the air, not just with him, but with everyone. True, the Reservicing Programme was putting people under pressure, but normally they pulled together as a team. There was the housekeeper's death, of course, but things had been wrong before that. They were wrong when Rozie first encountered Cynthia Harris. She remembered feeling it in the canteen. At the time, she'd felt like an observer, but now she realised she was caught up in it too. The note tucked into her folded clothes. Everything had changed with the note. She tried to pretend it hadn't happened, but she'd been on edge ever since.

Driving west through the dark, she saw her London life come into sharper focus. There was a force at work in the Palace that was undermining the 'happy ship', as Sir Simon liked to call it, that she had joined. It was hard to pin down, but it manifested itself in dark looks and broken friend-ships, in cruel messages and damaged personal possessions. And even in death. In such an atmosphere, how could the housekeeper's tragic fall possibly be accidental, as she'd just assured her sister?

The Boss had called in the police. She was worried too, but if she was trusting David Strong to find the answer, it meant she didn't know where to look.

Rozie rolled her shoulders. For now, she was just glad to be away from it all for a while. Eventually the road sign she'd been waiting for showed up in the beam of her headlights: ROYAL WOOTTON BASSETT.

She turned off the motorway. The sign brought back a whole different set of memories. The last time she'd been here, she was in the back of a four-tonner and the town had been plain 'Wootton Bassett'. At this time of night, for military personnel returning from active duty as she had been, the place was nothing special. But by day, when the dead from Afghanistan were transported in their flag-draped coffins from the military airfield at RAF Lyneham, the locals had turned out to pay their respects to each one. It must have been a strange sight. Hard not to be moved, and the Queen had granted the whole town the title 'Royal'.

This was the first time Rozie had seen the words written down and they brought a lump to her throat. They brought back the banter in the back of the four-tonner on the way home from Helmand, and unspoken thoughts about families who'd be meeting up with someone who had changed in ways the mums and dads would never really know; other families who'd be meeting a coffin . . . friends you'd never see again.

She drove on. According to the satnav she'd arrive at Easton Grey at close to midnight. Sholto Harvie had promised her that it didn't matter what time she got there. 'If I've gone to bed, help yourself to whatever you can find in the kitchen. Your bedroom's the first on the left at the top of the stairs. I'll see you in the morning.'

She parked up at two minutes past twelve. An owl hooted as she unloaded her bags from the car. The key to the house was where he'd said it would be, under a box plant beside the front door marked The Old Haberdashery. She let herself in.

Chapter 13

In one of the staff kitchens at Buckingham Palace, a debate was taking place between two liveried footmen, who had recently come off duty, and a telephone operator and a security night-shift manager who were about to start. The topics of conversation were the same as they had been for a week: England's chances in the World Cup, the Access Hollywood tapes, and the latest news regarding the body in the swimming pool.

'Word has it,' the junior footman said, casting his eye around his audience, 'Sir Simon came out covered in blood – face, hands, the lot – and went straight to the Queen's bedroom. She nearly had a heart attack.'

'He fainted in her room. They had to shut it up,' the telephone operator interjected.

'What? The bedroom?' the night-shift manager asked.

'No, the faint. Nobody was supposed to know, but I heard it from one of the housekeepers.'

'What was he doing in her bedroom?'

'You're over-exaggerating,' the senior footman said, casting a withering look at his companions. 'It's all rumours. Fainting in her bedroom? Don't be an arse. What you've got to ask yourself is: what was he doing in the *pool*?'

'What d'you mean?'

'When was the last time Sir Simon Holcroft went swimming? Tell me that.'

'Don't look at me. How would I know?'

'Never. That's when. That's all I'm saying.' The senior footman leaned back and folded his arms.

The operator wasn't quite sure what his point was, but it certainly sounded suspicious, now you came to mention it.

'What was *she* even doing there?' the junior footman said into the ensuing silence.

'Cynthia Harris?' the night-shift manager queried. 'That woman would get anywhere. Probably spying on someone. The family, I should think.'

'She'd never do that. She had her nose so far up their—'

'Spying on one of us, then,' the operator speculated.

'Maybe she had a secret drink habit. You heard they found her with a bottle of whisky?' the night-shift manager said.

'I heard it was gin,' the junior footman added.

'Did they?'

'Serves her right, anyway,' the senior footman concluded. 'The manky witch.'

'All the same,' the night-shift manager said – and this was something he *was* certain of, because he'd seen it with his own eyes – 'she was lying there all night, they said. You can still see the stain on the grouting, if you look.'

Rozie awoke to the smell of fresh coffee and the sound of virtuoso piano coming from downstairs. Eyes closed, she took a moment to remember where she was. Ah yes, a strange man's house in the countryside. All alone. In a very comfortable bed, to be fair, with smooth linen, soft pillows and a duvet light as air that enveloped her in a warm cloud of goose down. The room also smelled fantastic. Was it spices or woodsmoke behind that coffee aroma? She wasn't quite sure, but it was gorgeous. She just wanted to lie there forever, but the strange man would probably think that was rude. Reluctantly, she got up. There was a vintage green kimono hanging on the back of the bedroom door. She ran her hands over her very short hair (her mother was always telling her to grow it), slipped the kimono over her T-shirt and shorts and padded downstairs barefoot to say hello.

'Ah, you must be Rozie.'

The man at the ancient Aga was rotund, with swept-back hair and an easy, soft-lipped smile. He wore a striped cook's apron over French-blue cotton trousers and a crisp cotton shirt. Rozie was grateful for the kimono: it looked as though she'd made more of an effort than she had.

'And you're Sholto. Hi. Thank you for having me.'

'Not at all. So glad you made it safely. Was it easy to find?'

'It was, with your instructions.'

He smiled. 'Now, what can I get you? Coffee? Orange juice, eggs, sausages? What does your heart desire? I should say, the eggs are fresh this morning, from next door's chickens. The bread is yesterday's, but it's a good loaf – I pride myself on my sourdough. If you need to freshen the juice with some fizz, there's a bottle in the fridge.'

She laughed. 'No, really. I couldn't. Coffee's fine.'

He made a slight moue, but set about filling the base of a basic-looking steel pot with water from the tap. She watched as he added grounds to a middle section, screwed on an upper part and set it to heat on the stove. Meanwhile, she found she had sat herself at a stool at the kitchen island between them, where a couple of bowls of fresh berries were temptingly to hand. Sholto turned to say something, but instead murmured, 'I thought so,' and walked over to a fridge, from which he extracted champagne and sausages. Rozie was about to demur again, but realised she'd eaten half the strawberries and made a serious dent in the raspberries too. She was hungrier than she'd thought.

'Oh, I'm sorry!'

'Not at all, I bought them specially for you. Now, please don't offer to help, because I don't need it and I hate it. Just relax. I'll be with you presently.'

She rested her elbows on the island and watched as he worked. Sausages were put in a pan to sizzle, bread was carved and oranges pressed to make fresh juice. He seemed to move in a little dance to the piano music coming from a speaker on a nearby worktop, his movements practised and fluid, humming as he went.

'Who's this?' she asked. 'The composer?'

'Mmmm? Chopin. Played by Horowitz. Perfect for a Sunday morning. One, two, three . . . And!'

She thought he was counting to the music, but as soon as he said 'And', the little steel pot on the Aga started to bubble fiercely. Steam emerged energetically from its spout. Sholto watched it for a moment or two, conducting to the music with a wooden spoon he happened to be holding, then whisked it off and poured thick, dark coffee into a couple of waiting porcelain cups.

'Enough for us both,' he said. 'I've already had my first, but the day doesn't really start until the second. Chin-chin.'

He had heated some milk in a tiny copper pan and poured it into their cups. The resulting blend was the most delicious thing she had ever tasted. He waved a hand. 'It's the only way to make it. I learned in Florence, years ago. I'll teach you before you go.'

'Yes please.'

Rozie was starting to realise that this was not a work weekend to endure, but a masterclass in good living. Anything Sholto Harvie wanted to teach her was something she'd be happy to learn.

While he cooked the eggs and sausages, she took the chance to look around properly. The kitchen was large and square, with stone-framed windows overlooking a courtyard garden through a curtain of honeysuckle. Old oak beams were hung with copper pots and sheaves of lavender. Cream-painted cabinets displayed mismatched china, artfully arranged, and an open door led to a neatly stocked larder. This was a cook's kitchen, full of well-used implements, but an artist's space too. No doubt the lustrous green platter of fresh lemons in the corner would be useful if you wanted to make lemonade, but its principal job was simply to look fantastic, which it did.

Rozie very, very much wanted all of it, just as it was, for herself. She hoped it didn't show.

'Here we are. Let me know if you want brown sauce or ketchup. Bon appetit.'

Sholto served her where she sat. The smell of fresh-cooked sausages was only beaten by the tingle of champagne and orange juice on her tongue. The room by now resounded with the orchestral crescendo of Gershwin's *Rhapsody in Blue*, which she had loved since uni.

If he's awful, she thought, remembering Lulu, he's my kind of awful.

'Now, tell me all about *you*,' Sholto said. 'You must have led a fascinating life to be working so closely with Her Majesty. I want to know every little thing.'

They spent the day in conversation, doing some light gardening in the courtyard and cooking together in the evening, where Sholto allowed Rozie to prepare a salad while he put the finishing touches to a casserole.

Sholto had been surprised when she called, out of the blue, and a little nervous about entertaining her, but it was really very pleasant to remember his time working for the Boss. It was a privilege that few get to experience – a bit like going into space. They had formed a connection back then, he thought, he and the Queen. He was touched to think she must have thought so too. Rozie, he could tell, had also fallen under the Boss's spell. It was easily done. He was a little jealous of the girl right now, if he was being honest with himself.

She had been fascinating on the subject of her childhood in Notting Hill, and her rather brilliant – though she was reluctant to share details – army career. All very impressive. Now it was her turn to ask about his time in as Deputy Surveyor. She'd asked about the summer of a particular year, but he wasn't sure what he'd be able to tell her. However, he could give her a flavour.

'London in the eighties. I can't tell you how glamorous it was. Were you born then, Rozie?'

'In 1986.'

'Oh, just the time we're talking about! Where?'

'In Kensington.'

'That's where I lived, in Kensington Palace. Don't laugh at me – lots of us did. I had a little flat at the back. It was fantastic. It was the days of Charles and Di, when it was all starting to go pear-shaped, of course, but hardly anybody knew. He used to weekend round here; Highgrove's just up the road. She'd stay in town with the boys. I used to see Diana at KP all the time. Cigarette pants and fluffy jumpers, great ankles, great hair. She had the dirtiest, sweetest smile from under that blonde mop. "How are you doing, Sholto?" She always gave the impression she thought – hoped, even – you were up to no good. I only wish I was.' He sounded wistful.

'What was your job, exactly?'

'I didn't have a job *exactly*.' He took a swig of wine and poured some into the casserole. 'I mean, I had a job, but it wasn't exact. The Surveyor's department was terribly old-fashioned then. It was all very serious art history, don't you know, like it was some sort of Oxford college, or the Courtauld. But we had this fabulous collection, and people needed to know about it and see it. *The* people, I mean. Everyone, not just us courtiers. It needed cleaning and cataloguing properly and . . . Oh, we were very busy. We made it up as we went along, but we were very good.'

'I don't think they do that now. Make it up, I mean.'

'Oh no, they don't!' He laughed. 'There's an army of them now at the RCT – it's a *Trust* now, of course – hundreds of 'em. You lose track. All those job titles! We were only a dozen or so. We had more of a free hand . . .' He paused and Rozie looked up. She must have seen the bittersweet look on his face. 'I helped to set up the conservation department. Probably the most important thing I did.'

They ate at a round table draped in a vintage tapestry. He explained that the 'cottage' was in fact an old haberdashery, converted from a shop a hundred years ago. Sholto watched Rozie drinking in what he'd done with the place, seeing what she could learn. In this room, an antique Venetian mirror above the mantel was flanked by symmetrical collections of modern porcelain and vintage glass. Elsewhere, he was more abandoned in his taste. There were paintings wherever the bookshelves allowed: oils and watercolours, old and new, in a wide variety of frames, hung from floor to ceiling in unpredictable patterns. He was convinced that in a few years' time, when she could afford it, she'd do the same.

Once they'd finished their casserole, and the claret, and the cheese she'd so kindly brought from Fortnum's, they took their drinks into the sitting room. Rozie curled her feet under her on one of the sofas. He asked what she was thinking about.

'I was thinking how comfortable this room is. And wondering who painted that picture of trees on the stairs near my room, whose signature looks like Cézanne. And why you left London, if you loved it so much.'

He drummed his fingers against his glass for a while, reflecting.

'Well, it took me twenty years to get this room right, but thank you for noticing. The rug was lugged back from Kathmandu, for example. My wife had some rather nice furniture.'

'Oh, I'm sorry,' Rozie said. She must have picked up on the past tense. 'Did your wife pass away?'

He nodded briskly. 'Yes. Heart attack. A long time ago. Sorry, what else? Ah – the artist on the stairs. That is indeed, well done you, Cézanne.'

'What?' She stared at him. 'Really?'

'Very small. Very pretty. I do adore his trees.'

'Was it your wife's?'

'No, but good guess. I admired it when I was working for a wealthy widow in Hampshire. I advise on art collections, you see, and hers was outstanding. It helped that her husband had been a Scandinavian billionaire, but she had a good eye. Anyway, when she died . . .' He waved a hand.

'Lucky you.'

'Lucky me, as you say.'

'Why put it up the stairs?'

'Because it's funny,' he explained. 'Of course, it's the most valuable thing I own. Like keeping your Oscar in the downstairs loo. What was the other thing? Oh yes, leaving London. I had to move out. I lost a friend there and it was too painful. But I still miss it. The palace, particularly.'

'I can imagine,' she said. 'I have a room there, overlooking the lake. It's—'

'I don't mean Buckingham Palace – I mean St James's.'

'Oh?'

'It's *much* more interesting than Buckingham Palace. Did you know it's still the official residence of the monarch?'

Rozie shook her head. 'So *that's* why the ambassadors are appointed to it.'

'Exactly. Henry VIII had it built on the site of a leper hospital.' Sholto warmed to his theme. 'And Buckingham Palace was built on the site of a failed mulberry orchard. The Boss once told me that James I wanted to produce silk, but got black mulberry trees instead of white ones, so the silkworms weren't interested. She loves it when things go wrong in history. I find Buckingham Palace so ugly, don't you? That awful façade. They should get rid of it.'

Rozie stared. 'No façade? But what about the balcony?'

'Oh, they'd cope.' Sholto waved a hand dismissively. 'They could build another one. The whole East Front has only looked that way since 1913. We think of it as ancient, but honestly, it's *nothing*, in royal terms. Now, I really think we need a little whisky, don't you? I'll find us a decent bottle.'

In her bedroom in the North Wing, the Queen reflected on how she used to be able to see the Palace from her parents' house on Piccadilly and wave to 'Grandpa England'. It had seemed magical then. Today, it was grimmer than she'd known it for a long time.

The servants' hall, she knew, was still rife with speculation about the body in the pool. The press and various magazines were offering huge bounties for recent pictures of the inside of the north-west pavilion, and so far they hadn't got any. The staff were behaving with admirable decorum on that front, though it helped that there was a permanent guard at the door these days.

The media were far more obsessed with the fact that Buckingham Palace *had* a pool. Philip's alarm had been well founded: there were screeds of articles speculating on the royals' 'luxury spa' lifestyle and complaining about the 'extortionate' Sovereign Grant paid by the Treasury each year to fund it.

She was waiting for them to pick up the story of the poison pen campaign. They called that sort of thing 'trolling' these days, apparently. At least if they did, one could point to an ongoing police investigation into the matter. It made it look as though one was actually *doing* something – which of course one was, though she suspected it was not enough.

Was it possible that, in the midst of a cruel campaign against various female staff members, the violent death of one of them could be an accident? The Queen longed for reassurance that it was, but she was equally certain, deep down, that she wouldn't believe it if she got it. The chief inspector was due to make his first report tomorrow. She looked forward very much to hearing what he had to say.

David Strong, for his part, was not particularly looking forward to reporting to Her Majesty. He found her faintly terrifying, for reasons he couldn't quite pinpoint. She was hardly known for her towering intellect, but he had found, on his first case working for her at Windsor, that she was a hell of a lot sharper than she looked. Mistakes were picked up on. Dry comments were made. Eyes were rolled. He didn't want the Queen of England rolling her eyes at him tomorrow afternoon. Seriously not.

Which was why, at half past eleven at night, he was still up with his sergeant, in their makeshift office at the Palace, going over what they knew – which wasn't as much as he'd have liked. It had taken time to set up and get to grips with the environment. Far from a bank of computers in the Ballroom, he and Detective Sergeant Highgate had a padlocked cubbyhole in the South Wing on the floor above the Master's office for conducting interviews, two secure office laptops, some notepads and a couple of wonky chairs that had seen better days. The air vice-marshal didn't want them to get too comfortable, he assumed. No problem. Strong always worked better when he was uncomfortable.

To start with, there was just the language. He and DS Highgate were working their way through acronyms and nicknames as fast as they could. They were almost as bad as the Met. SJP was St James's Palace, KP was Kensington Palace, the APS was that lovely, capable Nigerian girl, Rozie. Could you call her Nigerian when she came from London? He wasn't sure. Nigerian *heritage*, that was probably it. The D of E was the Duke of Edinburgh (he knew that). Welly B was Wellington Barracks, where the soldiers who guarded the Palace were housed. The current lot were the Welsh Guards, who were known as the Foreign Legion for some reason. Strong's mother was Welsh and he felt slightly offended, but hadn't said so. For professional purposes, he greeted everything he was told with a smile, a nod and silence, which was generally interpreted as approval – whether it was or not.

He didn't smile about the poolside accident, though. The woman sounded like an old bat, but still . . .

'First off, the cause of death,' he said to his sergeant. 'Nothing new on HOLMES?'

DS Highgate, who had been tasked with checking up on the Met's incident room database, shook his head. 'No updates to speak of. The pathologist didn't find any signs of violence, other than what can be explained by the dropping of the glass and the fall. "Laceration of the posterior tibial artery". Looks like nothing, but you can easily bleed out if you don't get to A & E in time.'

'What d'you think of my suicide idea?' Strong said. 'She was under pressure, and the harassment was escalating in the days before she died?'

'Nah.' Highgate was unconvinced. 'Too nasty.'

'People cut their wrists. Why not an ankle?'

'Why do it there? She had access to a bathroom with a bit of privacy. Everyone says she was a massive Queen fan. Person, not band. Why subject Her Maj to the publicity?'

'Fair point,' Strong acknowledged. The good thing about Andrew Highgate was that they tended to disagree about things. It kept Strong on his toes and lessened the risk of confirmation bias. He'd done the same for *his* boss in times past. 'ABC, though,' he added.

'I'll keep it in mind,' Highgate promised. Strong had re-inforced the mantra from day one: *Assume nothing; believe no one; check everything.* Or as Strong generally preferred: *Arrest everyone; believe no one.* Except you couldn't really do that here.

There was nothing suspicious in Cynthia Harris's phone records, but they were still looking into that. They ran over the poison pen letters she had received. There had been eleven of them, all told, including a couple the year before her so-called 'retirement'. All handwritten on cheap paper, some in pencil, some in biro, done with stencil sets to disguise the handwriting. No prints, beyond those of the woman herself, the Master, and the four people in HR who'd handled them. All correctly spelled and punctuated, which was unusual for this sort of thing. Three found in coat pockets, four in her locker, two in a handbag, one in a tote bag, one in a room she was about to clean. All containing personal information referring to private moments in her past.

'The fake marriage,' Strong noted. 'She was accused of making it up just so's she could change her name. I'm inclined to believe that's true. The various demotions in her early days. We have a list of those, don't we?'

'We d-o-o,' Highgate said, hesitating on the second word. 'It's a bit vague. HR are going to try and get us a better one.'

'See if you can get it first thing. And then the abortion in 1987. She claims no one at the Palace could have known about that. Yet someone did.'

'We also have a list of the physical attacks on her property,' Highgate went on. 'All fairly recent. Twice, in June and September, clothes marked with an indelible marker. Once, in early July, her locker emptied and contents scattered about.

A make-up case "of sentimental value" was reported missing at that point.'

'And the cut-up clothes three days before she died.'

'Yes.'

'Curious, those clothes,' Strong said in passing. 'Did you see the descriptions? Antique stuff – what d'you call it? – vintage. Designer, some of it. Makes her sound quite . . .'

'Unusual?' Highgate suggested.

'Outgoing. Extrovert. And yet, everyone says she was a self-contained—'

'Superbitch,' Highgate finished off for him, roughly quoting what they'd been told. They agreed it was odd.

'Main suspects were the Simpson woman and Mrs Arabella Moore, whose husband was sacked when he failed to replace Harris successfully,' Highgate said. 'The Simpson woman's out, because she wasn't in Scotland at the right time. But from what I've heard around the Palace, they were practically queueing up. Do these notes strike you as a woman's work?'

They looked at them again, together, studying the style and content. It was hard to decide. Words such as 'hag' and 'harridan' were regularly repeated, along with 'shrivelled-up' (hyphenated) 'shrew' (alliterated). They knew from experience that on paper a woman could be as cruel to another woman as a man.

They moved on, running through the messages received by the lady in the catering office, Leonie Baxter, who'd been up in Scotland in the second wave of servants, but had come back early to help prepare the Palace. Her harassment had started in July and included misogynist Twitter trolling as well as notes. Cynthia Harris didn't have a social media account, which might explain the difference. The paper notes, all in stencilled capital letters, were left in similar places: bag, coat pocket, desk drawer. Mrs Baxter, too, was unpopular in certain quarters, with a reputation for being 'difficult'. She was a junior manager on the team that dealt with the entertainment budget – but most of her time was spent advocating for women's rights within the Household: more comfortable uniforms, more women's toilets, better career structures. She regularly pointed out that all the senior positions were occupied by men.

'Except at the very top, ha ha,' Highgate noted.

'She sounds like a bit of a pain,' Strong muttered.

'You can't say that these days, boss,' Highgate warned him. 'Women's rights are human rights. Or equal rights, same difference.'

'Yep, no problem, but there's ways and ways of asking for them.'

'Politely, you mean?' his junior suggested.

'In a friendly sort of way, yes. What's the matter with that?'

'Thin ice, boss,' Highgate said with a shrug. 'That's all I'm saying. Thin ice.' He scrolled through his notes. 'Anyway, she's disliked, but no obvious enemies. If anything, she was quite friendly with Arabella Moore. And then there's the van Renen girl, and everyone likes her. No enemies at all.'

'Or someone who's keeping himself well hidden.'

'If he's even a part of this. He could be what he says he is: a Tinder date from outside the Palace.'

'Except van Renen says he isn't,' Strong pointed out. 'When are you seeing her?'

'Next week,' Highgate said. 'She wasn't happy about it, but when I told her the Queen had personally asked us to sort it out, she said OK.'

'Good. And when do we get the handwriting analysis back on the stencils, by the way? I'm expecting a full character analysis from how much pressure he uses to dot the i's.'

Highgate threw him a look. 'God knows. Two to three weeks, they say, and I've pulled the whole royal thing, honestly. It's austerity cuts. Everything has a waiting list. Same story with the tech guys looking into the social media stuff. They're knee-deep in kiddie porn. It's a long queue.'

Strong grunted. ''Twas ever thus,' he said. 'Believe me, it wasn't all exactly a bed of roses ten years ago.'

'I was in sixth form then,' Highgate said cheerfully. 'I wouldn't know. Of course, if Mrs Harris was *murdered* . . .'

'We'd be at the front of the queue. Trust me, I've thought of that,' Strong assured him. 'Not that I'd wish it on her. But it would make our lives a hell of a lot easier.'

They wound it up for the night.

Despite his experience at Windsor Castle, Strong had somehow assumed that solving a crime at Buckingham Palace would be easier than normal. In fact, it was harder. He'd liked to have seen evidence of how Cynthia Harris was feeling the night she died. It was a shame there was no CCTV of her. The one interior camera on the ground floor of the North Wing had been on the blink for weeks. You'd think the place would be bristling with them, but apparently Prince Philip didn't approve of 'bloody spycams everywhere', despite the Queen once being hassled *in her own bedroom* by a man who literally wandered in. She'd kept the man talking until a servant arrived, *as you do with a total stranger in your bedroom*. That woman was made of steel – another reason he was nervous about tomorrow. There was a plan to upgrade the security system, about thirty years too late, but it was waiting for some sort of parliamentary approval. Who'd be a royal, eh?

Chapter 14

Sholto Harvie came downstairs on Monday to find Rozie surreptitiously taking pictures of his sitting room on her phone. She quickly pocketed the offending article, but he'd heard the shutter noise from the stairs. She grinned at him guiltily from the hearth.

She was beautifully lit by the morning sun that poured through the east-facing window. She would make a wonderful model, he thought, for a man who knew how to paint. Or, rather, who *could* paint. Sholto knew exactly how, but what he'd gained in understanding, he almost entirely lacked in talent. He could still admire the rounded planes of her face, the strength of that short, sharp hair, counterbalanced by the sculptural quality of her smile. More than that, he liked the way she inhabited the kimono, the room, the house. She was a girl with the world at her feet and her life ahead of her. She thought she knew, but she had no idea, really, how far this job could propel her. She needed it to, he thought. She didn't strike him as the sort to marry a man for his money, so she'd have to find a way of making it herself.

Was it Rozie he wanted to help, or the Boss? He couldn't really decide. One had charmed him thirty years ago, and one was doing it now. He felt guilty that she had come all the way here to talk about a painting that was obviously very dear to Her Majesty, and which must have disappeared while he was working at St James's Palace, but he couldn't give her the information she needed. He wasn't sure what help he *could* provide – very little probably – but he'd do as much as he was able, to make amends.

After breakfast, she asked him again about a refurbishment in the summer of 1986. He knew he'd been vague last night. It was all a very long time ago.

'I'm racking my brains,' he said, rubbing vigorously at a pot with his drying-up cloth, 'but I didn't have much to do with BP – beyond the objects inside it. I don't think I even knew there *was* a refurbishment.'

'Ah, well. It was a long shot.' Rozie was disappointed. The Queen had seemed so optimistic.

'I'm so sorry. I hate to let Her Majesty down. Absolutely hate it. I'll keep thinking.'

Rozie thought he'd forgotten, but after lunch he suggested a walk in the woods behind the house and, as they tramped up the path, he said, 'There's something the Boss perhaps ought to know.'

'Yes?'

'Watch out for roots and rabbit holes. They're a terrible hazard. Oh, I forgot – you've done obstacle courses in the army. What was I . . .? Oh, yes. Things going missing back in the eighties. I wonder if she's aware of the Breakages Business. I think probably not.'

'The Breakages Business?'

'Yes.' He gave a little laugh. 'Up to the left here and over the stile. There's the most marvellous view coming up. Where was I?'

Rozie reminded him.

'Aha! Sorry. I just love it out here, don't you? Especially on a day like this. Turn right along the path. We're nearly there. You see, if you lived round here you could keep horses. I don't ride, but I suppose you must, if you were in the Royal Horse Artillery. You do? Oh yes, sorry, sorry, the Breakages Business. I s'pose they got the name from insurance fraud. You know . . . "breakages". There were a few of them in the gang, not more than three or four, I should say, but their racket was to offload things that weren't needed any more. Or sometimes suppliers would be told a delivery wasn't up to scratch and it would be replaced, without letting the finance people know. That sort of thing. Ah, *here* we are. If you stop right there and look through the gap in the hedge, isn't that marvellous? I like to think you can see halfway to Bath. Just glorious, rolling countryside. It makes you glad to be in England, doesn't it?'

Sholto stood beside her in his battered shooting coat and country boots, puffing and grinning. His cheeks were red from exertion and he steadied himself with a hefty walking stick. Rozie dutifully admired the graded greens of hills and hedges, but she had suddenly lost interest in where they were going.

'Insurance fraud?'

He shrugged. 'Not exactly, but that's what it was like,' he conceded. 'I never got the full gist of it. Just the odd mention in the staff club, in the days when we were allowed to drink.

I should have said something – and I did – but it wasn't really my job. I was just a painting filer.'

'So what exactly *were* they doing? As far as you knew?'

He sighed. 'I think it worked like this. Things were catalogued across all the royal palaces in London. If it counted as art or antique furniture, it was done by the Royal Collection. If it was standard furniture and fittings, it was done by the Works Department, I think it was. That probably doesn't even exist now – there have been so many reorganisations.'

'I know,' Rozie agreed. 'I found that out the hard way.'

He looked sympathetic. 'Anyway, some of it's on display, but a lot is in storage. If you want to find something, you consult the catalogue. If it's not in the catalogue, it kind of doesn't exist. The Breakages Business was all about spiriting things away that wouldn't be missed. Small things, weird presents that were given a hundred years ago and never seen since, slightly worn-out things. There's an art to working out when something's beyond repair. The Queen has always run a tight ship and they were supposed to pass things on to Balmoral or Sandringham, but it wasn't always appropriate, or possible. And they worked out a way of – at least, this is what I *think* they did, from conversations in the bar, just the odd passing reference, you know – they worked out how to siphon them off. Sell them on and keep the profits. Nice little earner. Not Gainsboroughs, or Crown Jewels or anything. Plates. Rugs. Unwanted gifts. I mean, the Queen gets hundreds of gifts a year. Did you know she was given hundreds of pairs of nylon stockings for her wedding? Literally hundreds. And five hundred tins of pineapple. It mounts up. You can't give them all to charity. Where d'you put them? The clever part was having someone who worked in the archives, who could adapt the catalogue to fit. As I say, they didn't do it with paintings, as far as I know, or I'd have put a stop to it myself. But maybe there was one. It would make sense, if they'd been refurbishing the Queen's bedroom. Anyway, it was decades ago and it probably won't help you now.'

'It might,' Rozie said.

He smiled and turned to lead the way back downhill towards the house. 'I hope so. If it does, tell the Boss you got it from me.'

That night it was cold enough to justify a log fire. The woodsmoke reminded Rozie of the gorgeous scent in her bedroom.

'What is that?' she asked.

'My dear, you can't afford it. A candle called "Ernesto". It's supposed to remind one of the cigar smoke of revolutionaries. I've always adored it.'

He played Nina Simone and a French rap artist called MC Solaar – his musical tastes were broad – and they got talking about Paris, where she had spent one idyllic summer before joining the bank, and he'd spent two years studying Leonardo at the Louvre. She introduced him to Fela Kuti and some of her favourite Afrobeat stars. He was instantly into it. It was as if they'd known each other for years.

'You can come here any time, you know,' he said. 'Just call. If I'm on a cruise, I'll arrange for someone to give you the key. Think of it as your second home. I know you'd look after it. And the herbs could always do with cutting.'

She could tell he meant it. Rozie wondered what it was about her that had fired this connection. She sensed they shared something that neither found very often in other people. A love of art and music and beautiful things, yes, but she knew loads of friends who had that too. It was something about *this* art, *this* music, *these* things. And it wasn't in any way sexual or crude, as Lulu Arantes had suggested. She felt perfectly safe with him.

Sholto made it easy. He understood the difficulties that normally came with her job. Most new people she met wanted the low-down on the Queen, Kate (always Kate) and the politics. Sholto asked about none of it, which was refreshing. Even the body by the pool. She'd mentioned it, but when he saw the look on her face he said, 'I know. It must be very hard,' and didn't push it. He didn't want the Queen's inner thoughts on Brexit. 'Let us never talk of it.' Amen to that. She should really be driving back this evening, to be fresh for work in the morning, but he had offered another night and she couldn't resist. She'd rise at dawn and burn up the motorway in the Mini.

And as soon as she got to London, she'd buy that expensive candle he said she couldn't afford.

Chapter 15

Up at dawn on Tuesday, Rozie breezed up the M4 to the sounds of *Farming Today* on Radio 4. It was almost a straight line due east to the Palace. She was back in London before the traffic clogged the roads, feeling fully recharged, and managed to wangle a precious parking space in the Royal Mews, so that she even had time to nip up to her room in the West Wing and change.

Buying the candle would be a crazy extravagance. She'd looked it up online and the cheapest version was over sixty pounds. Her mother must never know. But she could imagine it now, as she fetched a skirt and jacket out of the wardrobe, filling this little room with heady scents of tobacco, leather and rum. She would have flowers by the bed: just a small posy of . . . something. She wasn't an expert on flowers, but she was pretty sure she could do a deal with the Palace florist, and she would learn how to make coffee that fantastic if it killed her.

Had Sholto really meant it about the spare room in The Old Haberdashery? He'd seemed sincere enough. The idea of having a bolthole to escape to whenever she needed it was . . . it was almost unimaginable for a girl from a Notting Hill housing estate. It was the kind of thing her posh friends had had at uni and in the army. 'Oh, you must come to Shropshire this summer. My parents will be away. It'll be just us and the dogs. It's an absolute tip and a bugger to heat. You can have one of the spare rooms.' And her bosses at the bank, of course, whose houses were never 'absolute tips', thanks to small armies of housekeepers and gardeners. The Queen had three such places: two castles and a country estate – but she was the Queen, so fair enough. For Rozie, a cosy single room with a Cézanne on the landing wall outside would do nicely.

She put on the skirt, changed her shirt for a fresh one, and was slipping into her signature heels when she noticed something peeking out from between the pillows on the bed. It was the pale white corner of an envelope.

For a moment she felt as if she was free-falling into an abyss, so hard and fast she almost reached out for a belay rope. Her head was full of the buzzing of bees.

Knowing what it was, she forced herself to walk across the floor, bend down and pick up the paper that burned at her touch. *In here. In her bedroom.* With slightly shaking hands, she had to press hard to get the traction she needed to tear it open. The sender had gummed it closed. Would there be saliva traces? Even now she was wondering how to find him and stop him. Her chest was tight, her heart pumped fast. Her mouth was dry.

The note inside was folded three times, like the last one. She pulled it out between two fingertips. Same cheap paper as before. Heart hammering, she scanned the contents. Under two lines of writing in capital letters like before, there

135

were the same crude doodles of jungle life, and a new one, horizontal across the bottom: a knife.

She even recognised the type. Though roughly sketched in blue biro, it was clearly a double-edged fighting knife, a Fairbairn Sykes, shaped like a dagger, as used by the Commandos in the Second World War. Those knives were legendary in the forces. She had seen a couple out in Afghanistan and been offered one as a gift. Outside the kitchen or army-sanctioned combat, knives were not her thing, though, and she had politely refused. Now, she folded the note, put it back in its envelope, and stood for a full minute, trying to numb herself to the shock.

You thought you fitted in. You grew up within walking distance of this place. You got the grades, learned your manners, made your family proud. The army used you as a bloody poster girl – which was one of the reasons she'd left it in the end – and yet whatever you did, wherever you went, there was always *someone* ready to shame you, dismiss you, erase you. The hurt burned. She wanted to punch something very hard. She wanted to tear this room apart and scream until she ran out of breath.

But she stood silently, listening to her shallow breathing, waiting for the moment to pass.

Because it was what he wanted, this private humiliation she did not deserve. He would not get it.

When she had decided what to do, she slid the envelope into the front pocket of her laptop bag, next to her office pass. Then she went to her wardrobe, pulled out a pile of hoodies and tracksuit trousers and retrieved a box of trainers at the bottom. From this, she took out the first envelope, which had been sitting underneath the trainers inside. She slid it into the laptop bag beside the new one.

From the moment the first note had arrived, she had tried to suppress her feelings. Then the death of Cynthia Harris a few days later had given her other things to think about. But it wasn't that easy. The shock was still raw.

Soon she would go downstairs and deal with this. Her regimental specialism had been 'find, strike, destroy, suppress'. She wasn't going to let herself get derailed by some words and doodles on a scrap of paper. First, she needed to sit on the edge of the bed for a moment. Breathe, and count to twenty. Count to twenty again, get up and move on.

The Queen emerged from under the hairdryer hood and sat quietly as Ellie, her hairdresser, removed the rollers at her dressing table. She noticed Ellie squinting at the results and looked more closely herself.

'Oh dear. What did we do?'

Their eyes met in the glass.

'I don't know, ma'am. I could swear I put them in exactly the same as always.'

Ellie looked mortified. But the Queen could have sworn to it too. Nothing had seemed out of the ordinary as each roller was systematically applied – and yet here were two curls, far too tight and entirely out of place, making her look like an elderly Shirley Temple (Wallis Simpson used to call one Shirley, not out of any kindness), and resisting all Ellie's attempt to tame them.

'More lacquer?' the Queen suggested.

'I'll do what I can, ma'am. Do you have a quiet day?'

Her voice was hopeful, but the answer was sadly no, unless you counted the Patriarch of Moscow and various other religious potentates in the morning, and the combined medallists of the British Olympic and Paralympic teams in the evening as 'quiet'. Half the family would be there to attend the reception. She needed to look, if not her very best, then at least presentable.

'Let's try again after lunch,' she said with a sigh.

'Very good, ma'am. I'll have everything ready.'

Half an hour later, when Rozie entered her study, she could have sworn the girl did a double take. The Queen would have liked to say something about the wayward curls and laugh it off, but she couldn't quite bring herself to this morning. Hair was too important. It shouldn't be, but it was, and that was that.

'Did you have a successful time in the Cotswolds?' she asked, hoping to be cheered up by news of Sholto Harvie's famous hospitality.

'Yes, Your Majesty. In a way. Very.'

The young woman's bleak tone entirely belied the words she spoke. The poor thing sounded if anything more edgy than before. This was not about curls. The Queen peered at her from over her bifocals.

'Are you all right?'

'Yes, ma'am.'

'You're not.'

'No, ma'am. Not really.'

'We can talk about the Cotswolds in a minute. What is it?'

Whatever her APS had been holding back – and the Queen now realised there had been something for a while – the time had come for her to share it. Rozie took out a folded piece of paper from the folder she was holding, opened it up and handed it over. The Queen read it.

'Oh,' she said, her voice crisp and icy. She turned it face down and placed it on the desk in front of her. 'When did you get it?'

'This morning. But I should have said something earlier. It's the second one.'

'The second?'

'Yes. I got the first three days before you came back from Scotland.'

The Queen was silent. That explained it. She should have paid more attention. One should have *known*. Then she roused herself and said, with feeling, 'I'm so sorry, Rozie. This is inexcusable. We must tell the chief inspector straight away.'

Rozie was nervous, but firm. 'I know what you mean, ma'am. But I want him to keep it private. If he can.'

'You mean, not tell the Master?'

'Or anyone at the Palace.'

'Why?'

'Because . . .' Rozie, so articulate in university debates and tutorials, in presentations at the bank or preparing speeches for national events, found it hard to vocalise what she was feeling. The notes were classic racist nonsense. They were designed to subdue and hurt – and Rozie didn't ever want to be seen as a victim, or singled out for being anything other than brilliant at her job. That was how she'd always identified with herself. 'I'd just rather . . . keep it to myself, if you don't mind, ma'am.'

The Queen gave Rozie a long, unblinking look. She saw how much her APS was struggling, and although she didn't fully understand why, she trusted the girl's judgement. 'All right. If you say so.' Carefully, holding the grubby little piece of paper by one edge, she handed it back.

'I'll tell the chief inspector this morning,' Rozie promised. 'Meanwhile, would you like me to update you on what Mr Harvie told me? He was very forthcoming yesterday, though I don't know how helpful we'll find what he had to say.'

They moved on to a discussion of Rozie's recent visit. The Queen thoroughly appreciated the girl's professionalism and poise. It was just such a shame that a trip she had so obviously enjoyed – once she started talking about it – had been torpedoed by the despicable note awaiting her return. For both their sakes, she focused on the matter in hand. And it seemed Sholto had not let them down with his disclosure about the Breakages Business.

'Do you think that could be how your painting disappeared?' Rozie asked.

'Yes. That's *exactly* what must have happened. If it was left lying around while I was away . . . If someone saw it and thought it wouldn't be missed . . . If they didn't realise where it had come from . . .'

'Would you like me to find out who was in the Works Department in the eighties, and if any of them are still here now?'

'Yes please, if you can. And I think it might be useful if someone started a little rumour about the Breakages Business and Sir James were somehow alerted to it. It would fall within his purview.'

'I'll see what I can do, ma'am.'

'Naturally, you wouldn't be the one starting the rumour, Rozie.'

'Of course. I can mention to Sir Simon that I heard something in the canteen. He's bound to tell Sir James. I can't imagine he wouldn't.'

'Absolutely. They're thick as thieves, those two.'

Rozie went back to her office and the Queen was left deep in thought. The Breakages Business issue she would deal with later. For now, there was the more immediate problem of the poison pen letter-writer.

If Rozie, too, had been targeted by vicious notes, were there still others they didn't know about? This had worried her from the start. Meanwhile, the drawing of the knife was a huge concern: if this was the same person who had stalked Mary, then did that mean Rozie was in real danger?

The Queen tried to concentrate on the day's agenda and the religious leaders who would soon be lining up to meet her. But her mind kept wandering.

Was he a racist, or a woman-hater, or both? Was it even a man? Or, rather, men. Ah, yes! That was one of the things that had bothered her about Rozie's account. *'Three days before you came back from Scotland.'* Until now, the Queen had assumed that one person was behind it all. Someone who had gone from London to Scotland with the second wave of staff who had arrived early in September and targeted Mrs Harris there. All the attacks were consistent with such an idea – except that whoever cut up all of Cynthia Harris's beautiful, treasured clothes in Balmoral (who would *do* such a thing?) could not, the same day, have been targeting Rozie with a racist note at Buckingham Palace.

She distinctly remembered the chief inspector telling her about that last attack on the housekeeper's possessions, and she remembered specifically because it coincided with the horrible afternoon they had buried Holly. If Rozie's note had also been delivered three days before the family left Balmoral, then the note and the attack must have happened only a few hours apart, and though she herself could have managed such a task if so inclined, not everyone had ready access to a helicopter.

The Queen had watched a lot of detective programmes with her mother in her later years and knew all about copycat crime. Was that what this was? Had someone learned from what was happening to Mrs Harris, Mrs Baxter and Mary van Thingy, and adapted it for Rozie? Or had more than one person been targeting Cynthia Harris? The housekeeper was really *very* unpopular. The Household had been more intrigued than devastated by her death. The Queen, as a woman not in the first flush of youth herself, found the general lack of interest somewhat alarming.

At least Mary van Blank – she really *must* learn the girl's name – was out of harm's way in Shropshire now. Or one hoped she was. She wouldn't be fully safe until this was all resolved. There was a pattern to all of the attacks, the Queen felt certain, though it eluded her every time she tried to fix on it. A hatred of women, certainly – but something more.

A memory jolted into place. Hiding in the cedar-lined wardrobe and that male/female voice saying *'Do you think I give a rat's arse about her feelings?'* And he, or she, was giving something that was to be distributed later. Was it notes?

If so, they were given to Spike Milligan, who was to pass them on. Spike Milligan, who had come up to Balmoral with the second wave of servants. He couldn't have given Rozie *her* note – but he might know who did.

She made a mental note to let the chief inspector know – as soon as she thought of a way of doing it without explaining where she had been when she found out.

Chapter 16

The army had taught Rozie how to strip and reassemble an assault rifle in under sixty seconds without looking; how to avoid blisters while running twenty miles in boots; how to survive in the Arctic wilderness and the Brecon Beacons – and how to deal with regular, low-level racism and misogyny and come up smiling. You don't get through years in the armed forces as a black woman without developing a few coping strategies. So she refused to let a couple of doodled notes get to her, even if one of them featured a fixed-blade fighting knife.

But her brain wouldn't always obey her. It kept throwing up memories of odd glances she'd received from Palace servants: Mrs Harris's clumsy failure to shake her hand, the woman who took one look at her in the canteen and said, 'Of course, I have *several* friends in Africa. They're all *so intelligent*.' The time she'd encountered Neil Hudson, the Queen's Surveyor, coming out of the pool this summer, and he'd said, 'My God, you look magnificent. Like some sort of Nubian queen.'

Did he have any idea how racist that was? How it sounded? She had tried to shrug it off at the time. Could Neil Hudson – he of the yellow waistcoat and the quill pen mentality – be the sort of person who would draw a fighting knife? Wouldn't he have chosen a cutlass, or a sabre?

Would he even have written that note at all, Rozie?

She was in danger of going crazy if she didn't just bury the whole thing again and carry on. She couldn't even bear to tell her sister about it: her sister who was a trained counsellor. If she told Fliss, it would make it more real – and that was the last thing Rozie needed right now.

A week passed. After a moderately busy day, the Queen was relaxing in her private sitting room, watching the late-evening news with her lady-in-waiting and the usual gin and Dubonnet. The news itself was far from cheerful. Theresa May had not exactly been feted in Brussels, despite assurances afterwards that it had gone very well. In newsreels of the visit, she reminded the Queen rather of the girl at a party that none of the others wants to play with, left by herself in a corner and pretending she likes it. In America, Donald Trump had called Hillary Clinton a 'nasty woman' in a debate. Was this really what statesmanship had come to? Where was the oratory of Kennedy, or Lyndon B. Johnson? Mrs Clinton seemed to be doing well, but the Queen didn't envy her the exhausting rounds of constant scrutiny. The whole tone of the election descended almost daily, in the Queen's opinion.

But one's opinion was not called for in these circumstances. One could only watch and wait.

Her attention briefly strayed to the lamp behind the television set. It was an old silk shade on a utilitarian wooden stand from the war and was flickering slightly, which was always a little unnerving. One never knew quite what the electrics were going to do in this place. In ten years, it would all be fixed. She would have to move out of these rooms briefly – to Windsor or the East Wing. And the workmen would move in. She was still waiting to hear back from Sir James about the Breakages Business. Would everything be returned, or would little objects be 'damaged' and 'lost' – and if they were, could she completely trust the person who came with the bad news? Up to now, she would have done so implicitly, but Rozie's chat with Sholto Harvie had cast a different light on things.

Mind you, by then she would be a hundred. Perhaps she would be past caring.

She sensed not. One had always cared. And at a hundred Mummy was still going strong. She'd have been furious if something of sentimental value was gone.

'Want another?'

The Queen came back to the present. Sitting in a nearby armchair, Lady Caroline Cadwallader was waving her empty glass of gin and tonic. The Queen looked at her own glass, which was still half-full.

'Not yet. I was distracted.'

'Yes, I can see that. Are you worried about the body? Or the notes?'

She hadn't been thinking precisely about either, but the Queen felt guilty to suggest it had been the electrics. She nodded vaguely. 'Mmmm.'

'Too dreadful. How is that nice policeman getting on?' Lady Caroline asked. 'Strong, isn't it? I gather he's quite popular with the staff. Polite and discreet.'

'Oh, good. That's what I asked,' the Queen said, glad to be talking about something that approximated progress. 'He's very diligent. He has a lot to keep him busy.'

'How encouraging!'

Reluctantly, the Queen said, 'Not quite. His latest line of enquiry came to nothing.' She wasn't going to explain that she herself had suggested it. She had had high hopes for the questioning of Spike Milligan, but apparently the footman had furiously denied everything.

'Oh dear.' Lady Caroline stared glumly into her empty glass. The Queen rang for her page and got it refilled. Lady Caroline remained thoughtful.

'You know, this nastiness takes me right back to my schooldays.'

'Does it?' The Queen was surprised.

'Oh yes. I've been thinking about it since you told me. We had the most awful scenes. They lasted about a year. I was at St Mary's, and we were in the first form or second form – I can't quite remember – but we were little squibs, eleven or twelve, and missing our ponies and our mummies and try-ing to be brave about it. And mostly, we were. I had quite a decent time, actually, but some girls were floored by it. And there was this one girl, Peggy Thornicroft, who just had the most dreadful, horrible time.'

'Oh dear,' the Queen said, hoping to bring this topic of conversation to a halt, because it was really quite depressing and there was already enough to test one's good spirits at the moment, surely? But Lady Caroline was too involved in her story to notice the tone. The Queen sipped her gin and stuck it out.

'It was too, too bad. We all suffered. Because of course, we all came under suspicion. And we felt so *sorry* for her.'

'Why? What was going on?' the Queen asked.

Lady Caroline thought back. 'It started with an apple-pie bed, I seem to recall. Something very innocuous – you know, when you try and get in but the sheet's folded back on itself and you can only get halfway down. Or perhaps she got in and the bed was wet and we helped her change it. But then her letters from home went missing. Peggy was quite distraught about it. Her mother was very good and wrote at least once a week, but the letters were stolen – the old and the new – and she was practically beside herself. We all had our lockers inspected, and I think eventually they were discovered stuffed down one of the loos.'

'The poor girl. What was she like, by the way?'

'Peggy?' Lady Caroline made a moue with her lips. 'Well, you know, not the most *likeable*. I don't remember her very clearly. She left after a couple of years. She wasn't particularly clever, or stupid. She had a perfectly nice face and brown hair in plaits, but didn't we all? She was an early developer, I do remember that. The poor thing got her monthlies early, she smelled of . . . you know . . . body odour. She got spots. Nothing too dreadful, but I think she found it hard. She was very good at drama, but nobody really cared about drama at St Mary's, so it didn't help.'

'And what happened? Did they find the letter-stealer?'

'Oh, it got much worse. That's what reminded me about Cynthia Harris. Peggy got anonymous letters, hidden in her bed and her locker and even her blazer pocket. I never knew exactly what they said, but we were led to believe they were pretty frightful. The police were brought in at one stage and we had to give examples of our handwriting. They questioned us and the staff. It was very serious and frightening. And then her bunny, or teddy or whatever she had on her bed, went missing and it was found a few days later, cut up and partially burned on the gardeners' bonfire.'

'No!'

'I know. Very personal. Just like Mrs Harris. One of the groundsmen came under a lot of suspicion after that. *We* all thought it must be someone in her dorm. And then, worst of all, there was the guinea pig.'

The Queen felt her heart drop. 'What about it?'

'We were allowed little pets from home, you know – things you could keep in cages. They were all in a converted stable behind the sixth-form block that we could visit before and after school. Peggy was very attached to her guinea pig, as you can imagine, with everything that was going on. I remember it was a sweet, fluffy little thing. Not so little, actually. And then one day it was found at the bottom of its cage with its neck snapped.'

'Oh!'

'I know!' Lady Caroline said, seeing the shock on the Queen's face. 'Simply awful.'

'*Dreadful*,' the Queen agreed. 'Did they find out who did it?'

'Yes, they did. The police were hopeless, mind you. We were far too scared of their uniforms and craggy faces, and nobody would really talk to them. But our headmistress brought in this sweet little man – I think he was a priest, but he didn't act like one, if you know what I mean. I don't remember his name. He was very calm and friendly and just sort of hung around and chatted. You never particularly noticed that he was talking about Peggy. I don't recall telling him anything remotely useful. But after a couple of days, he worked it out.'

'And . . .?'

Lady Caroline held her hands out wide, theatrically. 'It was Peggy!'

'The girl herself?'

'Absolutely.' Lady Caroline shrugged. 'Isn't that a strange story? It was awful to go through at the time, as I said. So disconcerting. I don't know how the priest man did it. But Peggy sort of admitted to it in the end. It was definitely her. She was doing it for the attention – which, of course, she got. For a year she was the main topic of conversation. She must have been very unhappy at home, my mother always said. But we never knew what caused it. Her parents came and took her away, but she was back the next term.'

'No! Really?'

'Yes. And we never talked about it. We tried to be nicer to her. Obviously, the girl had some sort of mental problem. And when you think about that poor little guinea pig, and what it must have taken . . .'

150

They looked at each other, both animal lovers, both trembling a little bit.

'What happened to her in the end?' the Queen asked.

'I'm not entirely sure,' Lady Caroline admitted. 'I did try and look her up, years later, on Facebook, and there was a woman with her name who *could* have been her, who had lots of pictures with her happy little family, sailing about the place and looking perfectly normal. But if it was Peggy, she would have changed her surname, surely, when she got married, so I don't know for certain. She didn't put where she went to school – which suggested to me that it *was* her. I mean, she wouldn't have wanted us all finding her and raking all of that up, would she?'

'No. I suppose not.'

'Anyway, goodness, I've been rabbiting on and it's not remotely helpful. I *am* sorry, ma'am.'

'Don't be.'

'A bit ghoulish.'

'Yes. But isn't human nature interesting?'

'It really is, isn't it?' Lady Caroline agreed.

The news was over by now and a panel show was on, which they watched for a little while before retiring to bed.

As she settled against the pillows to write in her diary, the Queen was still thinking about Peggy Thornicroft. Lady Caroline had apologised for not being helpful, but the Queen wasn't so sure about that.

Chapter 17

'So you're suggesting, ma'am, that Cynthia Harris wrote those letters to herself? And cut up her own clothes?'

There was a strong note of scepticism in Chief Inspector Strong's voice over the phone, though he was trying to hide it.

'Only that it's possible,' the Queen said, from her study at Windsor, where she was weekending as usual.

'We've been considering it as a potential line of enquiry, of course. It happens. But this would be a pretty extreme case.'

'True,' the Queen acknowledged. 'But I can think of lots of reasons why Mrs Harris might have wanted to attract attention and sympathy, a bit like Lady Caroline's schoolmate. She wasn't popular. She knew she was disliked. Having managed to come back after retirement, she may have wanted to make it difficult for the Master to get rid of her.'

Strong agreed, somewhat reluctantly. 'Well, that was certainly the effect.'

'If it's possible for someone to behave that way – to do themselves so much damage – then I wonder if she did. You haven't managed to establish how anyone here could have known about her abortion, have you?'

'Er, no, ma'am. Excuse me.'

He was having a coughing fit. Was it because she had said the word 'abortion'? It was written in his own report to her, which he had talked her through. It was very tiresome, sometimes, how even sensible people expected one to think and speak like a medieval princess in an ivory tower. Although, goodness knows, they were probably familiar with abortions too.

'That's what I thought,' she said.

'She might have done it,' Strong admitted. 'But if so, what about the other letters? Like the ones to Mrs Baxter and Miss van Renen. Are you suggesting she sent them to cover her tracks?'

'I don't know. It's just an idea. But I did wonder . . . If she was trying to attract attention to herself, why dilute it by creating other victims?'

'Out of sheer spite?' he suggested. 'Because she was a fundamentally nasty woman?'

The Queen bridled at the words *nasty woman*. She had heard them recently in another context and they brought her up sharp. Peggy Thornicroft had been unhappy at home, according to Lady Caroline. The Queen wondered what might have caused Mrs Harris similar pain. 'Was she? Perhaps that's something you could check?'

Strong agreed that he would. 'She couldn't have sent the notes to your APS, though. Wrong place, wrong time, and she was dead by the time Rozie got the second one.'

'Yes, it makes the question about who sent those rather interesting, don't you think?' she remarked, because it was on her mind. And instantly regretted it.

There was a note of real intrigue in Strong's voice when he replied, 'Yes it does, ma'am. It *does*.' He was silent for a moment. 'If it was someone else, they'd've had to've found out what the original notes looked like. Not super-difficult because, to be brutally honest, ma'am, your HR department leaks like a sieve. It's certainly a thought.'

'Anyway, I've no idea what you'll find, but you're very kind to look into it,' she said hastily.

After she put the phone down she let out a deep sigh. *Must be careful*, she thought. Strong was a useful resource, but she didn't want him getting any ideas. Among her aides, only Rozie knew how far she was prepared to go to solve a problem. The chief inspector was the professional. One tried to be helpful, that was all. God forbid she should ever be seen to do the police's job for them. That would never do.

On Sunday, Rozie got up early and took a bus to Portobello Green. She'd always loved the flea market here, with its vintage fashions and antiques. Since her schooldays, when she wasn't riding or doing homework, a lot of her free time had been spent visualising the life she would have one day, when she was a proper grown-up: the offbeat dresses she would wear; the furniture and fittings she would display; the perfect jewellery collection she would own. Her visit to Sholto Harvie's home last weekend had only sharpened and intensified her vision. She wanted to touch it, smell it, put a price on it. She wanted to buy at least a perfect coat, or a vintage cushion, as a down payment on the dream.

Today, nothing was quite right though, and it wasn't the real reason she'd come back to the area anyway. After an hour of window-shopping, she bought a bunch of dahlias from a flower stall. In her bag was a jar of chicken soup she had begged from the Palace kitchens, and a big box of Roses chocolates – because Mum always said you couldn't visit the sick without a box of Roses.

The block of flats she was heading for was sandwiched between a primary school and a busy road. Rozie knew it well, because she had been a pupil at the school twenty years ago. Which was why her ears had pricked up on Friday when she overheard a couple of housekeepers talking about where Lulu Arantes lived.

'She said it was a terrible accident at Vincent House.'

'In Pimlico?'

'No – Ladbroke Grove. She fell straight down the stairs – voom. Right onto that shoulder. Yeah, *that* one. And broke her collarbone, again. And two black eyes. She said she'd be in on Monday, but d'you really think so?'

Rozie certainly didn't think so. Even for Lulu, working with a freshly broken collarbone would be insane.

She had got hold of Lulu's number from another housemaid and texted to ask if she could visit. Rozie had said, truthfully, that her mum lived nearby and blatantly lied that she was coming over anyway and would be just around the corner. Lulu had said it would be nice to see her.

Rozie had a very bad feeling about this.

Her thoughts were dark as she walked along the familiar streets she had trodden as a schoolgirl in braids, back in those days when the worst that could happen was forgetting your homework or wearing the wrong kind of shoes to church. Now, she had a bad feeling about almost everything. Cynthia Harris was dead, Mary van Renen was so scared she had left London, Lulu's own sister-in-law had been killed by her wife-beating husband, and in the back of Rozie's mind was always that image of the elegant, deadly fighting knife, drawn so accurately, down to the ringed-grip handle.

Had Lulu *really* fallen down the stairs? Is that how she got those two black eyes? Who did she live with? They'd never socialised outside work and it wasn't really any of Rozie's business, but the feeling in the pit of her stomach told her that perhaps it should be, and if she was wrong, then at least there were the Roses.

At her knock, the door was opened by an elderly gentleman with unnaturally black hair, smartly dressed in chinos and a fitted cotton shirt. He had once been tall, but now had to straighten up a bit to look Rozie level in the eye.

'Yes?' His voice was croaky, his expression curious and wary.

'I'm Rozie Oshodi. I know Lulu from the Palace. She said I could come over.'

At once, his face lit up.

'From the *Palace*! Come in, come in. I'm sure she'll be happy to see you. She's in bed. She will try and get up and move around but every movement hurts, you can see it. It's the devil's work persuading her to stay put. See what you can do, will you?'

156

Rozie promised. She realised, relaxing slightly as she followed him through the narrow flat, that she had been half expecting a muscle-bound partner in a wife-beater vest. But there was no sign of such a person. She really did *not* know Lulu's situation and tried to be a bit more open-minded.

In fact, Lulu was sitting up in bed in a bright single room, cheerfully decorated in yellow and green, next to a table heaving with magazines and grapes. She grinned at Rozie as the older man walked away.

'That's Uncle Max,' Lulu explained. 'He lives with me – I live with him, really, it's his flat – and he's nursing me like a professional. He's such a dear. Oh, soup! And chocolates! And flowers! You shouldn't have. You really didn't need to come. I'm fine!'

Rozie settled in a nearby chair. Lulu was chatty as ever, but the dark patches under her eyes were almost black. She winced whenever she moved. Rozie got her to admit that as well as fracturing her collarbone, she'd bruised three ribs.

'On the stairs?' Rozie asked.

Lulu sighed, winced and nodded. 'I know. I don't know what it is about me. I must have been thinking about my shoulder. Carrying a heavy shopping bag. Reached out to grab the handrail, missed, started to fall backwards, twisted and fell right on my face. Stupid thing to do.'

'Where were you?'

'She was right outside this flat.' Uncle Max was standing in the doorway, holding a tray with tea things. 'I heard a yelp and ran out and there she was, face down, arms akimbo. You could tell she'd done something awful. She let me ring the ambulance this time and she never does that, do you, darling?'

Rozie started at the word 'darling'. What kind of 'uncle' was he?

He put the tray down on the floor, moved some magazines to make space for it and told them to wait while the tea brewed in the pot. Rozie asked how he and Lulu knew each other, and he parked himself on the end of Lulu's bed to join in the conversation.

'I've known Lulu since she was a baby, haven't I, darling?' he said. 'She's my sister's girl and my god-daughter.'

OK, so he *was* that kind of uncle. Their close relationship was obvious from the way they interrupted each other's sentences and finished each other's jokes.

'We've always lived in each other's pockets, haven't we?' he said.

Lulu agreed. 'Uncle Max was my coolest uncle by far. He was the person who took me dancing.'

'You look surprised, Rozie,' he said from the end of the bed. 'Lindy Hop dancing, d'you know it? It's a style from the forties, quite gymnastic. You should see me in my bags and spats and Lulu in her circle skirts. Although, for Lulu it's a dangerous sport, isn't it, darling?'

'I'm always bashing myself,' Lulu said with a grin. 'I don't know how I do it, really. Not just me. I gave my partner a black eye last month. I've crashed into you a few times, haven't I, Uncle Max?'

'More than a few. But hey, Rozie, tell me about the Palace. Lulu's bored with keeping me up to speed. What's the gossip?'

Lulu laughed again. 'Uncle Max used to be a butler in the Household, did I tell you? It was the reason I applied.'

'I've been hors de combat for ten years, though,' he added wistfully.

They spent half an hour talking about how things had changed since he'd left. He was misty-eyed.

'Every day, I miss it.'

Rozie laughed. 'I doubt that. You must have worked incredibly hard.'

'Oh, I did. We all did. Lulu does too, don't you, darling? But with such *pride*.' His eyes sparkled. 'Where else could you do such a job, with people you love and trust like that, eh? Tell me?'

Rozie wasn't feeling it right now. But she nodded anyway.

'And then, of course, that horrible death,' he went on. 'Two deaths – one at Windsor, and one at the Palace. I'm sure you know much more about them than you'd ever tell.'

Rozie gave the quick-fire response: 'I really don't.'

Uncle Max merely raised an eyebrow. 'That's exactly what you'd say, though, isn't it? I won't press you. I knew Cynthia, of course. Can't say I liked her, but you had to feel sorry for her.'

'Did you?' Rozie thought of the horrible old woman who had sat beside Mary van Renen in the canteen that day.

Uncle Max nodded. 'It was such a comedown, from the Royal Collection to Housekeeping. I think she started as a picture restorer, something like that – she had a degree in art – then she went to the Works Department and got briefly engaged to the boss. What was his name? No, can't remember. Someone

159

else I didn't have much time for. But she didn't give up, I'll give her that. Went to Housekeeping, kept her head down, learned her trade, got good at it. No one ever questioned her work. But she wasn't very *nice*, d'you know what I mean?'

'She was an absolute bitch,' Lulu interjected emphatically from her sickbed. 'A total cow, and I don't care what her sob story was. She should've dealt with it and moved on with her life.'

Rozie realised they were both looking at her for comment and she couldn't think what to say. So many sudden possibilities were jumbling round her head that she needed to be alone to straighten them out. 'I – I'm really sorry, it's been lovely. But I should go. It was good to meet you, Uncle Max. I've taken up too much of your time, Lulu.'

That was true. Her friend protested otherwise, but the shadows under her eyes were deepening. Her shoulders drooped. Uncle Max promised to cook the soup for them both that evening, after she'd had a nap. Rozie left, feeling that she had been wrong about her sense of disquiet on arrival – but that she had a new reason to be uneasy now.

Chapter 18

Grace Oshodi had been cooking. This was entirely normal for a Sunday, and equally normal that, even though Rozie wasn't expected, there was more than enough for her. She needed to think and she did that better on a full stomach. Or that's what she told herself, anyway. She was six streets from home and Mum's after-church Sunday feasts were legendary.

Having called ahead to announce her arrival, Rozie used the walk to Lancaster Road to do some mental maths. Cynthia Harris was sixty-three, according to her file. If she had joined the Household at, say, twenty-two, after an art degree (assuming Uncle Max knew what he was talking about), then the earliest she could have arrived was in . . . Rozie did a rapid calculation . . . 1975. That made sense. That was fine. It did not explain the bugs under Rozie's skin, or the buzzing in her brain.

When did she go to the Works Department? her brain persisted in asking. *Why did nobody say?*

But she ignored it, and bought a second colourful bouquet, to take to her mother this time, and a good bottle of red wine.

For the first, fantastic forty minutes, it was as if she had never been away.

In the dining room, which played host to an upright piano, three guitars, two tall bookshelves and a small TV, as well as a table for six set awkwardly for eight, the family were helping themselves to the feast. The aroma of sweet peppers emanated from the tiny kitchen where every other Sunday her mother concocted meals big enough to feed the five thousand. She alternated with Auntie Bea, her sister, who was here along with her husband Geoff and sons Ralph and Mikey, whom Rozie and Fliss had grown up with like brothers. Rozie's dad, Joe, sat at the head of the table with his eyes on a silent TV rugby match. On his right was a young woman she had never seen before.

This was not unusual. While her dad collected guitars, vinyl dance music from the fifties and vintage maps of the London Underground – all of which littered the flat – her mother collected people. A Sunday meal that didn't include at least one old friend or new acquaintance was an opportunity missed, in Grace Oshodi's opinion, and an affront to God's bounty. In many ways, her mother reminded Rozie of the Queen at Windsor and Balmoral: it was all about sharing, hosting, connecting. When work permitted, they were both very social women who loved a laugh.

The latest addition to the Sunday table was a student called Yeshi Choen, a visitor from Bhutan studying for a masters in political history at the London School of Economics. The new guest barely glanced up from her food when Grace introduced 'my daughter Rosemary', which suited Rozie nicely. It meant she could catch up with her cousins as she loaded her plate with rice and beef stew, squeezing into a corner seat and patiently asserting her right to what little elbow room there was to be had.

'So, are you still seeing Janette?' she asked Mikey, to her right, secretly high-fiving herself for remembering the girl-friend's name.

'Uh-huh,' he grunted, through a mouthful of stew. He swallowed. 'And are you still tragically single?'

'Mm-hmm.'

'Don't tease the girl!' Grace implored good-naturedly.

'Don't wha-at? You do know that is what she was put on this good Earth for? If we can't have a go at her, what's the point? Anyway, aren't you always telling her you had two kids by now?'

'I'm sure I'd never mention such a thing,' Grace said primly, to general laughter round the table.

Rozie settled in as the mountains of beef and jollof rice, stewed beans and fried plantain disappeared into hungry mouths. Gradually, stomachs were filled, the frenetic pace of eating began to slow, and even Ralph, who was famous for how much rice he could put away, turned down a fourth helping and slumped back in his chair.

'So, Rozie,' he asked, 'wassup at the Palace, girl? You got any news we oughta know?'

'Not really,' Rozie said lightly. 'Same old, same old.'

'You're famous now, you know?' Ralph said it like it was a challenge.

'I am not,' she assured him firmly.

'You're on Wikipedia. You've got your own goddam page. I looked you up.'

'I—'

'I beg your pardon, what is this? Where does Rosemary work? I do not understand.' Yeshi had finished her stew and was looking at them with an expression of polite confusion.

'She works for the Queen,' Grace explained. 'At Buckingham Palace. And Windsor Castle. And wherever else the Queen goes.'

'I see. And what is the nature of the work she performs?'

Yeshi addressed her question to Grace, who explained as best she could. Rozie left her mother to it. She just wanted this topic of conversation to be over.

'I see. She is a very senior person. I congratulate you, Miss Rosemary.' Yeshi bowed gently in her direction. She leaned forward. Her gaze was very intense now. 'And so, tell me please, what does your Queen think about the United Kingdom leaving the European Union in this Brexit situation?'

Rozie's heart sank. She *would* be studying for a masters in political history, wouldn't she? Not marine biology, or fine art.

'I'm afraid I couldn't tell you.'

'Her Royal Majesty's opinion is important, no?'

'The Queen is neutral,' Rozie explained. 'She's above that sort of politics. It's important that she—'

'I heard,' Auntie Bea said, leaning into the table too, 'that she was super-thrilled. Like, she's a total Brexiter because of Commonwealth countries like Nigeria. I read it on Facebook.'

'How would they know?' Grace said hotly to her sister. 'Did she make a speech about it?'

'She didn't have to. One of her friends said.'

'What friend?' Grace's voice was raised. Her eyes blazed. She was a passionate Remainer and an equally passionate royalist – more than ever since Rozie started her new job – and in her mind, the two things went together.

'I don't know!' Auntie Bea countered just as loudly. 'They were anonymous!'

'Ha! Tell her, Rozie!' Grace turned to her daughter in smug expectation.

'I can't!' Rozie said, uncomfortably. 'The Queen will follow whatever people voted for in the Referendum.'

'But it was rigged!' Grace expostulated. 'And anyway, I'm not asking you what she'll do, I'm asking what she *thinks*.'

Rozie held her breath for a moment. She couldn't bear to argue with her own mother about this, and she'd explained often enough that she couldn't, and wouldn't, answer for the Queen on anything. This was the first time her mum had challenged her.

'Oh, Rosemary doesn't know.'

Everyone turned to look at Joe, who had the air of a wise old owl at the other end of the table. He smiled knowingly at them all. Rozie mouthed 'Thanks,' at him, but he wasn't being kind.

'The Queen plays her cards close to her chest. She wouldn't trust a girl like our Rosemary with her deepest thoughts. You just take in the boxes, don't you?'

'Well, I—'

'She does not!' Grace insisted, affronted. 'She's one of the inner circle now. Did you know . . .?' She turned back to her sister. 'Rozie went on holiday to St Barts with some aristos she made friends with at the Palace?'

'Ha! You might have mentioned it,' Auntie Bea said with a sarcastic grin. 'About forty thousand times.'

'I did not!'

'You did. And you said she played catch with Prince George at Easter, and lent Kate her shoes when there was a crisis.'

'Mu-ummy!'

But Grace ignored her daughter's protest. 'Well, you seemed interested enough at the time, my dear. You were all, "Oh, I remember that picture. I saw it on *What Kate Wore*". You stalk that poor girl online.'

'I do not!'

And so the conversation degenerated into speculation about the Duchess of Cambridge, whom Rozie now thought of as 'Catherine' – not that she said as much here – and how *great* she looked in Canada, when she would get pregnant again, and whether she was feuding with some of her inner circle, and why she never seemed to have any 'best friends'. And Rozie, who knew the answers to some of these questions, and thought the others absurd, and all of them uncomfortable for the woman in question, was grateful to be left out of the chat. Instead, she silently helped Mikey and Ralph clear the table, carefully stacking the dishes on the minimal counter space in the kitchen, as she'd done since childhood.

Mikey turned to her as she finished balancing a pile of plates on the still-warm cooker. There was a look in his eye that made her wary.

'You went to *St Barts*?'

She nodded.

'You never said.'

'No need.'

He grinned. 'Yass, queen. Classy. I like your style.'

She smiled back, breathing a bit more deeply, enjoying the relative peace.

'What's it like, though? The island?' Mikey asked.

'Incredible. French. Laid-back. Good food. So expensive that it makes your eyes water. It's how very, very rich people imagine what it's like to relax.'

'Did you relax?'

'Actually, I did,' she laughed. 'They did this dish with fresh fish that was . . .' She gave a chef's kiss. 'Yeah, I kinda liked it.'

He shook his head with mock seriousness. 'We're losing you, Captain Oshodi.'

She moved in for a cousin hug. Her voice was low and she was suddenly very serious. 'You'll never lose me, Mikey.'

He sensed something inside her and hugged her back. 'It's OK,' he murmured. 'I was joking. We got you.'

He didn't understand why his cousin, officially the toughest woman he knew, was holding him tight. 'Hey, let it out, girl,' he said gently, patting the back of her head with gentle hands. Her shoulders heaved a couple of times. 'It's OK,' he repeated. 'I got you.'

She took a breath and stood back. He hadn't seen streaks of tears on that beautiful face since she was about fourteen and Patrick Stryker, the Year 10 football captain, broke her heart in assembly.

Taking his hands in hers, she asked him, 'What do you see, Mikey?'

He didn't know what he was supposed to answer. He shook his head. But she was firm.

'What do you see?'

In confusion, he said, 'I see you, Zee. What else am I supposed to see?'

She squeezed him close again and murmured, 'Nothing,' just as Ralph came through the door, armed with a dangerously tall pile of serving bowls and said, 'Hey? Wassup, guys? Spill the tea.'

Rozie needed a moment to herself, and Mikey steered his brother back out of the little kitchen and shut the door behind them. Staring out of the narrow window, at kids playing ball in the communal yard, Rozie thought of the notes and the drawing of the knife, and promised herself she would not let the bastard do this to her.

He was trying to take her apart. He had chosen the wrong target and he would live to regret it. Meanwhile, she wrapped the love of her family around her like a force field. Mum arguing with Auntie Bea, Dad not quite getting what she did, Ralph eternally teasing, Fliss *listening* from Frankfurt, all of it. She had better things to do than let him into her head. He wanted her out of the Palace? She would insert herself ever more closely into it. She would find him and get under *his* skin. *Let's see how he likes it.*

Chapter 19

It was dark early. Tomorrow would be Hallowe'en. The bus back to the Palace passed little shops selling masks and tridents. Rozie noticed how many rubber masks were of politicians' faces these days. If you wanted to scare your friends, you went as a prime minister, or a European bureaucrat, or a would-be president.

She showed her security pass to the guard at the forecourt and made her way straight to her office. One of her jobs was to keep the file of all Chief Inspector Strong's reports to the Boss. This included copies of the notes that Cynthia Harris had been sent – or sent herself – and a biographical note that his sergeant, DS Highgate, had put together after talking to HR.

Rozie checked through the notes first. Two of them mentioned Mrs Harris's early demotions. 'YOU USED TO BE SO HIGH AND MIGHTY NOW YOU'RE JUST A DIRTY LITTLE SCRUBBER'; 'THEY DIDN'T WANT YOU AT SJP AND THEY DON'T WANT YOU HERE YOU VICIOUS SHREW. NOBODY WANTS YOU. **** OFF AND KILL YOURSELF'

Following these up, DS Highgate had traced her career in a stark, printed note.

BIO

Cynthia Harris, née Butterfield

b.1953, Brighton, E. Sussex

MA Art Hist, Uni of Edinburgh

Joined 1982, age 29. Asst curator, R. Collection. SJP.

Promoted Asst to D Surveyor QP 1983

Moved Works Department 1986

Moved Housekeeping 1987. Housemaid?

Promoted senior hk 1992

Promoted Head of N Shift 1996

Windsor C 1998–2002

Senior hk BP 2002–2016

Rozie stared at the notes for some time, standing at her desk with her coat still on. Just as Lulu's Uncle Max had said, Cynthia had joined the Household as an assistant curator of the Royal Collection. And she'd gone from that to a house-maid? Really? It was Cinderella in reverse. What DS Highgate didn't seem to have learned, but Uncle Max had remembered, was that when she moved to the Works Department she got engaged to its head. That had obviously gone sour: if a 'Mr Harris' had been head of the department, somebody would have said. Then promotion, promotion . . . then moved away to Windsor Castle. Was she already making waves by then?

But all that was incidental. What mattered were the dates, and they were exactly what had caused the bugs under Rozie's skin. Cynthia Harris had been working for the Surveyor of the Queen's Pictures in the early to mid-eighties. She had been *assistant to the Deputy Surveyor* himself, for goodness' sake. She must have moved from the Royal Collection to the Works Department around the time the Queen's oil painting went missing. She was, it turned out, the person who could, quite possibly, have shed more light than anyone else on Rozie's enquiries over the summer.

Except nobody Rozie spoke to had ever mentioned her.

Of course, even if she'd known, Rozie couldn't have talked to the housekeeper directly in the summer months, because she'd been in London while Rozie was in Balmoral and vice versa. Rozie would have had to wait until Cynthia came back to work at the Palace in October, but by that time . . .

This is what the bugs were all about. She pictured Cynthia on her first night back, losing her balance and the crystal tumbler dropping, the glass smashing, the jagged edge fatally piercing the skin as she fell, then the artery. She imagined her lying stretched out on the green tiles, as the reports had described her (Sir Simon would never discuss his discovery in detail), and the blood pouring from the wound.

Had Cynthia simply slipped in her bare feet on those tiles? Rozie had never truly been convinced, and the Queen obviously wasn't either. She had called in a senior policeman within days of the housekeeper dying. She knew, intuitively or otherwise, that there was something more.

Rozie knew *she* was adding two and two and making about two hundred and fifty, but the feeling wouldn't go away.

Why did nobody tell me?

In the morning, she would talk to Her Majesty.

Part 3

A Three Dog Problem

Chapter 20

It was to be a month of diplomacy and death.

Back from a refreshing weekend at Windsor, the Queen was on her way downstairs to have lunch with Philip, Charles and Anne, to talk over a few issues surrounding the wider family. It was agreed that when Charles took over, the Firm would be slimmed down, for public purposes at least. Fewer faces on the balcony overlooking the Birthday Cake, fewer close protection officers required; more work for those that remained visibly royal. But the senior royals – her own children and Charles's boys – were ready for that. It was the lesser family members who would kick up a fuss. They liked being seen to be useful – and all the jollies that went with it. One had to let them down gently, and Charles still had a list of details to discuss.

Her equerry interrupted her at the foot of the stairs with the news that her APS would like a word, and it was rather urgent.

'She said it's to do with the enamel box, ma'am.'

The Queen sighed briefly.

'Tell them to keep the soup hot. I'll be as quick as I can. I'll see her in the 1844 Room.'

She walked swiftly towards the nearest unoccupied room where they could shut the door with the certainty of not being overheard. Willow, Candy and Vulcan padded happily at her heels. As she strode past portraits of ancestors clad in velvet and ermine, she vividly remembered the day she had given Rozie the box the girl was referring to, at the end of the first mystery Rozie had helped with, as a token of her gratitude. If Rozie had mentioned the box, then it would be with good reason.

The Queen reached the 1844 Room, which sat among the semi-state apartments on the ground floor. This was where she held audiences with her most important visitors. Its peach-pink walls were calming to nervous guests, but there was a formal grandeur to its twenty golden marble pillars, its malachite candelabras and the blue and gold Regency furniture. Like many of the public rooms in the Palace, it was multi purpose. She thought of them as stage sets, ready to be transformed as the occasion required. Yesterday, Philip had used this one to host a lunch and today the furniture was arranged along one side as the porters readied it for a reception. Fortunately, it was empty for now.

'Make sure we're not disturbed, will you?'

The equerry took this as confirmation that his presence wasn't required and remained in the corridor outside. Rozie arrived a couple of minutes later.

'You'll have to be quick. I only have a minute.'

'Yes, Your Majesty. It's about Cynthia Harris.'

'Oh?'

Rozie rapidly explained about her brief discussion yesterday with Uncle Max.

'I looked up Mrs Harris's employment record,' she went on, 'and it turns out she was almost certainly at the Works Department, as it was called then, in 1986 when the refurbishment was done. The current team in Operations pointed me towards a man called Joe Flowers who used to work there as a superintendent. But he's struggling with Alzheimer's. I went to talk to him at his care home when I got back from Balmoral, but I couldn't get any sense out of him.'

'They may well not have known about Mrs Harris.'

'True,' Rozie said, trying to keep the urgency out of her voice. 'But before that, she was assistant to the Deputy Surveyor at the Royal Collection, ma'am, and at the time, that would have been Sholto Harvie.'

'Sholto? Gracious!'

'If a painting had gone missing, surely she would have known about it, and she'd remember? I know it seems minor, but you said you were surprised I couldn't find the right link in the picture's journey, and it seems to me that Mrs Harris could have been that link. If we now think there was a racket going on . . .'

'The Breakages Business. I see.'

'Perhaps Cynthia knew about *that*. Perhaps they suspected she did. I just find it . . .' Rozie searched for a reasonable description of her state of mind. '*Of concern*,' she said, though the feeling was stronger, 'that there was somebody right here all along, who was on the spot at the time, and nobody mentioned her to me. We were in separate places over the summer because I was in Scotland when she wasn't, and vice versa. When you came back from Balmoral, I would have had the opportunity to talk to her face to face at last – if I'd only known how useful she could be. But of course, that never happened.'

'Yes, I see,' the Queen said.

'Your staff tend to stay a long time. Everyone tells stories. I can't believe Uncle Max was the only person who knew about her previous jobs. And afterwards, Mr Harvie saying nothing about her death? It just doesn't make sense. At the time I thought he was being reserved and diplomatic, but if she worked for him directly – well, it's just weird. He was very conversational most of the time.'

The Queen pursed her lips. She looked very grim indeed. 'You do know what you're suggesting, don't you?'

Rozie said quietly, 'Yes, ma'am.' She swallowed.

There was the sound of snuffling and the pattering of doggy paws on the carpet as the two women stood quietly, considering the body lying in a pool of blood.

'Well,' the Queen said at last. 'Do you have anyone in particular in mind?'

'I don't. Not that I can make any sense of, anyway.'

'Have you talked to Chief Inspector Strong?'

'Not yet.'

'Let me think about it for a while.'

'I—Of course. Yes.' Rozie relaxed a little. 'I didn't think you'd believe me. I thought I was getting a bit dramatic.'

'And yet you came to find me,' the Queen said, 'and kept me from lunch with the Princess Royal. You must have thought it was important.'

Rozie tried to hide her smile. Princess Anne was known for her punctuality. Even her mother might be on the receiving end of a sharply raised eyebrow. 'I did. I'm sorry.'

'Don't be. And now I really must go.'

However, after Rozie left her, the Queen remained in the calm stillness of the room, grateful for a moment of solitude.

Rozie had been on her mind yesterday while she was out riding at Windsor. She had been thinking about the notes. If Cynthia Harris had targeted herself, one had to wonder who had targeted Rozie and why. The notes seemed designed to get rid of her and the Queen had wondered if there was a specific reason why somebody wanted her out of the way.

And now this. The idea that Mrs Harris had been deliberately killed, almost the moment she got back to the Palace from Scotland, to stop Rozie from talking to her. Why? Because Rozie had been asking about a painting by a fairly unknown Australian that went missing thirty years ago. It was outlandish. It was outright ridiculous. And yet . . .

The strangest thing of all was the behaviour of Sholto Harvie, who had failed to mention that he once worked closely with a woman whose death was in the news, along with fanciful stories of young princesses and bottles of champagne. Why stay silent about that, but disclose the story of the Breakages Business?

Sholto couldn't be the killer – if indeed there was one. What harm could he have done from the Cotswolds? And anyway, why help and hinder at the same time?

There was a gentle knock at the door. 'Ma'am?'

Damn. The soup would be cold, or boiled, and Anne, Charles and Philip would be livid. She called out that she was coming and followed the dogs as briskly as she could.

Chapter 21

That afternoon, Anne put her head around the study door.

'Not disturbing you, am I?'

She was. The Queen was catching up on some private correspondence. But it didn't matter. Anne, who was in town for various work commitments, sat on the comfy armchair she generally used if she came to visit and accepted the eager, nuzzling curiosity of Vulcan and Candy as they came to settle at her feet. Willow remained by her mistress, but cocked an ear in acknowledgement.

'It's not the same, is it?' Anne said. Her tone was matter-of-fact, but her eyes were full of sympathy. 'D'you miss her badly?'

She meant the dog. It was only four weeks and a bit since the vet had performed his final, inevitable task on Holly, and several times a day the Queen felt a sudden tug at her consciousness: the different sound made by three sets of paws, not four; wondering what treats one might persuade the elderly dog to eat, and remembering that there was no need; the sight of the corgi's eager body waddling and waggling ahead of her down the corridors, snaking round her ankles as she tried to sit down and lying in all the most unfortunate places – a ghostly memory now.

In fact, the Queen had been responding to a couple of old friends who'd been offering their condolences. Dog-lovers, they understood.

'Yes, I miss her very much,' she said. 'But life goes on, doesn't it?'

'I know, Mummy, but you can talk to me. I bawled my eyes out when Mabel died.'

'You did,' the Queen remembered.

That was the thing about Anne: tough as old boots, which meant she hadn't cared a jot if the family saw her blubbing at the death of a precious pet. Mind you, one of her bull terriers had caused a corgi to be put down once. *Not* a happy memory.

Who, the Queen thought, *could kill their own guinea pig?* Her mind was back with Peggy Thornicroft, and from there to Cynthia Harris again.

'You seem very distracted,' Anne said. 'I thought so over lunch. Anything I can do?'

She reflexively declined the offer. 'No. It's not Holly.'

'Oh, God – it's not the President of Colombia, is it? He hasn't asked for anything outrageous in the Belgian Suite? D'you remember that prince who wanted an open fire?'

She did. He wanted it so his chef could cook appropriate meals the traditional way, but it had been agreed that such a fire in the kitchens might be a safer option.

'I do. Not that.'

'Oh, not the housekeeper in the pool? That was bloody bad luck. I haven't told the little ones about it. They'd go apeshit.'

'Not that either,' the Queen lied. 'But I do have a problem. I sense I should alert the authorities about something, but if I do, it will go from something very small to something very big very quickly, and I won't have the power to stop it. And I might be wrong.'

'Can't you get Sir Simon to fix it?'

'No, I don't think so.'

'Really? There's not much he can't do. Except find meaningful jobs for Beatrice and Eugenie, I s'pose.'

'Not this.'

'Can you wait? See if it sorts itself out?'

The Queen smiled fondly at her daughter. She loved Anne's practicality and instinctive desire to help, combined with the tact born of a lifetime of knowing that Mummy had to deal with secret things on a regular basis, and if she didn't want to tell you, you didn't ask.

'I don't think it will,' she answered. 'I wish it could.'

Anne stood up. 'Well, I'll leave you to it. But when I had a problem setting up the horse trials at Gatcombe, I remember I was calling up all and sundry, making my presence felt and being a bloody nuisance, and you said to attack it one piece at a time, and do nothing until I was sure of my facts.' She walked over to give her mother an affectionate kiss. 'I'm off to get changed. Black-tie dinner in the City to raise wodges of dosh for the Royal Voluntary Service. I'll see you tomorrow.'

Alone again, the Queen pushed aside the letter she'd been writing and considered her daughter's advice. Her duty told her to raise her concerns about Mrs Harris with

Chief Inspector Strong as soon as possible. If Cynthia had died to stop her from talking to Rozie about what happened in the nineteen eighties, then murder had been committed within the precincts of the Palace and of course the police must know.

But had it?

Despite the Queen's misgivings from the start, the police were still content that Mrs Harris's fall was a tragic accident. Had someone really masterminded that trick with the tumbler? (The Queen couldn't help seeing it as a trick.) All Rozie had done over the summer was ask around about the long-ago disappearance of a minor oil painting. Would someone plot and kill to stop her making progress? Really?

If one did talk to the chief inspector, he couldn't possibly keep it quiet while he made a few discreet enquiries. He wasn't like Billy MacLachlan, her old protection officer who occasionally helped out in his retirement. Strong would be duty-bound to report his findings up the line. Even if his bosses tried to keep it quiet, it was *a murder at Buckingham Palace*. She could imagine the headlines and endless updates in the news.

The Queen gazed out of the window. The gas lamps were on in the grounds – relics from a Victorian age, though her great-great-grandmother had found them too newfangled for her taste. Beyond the walls, London went about its business, oblivious. She could feel a headache coming on. To talk or not to talk? All she had was a hunch, although when Rozie had spoken to her in the 1844 Room, their joint conclusion had felt much more than that.

Anne's advice, though given without much context, seemed sound. If she were a minister, preparing to present to herself, she would endeavour to put a decent case together and be sure of her facts. She must do the same for the chief inspector.

Yes, that was the answer. She sat back in her chair with relief. She knew where to start. But she couldn't do it yet.

Chapter 22

The State Visit of the President of Colombia began on Tuesday. This was a highlight of the calendar that the Queen cared about tremendously, and she wanted London and the Palace to be at their best. Over the years, there had been some leaders of Latin American countries one had found more congenial than others. Mr Santos, who was on the brink of achieving a historic peace agreement at home, was a man she was pleased to welcome with all the pageantry State and Crown could command. He had once been a student here, and now he was the most recent recipient of the Nobel Peace Prize, due to give a speech at the London School of Economics about the role of young people in the peace process. He would visit Northern Ireland, hot on the heels of her own recent trip, and see the tremendous progress that a community could make when it actively turned away from conflict. She was grateful to Rozie for finding a suitable quotation from a Colombian writer for her own speech of welcome. *Which is harder to fight: war or indifference?*

That night, she gave the speech in the gilded Ballroom, at a banquet for a hundred and seventy. The tables, positioned in a U shape, were so wide that footmen had had to walk across them in stockinged feet to smooth out the cloths and position the silver gilt dessert stands and branching candelabras from the Grand Service, dating back to the early nineteenth century. Each place was set with six cut-crystal glasses. The flowers included choice varieties from Colombia alongside home-grown blooms. The Master had checked – with a ruler – that the knives and forks were set the correct distance from the edge of the table. She herself had closely inspected the settings beforehand, to ensure everything was right.

Sitting beside Mr Santos at the head table in the Ballroom, she wore the Victorian Suite diamonds and sapphires. The overall effect, with matching tiara, was suitably large and showy, to match the banquet. The Queen liked to break out all the rocks for occasions such as this. She had already given the President a formal reception on Horse Guards Parade, a carriage-ride up the Mall and lunch in the Bow Room. There was more to come tomorrow. It was the chance to connect with a world leader at a personal level and spread a little dazzle.

At times like this, and during the investitures and the garden parties, one could forgive Buckingham Palace for being so large, so extravagantly redesigned and decorated by her third-great-grand-uncle, George IV, and so difficult to maintain. It was not ideal as a home in many ways, but when the nation wanted to extend its thanks or hand of friendship, there was nowhere quite like it for doing the job. She and the rest of the family went out of their way to make the once-in-a-lifetime experience as delightful as they could for their visitors.

During the dinner, she was very glad to think that Mr Santos and his wife would have no idea of the horrors going on above their heads, where the space above the Ballroom ceiling had been recently inspected to make sure it wasn't as critically dangerous as the one above the State Dining Room, which was still out of use. The Palace was a bit like a swan on the lake: gliding gracefully on the surface, paddling like billy-o underneath.

To her relief and the Master's, no ceilings fell. After two nights in the Belgian Suite and a packed agenda of events, Mr Santos left for Northern Ireland and the Queen had a bit of breathing space.

On Thursday morning she travelled to Newmarket to unveil a statue of a racehorse in honour of her long and happy association with the town. In the helicopter on the way to Suffolk, she read a note from Sir James giving her a quick update on the new investigation into the Breakages Business that Rozie had covertly instigated. Her heart sank. It was half a page.

Initial enquiries suggest that there was a problem with a manager in the eighties called Sidney Smirke who became head of the Works Department. He was known as a bit of a character, but towards the end it became sadly obvious he was a raging alcoholic. He got a criminal record for beating up a man outside a pub and my predecessor at the time had to get rid of him. It's not impossible that he tried to run some sort of racket, but I can absolutely assure you that any possible issues with a 'Breakages Business' are purely historic. If I come across anything else, I'll let you know instanter, but I don't need to assure you that my team have management of your assets under tight control.

She looked up from the note with a sigh. There it was again. If anyone else told her everything was 'under control' she might be forced to break something herself.

She tried to use the rest of the journey to make sense of it all, but helicopter rides are not designed to aid the thinking process. This was a three-dog problem. She resolved to give it her full attention when she got back.

Chapter 23

For years, it had been the Queen's habit to take a few dogs for a walk in the grounds if she had a big problem to consider. Too many, and one ended up spending more time calling them to heel than thinking. Nowadays, she didn't have the luxury of choice.

On her return to the Palace that afternoon, there was a small gap in her schedule before tea. She put her papers aside and checked the sky outside her window. It was grey and gloomy, with a likelihood of rain. No matter. She told her page to explain to anyone who asked that she was going out and she might be some time.

The dogs accompanied their mistress to the boot room, where she slipped into a raincoat, headscarf and sensible shoes before heading out into the garden. Candy and Vulcan's dorgi ancestry resulted from an encounter years ago between her corgi, Tiny, and Margaret's dachshund, Pipkin. Despite their stubby legs, these two were energetic creatures who appreciated the exercise. Willow, the corgi, did not look convinced she needed another walk after the one she'd had with a footman this morning, but she came along out of curiosity, if nothing else.

The cool, tangy air outside was an instant reminder that it was the first week of November, and winter was on its way. The Queen felt it prick her skin and catch in her throat. Ahead, the lawn stretched down towards the lake. Two weeks ago, with autumn at its height, the view had been awash with vibrant colour from the bright yellow ash, the flaming swamp cypresses and tawny horse chestnuts that flanked the lawn and encircled the water. Today, the trees were a patchwork of gold and brown, and the lawn was edged with flurries of fallen leaves. In the past, there would have been bonfires; now there were composters. Philip ensured they were all environmentally efficient, but she missed the smell of woodsmoke on the air.

She turned along the West Terrace, keeping the Palace to her right as she headed for the kissing plane trees. The dogs were already ahead of her; they knew this route. They padded along the path, sniffing the borders and pausing occasionally if she called. At the end of the terrace they trotted past the north-west pavilion, which Papa had converted into the pool. From here, it looked like a Greek temple with Georgian windows. The Queen looked up as she passed, considering its interior and the night the family got back from Balmoral.

'What had happened to Mrs Harris, then?' she asked the dogs, who were more inquisitive about what lay under the leaf piles than their mistress's musings. She kept the rest of her thoughts to herself.

Why on earth would Cynthia Harris go there? The police were happy enough that she had done so alone, out of mere officiousness, or on a whim. She had arrived in her slippers,

191

which were found in the ladies' changing room, so it didn't look like a romantic encounter – not that anyone had expected it to be. Outside, the grounds were full of hidden CCTV cameras that could be triggered by the slightest movement, all of which were working. No one had entered the Palace unofficially that night. If the housekeeper had met anyone, it was an insider. There were no signs of trauma on her body, other than the knock on the head and the cuts to the lower leg, no indication that she was hurt or forced.

Even the newspapers were happy: they had run dozens of articles about the dangers of cutting yourself on the ankle. In the absence of photographs, they had mocked up endless pictures of what Mrs Harris must have looked like, lying there, with images of crystal glasses of all shapes and sizes, and advice on where to procure similar items from Harrods and Thomas Goode.

Surprisingly, they never had picked up on the poison pen campaign. Their angle was that Mrs Harris was a tragic victim of cut crystal and bad luck – or possibly the lax habits of poor Beatrice and Eugenie, who were in fact several miles away at the time – so it didn't fit that she might be unpopular. Simon had tried to explain this, but the Queen was quite aware of it already. She knew precisely how certain elements of the press decided their story first, then found the facts to fit. Her family had been at the receiving end of it all her life.

By now she had reached the plane trees planted by Victoria and Albert either side of the path, a hundred and fifty years ago. They arched above her, high into the sky, their spreading branches intertwining just as her great-great-grandparents must have planned. At this point she followed the path to the left, towards the rose garden. Was she stirring up trouble for nothing? What could she prove? Given all the trouble it would cause, why would she even want to try?

She passed the little summer house, where in warm weather she liked to give tea parties to the great-grandchildren. Willow stayed nearby on the path while Candy and Vulcan nosed about outside.

Because she knew something was wrong. One did not give up so easily.

'Motive, means, opportunity,' she muttered. 'You know that, Willow, don't you?'

The corgi panted at her in a non-committal way. They carried on.

Rozie had provided the motive. But while it gave the Queen pause for thought, it was so weak. Even if Cynthia Harris knew all about the Breakages Business and the purloined painting, who would commit murder for the sake of protecting a small-time art thief and a racket to sell unwanted presents? Not that they were ever *unwanted*, of course, just difficult to store.

As for means, the Queen had nothing but conjecture. Her knowledge of her staff did not extend to any unusual proclivities they might have for piercing arteries on demand – so this didn't narrow the field in any useful way. And opportunity . . . If Cynthia Harris *had* been murdered, it must have been by someone who knew the Palace well, was staying there that night and could avoid the internal CCTV. At the moment, three-year-old Prince George could evade that if suitably determined. About fifty servants had been at

193

the Palace that night. She had watched MI5 put all her staff under suspicion recently and had no intention of doing so again without due cause. No, she would have to unlock the motive first, before she could consider making any headway on how it was done, or by whom.

The rose garden in November was not at its best. She called out some encouragement to the dorgis and kept moving. Traffic bowled busily along Constitution Hill beyond the wall to her right. Ahead, the path under the trees took her past the old tennis court, where she had played some great games with Papa as a teenager, and a few with a young Philip Mountbatten, when he was courting her and keen to impress. Beyond that was the 'worm pie corner', where he and the gardeners experimented with the latest recycling and composting techniques. Philip was always keen to stay ahead with the help of the latest science. His diary, even now, was full of visits to medical research centres and universities. In fact, he was off in Hertfordshire today, opening a new science building. He was the Prince Albert of his day, she thought: progressive, eager, indefatigable. And somewhat foreign, when he arrived. Misunderstood by many and much loved by the people who knew him best.

She dragged her attention away from her husband and back to the matter in hand. Willow had to be persuaded away from a particularly smelly set of bins. By now she was at the far end of the garden, where the diesel chug of buses and taxis from Grosvenor Place created a steady bass note under nearby birdsong and the distant sound of a leaf blower on the lawn. The path turned once more to the left.

In a couple of minutes, looking back, she'd be able to see the West Terrace again behind the lake.

Somehow, in the strange way that meditative walking sometimes did, this suggested a different way to attack the problem. *Turn it around.* If she couldn't persuade herself that Mrs Harris was murdered, she should try and convince herself that she *wasn't*.

Very well. The Queen strode with more purpose now, counting off the arguments for an accident. First of all, Cynthia herself. It seemed unlikely that the housekeeper would have gone to the pool at night merely on the off-chance of clearing something up – but if anyone was going to behave in an odd, excessively conscientious way, it would be Cynthia. Second, it was perfectly possible she had *not* been killed by a poison pen letter-writer, because Lady Caroline's theory about her writing to herself was quite compelling. Especially if there was something in her past that had made her unhappy. That was in the hands of Chief Inspector Strong now. And the stalker? The Queen was sure that was a separate business regarding Mary van Renen, and possibly Rozie. It hadn't led to violence – yet. Thank God.

What about the Operations Team, who never mentioned Cynthia to Rozie? That was odd. Was it possible that *none* of them knew the history of the housekeeper – unpopular as she was – who came from the Royal Collection and used to work there when it was the Works Department, years ago? Cynthia had even been engaged to the manager, apparently. But 'apparently' wasn't good enough. Perhaps the engagement was idle speculation, or a false memory. In the Queen's experience, the Household loved nothing more than passing down Palace lore from generation to generation, but it was also possible that some details would be changed or forgotten over time. Cynthia herself might have been glad of it. Yes, she could accept the idea of collective amnesia about the housekeeper's history, if she had to. And anyway, even if the Breakages Business was still running, and Cynthia knew about it, and Rozie was onto it, she was back to her first question: who would commit murder for the sake of a few gifts and bits of furniture that nobody had missed?

Vulcan appeared from the bushes with a disgusting tennis ball that must have been last used on a dog walk in the summer. It was green with slime, and slobbery. She told him to get rid of it and glanced to her left, where the lake was now fully visible through the trees.

What about Sholto Harvie? If Strong's research was correct – and Rozie could check it for her – Sholto and Cynthia must have worked together closely in the mid-nineteen eighties. Was he being polite when he didn't discuss Cynthia's death with Rozie, beyond acknowledging that he knew she was dead? The Queen strode on, trying to fit the psychology to an innocent explanation. She remembered vividly how much he'd loved his job as Deputy Surveyor. She didn't remember Cynthia being his assistant, but it was quite possible she simply hadn't known.

From what Rozie had said, Sholto still thought of those days with immense fondness. It was such a pity he had left so soon. He had the makings of an excellent curator and art historian, and he was popular with the other staff at the Royal

Collection. She had half expected him to run the department one day. No, it was not obvious to her why a man like Sholto would have lost interest in someone he'd been close to in those days that were so special to him. He had only been there a few years, and Cynthia must have been his assistant for at least two of them. One couldn't help wondering why on earth she had left. And for a job that was much more menial.

The Queen slowed down and looked back at the shadowy grey-brown outline of the Palace emerging through the trees. It was so richly full of history – even if bits of it were practically falling down. The first-floor rooms had played host to a major statesman last night. They were lined with historic art and treasures that might be worth killing for, perhaps, if you were that way inclined. Sholto, indeed, had been partly in charge of looking after those treasures. But that's not what Rozie had been asking about when she went to stay. Anyway, Sholto had been helpful. Even if he didn't know what had happened to the 'ghastly little painting', he had given them the Breakages Business. She was back where she started.

Except . . .

What if it wasn't that at all? Sholto had brought the Breakages Business up, but she began to wonder if it had been a screen for something else. In that case, the question was – *what*? This was all about Cynthia Harris in the end. What else could Cynthia have known about?

Picking up the pace of her walk again, the Queen cast her mind back furiously over those happy years when she had consulted him about her art collection. Try as she might, she didn't remember anything of major interest going missing. Nothing she hadn't subsequently resolved, anyway. There were only the Thingummies, and they were the opposite, really: they were *found*.

Three Renaissance paintings – no, it was four – had turned up at Hampton Court Palace having been lost in storage for centuries, and one had been really quite excited for a while, but on closer inspection they'd turned out to be copies. Wasn't it . . .? Yes, it was Sholto who was in charge of that whole episode. He'd had the paintings cleaned and checked by experts. It had all taken an age because . . . Hmm. Yes, why had it taken so long? She racked her brains again and shouted quite harshly at Candy, who was burying her nose in something repulsive further down the path. This had all happened when Diana was around. Life had been a series of little dramas. Ah! Now she had it, and it was very sad. The young curator who was supposed to be working on the paintings had suffered a terrible accident that had set everything back by weeks or months.

What *was* the artist called? It was a woman, and she was famous. Sholto had been terribly excited. She was a bit later than the Renaissance. Seventeenth century. Gentileschi – that was it. Her work was worth a lot of money, quite rightly so because she was brilliant. The Queen had loved the paintings and was so disappointed to find out they weren't originals after all.

How much money? Was it thousands, or hundreds of thousands?

A man could kill for hundreds of thousands.

She began to see a pattern. It was dim, and it didn't fully fit together, but two 'terrible accidents' was starting to feel less like bad luck and more like a dark and sinister pattern that started and ended with Sholto Harvie.

Overhead, the clouds mirrored her thoughts and shifted from polished steel to gunmetal grey. Rain wasn't far away. Rounding the lake, she bowed her head, called the dogs to her side and took a rapid shortcut home across the lawn.

Chapter 24

Billy MacLachlan was FaceTiming his granddaughter in the Isle of Wight from his flat in Richmond upon Thames when a call alert flashed up on his screen. It was seven-year-old Betsy's bedtime and he was telling her a story. The screen was filled with her pink, chubby face contradicting him and instructing him to do it differently at every turn. It was exhausting, and the best bit of the day by miles. Almost nothing short of a national emergency would drag him away from Betsy at this hour . . . But the number on his screen was in the nature of a national emergency.

'Sorry, love, got to go.'

'Why, Grampa? You were just getting to the good bit with the can-tank-rious fairy.'

'The Queen of England needs my help.'

'But Grampa—?'

Already, he was gone. Betsy would tell her parents that Grampa Billy had said the Queen of England had called again, and they would laugh and explain that that was Grampa's little joke, because he used to work for her a long time ago. They probably suspected that this was really his code for problems with his waterworks, or maybe a secret girlfriend – who, frankly, he would be perfectly entitled to since Grandma Deidre died twenty years ago. MacLachlan didn't really care what they thought, as long as it was not the suspicion that he might be telling his granddaughter the truth. Anyway, it wasn't the Queen of England exactly: it was 'Queen of the United Kingdom of Great Britain and Northern Ireland, and of her other Realms and Territories, Head of the Commonwealth, Defender of the Faith'. He had used a kind of shorthand: synecdoche – the part for the whole.

'Yes, Your Majesty?'

'I hope I'm not disturbing you this evening?'

'I was just talking to my second-favourite Elizabeth, ma'am.' This wasn't entirely true – Betsy was the light of his life – but Disraeli said that when talking to royalty, flattery should be laid on with a trowel. 'What can I do for you?'

This time it was the Queen's turn to tell him a story. It started with some forgotten paintings found in storage at another royal palace, and ended with the body in the Buckingham Palace pool last month, which he had always thought extremely fishy, despite what the media said.

It was only a few months ago that he and the Boss had discussed another murder. After working as her protection officer, he'd risen through the ranks to chief inspector, built up a tidy pension and retired to the genteel borough of Richmond, where he was bored witless and grateful for any opportunity to stretch his brain beyond the *Times* crossword and the Polygon. The Queen turned to him every now and again. It was always on the QT and he was glad when she did.

'So if I've got this right, four paintings were discovered, but they weren't by the artist everyone hoped they were.'

'Exactly. It looked as though they must have been copied from the originals. It was quite a common practice in the seventeenth century, I was told. They were quite well done, but once they were cleaned up, they weren't nearly as impressive as we all at first thought.'

'And you say a curator was injured, ma'am. Is that where you'd like me to start?'

'Yes, please. It was in the mid-nineteen eighties. I don't remember the year precisely, but I'm sure the Royal Collection Trust will be able to tell you exactly when the paintings were discovered, and it was a few weeks after that.'

'Can't Rozie help?' He wasn't trying to be difficult, but he knew the Queen's APS had done sterling work last time and was surprised she wasn't better suited to this particular task, being on-site, so to speak.

'I fear she might have disturbed a hornet's nest already. As I say, she was talking to the Surveyor shortly before Mrs Harris died. If it was someone there that she alerted . . .'

'I get it, ma'am. New face, different story.'

'Yes. But I don't know how you'll do it.'

'Nor do I, ma'am. That's the fun of it. I'll let you know as soon as I've found anything. Actually, I've got a few mates from my old days working in your service. I can ask around. I don't think it'll be a problem.'

'And there's one other thing.'

She asked him to look into the recent whereabouts of an ex-staff member of hers. After he put the phone down, he went over to his drinks cabinet and poured himself two fingers of Johnnie Walker Red Label. Then he sat for an hour with his laptop and a notebook and pen, researching, writing, thinking. He hadn't felt this energised for weeks.

Maybe she and Betsy were his joint-favourite Elizabeths. Was that really bad? One was named after the other, so perhaps that made it OK.

Chapter 25

Rozie came out of the Queen's study the next morning feeling relieved and anxious in equal measure. The Boss had made it clear that she'd been doing a lot of thinking. She'd found a potential motive for the killing of Mrs Harris, but it was still tenuous. She didn't go into detail; they were so busy discussing next year's schedule there was hardly time for murder.

Nevertheless, she could sense the Queen was making progress. It was unnerving to think that if she was right, she, Rozie, was the cause of Cynthia Harris's demise. Meanwhile, as requested, she had made a handwritten list of all the people she had spoken to about the *Britannia* painting over the summer. She had written each name with thought and care, knowing it might lead to a killer. She was off to double-check Mrs Harris's records with HR.

Reaching her office corridor, she encountered Sir James, who looked like thunder and didn't say hello. She popped her head round Sir Simon's door to see what the matter was.

'Don't worry,' the Private Secretary said, waving a hand at her without looking up. 'It's under control.'

'Are you sure?' Rozie asked. Sir Simon's eager-beagle face looked just as miserable as his friend's.

'It's fine,' he insisted. He was still cross with her about the unnecessary policemen. 'It's just the final Reservicing figures. They don't quite add up and it's got to go to print first thing tomorrow. Mary van Renen was working on it and the temp . . . Well, the less said about the temp the better.'

'Can I do anything?'

He raised his head to gazed at her wearily. 'D'you know of an Excel wizard who understands databases and the ins and outs of BP refurbishment issues and has a free morning? Because I don't.'

Rozie smiled. 'I worked at an investment bank, don't forget. They made me go on courses.'

'But it's . . .'

'What?'

'Secretarial.' He looked apologetic.

She shrugged. The old 'secretaries-who-aren't-secretaries' thing.

'This is important,' she said. 'If you show me where to look for problems, I'll probably find them faster than anyone else who might be available.' Mrs Harris's HR records could wait an hour or two.

'Really?'

Sir Simon's features rearranged themselves, as if by magic, into their traditional combination of intelligent, curious hopefulness and Rozie made her way to the outer office in the South Wing where the Keeper's harassed assistants worked. Here, she acquainted herself with the issues and made herself comfortable at a free desk, which happened to be the one where Mary used to sit. She was the first person to think to call Mary herself, who talked her through the numbers.

Then she delved deeper into the databases to understand the discrepancies and lost all track of time.

The Queen was in her study when Philip popped his head round the door in passing to tell her some hair-raising stories about the US election that she would rather not have heard.

'I suppose the spooks have told you it's all being run by Russia and Facebook?'

'Not entirely.'

'Don't count on it. I got a sit-rep from someone at the Guinea Pig Club memorial thing.'

For a moment the Queen had a vision of Peggy Thornicroft's poor creature in the outhouses at her boarding school, but this was a club for aviators who had been guinea pigs in quite a different way. They were the men who had been shot down in their planes in the Second World War and suffered horrific disfigurement through burns. A surgeon called Archibald McIndoe had put them back together as best he could, feeding them barrels of beer to keep their hydration and their spirits up. He was a pioneer of plastic surgery and one of Philip's wartime heroes – and hers too – as were the young men (old men, now) who had been in the surgeon's care.

She had been entertaining Mr and Mrs Santos at the time, but in a perfect world she would also have liked to go with Philip and to spend an hour or two with the few pilots who remained. They were of one's own generation, they had been to hell and back and nothing could faze them. No doubt the visit would have been full of off-colour jokes and bonhomie. Her own events were never like that. There was something about the way men relaxed in each other's company . . .

She sighed briefly. 'How many of them are left?'

'Seventeen,' he said.

'Out of how many?'

'Six hundred and forty-three.'

But even seventeen still alive today wasn't so bad, she considered, given that Philip was ninety-five and most of them would have been the same age as him. She remembered so well the dances they'd held at Windsor Castle, and how bright and charming all the young men were who came, and how so very many of them never came back. One after the other, after the other. It was dizzying, sometimes, to think of those names and handsome faces, and how one had twirled around the floor with them. And then the telegram.

These men must have believed, as their flaming machines plunged towards Earth, that their time had come. How many might have guessed they would live to their hundredth year, and some beyond it?

Sir Simon and Sir James arrived, to talk her through the Reservicing Programme proposal for the last time before it was submitted. The Keeper happened to mention that Rozie was busy sorting out a last-minute issue with the numbers.

The Queen smiled. 'She's a woman of many parts, isn't she?'

'Yes,' Sir Simon gruffly admitted. 'And she offered to help – she didn't have to.'

This pleased the Queen even more. She liked people who pitched in and got on with things. One of her pet hates were the other kind: the prissy ones who stood on their dignity and watched chaos swirl around their ankles while they did nothing to avoid it. But it was awkward not to have Rozie here just now. She would have understood the following request and obeyed it without question. Sir Simon, on the other hand . . . Oh, well. One was the Boss, after all.

'Simon, before you go, I'd like you to find the young woman who's curating the Canaletto exhibition for the Queen's Gallery next year. I particularly want to speak to her.'

'Today, ma'am?'

'Yes.'

Her look was firm. His half-raised eyebrow descended obediently to its natural plane.

'Of course. But I'm sure Neil Hudson would be more than happy to come over if you wanted to discuss anything. He's in overall control and he—'

'There's no need to disturb my Surveyor.' Neil Hudson's name was on Rozie's handwritten list, which was folded in the top drawer of her desk. 'The curator will do perfectly well. You know my schedule. If you could fit in half an hour this afternoon, that would be very kind.'

Sir Simon nodded. *That would be very kind* translated as *Shut up and get on with it*. He had learned this early, and did both.

Chapter 26

By sheer luck, the Queen's next appointment quite naturally provided plenty of opportunity to talk about what was on her mind. With her page in attendance, she made her way to the Yellow Drawing Room again, where plastic sheeting had been liberally spread out on the carpet and Lavinia Hawthorne-Hopwood was waiting for her, along with the documentary crew. Over the summer, Lavinia had created a clay bust from her drawings. Unlike many other portrait artists, Lavinia didn't like to work from photographs. 'They kill the image for me,' she explained the first time they worked together. 'If I can't capture it with my hand in the moment, then it doesn't feel part of the process.'

This part of the process was something the Queen always marvelled at. A damp clay sculpture, built around a metal armature, had been somehow manhandled from Lavinia's studio in Surrey to this room in the Palace, where it stood on a rotating modelling stand, draped in wet muslin. Nearby, a velvet-lined box displayed the Girls of Great Britain and Ireland tiara, ready for the dresser to help her put it on. She had chosen this particular piece for the portrait because it somehow managed to be delicate and dazzling at the same time. This was 'Granny's tiara'. Her beloved grandmother, Queen Mary, had given it to her as a wedding gift and she had worn it so often since that it was an old friend. It had not escaped her notice that she thought of her tiaras the way other women might think of their hats or – what? in these more modern times – their favourite handbags, perhaps.

Lavinia chatted as the Queen applied the diamonds, checked herself briefly in a mirror and made herself comfortable in the designated chair. When she was ready, the artist carefully unveiled the work in progress and the Queen was delighted to see that, once again, Lavinia had done a splendid job. One looked like oneself, but ten years younger. She had indeed captured some sort of sparkle about the eyes, as she had promised, and how she could do that in rough clay the Queen couldn't begin to understand.

Now, with a couple of precious hours ahead of them, Lavinia worked directly into the sculpture, pausing occasionally to check the dimensions against the original flesh and bone with callipers, talking as she went. The Queen had requested that the camera crew only stay for the first hour, so the second hour was much more relaxed. They discussed the Olympics, the garden, the racing on Channel 4. The Queen said she had recently seen a fascinating programme about art forgery and fakes. (She had, but it was about five years ago.)

'I had no idea there were so many. I hope I don't own any!'

The artist pushed a strand of hair out of her eyes with putty-smeared hands. 'I hate to say it, but you probably do. It's endemic. Most galleries have the odd fake or two, whether they know it or not. Of course, they'd never admit it.'

'But how do they manage it?' the Queen wondered. 'The forgers, I mean. There are all these techniques for examining paintings these days, aren't there? X-rays, I mean. And that thing they do with colours, to test what they're made of.'

'Mass spectrometry? Yes, you're absolutely right. Technology's come on in leaps and bounds. Forgers have to be so much cleverer today.'

'Oh? Since when?'

Lavinia didn't answer for a moment. She was busy with the slope of the nose and needed to concentrate. When she was happy with the line she said, 'The science gets better with every decade. But when I was an art student – and I used to love this sort of stuff – you would hear tales to make your hair curl. Back in the seventies the experts did it mostly by eye. They used to check the materials, of course. I mean, if you did a Botticelli portrait on canvas, when everyone knew he used wood panels for portraiture, then you were in trouble. Or if you were stupid enough to use titanium white, which only came in in the twentieth century. But a lot of it was around provenance and whether a painting had the right "feel".'

'That's so interesting.' The Queen looked and sounded distantly composed. In fact, her mind raced and her nose itched, but her hands remained loosely clasped in her lap. A lady did not touch her face in public; Queen Mary had taught her that, as well as giving her this tiara. And a queen did not look unduly fascinated by crime. 'So if you wanted to forge a painting, back in those days, how would you do it?'

'Really, ma'am?'

The Queen glanced over at Lavinia, who was smiling. Her cheeks and forehead were smudged with wet clay, her hands busy as she sculpted the face. She was working hard, but a lot of it was about looking and muscle memory. It left her free to consider the Queen's suggestion.

'I often wondered. It would be a nice way to make your fortune – as long as you didn't get caught and go to jail. So many forgers did. But I secretly admired a lot of them. They were really good painters and craftsmen in their own right. The detail of getting it perfect: that's a challenge in itself.'

'What sort of detail? Let's say it was a Rembrandt.'

'Oh, OK.' Lavinia grinned. 'Wow, that's a toughie. Well, let's assume I'm a genius-level copyist, to start with. We're talking the golden age of Baroque. First of all, I'd get hold of a painted canvas from the period. That's pretty important. It's got to be the right linen, the right weave, the right wood in the stretchers – even the right nails. I'd scrape off the oil paint until I got to the ground – that's how the canvas is prepared. It's got to be authentic, so I'd leave that in. I'd research what Rembrandt's paints were made of and make my own with the same ingredients. I'd use his method of drawing, and practise his style until I could do it in my sleep. But the painting itself is half of it, really. The rest is the provenance side, and often that's harder to fake. Has it been in a collection? You'd need the right inventory numbers, and they'd need to match the records. Faking a painting from *your* collection would be hard, ma'am, because it would be so easy to cross-check. Often the back tells you as much as the front. Is it stamped? How was the canvas attached? What kind of frame has it been in?'

'I suppose if you had the original to work off, that would make it much easier?'

'Infinitely,' Lavinia agreed.

'But if you wanted to move a painting secretly, how would you go about it? I saw a film once where a man put it in a briefcase, but that didn't seem very realistic.'

'Oh, *The Thomas Crown Affair*,' Lavinia said with another grin. 'I loved that film, and no, you can't hide a Monet in a briefcase. But if you were really desperate you could always take the canvas off the stretcher, roll it up and take the stretcher apart. You'd have to put it all back together of course, with the original nails. Fiddly job.'

'Can you really roll a canvas? A painted one?'

'Absolutely, if you're careful. You keep the painting facing out and do it like a carpet. It's not ideal, but I'm guessing your forger is a desperate criminal.'

'Hmm.'

'We had to do it for a painting my mother bought at auction once.' Lavinia applied some clay to an eyebrow and smoothed it, stood back and judged the effect. 'All quite legitimate, but the only way of getting it to her was in my 2CV, and it was six foot square. Dismantling the frame was heartbreaking, but by the time we'd put it all back together and touched up the dodgy bits, you'd never have known. There! I think I need a bit of a stretch myself.'

Later, Dr Jennifer Sutherland was amazed to find herself in the Queen's Gallery, beside the South Wing of the Palace, waiting to be joined by Her Majesty. They had met a couple of times, briefly, when the Queen had come to St James's Palace to inspect preparations for an exhibition. She had never been alone with the Queen before. And she was still regretting her trousers.

She looked down at them now. Three days in a row she'd worn them, because they were the comfiest ones she owned. They were expensive when bought, designer stretch jersey, black and figure-hugging, but overstretched and slightly baggy now, and still bearing the traces of yesterday morning's boiled egg, though she'd tried to wash the mark off in the loos.

Jennifer had pictured a moment like this, of course, up close with Her Majesty, but in her dream she'd been about to collect her MBE (or perhaps even her damehood), and was wearing Vivienne Westwood pinstripes and vertiginous Louboutins, her hair recently coloured and her mum in the audience. Not at three thirty on a Friday afternoon, in work clothes, and for no obvious reason. Neil Hudson had said the Queen didn't notice what you were wearing, but Jennifer didn't believe him. She was a woman, and women noticed. She might not care, but that was another matter.

The one thing Jennifer wasn't at all nervous about, though, was telling the Queen anything she wanted to know about the upcoming Venice exhibition, for which she was the senior curator. She had done her PhD on Grand Tour city views, or 'vedute' as they were called in Italian, and Canaletto was the most famous artist to produce them. In fact, it was a treat to have this opportunity to talk about her favourite subject with its most famous collector.

And there was the owner herself, suddenly, short and sturdy, in a skirt and cardigan and sensible heels, with a page hovering in the background and a couple of low-slung dogs for company, looking cheerful and relaxed.

'Did you know, this room used to be a conservatory?' she asked, after Jennifer had been introduced.

'I did wonder.'

'To match the one on the other side. Then it became the chapel. But it got a direct hit during the war.'

'Was anyone killed?' Jennifer asked.

'Miraculously, no. My mother said she was glad we'd been bombed, because now we could look the East End in the eye. It was rather alarming, though. She was at the Palace when it happened.'

Jennifer had always admired the Queen Mother. When the royal family were advised to shelter in Canada during the war, she had written: *The children will not leave unless I do. I shall not leave unless their father does, and the king will not leave the country in any circumstances whatever.* They were not just words, when bombs were falling. Another fifty feet to the right or left . . .

'We were hit nine times. It was my husband's idea to convert the chapel ruins,' the Queen went on. 'Now it's all much grander than it used to be. Every monarch likes to make their mark, and this was mine. Do tell me how the exhibition will look.'

Jennifer was surprised. The Queen wasn't known for taking such an interest in the build-up to a show. But they discussed where various paintings would go in the three available rooms, and it was increasingly clear she had her personal favourites from her collection. She reminisced about her own visit to the Grand Canal, and how it contrasted with her Canalettos.

'I suppose you're an expert on the seventeenth century?' the Queen asked in passing.

'Yes, ma'am. I am. Baroque and Rococo.'

'Oh, good. Are you interested in Gentileschi, by any chance?'

'Of course! Which one?'

'Artemisia,' the Queen said. She had done her homework.

Jennifer smiled widely. 'Absolutely! She's one of my favourite artists of the period. We've got a self-portrait of her in the current show, actually.'

'I thought so.' The Queen had opened the exhibition, called 'Portrait of the Artist', a few days ago.

At Jennifer's instigation, they walked over to look at the painting in question. Jennifer sighed in wonderment, as she always did with this one.

'Remind me,' the Queen said, 'how did we come to have it?'

Jennifer was on home ground. 'It was painted here, when she worked at the court of Charles I. He invited her over from Italy, where she was already famous.'

'Really?'

'Oh yes. She became well known when she was still in her teens. Her father, Orazio Gentileschi, was already a court painter here for the king. A lot of their work was lost after his execution, including this one, but it was recovered after

216

the Restoration. I think it's one of the highlights of your collection, ma'am.'

They stood in front of it together. The Baroque was all about light and shade, bravura painting and new perspectives. In this self-portrait – which Jennifer assumed was an attempt to get new patrons and show off the artist's skill – Artemisia captured herself brush in hand, gazing towards a blank canvas off to one side, on which she was about to start work. The bottom half of the painting was taken up with her elaborate green silk sleeve and her palette. Above, light fell on her corseted, lace-edged chest, highlighting her décolletage. But the head in the upper right-hand corner was not coquettishly posing, it was looking away from the viewer and concentrating on the job. Her dark hair was caught up loosely, with several messy strands escaping. Her eyes were hard to see. The viewer's own eye was drawn instead to her muscular raised right arm, holding the brush, as she prepared to mark the canvas. The sleeve on this arm had fallen back to reveal the flesh, but the exposure wasn't designed to be sexy – and this is what Jennifer so loved about it – it was just a casual result of her work. This was a woman saying what it feels like to be a woman, and getting on with things, and being bloody good at them. Watch her if you want to, but she's got better things to do.

'She reminds me a bit of Frida Kahlo,' Jennifer said.

'Oh, really?'

Jennifer sensed her remark hadn't landed. 'I don't think you own anything by her, ma'am,' she admitted. 'Mexican. Twentieth century. She had the same bold approach to self-portraiture.'

'I think this one's rather marvellous.'

'It is. Your ancestor had a good eye.'

'Why an allegory, do you think?' the Queen asked, peering at the label, which said it was called *Self-Portrait as the Allegory of Painting*.

'Oh, I think she was having a joke at her male colleagues' expense. In Italian it's "La Pittura". Painting is feminine. It was something the men couldn't be.'

The Queen stepped back. 'I remember the first time I saw her work and realised that a woman had painted so well in the seventeenth century. It was quite a shock.'

Jennifer nodded. 'It can't have been easy, though she wasn't by any means the only one, or even the only great one. I'm sure it helped that her father taught her how. She wouldn't have had access to the training otherwise.'

'Ah. Training from one's father.' The Queen's face lit up in a way that caught Jennifer quite by surprise. 'I'm familiar with the concept. Are her paintings very valuable?'

'Not as much as Orazio's. History tended to ignore her and favour him. Although as you can see from this one, she was just as good. Much better, in my opinion. I think she's finally reached the million-dollar mark. But she has her league of followers. She really was exceptional, and there aren't that many examples of her paintings.'

'Thank you,' the Queen said. 'A million dollars? How interesting. And I look forward to seeing the Venice scenes next year. Can I ask you a small favour?'

'Of course, ma'am.'

'Do keep this conversation between us private, if you would be so kind. Even among your colleagues. I'm afraid I can't explain why, but it would help.'

Jennifer promised. At first, she was disappointed that she wouldn't be able to savour every little detail with her fellow curators at the RCT, but on the walk back to St James's Palace she considered that an air of mystery might be even better. *Oh, we talked about her favourite paintings . . .* Something vague like that.

Chapter 27

At her temporary desk in the Keeper's outer office, Rozie looked up from her screen and was amazed to see that outside the light was fading. She glanced at the clock. It was nearly 5 p.m. The discrepancies in the finance spreadsheets had been tracked down to a couple of lines in the database: cross-checking with meeting notes from the relevant committees (Sir James Ellington was a stickler for record-keeping, for which Rozie silently saluted him), it was clear that certain cost projections didn't tally with the real figures in the accounts.

If you were to illustrate the problem, a graph that should predict a steady rise in some fairly low-level maintenance requirements suddenly took off two years down the line in an almost exponential curve. Thanks to Mary, the Keeper already knew roughly where to look in the database; Rozie had simply helped him pinpoint the mistake. Apparently, Sir James had asked various underlings to fix the issue several days ago, but they had merely assured him it was all 'under control'. He had found this, he said, infuriating – given that it so obviously wasn't.

Anyway, armed with pages of printouts and a borrowed lap-top, Rozie made her way to the property accounts department to get the problem fixed. It would have made sense for them to be in the South Wing, near Sir James himself, but it was in the nature of Buckingham Palace for the sensible thing to be completely different from what actually existed. For reasons nobody could remember, this particular team were buried in the basement, off a long corridor in the West Wing, opposite the kitchens. Rozie hurried down three flights of stairs, past the vast boiler room that fed the central heating, like something from an ocean liner, and on until she came to their unassuming office underground.

To her surprise, it was empty, but there seemed to be a bit of a party going on in the staff kitchen next door. After the focused energy of everyone upstairs, the new atmosphere was a bit of a shock.

'Is it someone's birthday?' she asked.

Four heads turned to look at her. Four glasses of Prosecco paused mid-air. She felt the festive mood shift.

'Er, sort of,' the nearest man said, with a half-smile she couldn't read. He was short and out of shape, Rozie saw, with a belly he could afford to lose. His suit was crumpled and his tie loosened. 'Care to join us?'

'I can't, I'm afraid. I just need someone's help with this.'

She noticed that two of the men were Mick Clements and Eric Ferguson from the Operations Team, whom she had spoken to over the summer. Now, as then, Mick, the head, seemed sullen and hostile at the sight of her, while his younger colleague tipped his head to one side, as if examining her in a glass case.

Mick put his Prosecco glass down with slow deliberation.

221

'I guess I'll be going, then.'

As Mick brushed past her, she felt his body bristle with barely contained disgust. She couldn't imagine what she had done to deserve it, and the others were hardly less hostile. Nobody invited her to go to their office, or offered to help. Rozie stood her ground and explained her problem, resting her open laptop on a kitchen counter. As the party atmosphere fizzled out, she felt a mixture of discomfort and annoyance. It wasn't yet five thirty and upstairs the workday was still well under way; here, they seemed to think it was over. They were not remotely interested in her problem, though they were quick to dismiss her afternoon's work.

'I think you've missed the point a bit, miss.'

The junior-looking accountant stuck his hands in his pockets and gave her a shrug. His colleague stared at the ground.

'I don't think I have. Can I ask who's in charge?'

The short man in the crumpled suit grunted something and reluctantly listened as she explained again what figures she needed. He shook his head and looked at her sadly.

'Like Andy says, you've got into a bit of a muddle with this one, sweetheart. You've got your databases mixed up.' He reached across her and tapped on the keyboard of the laptop, breathing noisily into her shoulder. 'This line here doesn't relate to that one there. Don't worry, we can sort this out for you next week.'

The air was thick and stale, and uncomfortably warm. Rozie stubbornly explained her calculations line by line, only gradually revealing – as they continued to shake their heads and contradict her – that she was as financially literate as they were, if not more so; that she was working on their boss's most important project of the year, and that if they couldn't help her in the next five minutes, she was going to have to report them for obstruction.

She watched their dismay, resistance and eventual capitulation. They went back to their desks reluctantly to adjust their projections in line with her new figures, and she couldn't get out of the office and their company fast enough.

Eric Ferguson accompanied her. Tall and lanky, he'd been lounging in the doorway since his boss left and she'd almost forgotten he was there.

'I'm going your way,' he said. 'Let me carry that laptop for you.'

'I can manage,' Rozie said.

When they were out of earshot of the accountants, he hooted.

'Phew! That was tough. I felt for you, Captain O, I really did.'

'They could have been more helpful.'

'Yeah, you could say that. I thought you went pretty easy on them. Mind you, they'd just had some bloody bad news.'

'Had they? I thought they were celebrating.'

'Commiserating. Drowning their sorrows. Pete – he's the fat guy – he thought he was getting this big bonus today, but it just got cancelled.'

Eric seemed to be waiting for a comment, so Rozie said, 'Oh.'

'He had the fizz anyway, so . . .'

'I see.'

'Yeah. Bad timing.'

They were back near the boiler room, big enough to power an aircraft carrier, which emitted a low, steady hum so powerful Rozie could feel it in her bones. She remembered something from her research today and nodded towards the noise.

'They'll be overhauling all of that before too long. I bet you can't wait for the Reservicing.'

Eric gave her his odd sideways stare for a moment, then his face melted into a grin. 'Loads of work for us, you mean? We'll be at it non-stop. Can't wait though, yeah. Tippety-top.'

With a nod, he indicated a nearby staircase and disappeared up it at a trot. Rozie shrugged to herself, thinking back to the accountants. That atmosphere had been *weird*. Only now did she fully take on board how unwelcome her presence had been.

Was it one of them who had sent her the notes? she wondered. Was it personal? It was hard to see how or why: she'd never met them before. *'Like some sort of Nubian queen'*, Neil Hudson had said, as if he was being complimentary. Sod him. She would *not* suspect everyone she encountered. She would *not* let the pathetic little knife-doodler drive her out of the job she loved.

But still. She picked up the pace and speed-walked back to the office with the new projections. Slightly out of breath, she accepted Sir James's fulsome praise for 'saving the afternoon'. Then she made her way to DCI Strong's little incident cubbyhole on the floor above, to let him know of a couple more poison pen suspects to investigate.

Chapter 28

The Queen fitted in one more meeting at the end of the day.

After dinner, Billy MacLachlan was also shown to her private audience room. He looked around briefly, pleased to notice that almost nothing had changed in the time since he last saw it. A few photographs of grandchildren had now been joined by those of great-grandchildren. Prince Harry, meanwhile, had changed from the nervous teenager with the cheeky grin into a more confident young man, whose star quality shone out through the ginger beard.

'It's good to see you again, Billy,' she said.

'Likewise, Your Majesty.'

She thanked him for his help at Windsor at Easter, and he refrained from thanking her for tasking him with this new job. It was better if your employers thought you were doing *them* the favour.

'Did you find the curator?' she asked, inviting him to sit down.

Dogs came to sniff at his trousers, then settled at the feet of their mistress.

'Not a curator, ma'am – a conservator,' he said, sinking into the sofa cushions and making a mental note to brush the dog hairs off his trousers later. 'They clean the paintings and reverse the ravages of time, but I'm sure you know that. His name was Daniel Blake, and he was hired by Sholto Harvie, the Deputy Surveyor, in 1982 to work for the Royal Collection. He was the first full-time conservator they had – now there's a whole studio of them. Anyway, Mr Harvie made the case for a full-time employee and Blake worked alongside him out of Stable Yard House.'

The Queen pursed her lips, then shook her head. 'I don't remember him.'

'No reason why you should. He was fresh out of the Courtauld. In his late twenties, with a degree in chemistry and another in the history of art. Harvie and he got on pretty well, from what my sources tell me. But you were right, ma'am – Blake had a terrible motorbike accident in 1986. It was in the summer, shortly after they'd discovered those Baroque paintings in Hampton Court Palace. He was heading out of town up the M1 to go and meet some friends. A climbing trip, something like that. The smash was pretty bad.'

'And he recovered?' the Queen asked. 'Where is he now?'

MacLachlan paused for a beat. 'No, ma'am, he didn't recover. I interviewed an uncle. Blake's mother died five years after the smash and the uncle thinks it was the grief that did it. Blake had a refurbished Norton Commando bike, ma'am – his pride and joy, sounds like. Nice bikes, but notoriously unreliable. Crashed into by a lorry at a roundabout and was in a coma for several weeks before Mrs Blake had to make the decision to turn off the machines. The uncle I spoke to had helped him refurbish the bike and got a report from a garage afterwards – he wanted to know if it was something they'd done wrong or whatever. They said there was a loose bleed nipple. It's a component in hydraulic brake systems, ma'am. It can happen. The front brake was leaking fluid and Daniel didn't stand a chance. He skidded into that lorry and went right under it. It's a miracle he survived at all. P'raps better if he hadn't. For his mother. Making that decision. I don't know . . .'

The Queen looked dour. 'Something no mother should have to do.'

'Quite.' MacLachlan was glad to change the subject slightly. 'You mentioned there was a delay at that time about looking into the Hampton Court pictures, ma'am. The Artemisia Gentileschis.' He had practised the pronunciation watching art videos on YouTube. Not what he'd have expected, it was sort-of *Gentilesse-skis*. 'You were right about that too. They were all pretty cut up about Blake at the Royal Collection. He would have been the one to clean them up, so naturally it put the work back quite a bit.' *Artistic types*, he thought, though he didn't say it. If policemen downed tools every time somebody got knocked about, they'd never get anything done.

The Queen nodded. 'Those brakes. Is it possible to loosen the . . .?'

'Bleed nipple, ma'am.'

'Deliberately?'

MacLachlan had of course considered this. 'Yes, if you know what you're doing. If I wanted to give a man on an

227

old Norton Commando a nasty surprise and get away with it, that's what I'd do.'

'Thank you, Billy. Now, the pictures. I'm keen to know what happened afterwards. I have a dim memory of the copies going into storage, once it was agreed Artemisia didn't paint them. And I'm sure . . .' She leaned forward, absent-mindedly stroking the corgi's ear as she considered. '. . . At least I *think* the Surveyor told me that two of the originals were later found elsewhere.'

She was silent for a moment, lost in thought. The one time she had seen the canvases, soon after their discovery, they had been laid out in a conservation studio at St James's Palace, two flat on a table and a couple of others propped in front of them, on the floor. Everyone had been very excited, Sholto most of all. They were portraits of women – more allegories, perhaps – very dirty and dingy, with the occasional flash of brilliance underneath the centuries of grime. She didn't remember them precisely, only that the light and shadow on the faces was very clever, and the women were beautiful but also *interesting*, like real women, women she knew, people with complicated interior lives, caught in the moment. They had been quite lovely.

Then there had been a long gap over the autumn when nothing had happened, and it was explained that the young conservator – Blake – had had his accident, so someone else had been called in to look at the Gentileschis and clean them up. Afterwards, when the experts came to examine them properly, it turned out they were copies after all, and not even particularly good ones, apart from the faces. She had been disappointed, but other things had demanded her attention. Of course! The trip to China. She was away for several weeks, working hard each day to make the tour a success.

'I was aboard the royal yacht at the time,' she muttered. 'Very busy.'

When she had come back, she was exhausted and the Gentileschis were a distant memory. Soon afterwards she was finalising the following year's trip to Canada with the Foreign Secretary. Meanwhile, after a mix-up that was never fully addressed, she chose Cuneo's sketch of the lake through the trees to fill the gap on the pale jade wall outside her bedroom, where once the vibrant, 'ghastly' oil painting of *Britannia* had been.

'Ma'am?' MacLachlan gently brought her back to the present. 'D'you want me to look into the other "accident" while I'm at it? The one in the pool?'

'No.' She was firm. 'That will be a job for the police if we come to it. The *official* police, I mean.'

She still dreaded alerting Chief Inspector Strong to a murder at the Palace. Now quite possibly two. First, she needed to assure herself of a connection between them. That reminded her.

'Did you find out where Sholto Harvie was the night Cynthia died?'

'I did. Somewhere in the Adriatic Sea, between Split and Ravenna, with three hundred witnesses. He was an expert guest on a cruise ship called the *Evening Star*, talking about the art of Greece, Venice and everywhere in between. Nice work if you can get it.'

229

'I imagine it must be.'

MacLachlan looked as if he was about to say something, hesitated, then summoned up his courage and said it anyway. 'You must miss her a lot, ma'am. *Britannia*. You sailed everywhere.'

'Yes,' she agreed, simply.

And the worst of it was, having taken her yacht away from her and made travel and official entertaining exponentially more difficult, Mr Blair later admitted it had all been quite unnecessary. Suddenly she was very tired. She thanked Billy again for his work so far and took herself to bed.

Chapter 29

The weekend at Windsor was beastly. One of her great pleasures, after church on Sunday, was normally coffee with her cousin Margaret Rhodes, who lived in the Great Park. She was one of the only people left who had known one all one's life. As a little girl, she had known one as Lilibet, and to this day she was one of the few people one could talk to with utter frankness about everything that was going on in the world. She was a year older, and to see her soldiering so magnificently on was always heartening. Except, this weekend it was clear she was unwell. When the Queen popped in to visit her, there was a frailty to Margaret that was distinctly worrying.

Life without her cousin, the Queen reflected, would be a different life altogether. It would be a new age, and with Philip retiring to Norfolk soon, it would be lonely in a new way. She had lost her sister fourteen years ago, shortly followed by Mummy, and one by one, close family and friends from the early days had followed with dismal regularity. Even the dogs. Since she was seven, there had been corgis in her life, in ever-increasing numbers, and now, with Holly gone, there was only Willow. The Queen had already decided not to breed any more, because she knew she would not be around forever to look after them, and from a strictly practical point of view, they were a trip hazard, and it was beholden to the monarch not to break her neck if she could possibly avoid it.

She would cope. She would move on, just as she always did. And perhaps she was being maudlin and her cousin would get better soon. But it was a cold, dank, November weekend and the mood in the country and elsewhere was increasingly rattled. Would the fissures in Europe and in America mend themselves easily, regardless of who was in power? The US elections were due to take place in two days and the media were obsessed. Philip might joke about Facebook, but even the White House was 'confident' that Russia had tried to use it to influence the democratic process. It seemed as if the very foundations of democracy were being undermined in ways she hadn't seen since the war, which was longer than many of her subjects' lifetimes. Like everyone else, she felt they were all on the brink of something they didn't fully understand, grasping around to hold onto whatever they believed in, praying that it would stand.

Philip had started a picture. He had his oils out in the Octagon Room – which stank of turpentine – and he was putting together a decent landscape of Balmoral, based on some sketches he'd done in the summer. It was the garden, seen from inside the castle. She marvelled at his self-control to do something creative and retrospective, and not to sit glued to the BBC.

'That's nice,' she said, standing over his shoulder.

He grunted.

'Balmoral?'

'No. Timbuctoo.' He had a recording of an old cricket match playing in the background, and she sensed she was distracting him.

'Have you heard a weather forecast recently? I missed my ride this morning. Is it going to keep raining like this?'

He turned round properly to face her. 'No idea. Look, I'm sorry about Margaret. You'll stop feeling such a misery guts if you go and find something useful to do.'

He was probably right. She half-heartedly started a jigsaw of Dunfermline at the finishing post of the St Leger, but found herself pondering on the connections between Cynthia Harris and Sholto Harvie, and Mary van Renen, the secretary who had left, and Mrs Baxter, who was 'difficult', and Rozie, who had merely asked about a painting but wondered whether she might have inadvertently caused a murder. Daniel Blake was one part of the puzzle, but even if Sholto had caused his 'accident', he couldn't have caused Cynthia's from the middle of the Adriatic.

The Breakages Business was another piece. The Queen wasn't sure if it was just a distraction set up by Sholto, or whether it was something more. She wasn't satisfied with Sir James's cursory look into the matter. If she was going to be useful, she decided this was where to look next.

By Monday morning she felt much better, cheered by a good night's sleep and a pleasant early ride in the park. She worked in the car on the way back to London and was ready to face the week with her normal vigour.

Rozie was in charge of the boxes today.

'There is something I'd like you to do for me.'

Rozie brightened instantly. 'Of course.'

'It's about the Breakages Business. I've been thinking about the tunnels under the Palace. You must have heard of them.'

'I've heard rumours,' Rozie said. 'That there used to be a network connecting all the royal palaces in this area.'

'Not "used to be",' the Queen corrected her. '*Is*. They were used to store lots of the more valuable furniture during the war, then rather forgotten about.'

It was hardly surprising. Papa had other things to think about, repairing the worst of the bomb damage, trying to make the place presentable again with everything rationed and much of the empire still cut off as trade routes slowly re-established themselves. It wasn't until she and Philip had been living here for a while that the Duke had grabbed his equerry and gone on an exploratory adventure in the bowels of the Palace and beyond.

You'll never believe what we've found, he'd said on his return, dirty and happy, covered in mud and dust, with wisps of cobweb in his hair. *Two crates of china. German. Looks important. Some nineteenth-century wine. Fourteen Regency gilt chairs. Seven mouldy mattresses, a portrait of George III, four marble fireplaces and a family of Romanian refugees.* At that, her eyes had widened. *Ha!* he'd said. He'd made the last bit up, but he was amused by her lack of surprise at the rest.

At the time, they had all been fascinated by the forgotten treasures, and Philip had explored the tunnels further to see where they went, hoping to set up a useful little route for staff and family to travel out of the public eye between Buckingham Palace and Clarence House, where Mummy and Margaret now lived. He eventually reported that while the tunnel was reasonably roomy under the Palace grounds, its offshoots became narrow, low and damp as they ran under Green Park towards St James's Palace. Walls seeped with slime and some areas were quite impassable. Philip had closed them off, giving instructions that the better-built parts near the Palace be used for storage only.

The Queen summarised this for Rozie.

'I believe there is a doorway of some sort that lies roughly under Constitution Hill. It cuts off the far section and it's supposed to be firmly locked. When things are quiet, might you perhaps be able to check that it really isn't being used?' She phrased this carefully. It was a genuine request to Rozie, with an opt-out clause framed in her eyes. The far end of the tunnels was unsafe, after all, and she didn't want Rozie to take any risks unwillingly.

In fact, Rozie looked so delighted at the idea that the Queen had to give her strict instructions not to venture beyond Philip's locked doorway, should such a thing be possible. She took care not to break her own neck and preferred her APS to do the same.

'And one other thing. I believe that Lavinia Hawthorne-Hopwood may know Sholto Harvie's background.'

'The sculptor who's doing your portrait for the Royal Society?'

'Exactly. I'm sure I remember her discussing a connection. You could perhaps ask her about him, privately. If you'd be so kind.'

Rozie nodded. 'What sort of thing would you like to find out?'

'I don't know,' the Queen said. 'It might be nothing. But ask, and see what you find.'

Chapter 30

In the South Wing office of the 'rollicking bollockings', Air Vice-Marshal Mike Green had not particularly been enjoying the last four weeks. Normally he was in his element in the run-up to Christmas, organising lavish dinners and banquets for the cream of international society. But this year there had been the unfortunate death of the terrible housekeeper and the extra pressure of the Reservicing Programme and, worst of all, the jumped-up policeman, Strong – or Bogroll, as he was known in court circles – was ferreting around the Palace and basically telling him how to do his job.

It was the Master himself who had come up with this particular epithet. There was that TV ad from his childhood about loo paper: 'soft, strong and very long'. Bogroll was certainly soft and meetings with him felt endless. It was in the tradition of Palace nicknames. Mike Green was well aware that he was 'Crabmeat' to his elders and betters. The army and navy had called the RAF 'crabs' for decades, so it was inevitable really. The Master took it in very good spirit and smiled indulgently whenever someone accidentally said it to his face.

He smiled to himself now because Bogroll had been defeated. *He* wasn't the one to spot the clue that solved the whole problem of the poison pen campaign. *He* hadn't conducted the crucial interview with the perpetrator. (Admittedly, the chief inspector was rather annoyed about that – but was it the Master's fault if he had been away on a training course on the critical day?) *He* hadn't obtained the signed confession. Strong hadn't looked convinced by any of it when faced with the evidence, but that was typical of the smallness of the man: he just couldn't accept when he'd been bested. A gracious 'Congratulations' would have been enough.

The Master was looking forward to his meeting with Her Majesty. He hadn't seen her alone for a week, in which time much had happened. He trusted she would be delighted. She might also be just a little penitent that she hadn't trusted him in the first place, though of course she wouldn't show it, and he wouldn't expect her to.

They had half an hour scheduled before lunch, in her private audience room. It was their first opportunity to catch up since the state banquet.

'Not too many disasters behind the scenes, I hope?' she asked.

'One or two, ma'am. I'm afraid Vulcan disgraced himself again. He appeared from nowhere when a guest was emerging from the loos and bit him in the ankle.'

'Oh dear! One of ours or one of theirs?'

'One of ours. A Permanent Under Secretary, as I recall.'

'Oh, that's all right then.' She grinned. 'He won't sue. Do send a note, though. "The Queen deeply regrets . . ."'

'Of course.' He smiled, feeling a bit like a magician about to produce a rabbit from a hat. 'I thought you might like to know, ma'am, that we've solved the nasty matter of those letters.'

Her eyes widened behind her glasses. She looked positively shocked.

'Really? I didn't know you were still looking into them.'

He assured her that he very much was.

'In conjunction with the police?'

'In a way, ma'am.'

The chief inspector and his man were always available to help out (she seemed ready to dispute this, but he hadn't produced the rabbit yet), but they were focusing mostly on Cynthia Harris, and he, the Master, had a broader view. He admitted that their general presence might have spurred the culprit on to come clean when caught. If so, he was grateful for the assistance. (He wasn't, but you had to make Her Majesty feel useful.)

'Come clean?' the Queen queried. She still looked mightily puzzled. 'Do you mean, he's admitted it?'

'*She*,' the Master gently corrected. 'And yes, ma'am, she has. She couldn't help it: she was caught in the act. I have her confession here.' At which point, he opened the leather folder he'd been holding to reveal the signed typescript in all its glory.

The Boss was too startled, obviously, for the delighted smile yet, but he would settle for astonishment. He had been quite surprised himself.

'And who is she?'

'A housemaid, ma'am. A woman called Lorna Lobb. She was seen at the canteen last week, hovering near the table where your APS was sitting. My team have been asked to be on the lookout, and it was one of my clerks who spotted her.

Rozie was busy talking to someone else and my clerk saw Mrs Lobb about to drop something in her bag. He managed to corner her before she could do it. It was all very discreet. I don't think Rozie even noticed, ma'am, but Lorna could hardly deny the envelope she was holding, or the fact she was wearing a single latex glove. She was quite terrified when we questioned her about it. And quite rightly. The note was absolutely appalling.'

'Lorna Lobb?' The Queen considered the name, her brow deeply furrowed. 'Which notes did she deliver?'

'All of them, ma'am, except the ones to Mary van Renen.'

'Are you quite sure? Including the notes to Cynthia Harris?'

'Absolutely. We have it here in writing.' He tapped the folder. 'She didn't do it on her own account. She was working for Arabella Moore who, by the way, denies everything, but the case is very solid. Mrs Moore is married to Stewart Moore, who you may remember left under an unfortunate cloud that was somewhat of Mrs Harris's making. There was bad feeling between her and the housekeeper.'

The Queen's brow remained stubbornly furrowed. 'But didn't Mrs Harris receive other notes years ago? Before she retired, I mean? Before Mrs Moore would have had any reason to resent her?'

The Master had considered this himself. 'She did,' he acknowledged, 'but Mrs Lobb claims to know nothing about those. I assume they were the work of someone else, giving Mrs Moore the idea. Mrs Harris was unpopular with some of the junior staff even then. She may quite easily have said or done something to create ill will.'

The Queen's gaze rested on a selection of photographs in silver frames. Her lips were pursed. 'Did Mrs Lobb explain what Mrs Moore's motives were for the other messages? The ones not received by Mrs Harris, I mean.'

'No. After a certain point she clammed up, unfortunately. But I did my own research. Mrs Moore was known to have had words with Mrs Baxter about the unrest she felt Mrs Baxter was stirring up in her staff. And with Rozie there was a racist element. I must say, this came as a complete shock. I'd never have guessed. Mrs Moore has always seemed a picture of propriety.'

'Yes, she has,' the Queen said quietly.

'I asked if Rozie wanted to make an official complaint, formally to the police, I mean. But she didn't. She was quite clear about that.'

'And what about Mary van Renen? You said Mrs Lobb didn't confess to those notes.'

'Ah. That's another matter entirely, ma'am. I don't know if you remember, but Miss van Renen was being harassed by a man she had met on the internet. He caused some unpleasantness, but it was unrelated to Mrs Moore's campaign.'

'I see.' Her Majesty didn't seem puzzled any more, thank goodness, merely grim: the way she looked when watching parade manoeuvres poorly executed by troops of foreign nations in the rain. 'And what does Mrs Moore have to say about all this?'

'As I said, she's denying everything, quite vociferously, but she would, ma'am, wouldn't she? There's a formal process we need to go through before we let her go. I have initiated it. She won't be with us for much longer.'

241

The Queen's brow furrowed again. 'You haven't sent her home already?'

The Master admitted that he hadn't. He'd been too busy recently to give it his full attention, and – this was something he kept to himself – it was in his interest to keep Arabella Moore on for as long as possible. She might be a nasty, racist bully in her private life, but she was an excellent man-manager at work, and her team was responsible for all the guest liaison for the upcoming Diplomatic Corps Reception in a month, which was the biggest, most glamorous event of the year, putting even the state banquet to shame. She was, in her way, a bit like Cynthia Harris: very good at what she did in ways that were hard to replace at short notice in a high-pressure environment. She'd be out on her ear soon enough, once the formalities were over, but he offered to put her on paid leave instantly if Her Majesty required it.

However, she didn't. She merely requested him to let her know if he discovered anything new, and asked to see a copy of Mrs Lobb's confession. It was only as he was leaving that the Master realised she hadn't looked delighted even for a moment. This, too, was a mark of the woman. Despite the fact that he had dealt with the issue for her, one of the victims had accidentally died in the process, and that was hard for all of them to take.

The Queen went upstairs for final fittings with Angela, her chief dresser, for the black coat and dresses she would wear at the end of the week. Afterwards, she caught up on correspondence and took the dogs for another walk in the garden.

Philip had brought up his latest painting to work on, meanwhile. It wouldn't be long before he retired to the Sandringham Estate – at ninety-six – and she knew how much he would enjoy devoting himself to his canvases. He had never been a fan of the Palace. He would much rather live in a farmhouse in the middle of nowhere, but, thanks to her, until next year he didn't get to choose.

She popped in on him in his study when she got back, to see how he was getting on.

He glanced up from his oils, in shirtsleeves, with an ancient cotton jacket thrown over them for protection. 'Oh, Cabbage, it's you.' His eyes narrowed. 'What was Crabmeat doing here earlier? I passed him outside your study looking about to explode with self-satisfaction.'

'The Master had some interesting thoughts on who was behind that poison pen campaign.'

Philip looked at her hard. 'I know you. You think his thoughts were bollocks. Did you tell him?'

'Not yet. He might be right. He has a confession.'

'Don't tell me. Sandy Robertson.'

This was the Queen's loyal page, who had recently been suspected of spying by MI5.

'No. A housemaid called Lorna Lobb.' She explained about Arabella Moore and the theory of revenge.

'What? Mrs Moore, from the Lady Clerks department? She used to be a secretary in my private office. Damned efficient, always polite, honest to a fault.' He looked scornful.

'All I can say is, if it's her, she's a bloody Jekyll and Hyde. She's a lot less useless than your average desk johnnie.' From Philip, this was praise indeed.

'I can't quite see her as a criminal mastermind,' the Queen agreed.

'Still, a confession's a confession,' he acknowledged. 'She owned up, did she?'

'No. She denies everything. It's Mrs Lobb who's confessed. She said your Mrs Moore put her up to it.'

He looked at her with frank incredulity. 'And Crabmeat believes her? Christ. He flew jet fighters, didn't he? All those G-forces must have addled his brain.'

The Queen wasn't so sure about the G-forces, but she agreed on the essentials. She also knew something he and the Master did not: Mrs Lobb had not been working directly for the poison pen letter-writer, as the Master so readily assumed.

It was quite clear to her now. This must have been the subject of the conversation she overheard from inside the wardrobe last summer. The voice getting instructions had belonged to the Goonishly-named Spike Milligan. That had become obvious enough after the incident with the bats in the bedroom at Balmoral and she was still sure of it, despite his denials to the chief inspector. He was acting as an intermediary. The voice giving him instructions could have been male or female. She thought more likely male, but it was definitely not that of Arabella Moore, whom the Queen had spoken to many times about guest invitations.

Back at her desk, she picked up the phone and asked Rozie to talk to Mr Milligan.

'Can you assure him he was overheard, and say it has come to Her Majesty's attention that he was involved? That ought to do it.'

Rozie promised she would.

At six thirty she managed to sneak in a quick gin and Dubonnet before Chief Inspector Strong made his appearance in her sitting room, to give her the latest progress update. She admired the man for not sending panicked messages after the Master had made his grand announcement about Arabella Moore. Strong seemed to trust that she would wait to hear from him before coming to any conclusions. She liked calm, confident people who expected others to do their jobs properly until proved otherwise. After all, she was one of them herself.

Her equerry showed him in and left them to it. Strong sat down in his usual place, at her invitation.

'What do you think of this Lobb confession?' she began.

Strong paused for a moment, while his gentle face turned from pale to puce and gradually back again. 'Not strictly the way I'd have done it, Your Majesty.' His voice was tight.

'I imagine not. I do apologise. The Master's very *enthusiastic*.'

'*Isn't* he, ma'am?'

'But the girl was caught red-handed, I gather.'

'She was,' Strong admitted. 'And it turns out she was in most of the right places at the right times to have done it. My sergeant's been doing some cross-checking.'

'Thank you for that.'

'Just doing our job, ma'am,' he said pointedly. 'Mrs Lobb came back to London ahead of some of the staff from Balmoral and wouldn't have been around to cut up Mrs Harris's clothes, however. Which I understand she fiercely denies, and which doesn't form part of her confession.'

'Yes, I saw that. The Master didn't mention it.'

Strong's silence spoke volumes.

'Tricky,' the Queen observed.

'Quite. The Master has a theory that the clothes thing was done by another servant with a grudge. I increasingly tend to lean towards your theory, ma'am, that Mrs Harris was targeting herself.'

'My lady-in-waiting's theory,' she was quick to correct him.

'Right. It does seem that Mrs Lobb was delivering the notes to Rozie, though, and she could have done it to Mrs Baxter, and possibly Mary van Renen. But once you take Mrs Harris out of the equation – if she's lying about that – it's hard to see why Mrs Moore would have tasked her to do any of it.'

'Oh, I *see*,' the Queen said, trying very hard to make it look as if this hadn't been her first thought.

'My sergeant's still researching Mrs Harris, ma'am, to see if we can get to the bottom of that side of it. Meanwhile, he's spoken to Mary van Renen up in Shropshire. That's of greater concern right now, assuming the notes *weren't* sent by Mrs Moore. The messages to her were full of menace. We've followed up with Mary's Tinder dates and, like her, we don't think it was them. There's usually some sort of pattern with a man like that. These men all have good ratings with their other dates, and we questioned several of them. They were willing to give up their devices if required to prove it. We've talked to her friends in London, but found nothing suspicious. I believe we come back to the Palace, ma'am, and someone she knew from here.'

'How unsettling. To think he's here, I mean. Or she.'

'I'm sure it must be. And as for your assistant, I haven't made much progress yet. I'm not convinced by the racist tone of the notes – nasty as it is. If it was, there are other members of your staff who might be targeted. I sense it's more personal. But I don't know what's behind it. Rozie's popular among the staff that know her.'

'So I gather.'

Strong's eyes narrowed. He rubbed his chin. 'In some ways, she's the one that most concerns me.'

'Oh? Why?'

'Someone doesn't want her around. Mary van Renen's home safe with her family, so that's OK. But Rozie Oshodi – she *is* around. I'm going to tell her to be careful.'

It wouldn't be the first time, the Queen thought. She wondered about Rozie in the tunnels. With luck, the girl would be in and out in ten minutes, happy to report on a bolted door and nothing else to see. But if she hadn't managed to go tonight, it might be better to call the whole thing off and come up with a safer plan.

'Absolutely,' she agreed. 'I will too.'

Chapter 31

Rozie always felt that the Palace changed character as day turned to night. Sometimes, it upped its sparkle for a reception or a banquet. Sleek Mercedes and Bentleys, and sometimes even old-fashioned horse-drawn carriages, arrived to disgorge guests in designer dresses and 'decorations' – which meant medals for the men, usually, but could just as well describe the diamonds on their wives. Golden light glowed in the quadrangle and, for those in the know, this was the most sought-after address of the night in London.

At other times, the change was more downbeat. The majority of staff went home, the flood of tradesmen, craftsmen and daily visitors slowed to a trickle, and the place was reclaimed by those who lived there or habitually worked late. The buildings stopped trying to impress and their occupants got on with the task of working as efficiently as they could in a rabbit warren of corridors that ceased to make sense two hundred years ago.

The Queen had a busy schedule for the next few days, so it was after eight when Rozie finally turned off her laptop and stretched her shoulders. The assistants had gone home at six, but Sir Simon was still in his office with the light on. Under normal circumstances, she would have popped her head round the door and said, 'Go home to your wife!' And he'd have made some quip back about her not recognising him before ten thirty. But now, with their strained relations, she thought this might come across as too unfriendly. She merely wished him goodnight and he glanced up at her and nodded. The air between them crackled with regret. She hovered in the doorway, trying to find a way through it. He asked her to close the door behind her, and she did.

A few hours earlier she had asked an assistant to procure a powerful torch and a pair of size nine wellingtons. Rozie guessed at the state of the electrics in the basement and was taking no chances: she wanted her feet to be encased in rubber. How the assistant found them, she didn't ask. You used your initiative in the Private Office. If you succeeded, you took quiet satisfaction in the fact that your boss would have noticed, which they invariably did.

Armed with the boots and torch, along with a spare jacket she borrowed from the security officers at the North Wing front door, she took the nearest flight of stairs down, feeling the air grow colder with each step. She walked under the North Wing until she reached the long, wide corridor running north to south under the West Wing, which housed the boiler room, storerooms and, as she now knew, the accountants. There were various other offices, too. The florists worked nearby, for example, resulting in a thick, earthy smell of vegetation that might have been unpleasant if it wasn't for a heady top note of jasmine in the air.

From here, Rozie took the narrow staircase that led down again towards the cellars.

To her left was an unlit corridor lined with trolleys and wooden crates. The wine collection was stored that way, along with various provisions that needed to be kept cool. To her right was a thick steel door marked, 'OPERATIONS. HAZARDOUS. KEEP OUT'. The space beyond must extend under the kissing trees, she judged. She had never had any reason to ignore the sign. Now, armed with her heavy-duty torch, she did.

When she found the switch inside the door, industrial strip lights buzzed into life. The room ahead was large – about the size of the swimming pool, in fact – and square. Suspended by chains from the ceiling, the lights illuminated a series of metal racks containing crates, pallets, rolled-up rugs, books, boxes of vintage toys, kitchen gadgets from the fifties, a washing mangle, and several pieces of old furniture whose purpose Rozie didn't even begin to understand.

There was a little room in the far left-hand corner: a small cube carved out by breeze blocks in the larger space. Rozie walked over to it, calling out, 'Is anyone there?' She realised her voice was sharper than usual. But there was no reply. The door opened at the push of the handle. Inside was a desk and shelving, stacked with miscellaneous boxes, battered tins of paint and neatly organised containers for screws and nails. It smelled faintly of sandalwood and musk. She searched the desk, where an old mug housed various biros, pencils and rulers. There was a pad of lined yellow paper next to it. Rozie tried out a couple of the pens, which were useless and dry. A rusty wastepaper bin contained a couple of screwed-up sheets of yellow paper. Rozie put them on the desk and smoothed them out. They were written on in pencil – numbers and letters jotted in neat little rows that made no obvious sense. She got out her phone and took pictures, then she re-crumpled the papers and put them back where she'd found them. Notebooks containing similar markings were scattered inside a drawer.

A nearby metal door led to another storage room. This one was long and thin, with an arched, low ceiling and walls lined with glazed tiles, like an old-fashioned Underground station. Rozie sensed that it marked the start of the tunnels. Its shelves held, among other things, at least two dozen hatboxes, several coils of thick rope, three child-size racing cars and four lifesaver rings. When she looked more closely, she saw the rings were marked HMY *Britannia*. There was another metal door at the end, partly obscured by two old-fashioned Harry Potter-style trunks and a tea chest. Rozie shifted the tea chest to one side and the trunks to the other. One of these was heavier than the other and, out of curiosity, she lifted the lid to find three magnificent blue and white Chinese vases, each half a metre high, nestled neatly among straw.

The metal door behind them opened with a shove. If there had once been a sign on it to warn against going further, there wasn't now. Beyond was a red-brick tunnel about five metres long and, at the end, yet another door. This one was different: lower, much older, set into a heavy frame. By now she must be under Constitution Hill, Rozie judged, turning on her torch. This was presumably where Prince Philip had required the staff to shut off the tunnels. The air was unusually still, resulting in a quiet that heightened her senses. She was aware of every buzz and flicker in the lights behind her, and the woody, masculine scent that lingered alongside the smell of damp and dirt.

The door itself was worthy of a museum: thick timber, mottled with age and studded with hefty metal bars to hold its hinges. There was a keyhole in an ancient plate below a rusty handle, but no sign of a key. Instead, the door was locked with a more modern hasp, hinged at the wall and held in place with a heavy padlock that fed through a staple attached to a steel plate. Rozie thought she might as well take a photo to show the Boss. She put down the torch, retrieved her phone from a jacket pocket and held it in place with the flash switched on, ready to press the button. But as she pulled the padlock towards her to get a decent picture, she found the lock swinging towards her, almost causing her to lose her balance.

The steel plate that held the staple was not attached to the door at all. Left flat, the mechanism looked sturdy, but if pulled it simply came away at the hinge, padlock and all, leaving the door unlocked. All Rozie had to do was tug on the rusty handle and the whole door swung aside.

The Queen's instructions had been clear and so was Rozie's army training: you took instruction from senior officers and did exactly what you were told.

But she was a battle-hardened veteran and every muscle and sinew in her body strained to go forward, into the dark.

If you went forward, you made progress. Stop now, and you could only report a problem. The big question was always, 'Who else do you put at risk?' But there was no one else to worry about. And Rozie was perfectly capable of looking after herself.

'Sorry, ma'am,' she muttered, picking up the torch and moving on.

The walls around her were brick-lined, wide and low. The ground was laid with uneven stone, patched with planks of wood over bare earth left by missing slabs. The duckboards were marked with irregular dark lines, which she judged to be tyre marks – from a wheelbarrow, perhaps? They looked freshly swept: free from the mud and grime she would have expected after sixty years.

Beside them, the torchlight picked out a steady stream of litter. There was an abandoned beanie, a mouldy leather glove, a snack wrapper from a brand she didn't recognise. What were Taz bars? Regardless, she was fairly sure they didn't have them in the fifties, or whenever Prince Philip had made his visit. Fairly sure none of this was supposed to be here at all.

By now she thought she must be under Green Park. The tunnel snaked along with occasional bends, making it impossible to see very far, but St James's Palace must be ahead and slightly to the right. It was one of the few times in her life Rozie wished she wasn't just shy of six foot tall. These Tudor guys must have been really short, or maybe they used children. Either way, Prince Philip's plan would never have worked. She couldn't see Prince William or Prince Harry crouching down like this to visit secret girlfriends. They'd need decent physio if they did. And the idea of an old-fashioned royal like Princess Margaret being down here in the cold and dark, for a quarter of a mile, to see her sister? No.

The torchlight caught something bright and golden, glimmering on the ground a few feet further on. Rozie was stepping forward to inspect it just as a distant thud made the air reverberate behind her. Jerking up in shock, she banged her head, hard, on the tunnel roof. Dazed, she tried to catch her balance as her mouth filled with the ferrous taste of blood.

Chapter 32

Billy MacLachlan had had worse jobs. Sitting in a pub in Tetbury, pint of ale on the table in front of him, he looked approvingly at the logs that crackled gently in an open fire, the decent list of beers, the decent-looking barmaid and the chalked-up menus of posh pub grub. Once upon a time he and the lads had been pretty scathing about 'triple-cooked chips' and half-baked steaks, everything resting on rocket leaves and costing a week's wages. But you got used to it. The food these days was good. He was very fond of a triple-cooked chip, especially if somebody else was buying. Today he was on expenses from Her Majesty.

'Now, the pictures. I'm keen to know what happened afterwards.'

The man coming back from the Gents had the look of someone who knew his way around beer and chips, posh or otherwise. His hacking jacket and smart jeans were carefully tailored to accommodate his waistline. He reminded MacLachlan a bit of Humpty Dumpty. The rosy face and receding hairline added to the impression. MacLachlan made a mental note to stick at one pint tonight, even if Her Maj was paying.

'Have you decided what to order?' the man asked. His name was Stephen Rochester and he was a Tetbury local and a regular at the pub. He ran a gallery-cum-antique shop in the high street. He'd come highly recommended and, so far, he wasn't proving a disappointment.

'Cod and chips and mushy peas,' MacLachlan said, glancing at the nearest menu. 'If it's on, that's what I'll have.'

'Not the duck? It's very good,' Rochester suggested.

'Not the duck.'

'Or the lamb shank?'

'You have the lamb shank, Stephen.' They were on first-name terms by now, although in this case MacLachlan's name was Charlie. 'And let me get you some wine. What do we think? The Merlot or the Cabernet Sauvignon?'

They chose a bottle, one of the more expensive on the list, and MacLachlan neglected to mention that he didn't drink wine any more. It didn't agree with him – gave him a headache. But if he was entertaining, for whatever reason, he liked to keep his interlocutors loquacious, expansive and well oiled. A good Cabernet could do that. Stephen was on his second glass before he noticed that 'Charlie' had stuck to his pale ale.

They were talking about Stephen's business. 'Charlie' had wandered into the shop not long before closing and explained he'd come into some money and he'd need some paintings and the odd stick of furniture to go in his new country home, once he found the right one. 'To make it look lived-in. You know.'

Stephen Rochester did indeed know and was very happy to oblige. Unlike the rich city-dwellers who were flooding into the Cotswolds – with money to burn, but no love for 'brown furniture', such as the Regency mahogany tallboy that 'Charlie' had admired as soon as he walked into Stephen's shop – 'Charlie' turned out to be a man who knew his Georgian from his Victorian and asked so many questions about the local area that they'd ended up agreeing to go out for dinner at the pub.

Comfortably installed at a little table by the fire, they chatted about the different Cotswolds towns and villages: which ones were dominated by yoga bunnies in designer leggings, which ones were mostly Airbnbs by now, and which were just about holding onto their character. Stephen was happy to share his expertise. They talked about art, too. 'Charlie' was interested – 'very much as an amateur, you understand. I don't really know anything. My aunt was keen, mind you. The one I inherited from, God rest her. She had this Renaissance painting – at least, she *said* it was. She was convinced it was by Caravaggio. Is that how you say it?'

'It is,' Stephen acknowledged. 'That would be very exciting, but unlikely. Caravaggio isn't Renaissance, by the way.'

'Oh?'

'No, he's the height of Baroque, but don't let me bore you.'

'You're not boring me at all, Stephen,' 'Charlie' assured him. 'Not at all.'

They finished their dinner and ordered dessert, although MacLachlan picked at his Madagascan Vanilla Panna Cotta with Chocolate Soil and Fresh Basil like a bird. 'So, if it *wasn't* a Caravaggio, how would I know?'

257

Stephen Rochester happened to be a bit of an expert on the period, which was no surprise because MacLachlan had done his research. Stephen had worked in the local auction houses for years before he set up the gallery, and the Baroque was his specialist subject. He explained about Caravaggio and MacLachlan, who didn't really care, was impressed with his scholarship.

'Amazing. You could write a book about it,' he said, grinning appreciatively.

'Perhaps I will.' Stephen was enjoying himself.

MacLachlan topped up Stephen's glass. 'What was the most interesting painting you've come across, then?'

'Well, there was one . . .'

Stephen launched into the story of a Peter Lely miniature, followed, when pressed, by another about a Mary Beale portrait of a young girl that had caused quite a stir when it was discovered behind badly installed panelling in a Victorian rectory near Stroud.

At last, MacLachlan felt one step closer to his quarry. 'Mary Beale, you say? I didn't know women painted back then. I didn't think they were allowed to.'

'Not many did. But Mary was prolific. Her husband was her studio assistant, you know. She was quite the portrait factory.'

'A woman painter, eh? Back in the – what? Seventeenth century?'

'Oh, you remind me,' Stephen said, leaning back in his seat, happy in a well-fed, well-watered haze, 'about the Gentileschis. I'd almost forgotten.'

'Oh?' Bingo. MacLachlan looked politely intrigued.

'Honestly, tell me to stop if I'm boring on about art, Charlie. All this was twenty years ago. No – thirty!'

'Not boring at all,' MacLachlan assured him. 'Tell me about the gentle-what-was-its.'

Stephen had to pause for a bit to marshal his facts. He explained how there had been a potentially huge discovery of works by a highly respected artist called Artemisia Gentileschi, who was a few years older than Mary Beale, but the same sort of period. Unlike Mary, she was a Continental artist, an Italian. A bit of a genius.

'There were four paintings. Oils. Dirty and badly varnished but otherwise OK. They'd been hanging in rooms used by one of the old ladies who lived at Hampton Court Palace at the time. Anyway, one of the Royal Collection people finally got permission to see around the place and discovered these priceless pieces dotted about. Well, not priceless, exactly, but Gentileschi is one of the greats and the paintings were possibly the only surviving portraits of her daughter Prudentia, posing as various classical muses. I *am* boring you.'

'You're not, I promise.'

'It's not as if the world went mad,' Stephen admitted, 'like they'd found a Leonardo or something. Although I wouldn't put it past them. Artemisia Gentileschi hasn't got the recognition she deserves, but still, those of us who were working in London at the time, who heard about this on the grapevine, we were agog, you know? Given the time frame, it was possible that the paintings were a royal commission for Queen Henrietta Maria, the wife of Charles I. It would fit with the way the queen's private apartments in Greenwich were supposed to be decorated. All those interiors are lost. It's a big gap in the art history of the times, but apparently they were designed on classical themes of art and desire, like these paintings of the muses. It was perfect. If someone could prove the link, once they were cleaned up, it would have been . . . extraordinary.'

MacLachlan looked sympathetic. 'But I gather from the way you say it that it didn't turn out that way?'

'Nope.' Stephen took a morose gulp of Cabernet. 'Copies,' he sniffed. 'Poor Queen. I mean, not *poor Queen*, obviously, but you know what I mean. Poor all of us who cared.'

'They were fakes, then, the paintings?' MacLachlan suggested.

'Not exactly. It's only a fake if you pass it off as the original. When they were cleaned up, these looked like copies that were probably made by someone at court, soon after the originals were painted,' Stephen explained. 'Almost like prints, if you like. But by someone not particularly talented, from what I heard. I never saw them.' He paused for more wine. 'I did see a couple of the originals, though,' he added quietly.

MacLachlan, who had already heard this on the art grapevine in London, but wanted to hear it from the horse's mouth, looked suitably fascinated.

'*What?* How?'

'At auction about two or three years later.' Stephen had a faraway look in his eye. 'The first one was found round here, and I was working in this area by then. Apparently, the owners had heard the royal story, gone hunting about in their attic and . . . whaddaya know? They discovered an original Artemisia Gentileschi painting of Thalia, the muse of comedy. The second one of Erato, I think – the muse of love poetry – showed up in America, but I saw the catalogue. Same story. They were examined by the experts and they were genuine. Amazing how those portraits had lain undiscovered for centuries and then . . . poop! Suddenly up they pop.'

MacLachlan adopted the slightly fuzzy look of a man who scents scandal but is also a little bit out of his depth. 'What are you suggesting, Stephen?'

Stephen shrugged. 'I'm just saying. A bit coincidental. A bit neat. Not many people knew the local scene like me, I suppose. It all seemed above board, but the dealer who'd come into the auction house with the first painting? Well, he was someone I wouldn't recommend to clients, put it that way. And I happened to know the second dealer too, in America, because he'd bought a couple of things from a friend. Same story.'

'Dodgy dealers, dodgy paintings? Is that it?'

Stephen shook his head. 'No, Charlie, it isn't what I'm saying. What I'm *saying*,' he spoke slowly, to make himself understood, 'is that the dealers were dodgy, but the paintings were real.'

'Charlie' looked confused.

Stephen managed to lower his voice and sound emphatic. The wine and the rapt attention of his companion had loosened his tongue. 'I'm *saying* that quite possibly someone

261

stole the Queen's paintings, replaced them with copies, and sold one of the originals at auction about three miles from here, and another the following year, in Texas. That's what I think. I mentioned it to a couple of people. They said I was mad, but d'you know what's interesting? After that, no more Gentileschis. There had been four portraits altogether. What happened to the other two? I think the man behind it all got scared. Scared of me. When I set up the gallery there were a few clients who'd never work with me. Bigwigs, you know, people who knew my reputation, knew the quality of my pieces. I think he set them against me. Petty revenge.'

'Fascinating. So the *copies* were fakes. Ta*da!*' 'Charlie' said.

Stephen looked as if he was about to contradict him, but 'Charlie' had just about summed it up. If Stephen was right, the four 'copies' now in the Royal Collection had been passed off as paintings made in the seventeenth century, when in fact they'd been recently faked to enable the scam. He nodded. 'I s'pose so. You could say that.'

MacLachlan offered to get them both a digestif from the bar, and Stephen wasn't one to say no.

'Why didn't you say? To the police, I mean?' MacLachlan asked when he came back, plonking two cognacs on the table between them.

'Nah, I couldn't prove anything,' Stephen shrugged. 'It was a feeling I had, that's all.'

'Did he get a lot for them?' MacLachlan asked. 'The two originals that found their way to auction, I mean.'

'Depends what you call "a lot",' Stephen said. 'He'd have had to give the dealers their cut, and the people who claimed

262

to be the original owners, I guess, and the forger, of course.' He stared into his cognac glass. 'If the paintings had been found at a royal palace . . . who knows what they'd have gone for? As it was, the provenance was shaky. If it wasn't for the brilliance of the brushwork, they might not have been accepted as genuine. The two I know about sold for five figures each. Even so, that was back in the eighties, when you could get a decent house for thirty grand. If he'd sold all four, he'd have *raked* it in. I like to think my little feeling cost him the price of a couple of houses. He got too greedy, that was the problem. He should've waited longer. But perhaps he sold the others privately. It's possible. But I kept an eye out. I think I'd know.'

He waited for 'Charlie' to ask him who this art world Machiavelli was, who'd stolen art from under the nose of Queen Elizabeth II, but his companion was looking tired by now. The barman called time and 'Charlie' rose to his feet unsteadily to settle the bill. As they said goodnight, Stephen was fairly sure he'd remember less than half of the story in the morning.

Back in his comfortable room in a small hotel near the Market House, MacLachlan unpacked his notebook and wrote down their conversation almost word for word.

Chapter 33

Upstairs at the Palace, Sir Simon sat back with his feet up on his desk, on his second call to a colleague in the Cabinet Office, smoothing the way. He was tired, and put every effort not to let it show in his voice. Calm, affable, on top of things . . . that's what was needed, and indeed expected, from the Private Office. You were supposed to know everything, anticipate the impossible, offend no one, and charm your way out of every awkward situation. He had learned many of these skills in the navy and others in the Foreign Office, but most had come much earlier, when his parents were planning to divorce.

Simon was at prep school then, a little boy of eight, already slightly lost in a big country house full of iron beds and bells, the ever-present smell of cabbage and masters who could slipper you if you misunderstood a rule or stepped on an untied shoelace. For a term and a half, he had longed for nothing but to be back with his mother and his sisters, their menagerie of animals and the gruff sound of his father arriving home after a long day in the City and an 'infernal' commute from Waterloo. At home for the Lent half-term, he had heard his parents arguing late at night. His sister Beatty wrote afterwards to tell him his father had moved out. She thought he might be living above a pub in the village, but she wasn't sure.

For the next eighteen months, every fibre of his being had been dedicated to bringing his parents back together. At school, young Simon put on a brave face, denying the circulating rumours and making sure that – when it all turned out all right in the end – it would seem as if it had always been that way. During holidays and exeat weekends, he and his sisters went to work on their mother, reminding her of happy holidays and helping out with whatever housework they could understand.

With his father, he somehow knew to say nothing about what was happening. On manly fishing trips and long walks in the countryside during exeat weekends, he spent their precious time together listening, allowing this man he had thought of as a mini god to share his insecurities and his misery, always in the third person, always as if they belonged to someone else. He stayed quiet but hopeful, and if at night he resorted to desperate prayers to God to save his family, by day he was a skinny little rock of encouragement.

He didn't bring his parents back together – luck, finances, and the fact that they were fundamentally suited to each other did that over time. The storm clouds passed. For his tenth birthday, they gave him a golden retriever puppy that he named Nigel. It was the best present in the world, because everyone knew his father was the fan of golden retrievers, but his mother was the one who would end up looking after Nigel when Simon was at school, so it was a compromise between them: a loving pact, by people who had worked out how to fit back together.

After that, Simon's memories of home consisted mostly of sunshine, hearty meals and soft, warm animal fur. For many years he had thought of the dark days of early prep school as his childhood hell, but now, in his fifties, he realised they had given him strengths that had informed his progress for the rest of his life. He knew nothing lasted forever unless you worked at it, by God; that love is all that really matters; that you cannot flourish if you don't listen, adapt, learn, hope.

He was listening now – to various concerns the Cabinet Office had about trying to persuade the British public to accept a third-of-a-billion-pound refurbishment bill for a building most of them would never get to see. Quietly, with funny and tragic anecdotes, he reminded his friend across St James's Park at Number 10 of the real danger that the Palace was in, from floods, fires and rot. He asked, in all humility, for suggested alternative venues for state banquets and investitures, garden parties to reward citizens for their civic contributions, displays of the Royal Collection treasures, balcony appearances when the country needed to come together, the Changing of the Guard . . . What would those alternatives cost? How would they work? The Queen would go wherever she was put, that went without saying. Windsor Castle? Certainly, but what about those balcony appearances? Wouldn't she become rather invisible? Yes, they would *love* to cut a hundred million out of the programme. No doubt his colleague was much cleverer than he, and could work out where.

Slowly, slowly, he heard the doubts recede and the arguments for countering them were played back to him from Downing Street. Call over, he poured himself a lukewarm coffee from a stainless steel thermos on the desk, checked his watch, saw that it was nearly ten and prepared to pick up the phone again.

Before he did so, he quickly checked the pundits reporting on the US election. Like most other senior courtiers and government officials, he was gripped by a morbid fascination with what was happening in Washington and around the fifty states. Polls showed Clinton ahead, but for two weeks she had been under investigation, yet again, by the FBI. She'd only had twenty-four hours in the clear. Was it enough to reassure her base? And what about the postal vote? Her opponent was still busy campaigning to the 'deplorables' she had inadvertently formed into a Trumpian tribe. Had he been on her speech-writing team, Simon would have counselled against using such a term. Not if you would prefer such people to vote for you instead.

He had loved politics since the age of eleven, when a master at prep school had brought the Magna Carta to life, explaining the delicate thread of democracy that wound its way through English history. Simon could have had a quiet life as an academic historian if he'd wanted. Instead, he'd chosen to be a part of it. Here he was, advising a constitutional monarch. If, right now, he'd rather be glued to his TV screen, analysing the polls and making predictions, well . . . it was his own fault that he was too busy trying to ensure this monarch had a working roof over her head at the time of the next election, and the one after that.

'Hello, Sarah. I'm sorry to call so late, but I wanted to check if everything's on track for next Wednesday. Do you have what you need? Of course. Let me take you through it . . .'

By now Rozie was filthy, cold and wet. The ground underneath her boots was half an inch deep in water. Her head ached from the knock, her back was killing her and she frequently bumped her upper spine against bricks held together with rough mortar that scratched at her jacket and caught in her hair. The object she had bent down to see turned out to be a Twix wrapper. Hardly worth it.

The roof became lower still and Rozie decided she had seen enough. She shouldn't have come this far. Turning round, she made her way back towards Buckingham Palace. The question was, what would she find when she got there? Only now did she truly accept the implication of the thud that had so surprised her. There should be light at the end of the tunnel soon – but there was none.

No fresh breeze down here to cause the door she had left ajar to shut of its own accord. No phone signal. No way to call for help. Nobody waiting for her upstairs.

Rozie's brain swiftly ran through problems and solutions. Whatever happened, she wouldn't panic. The Queen knew roughly where she was. If there was an issue, eventually she'd be found.

As she feared, the heavy wooden door was now shut. Rozie was ready to put her shoulder to it and give it everything she had. But in fact it gave way quite easily with a gentle push. She began to walk down the brick-lined passage to the vaulted storeroom. The adrenaline rush made her question her original decision to investigate the tunnels, but given what she'd found . . .

'One step closer and I'll kill you.'

A man was silhouetted in the doorway between the cellar rooms. His voice was low and menacing. He was guarding the only way out.

Rozie walked purposefully towards him, stooping slightly under the passage's rough brick ceiling. The adrenaline still pumped in her veins. The tomb-like darkness had held its terrors, but she fancied her chances against this short, squat opponent, if that's what it took. She shifted her grip on the torch, so she could use it as a weapon. It was over a foot long and heavy, and she had asked for one like this deliberately, just in case.

'Drop it,' the man said.

Rozie did not. She could see now that he was armed too, with something long and sharp, holding it up like a baseball bat. It was a crowbar. She pictured how he would come towards her, how best to use the torch to defend herself, how much damage she could allow herself to do.

'I said, drop it, asshole.'

Out of the tunnel proper, Rozie drew herself up to her full height. 'Er, no. And if you attack the Queen's APS here in the Palace, I wish you luck explaining why.' Her voice was as calm and steady as she could make it.

'Shit!' He lowered the bar so that its tip rested on the floor. 'I thought you were some kind of thief.'

'As you can see, I'm not. And watch your bloody language.'

The man in the doorway wore a managerial suit under an open warehouse coat. She could just about make out the hint of curl in his hair and the hint of disdain in his flat, south London voice. She recognised him from the summer – and from the accounts department. This was Mick Clements, the head of Operations. She recognised the woody scent, too: it must be aftershave or deodorant. He had definitely spent time in the makeshift office recently, before her.

'What are you doing down here?' she asked.

'I might ask you the same question.' Even at this distance, and backlit by the brighter room behind, she could see the rise and fall in his chest. He was afraid – or he had been. But he stood his ground. He still blocked the doorway, with the heavy bar in his hand.

'Is there a reason I can't visit?' She used the full force of her height to intimidate him.

'People like you don't belong in places like this.' He enunciated the words slowly. 'That sign is on the door back there for your safety. I'm going to have to report you.'

'You do that.'

'Hey, hey.' It was Eric Ferguson, who must have been there all along. He stepped into the doorway next to Mick and reached gently for the crowbar, which he rested against the wall. His smile was placatory. 'Let's not get carried away, OK? This is Captain O, Mick. Show her some respect.'

Mick grunted. His voice was low and hard, and he hadn't taken his eyes off Rozie. 'What I want to know is, what the hell were you doing in the tunnels? Don't you know they're dangerous?'

'Well, I did wonder,' she said. 'I came down looking for something and I thought I'd check them out. If the door wasn't locked that's hardly my fault.'

'And why are you in those boots? If you don't mind my asking. Ever so politely.' Mick was staring at her wellies.

'I'm half dressed for the shindig,' she said disdainfully. It was the best she could come up with. The shindig was the annual staff party in December, usually a fancy-dress affair, and this year the theme was Heroes. 'I'm going as the Duke of Wellington.'

Eric snorted with laughter. Mick peered at her, unconvinced.

'I was looking for some sort of frock coat thing,' she improvised. 'I thought there might be one here.'

Eric beamed. 'You mean the big wicker basket full of costumes we keep available for all the dressing up?'

Rozie nodded. 'Yeah.'

'Not a thing, love. This is a palace, not a theatre, or a fucking nursery school.'

He said it without breaking his smile. Mick sniggered. Rozie decided she'd had enough. 'Thanks for the advice,' she said. 'I'm leaving.'

She strode up to them both, pushing Mick firmly to the side of the doorway with her torch, and forcing Eric to make way beside him. As she approached, she felt the fear and hostility pour off Mick in waves. He had shut her in the tunnels, changed his mind, and still considered knocking her out: she'd seen it on his face. But he had decided the consequences weren't worth paying for.

'I've got my eye on you, Captain Oshodi,' he said to her departing back.

No doubt he had. Now, it was mutual.

Sir Simon was still at his desk, on the phone, when he saw Rozie walk past. This struck him as mildly odd, and then, as he thought about it more, very strange indeed. Why was she carrying a massive torch? Why was she even still here?

'Hello?' the Prime Minister's Chief of Staff asked over the phone. 'Are you there, Simon?'

'Er, I'll call you back,' he said. His hackles were up. He didn't know why exactly, but something was wrong.

When he got to Rozie's office, she was slumped in the armchair near the window, in stockinged feet. She looked utterly drained.

'I thought you'd gone home. What happened?'

'Don't worry about it,' she said flatly.

When she spoke, he noticed redness on her teeth. Her lip was bleeding. 'What happened?' he repeated.

She didn't want to tell him. His fear was suddenly of something truly dreadful. If she'd been attacked – assaulted – he wouldn't let her go through it alone. Funny, he realised: he'd always thought of Rozie as indestructible. He pitied any man who might come up against her. But, right now, he saw a vulnerable young woman. Whatever resentment he still felt towards her melted away. His instinct was to hold her, which was obviously inappropriate, so he stood like a lemon and waited for her to talk to him.

'I was downstairs,' she admitted eventually. 'In the cellars.'

'What, near the kitchens?'

'No. The ones underneath. The ones we're not supposed to use. It was . . . something to do with that picture for the Boss.'

'The navy's one from the summer? Really?'

'Yes.' Rozie sat up a bit. She looked slightly less queasy. 'I thought the original might be there. Stupid, really. But two of the Ops men came and found me. Said I was trespassing. That's all.' She smiled and shrugged, getting up as if to go.

'It's not all,' he said, motioning her back down. 'I know you, Rozie. Being shouted at wouldn't even register. What did they do?' His gaze fell on her bleeding lip again. 'You look like you've been in a fight. Or . . .?' He tried to give her the space to talk, to say the unsayable, if that's what it was. He saw her eyes cloud with confusion, but they brightened again.

'Oh, Simon, no. They were just a bit threatening, that's all. And I hit my head on the ceiling and bit my lip. I think they were more scared of me than I was of them. It was nothing.'

He kept scanning her face, looking for signs that she was lying or making excuses to avoid describing something unspeakable, but the longer she talked the more she came back to her old self. She wouldn't lie if the men had done something terrible, would she? Simon didn't know. He felt out of his depth, which was rare.

'I just think you ought to know . . . I'm here,' he said. How inadequate that sounded.

The smile that spread across her face was slow and genuine, and good to see after such a long time. 'I do know that,' she said. 'I'm OK. Really. Thanks for checking on me.'

He felt he was being dismissed. If it were the Boss, she'd say, *That's very kind.*

'I'll, er . . . Right. I'll leave you to it. See you in the morning.'

As he walked the short distance to his office, he wondered about the boots. Why did you wear wellies to go and inspect some cellars? Were they leaking? Oh, God – not something *else* for the bloody Reservicing budget, surely? Back at his desk, he poured himself another cold coffee and settled with his feet up, phone in hand.

Chapter 34

The Queen did not have any time with Rozie in the morning. She was holding the investiture in the Ballroom, and in the skylit Picture Gallery people were lining up with hooks pinned to their jackets, ready to take the medals she would hang. However, she diligently read the handwritten note that had been included with her boxes. In it, Rozie explained about the hidden hinge, the tunnel in use and the encounter with Mr Clements and his sidekick from Operations afterwards. Rozie didn't go into detail but the Queen imagined that, alone at night, underground, it had not been pleasant.

As she held the letter, scanning it through her bifocals, she was furious with Rozie for explicitly ignoring instructions and going into the tunnels by herself, guilty that she was secretly pleased her APS had done it, and above all relieved the girl had emerged unscathed. There had been one or two women in the past, the Queen reflected, who had shown the same initiative and grit. 'Derring-do', they used to call it. It could get you into all sorts of trouble, but it made solving problems so much easier.

Clements's behaviour towards her had been unforgiveable. The man should be sacked, and he would be, but if it *wasn't* he who was running the Breakages Business, the Queen didn't want to alert whoever it was by making too much of Rozie's encounter last night. Rozie was clear in her note that he seemed fearful when he found her. There was no obvious sign of theft of any sort: nothing in the storage rooms that shouldn't have been there. And yet, he had only reluctantly let her go. *It has to be the Breakages Business. I'm sure it's still operational. The tunnel had signs of being used that day.*

It wouldn't be used any more, the Queen reflected. After a shock like that, they would shut it down immediately. Even now, there would probably be no evidence at either end that it had been in service. Doors would be properly bolted; dust applied to surfaces; duckboards spirited away. Nevertheless, she mentioned casually to Philip that Rozie had been down there and it had reminded her to wonder when was the last time they had done a health and safety inspection? Philip wasn't sure, but said she was damn right to think about it, and he'd bloody well ask. It had been years since anyone checked, as far as he knew.

As she changed into a silk dress for the investiture, the Queen wondered what exactly Sholto Harvie had been thinking when he gave Rozie the tip-off about the Breakages Business. Should one be grateful? She had the strongest sense that he did it because he had something to hide. And yet, try as she might, she couldn't make an adequate connection from that to the Gentileschis, to the notes to Mary van Renen, for example, and the body in the swimming pool. She felt certain a clue lay in Cynthia Harris's former life. Chief Inspector Strong's report on that was due imminently. Perhaps it would contain enough for her to take decisive action against Clements and whoever he was in cahoots with. She very much hoped so, because Rozie's underground escapades had exposed her to potential danger. The girl could look after herself, but one didn't like to think this was something she would need to do.

She was too busy to give it much further thought. After the investiture and various meetings with ambassadors and officials, there was a reception to attend in Cheyne Walk, beside the river in Chelsea, to celebrate Co-operation in Ireland. Her visit in the summer had been deemed a big success. It had been a diplomatic skating pond: how does one greet former terrorists, and indeed, how do they greet a reigning monarch? But everyone had got through it, and it had felt like the positive contribution to history she wanted it to be.

She had been very aware, back in June, that she was treading a path of peace and reconciliation that had been laid by many others before her. So many of them women, she reflected now – with a woman on the brink of becoming the most powerful person in the world. Mothers, daughters, sisters had joined forces in Northern Ireland to condemn the violence and find another way. The stop-start process had been helped from the British side by another renegade woman. The Secretary of State for Northern Ireland at the time, Mo Mowlam, had been a brave and charismatic campaigner too. She died of a brain tumour a few years later and the Queen still missed her. This was the Labour MP who had called for Buckingham Palace to be pulled down and replaced with something more modern. They had joked about it, the two of them.

'There are times,' the Queen had admitted, 'when the soup is perfectly cold and the bill for new carpets arrives, that I don't disagree with you.'

'See?' Mo said, 'I'd be doing you a favour.'

Now, in a shimmering pink suit, with Philip at her side, the Queen entered the building beside the Thames that had once been home to Thomas More, transplanted brick by brick and stone by stone from one side of London to the other by someone with a greater love of history than common sense. Inside, among canapés and Tudor panelling, the mood was jolly.

The highlight of the reception was the unveiling of a portrait she had sat for in May, commissioned by the charity. After one ninety-minute sitting she had expected something small and neat. Instead, the canvas hiding behind the glossy purple satin curtain was as tall as she was – taller, in fact, balanced on its little stand. She hoped it wasn't ghastly. Standing so close, Philip would find it hard to restrain himself and now was not the time. Everyone clustered around and she was handed the rope attached to the curtain. Making sure to hide any hint of anxiety, she pulled and the curtain fell.

There were smiles, a couple of cheers, a ripple of applause. She stared hard at the pink and turquoise canvas and breathed a secret sigh of relief.

'I think it's got all your wrinkles,' Philip observed with a snort.

She stood back a little, to get a better view. It was true. Her face was the size of a horse blanket, with every crease and fold acquired over ninety years unflinchingly portrayed.

But one *was* wrinkled – what was the point of denying it? The artist had caught the hair, which was never easy, and done a decent job with the jewellery. Best of all were the mouth and the eyes. She was almost smiling, but not quite. She looked quite wise in it, she thought, rather liking it. She would have liked it even more if he could have made it three foot tall instead of five.

The artist moved towards her.

'What do you think, Your Majesty?'

'It's very big, isn't it?' she remarked.

'They pay by the yard,' he said, which made her laugh. 'I like to think it looks as if you're still talking to me.'

'It does, a bit. Did I talk a lot?'

'Oh, just the right amount, ma'am.'

He was being diplomatic. She remembered having a long, wide-ranging conversation while he worked. But the more she looked, the more satisfied she was, especially considering some of the horrors she'd unveiled in her time. He had captured something very few artists managed, which was a sense that she was reflecting on more than the act of being captured on canvas, or being Queen. In fact, she was rarely thinking about either. There was so much to absorb her attention. She was glad that future generations might get a glimpse of her actively contemplating a world beyond one's own.

Chapter 35

It had been a long day.

The Queen woke up to the news that Hillary Clinton, poised to celebrate her victory under the largest glass ceiling in Manhattan, had admitted defeat and that a rather stunned Donald Trump had been voted in as the forty-fifth president of the United States of America. Which was not quite what one had been led to expect. Not only that, but Harry had thought to put out a press release – in the form of a tweet, God help him – asking for his new girlfriend's privacy to be respected by the media. One sympathised, of course one did, but it never paid to take the press on at their own game. They always won. It was only a matter of time.

Philip had a lot to say on both subjects at breakfast.

'Bloody fool.' This in relation to his grandson. 'What is it that model said? The Moss girl. Could have been about you, I always thought. *Never* something, *always* something. No, I've got it: *Never complain, never explain*. She could teach the lad a thing or two.'

Everyone would have a lot to say. But with decades of practice – like Kate Moss, who was a friend of Eugenie's, the

Queen seemed to remember – she herself would be sphinx-like and inscrutable. She was not her grandson – and in her experience, anything one said would inevitably be leaped on, taken out of context and almost deliberately misunderstood. Silence was the only safe option. Or rather, saying nothing worth repeating. Unlike her husband, who didn't always practise what he preached.

Luckily, Philip was soon distracted. They went to open the new Francis Crick Institute in King's Cross and he was in his element, talking about science. They were given a rather fascinating little lecture about the flu. Quite terrifying, these viruses, if unchecked – and how wonderful to have places like the Institute to stay on top of them. Then there had been the weekly audience with the Prime Minister. Mrs May was already keen to build relations with the new leader of the free world and wondering about booking in a state visit. The Queen observed that it was normally a couple of years before such things were put into the calendar and asked the PM to take it up with Sir Simon. One didn't want to look too keen. If they weren't careful, the UK might seem rather desperate, which wasn't the impression one wanted to give at all.

At a pub in Pimlico, Rozie was on her third glass of Chardonnay. This had not been her favourite day. Her head still pounded with a dull ache from the crack it had got last night. If she closed her eyes for too long, all she could see was Mick Clements in the storeroom with the crowbar. Not a pretty sight.

At times like this, it was useful to know an equerry with benefits. She thought of him now: six foot three, military bearing, neck like a tree trunk, strawberry-blond hair and eyes the colour of the shallows near his parents' place in St Barts. She'd called him at lunch and he'd suggested a drink after work at this pub on Pimlico Green, walking distance from the Palace but far enough away that you weren't likely to bump into half the Household at the bar – although that turned out to be a miscalculation. A drink wasn't exactly what she had in mind, but that, too, seemed like a good idea.

After three glasses, she wasn't sure if the wine was making the pounding in her head better or worse. Either way, the blue-eyed strawberry blond still hadn't showed. She couldn't blame him. Anything might have cropped up at work: she'd let down more friends in cocktail bars than she cared to remember. She'd give him one more glass, then wend her way sadly home.

She'd just ordered it when she spotted a balding head above a broad-shouldered jacket among a group of men at the far end of the bar. She might not have recognised him, if not for the fact that as soon as he happened to catch her eye, he went white as a sheet. She concentrated for a moment, thinking back to the staff records she had recently been examining.

This was Spike Milligan. The Boss had tasked her with challenging the Palace footman about being involved in the poison pen campaign, along with Lorna Lobb. Rozie had tried to track him down, but so far he had evaded her. Now she held his eye and saw his Adam's apple bob. The slight nod she gave him said, 'We can do this quietly, or I can come right over and we can do it in front of your mates. You choose.' He seemed to crumple slightly. After a couple of muttered words, he headed for the door at the back of the room.

Rozie followed him.

The door led to a narrow corridor with the toilets to one side and the kitchen at the far end. There was also a staircase to a function room above. She motioned to it and they stood awkwardly halfway up. Though Rozie was on the lower step, it was clear she was in charge. Milligan's eyes darted around, looking anywhere but at her. His face was ashen. One of his fingers beat an unconscious tattoo on the bannister. But he jutted out his jaw and said, 'I dunno why you're interested in me, Captain Oshodi.'

'How could you?' Rozie said crisply. 'You haven't answered my messages.'

'Look, I'm not stupid. I assume it's something to do with the letters business. I already told the police everything I know. Which is nothing.'

'You were overheard talking about them.'

'Who by?'

'Never mind. But,' Rozie lowered her voice to a menacing hiss, 'HM herself is aware of your involvement. You'd better explain yourself now or it'll go badly.'

The footman pursed his lips for a moment and finally looked her in the eye. 'I'm sorry, right? About what happened to you. But it's got nothing to do with me.'

Rozie's eyes narrowed. 'What do you mean, "what happened to me"?'

He swallowed again and panic flickered across his face. But someone came out of the function room at the top of the stairs and walked down past them. It gave him time to think.

'That Lobb woman – that's her name, isn't it? She was seen trying to drop something in your bag. People talk, you know.'

Rozie cocked her head to one side. 'So you mean what *didn't* happen to me.'

She was convinced that he was lying – or rather, that he knew about the letters she had already received, which were a tightly contained secret shared only with the Queen and the police. This meant he had been involved in delivering them, as the Boss suspected.

Rozie had been sure, when given this task, that she could manage it dispassionately: 'find, strike, destroy, suppress'. But her heart hammered. They faced each other in silence for a short while, Milligan scared but obstinate, and Rozie fighting to manage the roiling fury and disgust that boiled inside her.

She hadn't expected the encounter to go like this. Normally the Boss's magic dust did its trick instantly: you asked, they answered. And yet here she was, accusing Milligan of something she was sure he was guilty of, and he was prepared to brazen it out.

Whatever he was scared of, it was more than the displeasure of Her Majesty.

He swallowed again. 'Like I say, I'm sorry if . . . whatever. There are some bad people out there. But I can't help you.'

He enunciated the last four words clearly and slowly, and she knew he wouldn't change his mind. She wondered, briefly, how many broken bones it would take before he did. But she wasn't that kind of girl, and it wasn't that kind of job. Breathe and let go. She couldn't even tell him to fuck off – he wasn't obviously threatening her, as Mick Clements had.

'This isn't over.'

She stood aside, so he could squeeze past her down the stairs. He did so fast, without another word, and by the time she entered the bar area again, he'd gone.

Breathe and let go. She rolled her shoulders, tilted her head and decided she needed a massage, a run . . . something to relax.

She was about to fetch her coat from the seat where she'd left it when she spotted a strawberry-blond head moving purposefully through the crowd.

'Hey! You stayed. Sorry I'm late.'

White teeth flashed in a sweetly lopsided smile. The equerry pulled in for the kiss-on-each-cheek that you could do in public without raising an eyebrow if you were posh. Rozie felt a whole new set of chemicals flood her body.

He looked at the empty wine glass on the nearby table and assumed it was hers.

'Fancy another?'

She absolutely did.

Chapter 36

This weekend there was no trip to Windsor. Instead, on Saturday evening, the family showed up en masse at the Albert Hall for the Festival of Remembrance. The Queen and Philip were accompanied by all the children, her cousins and William and Catherine. In fact, almost a full complement of royals except for Harry, who was otherwise engaged. The media were now obsessed by the absence of his new girlfriend at the rugby. Sure enough, whatever they did or didn't do, the press would have their say.

But the event at the Albert Hall was uplifting as always, though it marked the centenary of the Battle of the Somme and twenty-five years since the first Gulf War. There was a marvellous, moving piece to honour the ATA girls who had flown Spitfires to their bases during the war. The round auditorium was filled with uniformed serving personnel and veterans, who always sang with a lustiness particular to the armed services, she thought. It was always good to celebrate with the living.

Tomorrow would be devoted to the dead.

* * *

Sunday dawned dull and overcast, with a bitter chill. Her mother would have called it 'dreich'. Only the Scots could truly describe bad weather. Nevertheless, it brightened up in time for the Queen to lead the laying of the wreaths of poppies at the Cenotaph to mark Remembrance Day, in front of a silent crowd.

The moment was bittersweet, because she and Sir Simon had discussed the proposal that this might be the last time she would perform this essential task in person. Charles could do a perfectly decent job of it for her, and really it wouldn't do for an aged monarch to break a hip while stepping backwards on a multi level, rain-slicked stone platform in November. She understood the logistics – but her heart would always want to be there, doing the right thing, paying her respects as she was doing now.

On the balcony at the Foreign Office, overlooking the ceremony, Camilla, Catherine and Sophie stood together, all in black. For them, as for the vast majority watching on TV today, or lining the street to see the parade – or not watching at all, perhaps – most of the wars and sacrifice they were remembering today were distant stories, or an old-fashioned news report. But for the Queen and for those lined up in Whitehall they were vivid, lived experience. Though she had always been kept safe, she had lost men she had loved: friends and uncles, and ultimately her father, who smoking and the stress of the war had driven to an early grave. She had grieved with wives and girlfriends, sons and daughters, and now husbands and boyfriends in the later wars. Every military life was given in her father's service and then hers, and she never forgot it. Each one mattered. With so many gone, it was difficult to keep one's eyes entirely dry.

The mood was still upon her later that afternoon, when the family had gone and the Palace was quiet again. She was on her way to change out of her black dress when her Private Secretary caught up with her.

'I just wanted to let you know about the tunnels, ma'am,' Sir Simon said. 'The Keeper mentioned that the Duke had asked him to get them checked out. He wants you to know that Security went down to have a look and the door's shut tight with an outsize rusty padlock. You'd need bolt cutters to open it. We have nothing to fear from Health and Safety.'

'Isn't that a relief?'

She looked quizzically at the manila folder tucked under his arm.

'I thought you might like to read this later.' He held it out. 'It's the latest update from the chief inspector. I can leave it on your desk if you—'

'Thank you. I'll take it now.'

'I've added today's note at the top, ma'am.' Sir Simon positively bristled with efficiency. 'It makes very depressing reading.'

'Oh? You've read it?'

'Just a skim through, to keep myself up to speed. Strong's sergeant has found more background on Mrs Harris. It seems she was always difficult, regularly getting into trouble and making bad decisions. She had a rough start in life, so perhaps that explains it. The chief inspector seems to think

288

she might have written her own poison pen letters. Were you aware of that?'

'I was, actually.'

'I must say I find it hard to imagine, but he makes a good case for it. It's all in the notes. I can summarise them, if you like.'

'Thank you, Simon, but no. I'll read them myself.'

After he'd left, she permitted herself a little sigh of frustration. It was Rozie's day off and he was trying to help. Sir Simon hadn't got to be as good as he was without casting a critical eye over anything he deemed important. In this, she recognised a fellow spirit, but she didn't like the thought of him rummaging around in Rozie's files.

The Queen continued up to her bedroom to change, but found herself increasingly absorbed by the note in the manila folder that now rested on her dressing table. This was the report on Cynthia she had been waiting for.

DS Highgate's findings were certainly upsetting, given what had happened in the end. Cynthia Butterfield and her mother had been abandoned by Cynthia's father, who had set up with another woman when the girl was three. A second unhappy and possibly violent marriage had ended in divorce, and her mother had then lived as a bit of a recluse. Overcoming these early obstacles, the young Cynthia had left Brighton for Edinburgh, then London to study art history, and started a strong career.

Sir Simon mentioned 'bad decisions'. The report said that Cynthia's work as a curator had come under scrutiny in the summer of 1986. The personnel notes were sparse, but it seemed she was accused of making 'basic mistakes'. That summer, she had left the Royal Collection to join the Works Department. She was offered the job by Sidney Smirke, its head, now known to be occasionally violent, and a drunk. At that time, she became the only woman in a 'very macho' department and after a few months she transferred to House-keeping.

Sir Simon had drawn from all of this that Cynthia Harris was 'difficult'. But the Queen thought of the date. The Gentileschis had been discovered in 1986. She could well imagine that Sholto Harvie did not want a keen assistant looking over his shoulder. He must have been responsible for pointing out those 'basic mistakes'.

Had Cynthia made any mistakes at all? the Queen wondered. Or had she simply been told she had, by a popular and dynamic senior member of staff? And if she protested her innocence, who would believe her?

The thing was, where Sir Simon saw 'difficulty' and 'trouble', the Queen saw strength and perseverance in the face of increasingly unpleasant odds. DS Highgate had also con-ducted a recent interview with the person to whom she'd left all her personal possessions in her will. This woman – a Miss Helen Fisher – described a university room-mate who had become a friend for life. The Cynthia of those first days in Lon-don was confident and chic, basing her style on Louise Brooks, the dark-haired jazz age film star. She had loved to travel and had developed an abiding passion for great art. This was the character whose hopes had been dashed, her potential lost.

Nevertheless, the enduring friendship between these two women rang out through the clipped report. The Queen made a mental note to get Lady Caroline to write to Miss Fisher and express her condolences. She had been told that Mrs Harris did not have any close family still living, but that didn't mean that there was nobody to mourn her. Although it seemed there was nobody to mourn her *here*.

The Queen rose from her dressing table. Still wearing her black dress and with Willow and the dorgis at her heels, she descended the little staircase to the ground floor of the North Wing, where a corridor led to the north-west pavilion and the swimming pool. The footman who stood guarding the entrance looked very surprised to see her, but quickly hid it. She was grateful for his presence, as she realised she had absolutely no idea what the door code would be. Philip, who swam regularly, would know it, presumably.

'Your Majesty.' The footman bowed slightly and let her in, preceded by the dogs.

Beyond the tall, glass windows with their Georgian panes, the sky was dark, or as dark as central London ever got, bathed in its eerie orange street light glow. The pavilion itself was atmospherically lit with several spotlights just below the skylit roof, while inset bulbs under the water cast rippling reflections around the room. The dogs happily padded around on the tiles, but she called them to her. Their oblivious general curiosity seemed inappropriate somehow.

It must have been just about *there*, near the door to the changing rooms towards the shallow end, that the body had lain all night.

'*Exsanguination.*'

The word had leaped out at her from the first police report. The process of the blood flowing out of the body. Enough to cause death. Her equerry had told her – because she asked – that it could take the loss of between half and two-thirds of a person's blood to kill them. It was the sort of thing that soldiers knew. How heartening, in a way, that one could perhaps survive with only half one's blood still in the body. But Cynthia Harris had not survived, of course.

Standing here, in the rippling light, with the hum of the filter and the sloshes and plops of little waves, the Queen was aware that these were the last sights and sounds Cynthia had known before she lost consciousness. She felt the house-keeper's presence, or rather her absence, very keenly.

Memories came back to her in quick succession: the swish of chic, bobbed hair, once almost black, now faded to almost white; the harmonious composition of any room whenever she had finished with it, which nobody else could match; the flash of joy on her face – fully explained now – when a paint-ing had been reframed at her suggestion and they had jointly surveyed the happy result on a guest room wall.

The Queen felt a wave of sympathy for the woman. She was more convinced than ever of a different story to the one Sir Simon saw. This was not 'difficult'. It was . . . there was a phrase for it. It was on the tip of her tongue. She called out to the footman:

'What's it called when an employer makes your job so unpleasant that you can't do it?'

He thought for a moment. 'Constructive dismissal, ma'am.'

'That's it! Thank you.'

There had been times in her reign when it felt as if the tabloid press were trying to do as much to her. But she was a queen, and Cynthia Harris was a curator. So why not simply get a different curatorial job elsewhere? The woman described by Miss Fisher adored her work.

The Queen looked across to the spot where the body had lain. Instead of an embittered woman in late middle age, she saw the university graduate with no family support, who liked silent film stars and dreamed of rising up in the art world. She also saw the shadow of the young woman's boss, Sholto. The Queen knew from her personal experience how charismatic he could be. If he had wanted to prevent Cynthia from getting another decent job, he could probably have done so. In the tight-knit London art world, the word of the Deputy Surveyor could make or break a young career.

Why would he want to break it?

It seemed harsh punishment if all he needed to do was get Cynthia out of the way while he had the fake Gentileschi copies made and spirited the four originals out of the building. She was increasingly certain that was what Sholto had done – rolling them up like carpets and simply driving them out of Stable Yard under everyone's noses.

She parked the thought of his treatment of his assistant. Sholto had never struck her as remotely vicious or vindictive. But then, of course, he had never struck her as criminal either. Yet Daniel Blake, the young conservator he had hired, had died. One couldn't put anything past him, however eloquent he was on the subject of Leonardo da Vinci.

With the dogs beside her, she walked along the pool's edge to the patch of tiles where Mrs Harris had collapsed.

Ignoring her protesting knee, she bent over to inspect the grouting. It was far from pristine after several years of wear, but it was impossible to make out specific stains any more. She assumed the Housekeeping team had been extra diligent with bleach. Still, the woman had bled to death here, all alone. The Queen said a little prayer for her, hoping she had lost consciousness quickly, at least, and had not been afraid.

Sholto Harvie's shadow seemed to haunt this place. Everything came back to him. Every note reinforced her theory – and yet he *had not done it*. He was not here. He wasn't even in the country. If he had wanted to create a perfect alibi, he couldn't have done a better job.

The answer must lie in the Breakages Business – which Rozie had demonstrated so clearly was still going on. Who would have thought a chocolate bar wrapper would be such comprehensive proof of dark deeds underground?

That wrapper now sat in a sealed envelope (she hoped it was sealed) in Rozie's desk, in case they needed it. Meanwhile, there was no easy proof that the tunnels had been used. As she expected, they had acted fast to hide all trace of that secret hinge, and she couldn't move against them until she was sure of her ground. The question still remained: who were *they*, exactly?

She was working on it. Unless she found something soon, she would have to take her suspicions to the proper authorities.

They think it was an accident, she said to the rippling shade on the tiles in front of her. But her original presentiment remained, that even if Cynthia had died alone, the exsanguination had not begun that way.

Chapter 37

The following evening, Rozie felt much better. She was sitting in the billiards room of the Chelsea Arts Club, ignoring the half-hearted game going on nearby and focusing on the elegant woman who nursed a glass of champagne in front of her.

Rozie had heard stories of the Chelsea Arts Club. She knew of its famous balls and secret garden and had pictured something posh and well upholstered, like Claridge's perhaps. But it turned out that artists didn't want Michelin stars, marble floors and silk furnishings – they wanted (and could afford) cheap wine, café tables and somewhere friendly to relax. The white walls were hung with paintings for sale. The rabbit warren of little rooms was full of people in jeans, lounging in armchairs or laughing over candlelit dinners. Rozie's host, Eleanor Walker, was one of the smartest people there.

Eleanor wore a silk shirt and lots of gold jewellery. She explained that a friend was a jewellery designer and 'I simply love her stuff, can't get enough of it'. There were rings on most of her fingers, her ears were adorned with punkish gold spikes, and three chunky necklaces were hung with charms. All of which surprised Rozie, because Eleanor was in her sixties. She had briefly been a model in her youth. That bit didn't surprise Rozie at all.

They were here to talk about Sholto Harvie. Eleanor was Lavinia Hawthorne-Hopwood's aunt, and the artist had cheerfully put Rozie in touch with her yesterday. 'Oh God yes, she knows all about Sholto. Get her drunk. She's great company. And she'll love an evening out.'

They talked for ten minutes about the Palace and Rozie did her party trick of sounding entertaining while saying nothing of any value whatsoever. Eventually, she brought up the subject of the ex-Deputy Surveyor of the Queen's Pictures. Her excuse was that she was helping to collect anecdotes for a book about the Royal Collection. Eleanor's features rearranged themselves from curious and delighted to something more wary and disdainful. They reminded Rozie of someone else for a minute, but she couldn't think who.

'Have you met Sholto?' Eleanor asked.

'Yes, I have,' Rozie said. 'I stayed with him, actually.'

'You liked him?'

'Very much.'

'Of course you did!' Eleanor's smile was disarming, but knowing. 'Everyone loves Sholto. He's just so . . . *lovable*.'

'Go on,' Rozie said, cautiously. She sensed honesty and scorn. She wasn't sure what to make of it.

Eleanor rested her chin in a cupped hand and gazed at the bubbles rising in her glass. 'He's cultivated that image since childhood. You see, Sholto loves *things*. Beautiful things. He adores them. He covets them and cares for them and obsesses over them. He always did, even as a child. His mother always used to tell a story that at seven, he knew how to tell marble from alabaster.'

'Is there a difference?'

Eleanor laughed. 'Lavinia could tell you. Anyway, his parents were moderately well off. They had enough money to send him to boarding school and of course, once he was at Shadwell's he made sure to befriend anyone who had more than him. Sholto learned very fast that what rich people love, more than anything, is entertainment. Because, you see, they're so terribly bored. If they've made the money, or inherited it, what else is there to do? So Sholto became the party piece, the clown. He knew everyone who mattered across three counties. He was a gossip and a flirt, especially with the mothers. They adored that, of course. He was witty and well read, could cook divinely and deworm a recalcitrant dog. By seventeen, he was the most wanted party guest in the South of England.'

'Wasn't that a good thing?' Rozie asked.

Eleanor's face hardened. 'No, it wasn't. Because none of it was real. Sholto didn't want *friendship*, he wanted *access*. Close proximity to your Gainsboroughs and your Fabergé and your daughters.'

She eyed Rozie coolly across the table. Eleanor herself was all angles, high-cheeked and loose-limbed, dressed in faded, flared jeans and a man's jacket over the shirt. Rozie felt slightly wrong-footed by her shrewd, appraising gaze.

'I was in my last year at school,' she said, 'when I met Sholto at a London party and brought him down for the weekend. He was the same age as me: seventeen. I was the fourth child out of five and we lived in the grounds of my grandfather's house. A stately home, I suppose you'd call it. I was shy and biddable and loved horses and dogs. I wasn't sure what to do with boys. I was used to the look on my friends' faces when they saw Booke Place for the first time – but Sholto took it to the extreme. He fell in love with the estate,' she concluded with a shrug. 'With the situation, the architecture and everything in it. Including me, because I happened to be in it. He was obsessed. He was also a kleptomaniac.'

See what you find, the Queen had said. Rozie leaned in a little further. 'Oh?'

'He started off with small things: mementos of his stay. My mother was cross when a silver ashtray disappeared during his first weekend. They all assumed it had been misplaced by a cleaning lady, but I found it in Sholto's jacket pocket weeks later. There was a rather exquisite silver hummingbird that my grandfather had brought back from Geneva years before. A Fabergé egg. This was two years later. By now I was working in a little art gallery in Mayfair and Sholto was studying art at the Courtauld. He'd taken my virginity and I'd assumed wedding bells, though nothing was said. It was all very bohemian. He cooked me supper, very well, on two gas rings in his student flat. I found the bird and the egg when I was looking in his handkerchief drawer for something to use as napkins. Later, I discovered he'd also taken a portrait of my mother. At least, it disappeared that Christmas, and where else would it have gone?'

Rozie remembered a beautiful picture of a pale young woman – all angles, too – in a fifties evening dress, that hung in his dining room. Was it a sign of what was to come?

'He tried to take me, too.' Eleanor leaned back in her chair, examining her strong hands, adorned with little rings. 'I was madly in love. He knew what my parents thought of him and made plans to run off with me to Gretna Green and marry me the day he graduated from art school. I thought it was the most romantic thing in the world. Like an idiot, I told my younger brother, and of course he told my mother. Sholto came from what my parents called "trade" – which meant his father was a doctor and his mother's family were engineers. They bought their own furniture; Sholto needed to work for a living. Of course I didn't care – I *loved* that. Salt of the earth. I thought I was a socialist, but I was just a dupe. Sholto wanted beautiful things, and I was one of them. But my grandfather bought him off with a thousand pounds. He'd been prepared to go much higher.'

'Did they know about the bird and the egg?' Rozie asked, to try and take the sting out of the '*thousand pounds*'.

'And the portrait? No, I didn't tell them. They were being so snobbish. But it wasn't only that. Once they heard about Sholto's plan, my grandfather paid a detective to find out more about him. Of course, they didn't tell me at the time. Sholto loved to hang out with disreputable people. Aristocrats in the West End, drug dealers in the East End. Pimps. Petty criminals. He *liked* them. It was the seventies and art school was all about rebellion. He didn't take the drugs, but he liked the danger. I think he thought it made him cool. Anyway, it didn't make him a perfect suitor. I thought it was my grandfather who broke my heart, but . . .' She made a dismissive gesture with her beringed fingers to suggest she didn't think so now.

'Did he stay in touch?' Rozie asked.

'Of course he didn't. He bought a Ducati, slept with two of my friends and went off to India with Lydia Munro, whose family weren't as clued up as mine. He gave her crabs – God knows where he picked them up – and came back solo. I always wondered what would happen to him.' Eleanor drained her glass, her stacked diamond rings flashing in the light. 'Bizarrely, he stayed in touch with my brother for a while. Rupert was too polite to shun him, and Sholto was too crude to stay away. I assumed he'd end up in prison, but he worked for the Queen and retired to the Cotswolds. I saw his cottage in *House & Garden*. I must say, I searched the pictures for the bird and the egg, but I didn't find them. Did you?'

'I didn't see them,' Rozie said truthfully, keeping quiet about the portrait. 'And what about his time at the Royal Collection?' she asked, aware of her cover story.

'Oh, you didn't come here to ask me about that, did you?' Eleanor smiled her disbelief. 'What the hell would I know about that? Don't worry, I don't mind. I assume he stole the family silver. The Queen should count herself lucky he didn't run off with Princess Margaret. I bet he tried.'

Standing in Old Church Street afterwards, waiting for a cab, Rozie suddenly remembered who Eleanor had reminded her of, the moment she brought up Sholto: it was Lulu Arantes, who must have heard about him from Uncle Max. Lulu had been spot on about Cynthia Harris. She really ought to trust her more.

Chapter 38

Billy MacLachlan, too, had been busy. Back from Tetbury, he had visited one or two of his stomping grounds as a young detective, and reinserted himself into his old world as a royal protection officer. There were several networks for ex-royal servants, and for professional purposes Billy had kept up with more of them than he might have done otherwise – being a man very happy with a book and a crossword, most of the time. But he occasionally still golfed with ex-butlers, drank with ex-footmen, fished with ghillies and wine-tasted with sommeliers. They were in various stages of health and decrepitude, but they all had one thing in common: a love of gossip. There was a big pre-Christmas party at the Palace for old retainers coming up soon. On the pretext of making plans for this booze-up, Billy got to work.

After two days of nosing around, he finished his report for the Boss. He delivered it to the Queen and Rozie together as they all took a tour of the gardens at lunchtime. He sensed the Queen was getting antsy. She'd actually called him yesterday to ask about progress, which wasn't something she normally did.

'Do you know what a fence is, ma'am?' he asked, as they headed towards the lake.

The Queen looked slightly bewildered. She glanced at the wall beside Constitution Hill and then away again. 'I'm not sure I—'

'Oh, right, sorry. I mean, in the criminal sense.'

'Ah. I see. Isn't that someone who handles stolen goods?'

'On the nose, ma'am!' he beamed. 'Well then, you're with me. I've been talking to a man by the name of Frank in Bethnal Green. He has an interesting tale to tell. My suggestion that a few Palace items might have been half-inched in years gone by came as no surprise to him.'

The Queen looked resigned. 'I see. People can't help themselves. Or rather, they can. Guests have stolen our loo rolls, you know. Quite prestigious ones. Guests, I mean. I'm not sure you can have prestigious loo rolls.'

'They've stolen a lot more than that,' MacLachlan said. 'Of course, it's nothing new. You know about William Fortnum in the eighteenth century?'

'The man who started Fortnum & Mason? Who was a footman for Queen Anne?'

'Yes, him.'

'Indeed I do,' she said, smiling at the name. 'A very enterprising man. He started off selling half-used Palace candles to the ladies-in-waiting. You can see his point. The queen liked fresh ones to be lit each day and there were thousands. It must have seemed a pity to waste them.'

'He was quite the salesman,' MacLachlan agreed. 'And it worked out OK.' He was picturing the store that stood seven storeys high on a corner of Piccadilly, with its lavish windows and a musical clock his little granddaughter was very fond of. 'The thing is, Fortnum wasn't alone. The palaces have always produced their entrepreneurs, shall we say. Some more savoury than others. So . . . The Breakages Business. Sir James suggested there might have been a little racket going on in the eighties as a one-off thing. But I know it was still going in the nineteen nineties for sure, when a man called Theodore Vesty was running it, and there's no reason it couldn't have kept going after that. It's all rumour – nothing you could bring charges for. As I understand it, it worked two ways. There was the simple version, which was just smuggling things out that wouldn't be missed: old curtains that were being upgraded, a small proportion of the baby clothes that got sent every time someone got pregnant. Never a *large* proportion, ma'am – that was the thing. Nothing to raise eyebrows unduly. Nothing to make nervous underlings go to the authorities.'

'Hmm.' The Queen nodded grimly.

Rozie remembered the similar way Sholto Harvie had described the Breakages Business to her.

'Palace records were duly adjusted,' MacLachlan went on. 'They fenced the goods through people like my mate Frank. But I also looked into that Whitehall mandarin you told me about at the MOD, the one with the corner office – Roger Fox, his name was. He was a procurement manager in the eighties and early nineties who took early retirement for his health. That was the official story, but *unofficially* they caught him with his hand in the cookie jar. He was a crook through and through, basically. He may well have helped them out with finding willing buyers, no questions asked. He knew Vesty and, more to the point, Vesty's predecessor, Sidney Smirke, was his brother-in-law.'

'What?' The Queen stopped in her tracks.

'I thought you might be interested, ma'am. A nice little family business. Not hard to imagine your little picture going walkies from his storerooms to Fox's office, if it wasn't properly labelled during the refurbishment. The thing is, if it was usually hanging outside your bedroom, in your private apartments, I'm guessing most of the men in the Works Department wouldn't have seen it there so it wouldn't ring any bells. They must have assumed it was just general decoration and fair game. So it wasn't handed over to the Royal Collection and was miraculously "lost". That was the way they usually worked it, but only with things that didn't matter. That time they made a mistake.'

'Cynthia Harris would have known about it,' the Queen said.

'Even if she was with Sidney at the time, I doubt she was in on it. This was very much all the queen's *men*, ma'am. Sidney didn't tolerate women and she left soon after. But she might have guessed what must have happened if Rozie had had the chance to ask her. And it wasn't just you being defrauded, ma'am,' MacLachlan went on. 'Suppliers were, too. In a different scam, they were forced to resupply goods that were delivered but never officially received. It's hard to argue with Buckingham Palace. I mean, it can be done, but they'd have picked on small suppliers who wouldn't dare.'

'They used my name to threaten and defraud people?'

'Er, yes, pretty much. It took a fine network to pull it off and I'm guessing that when they didn't have everyone in place, they didn't run it. You need two or three people who are responsible for taking in deliveries and signing them off. At least one of them has to be fairly high up. Another needs to be fairly junior, so it looks normal for him to be carting stuff down to the cellars, where the tunnel starts, so it can be spirited away. And obviously you need someone at St James's Palace to receive the goods and get them out. Smuggling stuff *in* to the palaces would be pretty tough with all the security checks. Smuggling *out*? A child could do it, as long as it wouldn't be missed.'

'But what about receipts and invoices?' Rozie asked. 'There would be a paperwork trail. Someone in Finance would notice.'

'Which is why you need accomplices there too. You pay them off. They look away. If you poke about a bit, I'm told there's been an odd history of managers in the accounting team that looks after the property side over the last few years. They come and go. Some leave after hardly any time. I'm guessing the honest ones are put under pressure to move on. Maybe they're accused of something, or their lives are made difficult.'

'Constructive dismissal . . .' the Queen said thoughtfully.

'That's it, ma'am. You keep the ones you can manipulate, shift the ones you can't. Theo Vesty was a popular man in his day. He could get someone in with a good word, I imagine, and get them out again just as easy.'

'Was it an accountant who killed Mrs Harris?' the Queen wondered aloud. One never thought of accountants as being murderous types. Perhaps one should.

Rozie was thinking furiously. 'I was down there! In their office, the day we finalised the Reservicing Programme. That's the team you're talking about, Billy. There are four of them, but only two were there at the time, along with Mick Clements and his sidekick from Operations. They were celebrating and I ruined it. I was asking about some of the assumptions built into the financing model and—'

She looked from one face to the other. Not everyone found Excel spreadsheet modelling as compelling as she did.

'Sorry. Carry on, Billy. But I know who you mean. I think they thought they'd got away with something.'

'And you were announcing they hadn't?' MacLachlan asked.

'Without meaning to.'

'I bet their little scam was worth thousands, or would have been.'

'Ultimately, millions. And it was Mary van Renen who spotted it first. Perhaps they were onto her. It would certainly be enough to give them a motive to keep Cynthia quiet, if she had the slightest suspicion.'

MacLachlan nodded. 'Worth checking where they were the night she died. Do accountants ever sleep in the Palace?'

'I can't imagine why they would,' the Queen remarked.

'I'd look into it myself,' he began. 'Security keep a record. But I don't want to stick my head above the parapet, ma'am.'

She nodded in agreement. 'Thanks for your discretion, Billy. I'd rather you stayed out of this. I know Chief Inspector

Strong made a list of overnight guests that night. It's in the file, isn't it, Rozie?'

'It is,' Rozie confirmed.

'There are a couple of porters you might want to check too,' MacLachlan added to Rozie. 'I'll give you their names. I can't see them being criminal masterminds, but they've been spending more lavishly than their pay packets suggest. Watches, phones, the odd new car . . .'

'Stop that!' the Queen commanded, her voice ringing with authority. Candy emerged from a bush, looking apologetic. The Queen turned back to MacLachlan. 'I'm so sorry. Do go on. You were talking about criminal masterminds.'

He shrugged. 'Hopefully Strong's list will help narrow things down. There's those we've mentioned – Clements, the accountants and the porters – none of whom I'd put in that category at first glance. Plus maybe a security officer or two, though I'm afraid I can't give you names.'

'Oh?' The Queen turned her sharp, blue gaze on him, frowning.

'Yeah. Bit weird. Came from some gossip on the golf course. One of the old boys, ex-soldier, said he'd been having a drink with some of the current lads at the pub after work – someone's birthday – and they got on to battlefield injuries. Not in the best of taste, ma'am, but I asked about it for the sake of duty, you know.'

'I can imagine,' she agreed.

'Apparently a big group of them sat round and it got gory. They were egging each other on, sharing ugly ways to die. Quick ways, slow ways. One or two seemed to have encyclopedic knowledge. Ankle-slashing came into it.'

'And not one of them thought to mention it? When some-body actually died that way in the north-west pavilion?'

'This was after Mrs Harris died, ma'am. It sounded like the manner of her death inspired the conversation. Sadly, my contact couldn't remember who said what because there was a big group and he didn't know everyone. It certainly didn't make anyone suspicious.'

'Cynthia Harris had nobody to fight her corner,' the Queen mused. 'And if her death was deliberate, I suppose anyone might assume that it had been orchestrated by Mrs Moore, who had reason to hate her the most. She hardly strikes one as an ankle-slasher. Arabella Moore is very popu-lar, I understand.'

'Very much so,' Rozie agreed.

'We don't like to think of our heroes as being villains, after all.'

'Could she have done it?' MacLachlan asked. He had no problem thinking of heroes as villains or vice versa. He knew some women who would make excellent ankle-slashers.

'No,' the Queen said. 'When DCI Strong drew up his list, I distinctly remember him telling me that Mrs Moore was at home with her family that night. He checked, because she was a suspect for the poison pen letters. Her husband and three children can all vouch for her. By the way, did you manage to talk to Spike Milligan about the notes, Rozie? Could he shed any light on the affair?'

'I'm afraid not, ma'am,' Rozie said. 'I mean, I managed to speak to him, but he swore he didn't know what I was talking about. The poor man looked terrified.'

'Of you?'

'Partly.'

'You can be rather frightening.'

'Thank you, ma'am. I was trying. But he was more worried about something else. I didn't scare him into saying anything useful. He was definitely lying to me, but I had nothing specific to accuse him of. I said he'd been overheard, but I couldn't exactly say who by.'

'Who did overhear him?' MacLachlan asked.

'We don't need to talk about that right now,' the Queen said briskly. 'How irritating.' She paused, thinking.

Rozie said, 'So for now, we come back to Mick Clements.' She was remembering the murderous look in the man's eye when he found her in the cellars. He would have gone for her, she was fairly certain, if Eric Ferguson hadn't pulled him back.

'We do,' the Queen said. 'And he was one of the people who sent you on a wild goose chase in the summer, wasn't he, Rozie?'

She nodded. 'By sending me off to the old manager with dementia, yes.'

'Because you had started pulling on a thread,' the Queen continued. For a moment, it all made sense. But then it didn't. At worst, Mrs Harris might have told Rozie about the crimes of the nineteen eighties – if she even knew, for which they had no proof – but surely Clements could have distanced himself from those? He might have tried to threaten her into silence, but to go to all the effort and risk of actually killing her? He was impulsive – Rozie had seen that. Was that all it took? Could he have got away with it if it was?

'Are you all right, ma'am?'

MacLachlan was looking at her with some concern. She realised she had been staring at a spot in the distance without speaking for some time.

'Perfectly fine, thank you.' She felt close, but not quite there yet. She had a murderer in mind, and a victim. But they refused to meet. 'It's all deeply frustrating,' she admitted.

'We'll work it out, ma'am. There's the pensioners' party in a couple of days. I don't normally go, but I'll pitch up this time and see what I can winkle out of the old-timers.'

'Thank you, Billy. Of course, there's always the possibility there was never a murder at all.'

'I think we agree that's unlikely,' MacLachlan said, somewhat unreassuringly, as they tramped back to the boot room.

The Queen went off to get ready for her weekly audience with the Prime Minister. She gave herself seven days to prove to her own satisfaction that someone from Billy's list could have, and indeed would have, wanted to silence Cynthia Harris enough to kill her that night. If she hadn't worked it out by then, she would hand the whole thing over to Chief Inspector Strong, just as she had admonished the Master for *not* doing with his poison pen investigation.

The whole panoply of the press would descend upon them like a marauding horde. They would be besieged and no doubt accused of a cover-up. She sighed. Sometimes the punishment for doing the right thing could be daunting. But some things were too important to be left to amateurs, regardless of the consequences. She had indulged herself enough.

Part 4

Pentimenti

'You will find the spirit of Caesar in the soul of a woman.'
Artemisia Gentileschi, 1593–c.1654

Chapter 39

Helen Fisher sat at the kitchen window of her basement Chelsea flat, reading and rereading the letter with the red royal crest. She still couldn't quite believe that it started with the phrase, '*The Queen has asked me to write to you . . .*' and that the 'you' in that sentence was she, Helen, now linked to Queen Elizabeth II by a string of six short words.

Not many people had written to express their condolences when Cynthia died. In fact, Helen could count them on the fingers of one hand. Two by email, two by text (one with a thumbs-up emoji, which she assumed had been an unfortunate mistake) and this one, on good old-fashioned thick cream paper, typed up and signed in neat blue ink, above the words 'Lady-in-Waiting'. Helen had always assumed, when she thought about them at all, that such ladies held long trains and ran the monarch's bath and – actually, she had no idea what they did, but apparently one of the things was to write letters for the Queen, elegantly expressing her sympathy for Helen's loss of a long-standing friend, and remembering what a stalwart and dedicated member of the Household Cynthia had been.

Long-standing friend . . . How did the Queen even know? She couldn't have been getting all the police reports, surely? Helen had only talked to that one detective sergeant who'd come round. The 'copper-headed copper', as she liked to think of him. Nice man. Gentle. Not above sitting down for a cup of tea and letting Helen rabbit on about Cynthia's unhappy childhood and their days as uni students in the late seventies.

He was investigating those awful letters Cynthia had got – although why he was still bothering after she was dead, Helen wasn't sure. She'd asked, but he'd just said it was private Household business and he was sure she'd understand. Which Helen did, better than most, because Cynthia had always been a stickler for the royal family's privacy. She never let out a peep about what went on in those grand rooms behind the gates of Buckingham Palace. Only that the Queen was a 'darling' and Prince Philip 'not as bad as you'd think', and Prince Charles likewise, and Camilla was 'hysterical' – in a good way.

As for the rest, well, she rarely talked about her work, and nor did Helen, who'd been a translator for most of her life after her art career fell through, as most of them do, unless you're lucky enough or savvy enough to marry someone who'll bankroll you. They met once every couple of months on one of Cynthia's days off and went to galleries or concert halls together and talked about art and music, mostly. London was marvellous for culture. Worth, *absolutely worth*, living in a dingy one-bed basement flat, always lightly dusted in diesel particles from the passing buses on Battersea Bridge Road, instead of somewhere light and airy with a garden. Who needed a garden when you could have Tate Britain practically on your doorstep? And the V & A, and the Royal Opera House?

They *had* talked about that hideous campaign against Cynthia at the Palace, and Helen had spent many a Sunday afternoon in cafés at different cultural attractions offering tea and sympathy. She'd told the policeman all about this, and about Cynthia's strange, unsettled career, from art curator for the Royal Collection at St James's, to the Works Department that dealt with all the London palaces, to her eventual role at Buckingham Palace, where she seemed so settled, and Helen had tried to be happy for her. Though it was hard.

It was something Helen had never told anyone, because, frankly, nobody had ever asked, but she'd always felt the light had gone out of Cynthia that summer when she lost her job at the Royal Collection and set herself up with that hideous, *awful* man who belittled her in public (Helen had seen it with her own eyes) and ignored her at work (Cynthia said so), and quite possibly hit her. Cynthia had never admitted to it, but Helen had seen the way she shrank into herself near any man of roughly his size and weight for *years*. Why do it? She'd been such a confident, free-spirited girl at art school: like Helen herself. But it was the year her very good friend Daniel had died in that horrific bike smash, and she was grieving and unbalanced. That must have been part of it. Helen had tried to make her apply for other jobs in the art world. She was so *good* at it, and the Baroque was her passion. But Cynthia just said she was 'done for'. Her 'name was mud'. 'Nobody would look at her.' It was never clear exactly what she'd done, but overnight she'd gone from being the department's darling to persona non grata. It was almost as if they'd caught her stealing a work of art.

Cynthia was crushed after that. She'd already lost her friend Daniel, and she spent the rest of that year, and the next, pushing most of her other friends away. Of course, Helen hadn't told the copper-coloured copper all of this, because he just wanted to know about the poison pen campaign, but Helen always felt that summer was the start of it: the grief and loss and the inevitable shift in Cynthia's identity. Even as her best friend, Helen couldn't help but notice how sharp and judgemental Cynthia had become. She knew it came from a place of pain and so she'd found it easy to forgive, but others probably weren't as generous. Helen had no idea who might have sent the letters and cut up her beautiful clothes, but she found the copper's suggestion that Cynthia might have done it to herself offensive and bizarre. Nice though he was, this very idea had left a bitter taste in her mouth. But the lovely letter from the Queen was so wonderfully soothing.

She must write back, she decided. It would be impolite not to reply, and Her Majesty had been incredibly kind. Helen got up and went over to a wide pine dresser against the far kitchen wall, and pulled open its centre drawer. Here she kept many of the mementos of her trips with Cynthia: cards, mostly, from the gallery shops. They had beautiful pictures and she was sure she could find something appropriate.

Ah! This one. Perfect.

She sat back at the table, hovered her pen over the card's pristine white interior for a few moments, and began to write.

Chapter 40

'Shall we hit the road?'

It was Friday, November 18. Sir James Ellington took his coat, elegantly draped over one arm, and started to put it on. Mike Green, standing next to him in Sir Simon's office, did likewise. Sir Simon glanced at his computer screen and was about to shut it down when an alert popped up.

'In a moment. You two go on. I'll meet you at the door. I'll see if I can track down Rozie, too. She was just finishing up herself. You don't mind if she joins us, do you?'

Sir James hesitated fractionally.

'*Do* you?'

'No, no,' Sir James replied. 'The more the merrier. It's just, if we're with a woman we can't use the bar at the Rag. But we've still got the Ladies Drawing Room and the dining room.'

'I am *not*,' Mike said, quite loudly (he'd been celebrating already), 'drinking to a bloody fantastic result in a *Ladies Drawing Room*. For God's sake!'

'The dining room will be fine,' Sir Simon assured him, clicking on the message on his computer screen. 'I've often been there. They do a reasonable house champagne, don't they, James?'

'They do indeed. I've got them to put a couple of bottles on ice. Tell Rozie to get her skates on. See you at the door.'

Sir Simon raised a hand in acknowledgement. 'Two minutes.'

A new email had come in. Someone in the Hong Kong legislature wanted to know the Queen's thoughts on right of public protest. At nine thirty on a Friday night, when anyone who'd studied the Queen for thirty seconds would know she didn't make her thoughts public, whatever they were, if they might result in a war with China. But the Boss had enormous affection for Hong Kong. He'd write something conciliatory on Monday morning and, meanwhile, a holding reply would have to do. He was just finishing typing it up when there was a light tap on his office door.

'Can I help you?'

The door opened enough to admit a portly gentleman with rumpled hair, definitely two sheets to the wind, if not all three. He was wearing dinner dress, but his bow tie was askew and his extravagant, jazzy cummerbund was hanging low. 'Dunno,' he said, then smiled a soft-lipped, charming smile. 'I hope so. Have you seen Rozie Oshodi?'

'I was about to look for her myself, actually,' Sir Simon said. 'Can I give her a message?'

'No. It's . . . No. I'll wait.'

'I'm afraid you can't,' Sir Simon pointed out. 'Not here. It's the Private Office, and we're extremely keen on security. I'm surprised you got in.'

'I have an invitation,' the man said, digging around unsuccessfully in his dinner jacket pockets. 'To the party.'

He must be one of the pensioners, Sir Simon realised. They were having their reunion tonight. A big, pre-Christmas do for ex-staff, organised by the dining club they had. Sir Simon himself would be entitled to join it one day, but he probably wouldn't. Top brass tended to put a dampener on raucous celebrations. They had their own, more exclusive, club anyway, which no one talked about. It didn't do to make the others feel left out.

'Whatever you've got, it doesn't extend to this corridor,' he said. 'Don't worry, I'll escort you out.'

The rumpled man looked slightly desperate for a moment, but he got a grip of himself and accepted the offer with good grace. Sir Simon had used the brisk end of his voice and the man knew he had no choice.

'Just tell 'er,' he said – and Sir Simon sensed a wave of drunken emotion that the reveller found hard to contain – 'tell 'er I meant what I said. About visiting. She's always welcome. I think . . . I think she might wonder. But tell her I meant it.'

They had reached the door at the far end of the corridor that led towards the Great Hall. It was manned by a footman to whom Sir Simon gave a filthy look for letting the pensioner in in the first place. The man's minuscule nod was a promise he wouldn't let it happen again.

'What was your name?'

'Just tell 'er. She'll know.'

Sir Simon shrugged to himself and hurried back towards his office, just in time to see Rozie emerging from the ladies' loos, looking a million dollars and giving off waves of expensive scent. She was obviously going somewhere, but it was at least worth asking.

'We're off to the Army and Navy Club,' he said. 'Want to join us?'

'Celebrating?' she asked. The Reservicing Programme had been passed by the Prime Minister that day, having got the nod from the Public Accounts Committee.

'Celebrating hard,' he assured her. 'And for a long time. Come on, you've earned it as much as the rest of us.'

She grinned. 'So I get to join the triumvirate?'

'You do, my dear. What's the Latin for triumvirate when it's four people and one is a woman? Quadrangle? Tetragentes? Tetra's Greek, isn't it?'

'It wasn't a thing,' Rozie pointed out. 'Let's call it a quartet.'

'Will your friends mind? You look as if you were going somewhere lovely.'

'They'll deal with it.'

Only later did he think to tell her about the drunken pensioner. She was thoughtful for a moment, but didn't seem unduly sorry to have missed him. And by the end of the night they were not necessarily any more sober than he had been themselves.

The card was at the top of the basket of hand-picked, private correspondence on Saturday morning. Nursing a sore head, but giving no sign of it, Sir Simon brought the boxes to the Queen in her study, with the basket balanced on top of them. He saw the Boss do a double take when she saw the illustration and asked if it was anything interesting. She opened it, briefly read the contents, and wondered aloud if Rozie had put it on the pile.

'She did, ma'am. She said she thought you'd like to see it.'

'Mmm,' the Queen said. 'Do you think you could ask her to ask . . .' she peered inside the card again, ' . . . Miss Fisher why she chose this card particularly? I'm curious to know.'

'Of course.' Sir Simon smiled a courtier's reassuring smile and made one mental note to give Rozie the message, as requested, and another to have a closer look at the card itself when he had time. It hadn't struck him as anything particularly special: a woman playing a lute, early Baroque, by the look of it. The card was slightly nicer than average: thicker paper, nice matt finish – from the National Gallery, probably. It was the sort of thing he sent to his own siblings. Hardly the sort of thing to make the Boss excited. She normally went for horses, funny cartoons and dogs.

'The Queen wants to know,' he said later, in Rozie's office, 'why the sender chose this particular card.' He waved it at her. 'Can you ask?'

'No problem.'

'And can you tell me too? I'm curious that she's curious.'

Rozie narrowed her eyes a bit, but agreed. When she did so, a few hours later, the answer was nothing exceptional. The featured painting was by an artist called Artemisia Gentileschi, who had worked in the seventeenth century. The Queen might have noticed because, according to Rozie, there was a painting by the same artist in the Queen's Gallery at the moment. (*Was there, by God? And how astonishing of her to remember. But the Boss really did know her own paintings.*)

'And why *did* the sender choose it?' he asked.

It turned out, Rozie explained, that Miss Fisher had sent it in honour of her friend Mrs Harris, who was an expert on Artemisia Gentileschi in her day. At his slight incredulity that an elderly housekeeper could be an 'expert' on Baroque painting (very snobbish of him, he knew), Rozie said Miss Fisher had just explained that, as a history of art student, Cynthia Harris had done her Masters on the artist. She had hoped to write a book on Artemisia one day.

Which just showed, you should never underestimate the members of the Royal Household. He was proud of this little ship. Everyone was exceptional in their own special way, even the difficult ones like Mrs Harris. So, the woman had an artistic streak? Perhaps that explained why she had been so good at getting the best out of the Belgian Suite.

Chapter 41

On Monday, taking advantage of a rare free afternoon, the Queen found time to do something that had been on her mind for the last few days. She paid another visit to the top rooms in the East Wing, which had been fully redecorated after their late-spring drenching, when the antiquated water tank had sprung a leak.

She was attended by several people from the Operations and Property Departments and – somewhat to their surprise – accompanied them back to their offices in the South Wing to have a congratulatory word with their teams about the Reservicing Programme. *'Lots of work for you to do, finally getting this place in a fit state for us all to live in. I'm sure you'll do a marvellous job.'* She popped in on as many of the sub-teams as she could, catching up on their latest tasks and making encouraging noises. She even managed to make it to the property accounting unit in the windowless basement corridor.

All in all, the impromptu visit was considered a great success. The Master, who had rushed to her side as soon as he heard what she was up to, basked in her reflected glory.

He let it be known this was something they'd actually been planning for a little while, in gratitude for all the hard work everyone had put in recently. By the end of the day, it was his idea. The following morning, he humbly accepted the congratulations of Sir Simon and Sir James. It had been quite a coup. He was really rather proud of himself.

Six agenda-filled days had passed since the Queen's walk in the garden with Rozie and Billy MacLachlan. She was beginning to lose track of how many ambassadors and high commissioners she had received this busy season. With Great Britain now cast somewhat adrift in the Atlantic, keen to build on old ties to the Commonwealth, each audience mattered more and she was acutely aware of how important it was to say the right thing. The engagements were closely packed and she was already starting to think wistfully about Christmas, and the peace and calm of Sandringham.

Today, Philip was in Greenwich, visiting the National Maritime Museum, then attending a boozy lunch, no doubt, at Stationers' Hall in the City, with the colonels commandant of various regiments. Anne would be among them, which was always nice. Like her father, she wouldn't be drinking, because, like him, she had other engagements later on. The Queen had a brief gap to gather her forces and sort out her hair before an evening with the Royal Life Saving Society, where Philip would join her. They were celebrating 125 years, and she had been a member since she was thirteen, so for a dauntingly large chunk of its history.

Before retiring, briefly, to her private rooms, she'd observed the Household staff in action, moving furniture and bringing in glasses, setting up flowers and ensuring the lighting was right. She and Philip would greet the principal guests in the White Drawing Room before shaking hands with everyone else in the Picture Gallery and having a private word with a select few in the Ball Supper Room. Then it would be time to award the life-saving medals. She always enjoyed that moment, particularly having trained here for her own certificate. To know that someone was alive today because of something one of these brave souls had done . . . How splendid.

She needed to change and touch up her make-up first. If she was quick, she could sneak in a catch-up on the racing. But as she sat in her private sitting room, fiddling with the remote control for the small television in the corner, she found herself thinking of Cynthia Harris again. It was the life-saving that did it, of course. All those people one would celebrate tonight, and no one had been there for her.

The Queen had had no luck during her little tour of the Property, Operations and Accounts Departments yesterday. Almost everyone had said something, but no one had produced the distinctive voice she was sure she'd recognise: the one who had tasked Spike Milligan (she was certain of it) with getting Lorna Lobb to deliver the poison pen letters. It wasn't Mick Clements, with whom she'd had a two-minute conversation. His voice was a bass, whereas the one she'd heard had been a tenor. She had hoped to listen to Eric Ferguson and a couple of the porters, but they weren't there.

Meanwhile, Sholto Harvie's reasons for wanting Cynthia dead were stronger than ever. That card from Helen Fisher had been remarkably informative. It was Cynthia who had found the Gentileschis – it *must* have been. Unearthing those paintings should have been the highlight of her life. Her career was on the brink of a major coup, and then . . . Sholto's cruelty was worse than the Queen had imagined. She was appalled that Cynthia had been used in such a way by him.

What *was* it about the Surveyors of the Queen's Pictures and their deputies? She felt certain that Sholto had killed Daniel Blake. Cynthia would have known the young conservator quite well, working alongside him at Stable Yard. She might have had light to shed on that subject, if asked. But Sholto *couldn't* have killed her too.

Which left 'Mr X' from the Breakages Business. Rozie had established that four of the people on Billy MacLachlan's list had been at the Palace that night, working hard to finish off the leak-induced refurbishment and prepare the state and semi-state rooms for the family's return from Scotland. But why would one of *them* kill Mrs Harris, when it was Sholto who had the most to lose? If they were worried about Rozie finding out about the business in the course of her research, all they had to do was shut up the tunnel and lie low for a bit. Everyone would assume it was a historical scam, surely? And why had Sholto told Rozie about the business after all this time? He could have told someone at any point in thirty years.

There was a brief knock on the door and Philip put his head round.

'Ready to go soon, Cabbage?'

He'd come up to get changed for the lifesavers too.

'Quite soon. How was the lunch?'

'Spot on. Many war stories told. We'd heard them all before, of course, but they bear repeating. D'you remember Sergeant Pun in Afghanistan, during the elections, who fought off thirty Taliban single-handed? Caught by surprise in an ambush on his post. He ended up throwing the machine gun tripod at one of 'em. We got a blow-by-blow account of it. Extraordinary fellow. Typical Gurkha. His grandfather won the Victoria Cross in Burma. Are you there? You look as if you've gone gaga.'

'No. I'm quite all right. I just need to think for a minute.'

'If you must. See you in your glad rags shortly. I'm off to have a bath.'

He left her to it, and she let her mind drift back to the walk in the garden with Rozie and MacLachlan. There had been a discussion of war stories and something had struck her at the time. What was it?

She thought of Mick Clements, who was certainly aggressive. Look at the way he had tried to intimidate Rozie in the cellars that night. He was rash and impulsive, barely in control of himself, Rozie had said. But whoever killed Cynthia – if indeed someone had – had done it subtly, with premeditation. It was a bit like the way the Breakages Business was run: criminal, but not too greedy. Always flying under the radar. Dangerous, but restrained. Not like Mick Clements at all.

According to MacLachlan, one or two people discussing Cynthia's death over drinks after work had been 'encyclopedic' on the subject of battlefield injuries. *Quick ways, slow ways* . . . They could have been security officers, but not necessarily.

The knife on the note sent to Rozie had been quite specific. It was a type of commando knife the Queen recognised, used by the special forces. Not a kitchen knife, or a vague approximation, but an historic model that a military buff would know. So who had been talking in the pub? The same man who'd written those notes to Rozie, she felt sure.

Quick ways, slow ways . . . Perhaps *that* sort of man, he wouldn't need much . . . He'd do it as a favour. Do it carefully, so as not to get caught.

And then it all fell into place.

If she was right, *that* sort of man might even have taken pleasure in doing damage. He was quite possibly the same sort of man who would put a filthy message on Mary van Renen's bicycle, when no one was looking . . . just because he could. It would explain what happened to Mary and Rozie and even poor Mrs Baxter, whose suffering was just a distraction: the unnecessary cruelty, the instinct to hit where it hurt.

It wasn't Mick Clements, who might have the interest but didn't have the self-control. Not anyone she had spoken to yesterday, because none of them had the voice she remembered from the unfortunate episode in the attics. Someone made interesting, in fact, by his absence during her tour of the departments. Someone who took care to stay in the shadows.

But given the extreme nature of the act, when Cynthia's death hit the news, why didn't Sholto say something?

He had his own dirty secrets. There were the paintings. And the nobbled motorbike. Anyone who knew about the paintings would probably know about the bike.

The Queen reviewed what she knew and felt certain she had it now, but all of it was *perhaps* and *assuming* and *probably*. She wasn't absolutely sure she had the right person. She ran back over the events once more in her mind, looking for something that would constitute proof of the kind the police would need.

There was nothing. She might still be wrong. She would have to tell Strong anyway. If she *was* right, this was as far as she could go. Also, if she *was* right, there was no limit to what this man might do.

There was a phone on the desk and this time she had no hesitation. She used it to ask the Palace operator for Rozie, who answered promptly.

'Can I help, Your Majesty?'

'Rozie, this has gone far enough. Please can you fit in an appointment for Chief Inspector Strong to see me as soon as possible? First thing tomorrow, ideally. Half an hour will do.'

'Of course.'

'Meanwhile, can you find out what has happened to Eric Ferguson? I'd like to be sure one knows where he is.'

'I'll get onto it now.'

'Don't, for God's sake, go near him. Just his location – that's all I need.'

'I'll be careful, I promise. Have a good evening.'

The Queen intended to. She felt much better now. She glanced at her watch. In forty-five minutes she would be appearing through the hidden doorway in the White Drawing Room, and there were a few miracles to perform with lipstick, powder, diamonds and curlers between now and then.

Rozie made a succession of phone calls, all of which were dead ends. Eric Ferguson hadn't been at his desk for days, and he certainly wasn't at the Palace, or his team's second office in SJP. Sensing what the Boss might be thinking, she rang Mary van Renen's family home in Shropshire, trying to keep any note of panic from her voice. *She's out*, her mother said. *You can try her mobile, but reception's terrible in that place.* Rozie asked what place and Mrs van Renen explained, rather excitedly, that Mary was on a date with a new man, someone she'd met in London, who was visiting the area and who *between you and me, gave the strong impression he'd come up to see Mary specially. Isn't that lovely?*

Was it, Rozie wondered? Was it really? She felt sick.

Mary's mother was right about the mobile reception in the restaurant. Or maybe the date was going well. Either way, Mary didn't pick up, and the restaurant itself wasn't answering their landline number. Rozie wrote a brief but urgent text, asking Mary to call.

Sitting at her desk, alone in her office, she racked her brains about where else to try. Then she remembered the little breeze block office in the cellars. There had been various drawers that she hadn't had time to go through. She sensed that was where Mick Clements did his thinking. Perhaps Eric Ferguson did too. It was a very long shot, but she was really scared for Mary, and you never knew.

Chapter 42

It wasn't yet seven o'clock and Sir Simon was preparing to knock off early for once. He wasn't needed for the reception upstairs: that was the Master's domain, and no doubt he had it under control. There was a drinks party at the In and Out club across the square from the Rag, and another at the Foreign Office on Whitehall, and Sir Simon was wondering whether he had time for both. His wife was deeply into a drama series on BBC One and it was the finale tonight, so she wouldn't mind if he wasn't back before eleven.

As usual, before tidying up for the night, he scrolled through various newsfeeds on his computer. There was more fallout from President-elect Trump's decision to pull out of the Trans-Pacific Partnership. Definitely drinks at the Foreign Office: they'd all be apoplectic. More reports of Mr Trump's meeting with the press, post-election, which according to his new spokeswoman was 'very candid and very honest', and according to the *New York Post* was 'like a f---ing firing squad'. Drinks at the club, then, too, where one of Sir Simon's good friends had gone to the *Economist* after a short career in the navy. He'd have a thing or two to say.

He slipped on his coat and popped his head round Rozie's door to see if she was still working, and to say goodbye.

She was in her office, but not at her desk. In fact, she was standing in the middle of the room, wearing her coat and her emergency trainers. She started guiltily.

'Where on earth are you going?'

Rozie quickly recovered her composure. 'Just downstairs. It's nothing.'

'It's clearly not nothing.' Sir Simon gestured at her jacket and shoes.

She hesitated for a fraction. 'It's to do with that painting of *Britannia*. Just a couple of loose ends. I thought I'd look around and see if I can . . .' She trailed off with a smile and a shrug.

'Downstairs?'

'Yes.'

'Downstairs where?'

'Just, you know, the cellars. It's fine. I've been there before. I just thought I might find . . . Honestly, you go. Have you got something on?'

'A drinks, actually. Two. Look, stop trying to distract me. You're not going to the cellars on your own, Rozie. Definitely not at night. I saw what happened to you last time.'

'Nothing happened,' she said brightly. 'Honestly. Go.'

But he was already taking off his coat. 'You had blood on your lip and you scared the life out of me. Let's go down and find whatever it is you need and get the hell out of here. We've both earned a decent drink.'

She tried to remonstrate, but he wouldn't be moved. Sir Simon glanced at his watch: a quarter to eight. Hopefully they'd find this ruddy thing soon, whatever it was, and they could both get on with their evenings.

It was abominably cold down there. He regretted leaving his overcoat in Rozie's office. She saw him shiver and offered him hers, but naturally he refused. It would have to be a question of hypothermia or frostbite before a gentleman accepted warm clothes from a lady, even if she was a decorated army officer.

The door ahead was clearly marked with a freshly-made sign:

DO NOT ENTER.
PROPERTY DEPARTMENT ONLY.
BY ORDER OF THE DUKE OF EDINBURGH.

Rozie opened it and he followed. Inside, it was dark and she had to feel around for the light switch.

'You can't hear anything, can you?' she asked, just before turning it on. He listened. There was nothing.

'No. Why?'

'Just checking.'

She flipped the switch and the lights slowly buzzed into life, illuminating an Aladdin's cave of royal discards. They passed rack upon rack of fascinating artefacts peeping out of boxes or simply stacked on shelves. It was a bit like how he imagined the storerooms at the British Museum.

Rozie seemed to know where she was heading. Beyond the racks there was a small office with rough, unpainted walls, built into the far corner. She opened its door with some caution and poked around inside while Sir Simon waited nearby, rubbing his arms through his jacket and watching his breath form condensation in the air.

When she came out, he asked, 'Anything?' and she shook her head. He was about to head back, but she said she just wanted to have a quick look in the room beyond. This one had a barrel-vaulted ceiling that took him straight back to his history books. It couldn't be Tudor, so must be late Georgian, he judged. Berating himself for not coming down here before, he followed Rozie with considerable enthusiasm now, noting the old, thin bricks peeping through where a couple of tiles were missing, and the well-worn stones of the floor.

She looked around and, following her gaze, he spotted a trio of rather nice Chinese-looking pots standing in a row in front of one of the racks. Rozie glanced towards the far end, where another door was just about visible behind a tower of trunks and boxes.

He gestured towards it. 'I suppose that's where the tunnels start.'

Rozie murmured her agreement. But her attention was caught by a patch of something dark on the floor ahead of them. She went over, crouched down and put her finger in it, then stood to rub whatever it was off her hand.

'I think we should call someone,' she said, staring back at him.

'Oh? Why?'

'Because I think that's blood.'

He walked over and touched the stain too. It was like the swish of a paintbrush, rust brown, mixed with dirt on the stone. Adrenaline kicked in.

'Go and get help.'

'The blood's dry,' she pointed out.

'You're right.' He was overreacting. Perhaps this was an ancient storeroom injury, or rusty paint. He was just starting to relax when he happened to follow Rozie's gaze again towards the pile of trunks and boxes. 'Oh my God.' There was a smear of something ominous on the side of a tea chest in front of the tunnel door. 'D'you see that?' he asked, pointing it out.

'What?'

'On the tea chest.'

'Oh? Er, yeah.'

They went over together and Rozie lifted down the top trunk from the tower. He helped her lift down the tea chest, only to find it was nailed up.

'We need to open this.'

'I don't think—'

'It's not nailed hard. We can easily lever the top off. I'm sure I saw a crowbar leaning against the wall in that other room. Can you get it?'

She went off in search of it and, as she did, Sir Simon's attention strayed to the heavy trunk at the base of the tower, now sitting unencumbered. It was like the ones some of the boys had had at school. His own had been quite small, made of canvas bound with brass-studded wood. This one was similar, but larger and made of leather. Steamer trunks, they were known as. It was somewhat battered and there seemed to be a noise coming from inside it.

He bent down and listened harder. It was an unpleasant sort of scrabbling sound, reminding him of mice behind the wainscot at the cottage at Kensington Palace. With curiosity mixed with faint disgust – Sir Simon was no fan of vermin – he tested the lid. The two hinged buckles gave way easily; it was not locked. He lifted it up.

The smell hit him full on, sweet and sickly and nauseating, followed by the sight of a pair of small, frightened eyes that stared up at him, caught by the light, above a set of twitching whiskers. They belonged to a fat, filthy rat that leaped up at him suddenly, before throwing itself over the side and scuttling into the shadows. Holding his sleeve to his nose, he looked back at the hideous object the animal had been feasting on.

Inside the trunk, untidily folded, was the body of a man, face up. He had not been dead very long, Sir Simon judged – days at most – but the rat had been busy. The eyes and eyelids of the cadaver were already eaten away. Additionally, there were dark bullet holes in one marbled cheek and the opposite temple, and his navy waistcoat and white shirt were stained with blood. He'd been shot in the chest first, Sir Simon speculated, and then a lucky – or unlucky – bullet had caught his head as he turned it. Even so, enough of the face was left for him to know he had seen the man before, though he couldn't put a name to him.

Rozie came over, clutching the redundant crowbar. 'Shit!' she said, reeling from the stench. She peered over his shoulder.

'Do you know who this is?' he asked. 'I warn you, it's not pleas—'

'I met him over the summer,' she said, oddly calm. 'It's Eric Ferguson.'

Chapter 43

This time, there was no avoiding it.

MURDER AT BUCKINGHAM PALACE!
QUEEN'S AIDE FINDS DEAD SERVANT
SECOND BODY PALACE HORROR!
QUEEN ELIZABETH IN MURDER QUIZ

The news was halfway round the globe by breakfast and was even picked up by astronauts on the International Space Station. Twitter went into meltdown. The first conspiracy stories hit Facebook as fast as they could be written and fed each other in a frenzy. Instagram spawned a thousand memes.

The Palace communications team worked hard to make sure at least some of the news stories bore a vague relationship to the truth. The team reported to Sir Simon, who was the hero of the hour. He firmly instructed them to keep him out of it as much as possible, but it simply *wasn't* possible: everyone the world over was fascinated by the thought of the Queen's right-hand man discovering not one body but two (this news quickly spread, too). Pictures of Sir Simon landing a helicopter on a ship's heaving deck thirty years ago, or looking dapper in his current array of silk ties and Savile Row suits, only served to feed the fire.

LIFE STORY OF THE QUEEN'S REAL MR BOND!
YOU'LL BE AMAZED WHEN YOU SEE THE MAN
BEHIND THE ROYAL BODIES!
WHO IS THE SILENT COURTIER WHO SOLVES
MYSTERIES IN HIS SPARE TIME?

'But I haven't solved anything!' Sir Simon pointed out, self-deprecatingly, when lightly teased by Sir James and Mike Green over lunch in the canteen. 'If anything, I've only created problems for the police.'

He was working on it, though. They all were. It hadn't taken long for Cynthia Harris's recent, ugly death to be seen in a new light. The canteen was full of talk about how Eric Ferguson himself had been overheard talking about similar killing methods used during the Second World War. Several female members of staff had tales of times he had made them feel uncomfortable. Lots of people now reported their concerns to the Master, the Keeper, Sir Simon himself or DCI Strong – who was running a proper incident room now, based partly in Rozie's office, while she camped with the Private Secretary.

Had Ferguson killed Mrs Harris, or given someone else the idea of how to do it? The police had found a cache of historical guns and knives at his flat. The man seemed quiet enough, but he was plainly a psycho. This was the common consensus among the staff. No one could work out exactly why he should want to kill the old housekeeper, but it was still universally agreed that she wasn't missed.

Upstairs in her study, the Queen was slow with her boxes, which was very rare.

Suddenly, everyone around her was very sure of themselves – certain that Cynthia Harris had died violently, that Eric Ferguson had done it, and that he was therefore the person behind the poison pen campaign. Within minutes they had wrapped up the whole problem and tied it with a bow. Their very certainty made her more cautious. She had been considering this possibility far longer than they had, and saw more nuances to it than they did. For example, *had* Eric targeted Cynthia that way? The Queen had her own contradictory theory, but it was just a theory after all.

She picked up the phone and asked the operator to find Spike Milligan for her. They were quite miraculous in the way they could locate almost anyone at any time. Sure enough, four minutes later he was on the line, sounding slightly breathless and extremely nervous.

'Your Majesty?'

'I have a question for you, Mr Milligan, and I would be grateful if you would stop lying to me.'

She heard him gasp down the line. *Shock and awe*. Wasn't that what the Americans called it these days? Usually, good manners were called for, but not today.

'I-I'm sorry, I really d-don't know what you mean.'

'You do, Mr Milligan. Captain Oshodi asked you some questions about the poison pen letters two weeks ago and you pretended to know nothing about them. I happen to know this isn't true.'

'I-I don't know what to—'

'The problem has gone away now. At least, I assume that's right. There's nothing to stop you being honest at last, is there?'

He paused for a moment, clearly thinking. 'I-I s'pose you're right, ma'am. How did you—?'

'That doesn't matter. You were in cahoots with Lorna Lobb. She got the letters from you, yes?'

'Yes, ma'am.'

'And distributed them as you instructed?'

'That's right.'

'So, tell me . . . who gave them to *you*?'

He was a broken man, talking to the monarch directly on the phone. He dropped the pretence and did as he was told.

'Eric Ferguson did, ma'am.'

'Why?'

'He found out about Lorna and me. I think he overheard something in the canteen. Lorna's married, and so am I. Happily married, if you want to know – or good enough. He said he'd tell my wife and I'd lose my marriage, and Lorna would too. He would have, he was the type. There was nothing he wouldn't do.' Milligan sounded bitter now, glad for the chance to get it off his chest. 'Lorna didn't like it, especially after she found out what some of the notes said. She didn't know exactly, but the Master made it clear they were racist, ma'am. I'm very sorry about Captain Oshodi and so is she. Really we are, ma'am.'

'Sorry isn't good enough, is it?' the Queen said. She had seen that letter. Seen the knife. Felt the shock. Seen poor Rozie's distress.

'No, ma'am,' Milligan mumbled.

'So. I'd like you to confirm exactly who you told Mrs Lobb to give the letters to.'

There was a silence on the line as Milligan hesitated.

'Mr Milligan. I don't have long.'

'Sorry, ma'am. It was your APS, Mrs Baxter and Mary van Renen. But she didn't do the bike, ma'am. Only the notes in the palace.'

'Did Mrs Lobb also use social media for harassment?'

'No, ma'am, that was Eric, like the bike. At least, I always assumed it was.'

'And what about Mrs Harris?'

His tone shifted from shame to puzzlement. 'I thought it was weird. She was the one person we didn't do. Not even once, ma'am. Eric liked to laugh about that. He told Lorna to own up to it anyway, or else. *Keep them guessing*, he said. But on my honour—'

'What honour, Mr Milligan?' she demanded crisply.

'I-I know. D-do you need me to hand in my notice, ma'am?'

'I'll think about it.'

She put the phone down. A tiny part of her felt a scintilla of sympathy for the man. He was being blackmailed – but with cause. At any point he could have taken some responsibility for the damage he could see he and his lover were doing, but for many months he had sacrificed the well-being of her House-hold for his own interests. He had let his mistress, and the

341

entirely innocent Arabella Moore, risk their jobs and take the blame. He should go, of course. But, if she were to be brutally honest with herself, it would be very awkward indeed if he decided to explain what had precipitated his resignation. He had confirmed her assumptions about Ferguson, which was all she really needed. That was what mattered.

Eric Ferguson must have copied the style of Cynthia Harris's notes having seen them somehow (the Queen grimly remembered how Strong had told her the HR department 'leaked like a sieve'), but he did *not* target her as part of the poison pen campaign. He'd had other reasons for killing her, and the Queen was now confident that she knew what they were.

She had not yet had her proposed meeting with Chief Inspector Strong. When Sir Simon made his discovery last night, the policeman had understandably said he was very busy and had politely asked if she could postpone. Now, she wondered if she could, after all, stay behind the scenes. It was what she wanted, but was it perhaps selfish? It was her *duty* to tell him everything she knew. But then she would have to explain how she had worked out the historical connection between Cynthia and Eric, dating back to the nineteen eighties. That would bring Rozie in, and the awkward moment in the cupboard . . . Strong might start to wonder what else . . . It was all very difficult.

She lifted the telephone receiver again to ask to speak to him, then paused with it in her hand. She had, after all, been solving mysteries since her father was on the throne and so far, she had managed to keep it a secret. All it would take was a couple of carefully judged 'senior moments'. One had dug oneself into an awkward hole and now one must dig oneself out of it.

Chapter 44

Instead of Strong, the Queen asked to see Sir Simon. They had spoken briefly a couple of times since his great discovery of the body, but he had been rushed off his feet managing the consequences. She was relieved to see that this time, he was perfectly compos mentis. The discovery of Cynthia Harris had briefly undone him. Was it because she was a woman, the Queen wondered? Or was it just the unexpected pool of blood? Either way, finding a man with his face half eaten off by vermin was all in a day's work for her Private Secretary. He was, if anything, more on top of things than ever. As he entered her study in answer to her latest call, she was almost certain she detected a spring in his step.

'Your Majesty.' He gave the courtier's bow, which started and ended at the neck. Otherwise they'd be up and down like cranes in a dockyard.

'I thought I might be able to help,' she said.

'Oh, really?'

His face was a picture of politeness. She admired how it was almost, *almost* clean of disbelief.

'Yes. I understand that now the death of Cynthia Harris is being seen in a new light.'

'Yes, ma'am. Awful. It hardly bears thinking about.'

'I suppose one must face up to the fact that someone working at the Palace could be responsible for . . .'

'I know, ma'am. Dreadful. Ferguson, almost certainly.'

'But *was* it? You see, I've always liked the man very much—'

'Who? Ferguson?'

'No, no. And I find it very difficult to imagine him as a – not to put too fine a point on it – a *killer*. But I'm sure I remember seeing something about Mrs Harris having a relationship with him.'

'Who, ma'am?' Sir Simon asked. He looked utterly baffled, which was much as the Queen expected.

'Neil Hudson,' she said, assertively.

'*Neil*? At the Royal Collection? Your Surveyor of Pictures?'

'Yes.'

'That seems incredibly unlikely.'

'I know. It *all* seems unlikely, though, doesn't it? And we can't forget his predecessor.'

Anthony Blunt (he had been knighted, but his knighthood subsequently revoked) was a famous Communist spy, as Sir Simon well knew.

'But I don't think *all* your art experts can be criminals, ma'am.'

'I hope not.'

'And surely she was too old?'

The Queen frowned. 'I don't mean *that* sort of relationship. Was she an aunt? A godparent? I forget, but I'm sure it was *something*. I'd just like to be reassured that he didn't have anything to do with . . . any of this.'

Sir Simon regained his unflappable poise. 'I'll certainly look into it, ma'am.'

He was the consummate courtier. Eyes that refused to judge; a smile that refused to falter. Rozie couldn't do it yet. You could always tell at a glance if she thought you were being absurd. The Queen would miss it when she, too, employed a poker face.

'If you would be so kind.'

After he'd gone, she wondered if he would remember the little illustrated card. How fortunate that he had been the one she had mentioned it to at the time, even though she hadn't wanted to. With any luck, Rozie would have left it at the top of the file.

'Can you get me Bogroll's file on Mrs Harris?'

'Really?'

Sir Simon waited while Rozie rooted around in her desk drawer. She had had to empty the drawers before the porters shifted the desk into his office to make way for Strong and his team in hers. Inevitably, files got misplaced. Nothing was quite at her fingertips any more. It gave her a few seconds to think.

'Is this for the Boss?' she asked.

'Yup. She has some idea that Cynthia was Neil Hudson's aunt. And that therefore *he* killed her. Not Ferguson.'

'*What?*' Rozie popped her head up to stare at him. This was unexpected.

'I know. I think she's been watching too much *Death In Paradise*. Or what's that one with Angela Lansbury as the writer?'

345

'I have no idea.'

'*Murder She Wrote*. The Boss did a little binge-watch at Balmoral. It's given her ideas.'

Rozie nodded absently, turning back to her files. Her brain was working overtime. *Neil Hudson?* Was there something the Queen hadn't told her? She panicked for a moment, then realised – or thought she realised – what the Boss was up to. Sir Simon extended a hand and she adjusted some papers in the file and passed it over.

'Neil's aunt, you say?'

'Or something,' he muttered. 'Though why that would make him want to slash her ankle, I have no clue. Could you imagine him doing it? The blood on his shoes alone . . .'

'I'd say he was more of a poisoner,' Rozie agreed. 'Preferably with something used by Lucrezia Borgia.'

'Exactly. And I wonder how long we'll be playing the game of "favourite murder methods of fellow staff".'

Rozie eyed him reflectively. 'You'd use a Walther PPK, obviously, in keeping with your Bond image.'

'I wouldn't, actually. Barrel's too short, calibre's too low. You might as well just chuck it at your victim. Fleming was hopeless on guns. *You'd* do it with unarmed combat, no question.'

Rozie shrugged. 'So? What *would* you use? If not the PPK?'

He was about to say something flippant, but the image came back to him of the face with the holes in it, and the body on the tiles. He had started this game, but he was suddenly rather tired of it. There was a knock at the door and Sir James Ellington appeared.

'You two look like you're having fun.'

'Favourite murder methods,' Rozie explained.

Sir James didn't pause for a beat. 'The iron staircase at the end of my office corridor. There are a couple of newspaper editors I pray I never meet at the top of it. Look, can I carve out some time with the Boss tomorrow? Bogroll and I need to update her on Eric Ferguson. God, he was a nasty piece of work. It's pretty explosive, actually. We're still working on it, but I can give you the gist of the thing now, if you like.'

He did, and at some points even Rozie found that she was genuinely surprised. Afterwards, Sir Simon retreated to his desk with the file she had given him, to see if he could reassure Her Majesty that, unlike the latest murder victim, her Surveyor of Pictures was not a secret vengeful psychopath.

Chapter 45

It was not until ten o'clock the following evening that the investigating team had everything ready and Sir James managed to get his meeting with the Queen in the pale blue Audience Room. He was accompanied by Sir Simon and the Master, along with Rozie, who was there to take notes. They had all had a rather exhausting day, but the Queen, as always, looked fresh as a daisy. Nevertheless, she conducted the meeting standing up, which led Sir Simon to believe she wanted it to be a short one. This wouldn't be a problem: it would only take a few minutes for the Keeper to deliver his bombshell news.

'Is the chief inspector not with you?' she asked, looking somewhat surprised as the triumvirate gathered round her near the fireplace

'No, ma'am,' Sir James confirmed. 'He's away as part of the investigation. In fact, we're expecting news from him at any moment. Sir Simon had an extraordinary—'

'We don't need to talk about that,' the Private Secretary interrupted with a self-effacing flap of the hand. He'd been getting good at these recently. 'It may come to nothing. We'll let you know if there are any developments, ma'am.'

'Oh, good. So why are you here?' She looked expectantly back at Sir James.

'Since Sir Simon found the body on Tuesday,' the Keeper said, 'we've discovered an enormous amount about Eric Ferguson. None of it good, I'm afraid.'

'Go on.'

'Mr Ferguson – and as the ultimate head of Operations I take full responsibility for this, ma'am – was someone who should never have been allowed to come within a mile of this place. He was a very dangerous individual, with morbid tastes. The police discovered a lot of violent material on his computer and a large cache of weapons at his flat. The walls were covered in them, like the armoury at Hampton Court. Nobody knew, because it turned out he never invited anyone home. Not from the Household, anyway. They're all talking about it now.'

'I'm sure they must be.'

'But more to the point, ma'am, perhaps, is the fact that they also found half a dozen crystal tumblers in his kitchen, similar to the ones used at the Palace. His computer records showed he had ordered eighteen of them. It looks as though he'd been experimenting with making the damn things lethal.'

'Goodness. Really? Oh dear. Is this what the police think too?'

'It is, ma'am,' Sir Simon agreed, stepping in. 'They are convinced, now, as we had begun to fear, that Cynthia Harris's death was not an accident, far from it. I'm sure the chief inspector will be able to confirm it himself very soon.'

349

'And Neil Hudson? Was he involved?' the Queen enquired meekly.

Sir Simon noted the frank humility in her clear blue eyes and shook his head gently. 'No, ma'am, I'm afraid that was always an unlikely possibility.'

'I see. Never mind.'

'It did throw up a useful line of enquiry. But meanwhile, the police have uncovered some rather devastating details about Ferguson's work life, haven't they, James?'

'They have indeed,' Sir James said. 'It's why I wanted to talk to you, ma'am. We were rather lucky with a very talented young cyber security officer at the National Crime Agency. Digging around Ferguson's computer files, he discovered that for at least two years Ferguson has been running a major scam at the Palace. It's known as the Breakages Business. I believe you were aware of it.'

The Queen's eyes widened. They caught Rozie's for a moment, who nodded almost imperceptibly. 'Good gracious,' she said. '*Running* it? But he was quite junior, wasn't he?'

'Middle management, ma'am,' Sir James said, 'but that was the clever part. He was operating well below the radar. I must admit, I wasn't sure about his boss – a man called Mick Clements. But I'd never suspected anything of Ferguson. We might not have discovered him for months, or years.'

'How did he do it?'

'We're still piecing it together,' Sir James admitted. The thing is, ma'am,' and here he paused, so Her Majesty could keep up with all the revelations, 'we think this gives him a motive for being the true person behind the poison pen campaign.'

'Oh, *really*?'

'Astonishing, I know. You see, one of my secretaries was convinced there was an issue with the Reservicing Programme. We now think that what she had discovered was not a mistake, but a deliberate fraud, masterminded by Ferguson. Her name is Mary van Renen and she was one of the targets of the harassment. We believe that Ferguson mounted a successful campaign to get her to leave. Fortunately for us, her work was taken over by Rozie here, who was targeted for the same reason.'

The Queen glanced across at Rozie again, who kept her face entirely neutral. She was learning. The two of them had a lot to talk about.

'I see,' the Queen said. 'How fascinating, and how awful. What about the other letters?'

'Oh, they were pure misogyny,' the Master said, opening his mouth for the first time. He was here because of the relevance to his staff. 'Mrs Harris and Mrs Baxter were both highly unpopular. Ferguson may have chosen them for that reason, or he may have had his own personal motives. I imagine a psychologist would say he found strong-minded women a threat, ma'am.'

Not as much as they found him, the Queen thought to herself. She felt for Mrs Baxter, a 'difficult woman' who had been chosen for harm merely to cause confusion. And so far it had worked.

'Either way, it confused us for a while,' the Master went on, 'because of course we were focused on Mrs Harris and not Miss van Renen, who was perhaps the victim most in danger.'

'Except that it was Mrs Harris who died,' the Queen said drily.

'There is that, ma'am. There is indeed that.' He coughed and shuffled his feet. 'We're still looking into it.'

'You mean the police are?' the Queen asked, sharply enough to make them all swallow.

'Yes, ma'am,' Mike Green agreed swiftly. 'When I say "we", I mean all of us together. Now the police suspect Ferguson as a criminal and a murderer, they are re-examining all the evidence. Bog— I mean the chief inspector, has a large team working on it, reporting to his superintendent at the Met.'

'How reassuring. But there's still one thing I assume we don't know – or you'd have told me.'

'What's that?' he asked.

'Who killed Mr Ferguson?'

'Ah.' It was Sir Simon who answered. 'On that note, I trust we will have news for you in the morning.' His expression was bland, but inside he was as excited as the day he got his Wings. 'Along with a full report on what we've already told you. We thought you'd appreciate the headlines while they were fresh.'

'I do indeed,' the Queen said, smiling gratefully at all of them. 'It is always such a comfort to me to know that you have everything under control.'

Chapter 46

When the boxes came the following morning, the Queen hoped that it would be Rozie who brought them. Sir Simon's name was in the calendar, but it was her APS she really wanted to talk to.

She beamed when it was indeed Rozie who was ushered in.

'Well done,' she said, without asking how the girl had done it. One came to rely on people who knew what was required and somehow made it happen. 'That was interesting last night, wasn't it?'

'They missed a few things,' Rozie said, placing the red boxes carefully on the Queen's desk.

'Yes, didn't they?'

'They didn't seem to spot that I got my first note before I got involved in the Reservicing Programme stuff.'

'Mmm. Or that Mrs Harris got her first one years ago. They haven't had long though, have they? To think about it, I mean.'

'No. And they have a lot on their minds. Chief Inspector Strong has been very busy. He's not here today, by the way, ma'am. He still hasn't found what he's looking for.'

'The killer of Mr Ferguson?'

'Yes, ma'am.'

The Queen didn't press her. She was about to dismiss the girl and start on her papers, but saw that she was looking pensive.

'Was there something else?'

'Only . . .' Rozie sighed and shrugged. 'I should have got it before. Eric was always very strange. Always in the background and just a little bit creepy. I suppose I put it down to an odd personality. I thought he was holding Mick Clements back that day in the cellars. He was, but only because he knew they'd get caught.'

'I agree,' the Queen said. 'Mr Ferguson was the cunning one. It wasn't your job to catch him, Rozie. You've done well as it is. Whoever chose him to run the Breakages Business certainly knew what they were doing.'

'Sir Simon's looking into that, ma'am. He's looking into a lot of things.'

The Queen smiled up at her from her desk.

'Oh, good.'

Sir Simon's wife, Sarah, who had cooked coq au vin for them both, listened that night as he explained the last three days' proceedings to her over the dining table at Kensington Palace, while candlelight threw dancing shadows on his eager, intelligent face.

She loved him when he was like this. It made up, or at least sometimes partly made up, for all those nights he worked very late, and those weeks when he was away. There were three of them in this marriage, and the third person headed the Commonwealth and always held all the cards. But, in return, there were moments like this, when Lady Holcroft (Rah to her friends) watched as her husband held all the secrets of the realm in his capable hands, and she knew they were safe with him. He was even more of a hero than she had imagined. Not just brave but brilliantly insightful and clever. It was extraordinary the way he had made the crucial connection in absolutely record time. He was constantly checking his phone for updates, but they were of national importance, so she didn't mind.

'Are you really James Bond?' she asked, later.

'I'm afraid I can't answer that question,' he said, slightly breathless, in a gruff Scottish accent.

'Is that a gun in your pocket or are you just pleased to—'

He didn't let her finish. The last couple of months had been dark and bloody, but now he could sense the shadows lifting. Like Robert the Bruce, he felt his strength returning. He wanted to celebrate.

The news they were waiting for failed to arrive in the following hours, but the investigations continued apace. Along with several hand-picked underlings from his unit, Chief Inspector Strong returned to his temporary incident room at the Palace, whose corridor in the North Wing was vacuum-sealed against leaks. Rozie, who knew everything, was begged and bribed for whatever snippets she could share – but, like the senior men she worked with, she was incorruptible. She wouldn't even give any hints to her sister, who both respected and mercilessly teased her for it. More to the point, she didn't tell the Queen – who didn't ask.

'Are they on the right lines, would you say?' was all she wanted to know.

'I think so, ma'am. They've made the appropriate connections.'

'Splendid! Then we shall wait.'

On Friday evening, the day after her audience with the triumvirate, the Queen found out that her friend and cousin Margaret Rhodes had died. She spent the weekend at Windsor feeling very sad, and going over old photograph albums of her girlhood, accompanied by Lady Louise, Edward's lovely girl, which helped.

But Louise had to keep asking who everyone was. Who could she reminisce with now? All the official engagements were recorded in minute detail, but what about the unofficial ones? The private moments of hilarity and grief? First her sister, then Mummy, then Cousin Margaret, and even the dogs . . .

After dinner on Saturday, Philip spent the evening with her, instead of on his own pursuits. It was a thoughtful gesture. He presented her with the little oil painting he'd been working on in the Octagon Room in the Brunswick Tower, and then back in his study at the Palace. It was a perfect rendition of the lawn at Balmoral, seen from the castle, and in the very centre was the spot they'd picked for Holly's grave. So *that* was what had been absorbing his attention. She looked up with glistening eyes.

'You can hang it outside your bedroom at BP, if you like,' he suggested gruffly. 'In place of that ghastly Australian thing.'

'If you mean the *Britannia*, that's coming back soon, I hope. And I won't replace it. But I'll find this one a home.'

'You can use it to eat your toast off,' he said. 'I don't care.'

'I'll hang it in my bedroom.'

'You don't have to.'

And so, with gentle bickering, he took her mind off what she was feeling and made it easier to regain her normal fortitude and look to the future, as one always tried to do.

By Monday, Buckingham Palace was a hive of activity in preparation for the Diplomatic Corps Reception the following week. It would use every public room they had, to entertain a thousand guests from the ambassadorial elite to a buffet supper and dancing. The reception was a white-tie affair, dripping in decorations and diamonds, far more complicated to manage than a state banquet. The problem was that many guests came so regularly that their pet sport was to look for slights or mishaps. The Master's job, with the help of Mrs Moore, was to make sure there were none to find.

He was at full stretch, and yet he found time to join Sir Simon to compare notes on the rapid developments in the case. With the efficiency typical of senior courtiers, the triumvirate found themselves able to assist, if not positively lead, the police at every turn. Sir Simon in particular was proving quite spectacularly good at this. There were whispers in all the corridors that he had practically solved the crime single-handed.

On the last day of November, a week after Sir Simon's discovery of Eric Ferguson's body, Chief Inspector Strong received the final communication he'd been waiting for. He requested an audience and asked that the Private Secretary, Sir James and his chief superintendent (who was standing at his shoulder as he typed) could be there too.

The Queen graciously accepted. Privately, she wondered how much they really understood.

Chapter 47

At Sir Simon's request, the team met twice to rehearse in his office, as if they were preparing for a Commons committee. They each had roles and cue cards: it wouldn't do if they all talked over each other. The chief superintendent could take the credit in public. But they were generous men and, between themselves, they accepted that privately the honours should be shared.

The Queen agreed to grant them an audience in the blush and golden splendour of the 1844 Room. On the dot of twelve on December 1, an advance party of three dogs announced her arrival, as the men stood waiting within. Sir Simon, who was so often the person introducing her to others, felt his heartbeat quicken in an unaccustomed way at her approach. Rozie, walking in behind the Boss, gave him a surreptitious thumbs up. And then the Queen was smiling hellos at all of them, and it was time to explain to Her Majesty how three of her servants had ended up dead, and how he . . . with *help*, obviously . . . had solved the crimes.

At her invitation, the four men sat in front of her in a little semi circle of silk-covered chairs. Sir Simon and Sir James looked elegant as usual in their pinstripe suits. DCI

Strong had not tried to compete sartorially, but the Queen detected signs of a very recent haircut. The most splendiferous of all was the chief superintendent at the end of the row, who was a tall, urbane man with a sportsman's jaw, Hollywood teeth and silver buttons on his uniform that would pass muster on Horse Guards Parade.

Rozie sat further back, with a notepad on her lap. A footman had originally positioned himself just inside the door, but the Queen informed him she would ring if she needed anything. Her equerry, likewise, was not required for this conversation. Murder among the servants . . . It was too close to home.

'So tell me,' she said, sitting upright on a Morel and Seddon sofa, with Willow by her side and the dorgis at her feet, 'was it indeed Mr Ferguson who killed Mrs Harris?'

'It was,' Sir Simon informed her gravely.

'And you've found the man who killed Mr Ferguson?'

'We found him yesterday, ma'am,' the chief superintendent confirmed. 'After quite an elaborate investigation. I'm afraid it will come as a shock.'

The Queen blinked. 'I'm so sorry,' she said, pausing to adjust her handbag and looking up to give him a friendly smile. 'I'm getting ahead of myself. Do tell me everything.'

It was, by agreement, DCI Strong who began the story. His team, after all, had worked out the details of how Eric Ferguson practised his murder technique and prepared the way for Cynthia Harris to arrive at the pool.

'We don't have a record of Ferguson's contact with Mrs Harris before the fatal meeting, ma'am,' the chief inspector said. 'He was too clever to leave a trail – but we *do* know that it was he who consistently reported the internal CCTV cameras being out of action, and he, almost certainly, who had interfered with them to render them that way.'

'It won't be so easy with the new cameras,' Sir James assured her from the seat beside Strong. 'The old ones are practically museum pieces. Top of the list for change.'

'What a relief,' the Queen remarked. One might as well be living in the middle of a shopping centre. Although, on reflection, that would probably be better secured.

Strong returned to his theme. It was also Ferguson, they discovered, who had postponed delivery of the new carpet to the leak-damaged rooms in the East Wing, so their refurbishment ran over and there was a mad dash to get them ready in time for the family's return from Balmoral. This meant that he had a reason to request an emergency room at the Palace for a couple of nights, to oversee the results.

'This behaviour, along with the tumblers at his flat, leaves us in no doubt that he was the killer,' Strong concluded. 'We assume he lured Mrs Harris to the pool on some housekeeping pretext. Tumblers had been found there before and we think this was his doing too. She would have been tired after her journey down from Scotland, and unsuspecting. My thinking is that Ferguson had already arranged the broken glass in place. She bent down to look, he hit her over the head with something hard he'd brought with him for the purpose, and used the jagged tumbler base to cut the artery at exactly the right point on her ankle. We know from his reading material that collaborators in the Far East were killed this way in the Second World War. The blood loss would have been rapid. It's possible she never came round again before . . .'

'She died?' the Queen finished for him.

'Yes, ma'am.'

'That certainly explains how he did it,' the Queen agreed. 'Might I ask why?'

'Initially, as you know, we assumed it was pure misogyny connected to the poison pen campaign,' Strong said, 'while he targeted Mary van Renen because of a fraud he was operating here, called the Breakages Business. You're aware of that, I understand.'

'I am,' the Queen agreed. In his seat, Sir James blushed faintly.

'However, we then discovered that Mrs Harris was connected to the Breakages Business too,' Strong went on. 'We've traced the operation back to a man called Smirke in the nineteen eighties. Harris worked for him briefly at the time and they had a bit of a relationship. There were rumours of dodgy dealings, but everyone assumed they went away when he retired. In fact, he handed the business down to his successor, a man called Vesty, who handed it down to *his*. They kept it in the family, ma'am. It turns out they were all related. Eric Ferguson was Sidney Smirke's second cousin once removed. Not immediately obvious, but we got there with a bit of probing. No doubt that's how he was anointed as the new head, in his junior position, at the grand old age of thirty-two.'

'Oh dear.' The Queen's tone was dry. Her courtiers swallowed. They were not enjoying this bit.

'However,' Strong continued, 'we shifted our focus slightly, thanks to a suggestion by your Private Secretary. He gave us an invaluable insight.'

Strong nodded to Sir Simon, who smiled and did his self-effacing hand flap.

'I must admit, I had a huge piece of luck.'

'Oh, did you?' The Queen was all polite curiosity.

'It was your mention of Neil Hudson that started things off,' Sir Simon informed her – pleased to share credit when he could, however small. 'I can absolutely assure you there was no relationship of any sort between him and Mrs Harris. But in looking at her file I noticed that she had worked at the Royal Collection before working for Smirke. We were . . .' He corrected himself. 'The *police* were in the process of establishing the modus operandi of the Breakages Business. They had another look at the tunnels last week and found all sorts of evidence of activity between the palaces. We knew that they must have a man on the inside at SJP. If Mrs Harris was at the Royal Collection, she would have worked at Stable Yard. Was she the inside man, I wondered? Or woman, rather. I couldn't *quite* make sense of it all, but I spotted another name in that file. Sholto Harvie, ma'am – your old Deputy Surveyor. According to the file, Mrs Harris worked directly for him. Was *he* the link?'

'Oh, surely not Mr Harvie?' the Queen said. 'But he was so charming!'

'It pays never to be blinded by charm, ma'am,' the Private Secretary said wisely, crossing one pinstripe-trousered leg over the other and giving her a sad little shake of the head.

'I asked an old-timer if Smirke and Harvie had been friends, and he remembered that they were very pally. The thing is, I happened to see Harvie outside my office a few days before I found Ferguson's body. He was actually looking for Rozie. She told me later who he was, and that it was something to do with your old painting, which they'd discussed, I gather. Young Rozie had nothing to do with all of this, I hasten to say.'

'Thank goodness for that,' the Queen said, with a nod to her APS, who glanced innocently up from her notes.

'Although, to think, if it wasn't for your little picture, ma'am, I might never have put two and two together.'

From two seats away, Strong gave the Queen a brief, inquisitive look, which she affected to ignore.

'Goodness me. How lucky indeed. And how very sharp of you, Simon.'

'Thank you, ma'am. Just doing my duty.'

'And what were the two and two, exactly?' she asked.

'By then we were fairly sure Ferguson had killed Mrs Harris, and it seemed too coincidental that she had also known Mr Harvie, whom I had seen at the Palace on what was almost certainly the fateful night Ferguson died. It was just a *feeling*, ma'am. Hard to explain. Anyway, I told the chief inspector here and he agreed to visit Harvie in the Cotswolds and investigate. We still thought it was all about the Breakages Business, but then the police made a breakthrough.'

Strong took up the story again. 'We found Harvie's house locked up and he wasn't answering his phone, so I got a search warrant. We didn't find Harvie, but we did find *something*.' He paused, because he had been looking forward to this bit. 'Quite a momentous discovery, in fact, ma'am. Upstairs in the spare bedroom. Wrapped in blankets in a box under the bed.'

The Queen's surprise was real. For a fraction of a second, her eyes met Rozie's – whose expression read, *I know!* That very bed. The one she'd slept in. Like the Princess and the Pea. Except she hadn't noticed anything.

'Two original seventeenth-century paintings!' Sir James announced happily, leaping in. 'Of really quite exceptional quality, by an artist called Artemisia Gentileschi. Harvie had some good art on his walls, but nothing of that sort of value. We took them to the RCT to have them examined and it turns out they were part of a set of four, originally discovered in Hampton Court Palace.'

'And how did this connect to Cynthia Harris?'

'Ah.' According to the cue cards, this was Sir Simon's moment. The others duly turned to the Private Secretary.

'She was the original expert on Gentileschi, ma'am,' Sir Simon explained.

'Can I just say,' the chief superintendent interposed, his shiny buttons catching the light as he adjusted his pose to the benefit of his chiselled jaw, 'that Sir Simon makes this sound quite straightforward, but it was really his extreme alertness and attention to detail that enabled us to put everything together so quickly. He'd be welcome on the force at any time.' He hadn't spoken for a while. He smiled and sat back.

'Oh, please,' Sir Simon begged. 'Stop it. Pure luck. The Boss knows I'm just a simple sailor.'

'I know nothing of the kind,' the Queen said encouragingly. 'Do go on.'

Sir Simon flapped his hand again. 'All right, then. You see, a friend of Mrs Harris had recently written to you, using an illustrated card featuring Gentileschi, and I happened to find out – I think it was Rozie who told me – that Mrs Harris had once studied the artist.'

'How fascinating.'

'I asked the Surveyor about it. He's *very* dependable, ma'am. And he found out that when she was working for Harvie in the eighties, part of her job was to call in on the old gentlemen and ladies who lived in grace and favour apartments at Hampton Court, and find out what goodies they might be sitting on. She used to cycle over there and see. In this case, the four portraits had been hanging in an unused dining room for decades. Mrs Harris would have instantly recognised the quality. She not only knew about these paintings . . . she *discovered* them.'

There was a suitably long pause.

'Well,' the Queen said. 'How surprising.'

'Astonishing, isn't it? And Hampton Court Palace was a fire hazard in those days, so you might even say she saved them. But then they disappeared.'

The Queen looked appropriately curious, amazed and offended as the story of the theft and forgeries was explained to her, ending up with the disappointing copies she had seen. It was much as she had imagined, and the police had even managed to track down the niece of the forger himself.

'Apparently he'd told her it was one of his greatest jobs,' Sir James explained. 'It was Harvie who hired him. They'd known each other since their art school days. The tricky thing was not to make the fakes too good. They had to look like contemporary copies. The forger said he imagined he was a bored countess in the court of Charles II, practising her oil technique.'

'Harvie was known to hang out with a very *louche* set, ma'am,' Strong added. 'It was put down to youthful high spirits at the time, but apparently he never quite lost that attraction to danger.'

'And to crime,' the Queen pointed out.

'Exactly, ma'am,' Strong agreed. 'He made around seventy thousand pounds from the sale of two of the original Gentileschis—'

'*My* Gentileschis.'

'Yes. And kept the other two. But seventy thousand was a small fortune back then. He used it as a down payment on his house. He married soon afterwards and liked to give the impression his money had come from his wife, but it didn't. Her family always thought there was something dodgy about him.'

'It seems everyone thought so,' the Queen observed. 'Except us.'

'The one thing we don't know,' Strong admitted, 'is why Mrs Harris should have reappeared in his life after thirty years. In fact, my first thought, when Sir Simon alerted us to his association with her, was that perhaps they had a love affair long ago and Harvie might have killed Ferguson to avenge her in some way. Then we discovered the Gentileschis and a very different story emerged. We suspect she may have been blackmailing him, possibly through Ferguson.'

'Mmmm.' The Queen glanced briefly again at Rozie, who was looking at her shoes.

'We don't know that for sure,' Strong went on, 'but we *do* know that at some point in July, Eric Ferguson and Harvie were in touch by phone. A subsequent WhatsApp message from Ferguson said "things were hotting up re 1986". That was the year Harvie had the Gentileschis faked, ma'am. He had caused her to leave her job that summer, presumably so she wouldn't be around to see that the paintings she had just discovered were not the same as the "copies" he later revealed. The message from Ferguson said "it was on video". We don't know, but perhaps this was something Mrs Harris had made as part of a blackmail campaign. We know how difficult she was. Anyway, that's when Harvie replied with an instruction to "keep Cynthia quiet".'

'How on earth would Eric Ferguson know about the Gentileschis?' the Queen asked, with genuine interest.

It was Sir Simon's turn to reply. 'Ah. Well, it goes back to the family connection. He'd have heard it all from Sidney Smirke, who was running the Works Department at the time. Smirke was the person Mrs Harris had a relationship with after leaving Harvie. Given they were pals, it made me wonder whether Harvie fixed that too. Which he did, as it turns out. When that relationship went sour, she ended up making beds in Buckingham Palace. She probably felt bitter and vengeful about her treatment, even after all this time. No wonder Harvie was wary of what she might do or say.'

Difficult. Bitter. Vengeful. The Queen heard these words, nodded, and kept her thoughts to herself.

'Anyway, what matters,' Sir Simon continued, 'is that Harvie had stolen four of your artworks and subsequently sold two of them, and if Mrs Harris chose to, she could easily incriminate him, even if she didn't necessarily know the details of what he'd done. Hence, he asked Eric Ferguson to "keep her quiet".'

'And Mr Ferguson overreacted,' the Queen said, 'and decided to kill the poor woman?'

'Exactly, ma'am. Given what we now know about him, he probably enjoyed it.'

'It seems excessive.'

'It was. But this was a man who stalked a secretary here for weeks, online and in person, to get her to leave.'

'The timing was important.' It was Strong who pointed this out. 'Ferguson was in the middle of orchestrating his most daring move yet: the master-fraud embedded in the Reservicing Programme. Nothing must be allowed to draw attention to the Breakages Business – past, present or future. Still, to any normal person, a murder would seem, as you say, excessive. We wondered, ma'am, why Harvie said nothing when the body was discovered. He must have realised the death was highly suspicious.'

'Precisely. Indeed I—Um, yes. I see what you mean,' the Queen said, with a cough.

'We have reason to believe Harvie didn't know Ferguson's true nature at the time, or he'd have done things differently. Afterwards, it was too late. Because not only did Ferguson know about the paintings, it turned out he also knew another dark secret of Mr Harvie's.'

'Dear me. More secrets?'

They told her about Daniel Blake, and it wasn't difficult to look upset at the thought of the bike crash, because she was.

Strong explained, 'Harvie probably got advice from one of his dodgy friends on how to nobble the brakes. Harvie liked bikes, but he was hardly a mechanic. From what we understand, he was pretty devastated by the death. They were friends. He intended the young man to be injured, perhaps with a broken bone or two. He was a fool. A murderous fool, as it turned out.'

'Oh dear.'

'There was a sort of Mexican stand-off,' Strong explained. 'That's when—'

'Yes, I know.'

'Oh, right. Well, Ferguson knew Harvie had effectively killed Daniel Blake, back in the day. Harvie strongly suspected Ferguson had killed Mrs Harris. But Harvie also realised, ma'am, that Ferguson wouldn't let him live indefinitely, with the knowledge he had. He decided to kill the man before he became his next victim.'

'You're sure it was Sholto?'

'Yes, ma'am. The last call to Ferguson came from a landline at the Travellers Club, where Harvie regularly stayed when he was in London. We established he had been at the club the night of the murder, which was also the night of the pensioners' party at the Palace. He was our man, no doubt about it. He wasn't as clever or as thorough as Ferguson. Afterwards, he hid the gun in a Chinese vase in the cellars.

Assumed we wouldn't look there, I suppose. It was practically the first place we tried.'

'How, might I ask,' the Queen said, 'did he smuggle a *gun*
into the Palace in the first place?'

The men all looked helpless. It was collectively their job
to protect the Sovereign and this was a good question.

'We don't tend to frisk your old servants, ma'am,' Sir
James admitted. 'Perhaps we should. We ask for photo ID, of
course, and we had a bag search at the door for the party, but
Sir Simon suspects that Harvie had hidden the pistol against
his back, under a silk cummerbund that he was wearing.'

'It was particularly wide and garish, ma'am,' Sir Simon
explained. 'I remember noticing it later. Not the highest
form of tailoring, for a man who was otherwise well dressed.
The gun was a Colt .38 Special from the thirties. Small and
powerful – the sort of thing you might choose if you're not
sure of your aim and want to stop someone at a short distance. DCI Strong here subsequently discovered that Harvie
bought it as a deactivated antique and had it reactivated by
one of his more disreputable friends. He had a lot of those,
we now understand. It was another such person who must
have sold him the fake passport he used to get to France.'

'He was in France?'

'That's right. The French police found him in a hotel outside Paris yesterday.'

'Goodness.'

The Queen looked genuinely fascinated. Sir Simon was
relieved to talk more about this discovery, and less about
those moments when killers had been allowed to stalk the

Palace corridors uninterrupted, which was something the triumvirate and the police would rather put behind them.

'He was in the middle of writing a letter, which was more of a confession, really.'

'To what, exactly?'

'To the killing of Ferguson. By then we were already pretty certain he'd done that anyway. But also to the fact that he felt indirectly responsible for the two other deaths.'

'Three deaths,' the Queen mused. 'And to think I sent Rozie straight into his lair.'

'Hardly a lair, ma'am,' Sir Simon reassured her. 'Harvie was obviously taken with Rozie. He was very keen to see her that night at the party. I believe he had just killed Ferguson at the time, and was tired and emotional—'

'You mean drunk.'

'Very drunk, actually. It must have been quite a mental and physical job to deal with the body in the cellars.'

'Wasn't he covered in blood?' the Queen asked, suddenly wondering.

Sir Simon smiled. 'It seems he had the presence of mind to put on a warehouse coat he must have found down there. I saw it stashed with the body, but stupidly assumed it belonged to Ferguson. Anyway, it looks as though he cleaned off, went back upstairs, drowned his sorrows thoroughly at the bar and decided in a maudlin fug that he wanted to assure Rozie of his affection. In fact, he left her a painting, ma'am. He mentioned it in his letter. He said it was one she had admired when she visited.'

'I don't understand. You say he *left* Rozie a picture?' The Queen looked from one man to the other.

DCI Strong leaned forward. They had decided to leave this information until last, because of its upsetting nature.

'I'm sorry to tell you, ma'am, that when the French police found Harvie yesterday, he was dead.'

'Oh,' she muttered quietly, resting a hand on the back of the corgi curled up beside her. 'I see.'

'He'd taken a bunch of pills in a little hotel in the suburbs. It's the kind of place they don't clean as often as they might. They didn't find him for two days.'

The Queen nodded slowly. 'So that's why you called his letter a confession. The words of a dying man.'

'Exactly, ma'am. They were addressed to a woman called Lisa. We don't know who she is yet, but we're making enquiries. It seems the Private Secretary's quick thinking rather caught up with the man,' Strong added. 'Harvie mentioned that he'd hoped it would be months before anyone looked in that trunk in the cellars, and by then it would be difficult to know exactly when Ferguson died. When he heard on the news how fast Sir Simon here found the body, he knew the game was up.'

'What did he say to Lisa, exactly?' the Queen wanted to know.

'Oh, nothing too specific. Only that he was sorry. Not for killing Ferguson, which he seemed quite pleased about, but for Blake, and for Mrs Harris, and for introducing Sidney Smirke to the Palace in the first place. We didn't know this, but apparently it was Harvie who originally recommended him. Another dodgy, plausible friend from his art school days.'

'Was he sorry about the pictures?'

'He didn't mention those in his letter,' Strong said. 'I think it was more the lives that mattered to him.'

'Well, at least there's that. And the Breakages Business . . . have we finally put an end to it?'

By 'we' the Queen meant 'you', and Sir James and Sir Simon knew that.

'We have indeed,' Sir James said firmly. 'Ferguson was good at deleting things from his phone, but he kept a detailed record of the frauds on his computer. He assumed it was hack-proof, but thanks to the whizz-kid at the NCA, it took less than a day to give up all its secrets. Including Ferguson's associates inside the Palace and out.'

'We've arrested most of 'em,' the chief superintendent announced, buttons twinkling. 'Some we're just keeping an eye on. They might lead us to more syndicates we've got an interest in. And meanwhile the media can feast on the fact that yes, there might have been two bodies, but with Sir Simon's help we solved the mystery of both of them in record time. All in all, it's been an excellent team effort, I'd say.'

On that note, the four men sat back, satisfied.

'Well, I must congratulate you all,' the Queen said. 'This has been most informative.'

'All in a day's work,' Sir Simon said with a grin.

'Oh, absolutely,' the Queen agreed, rising. 'It's just what I'd have expected. Very well done.'

If he did that hand flap again, she thought, he might get RSI.

Chapter 48

As they left, the Queen asked Rozie to stay behind. They stood together quietly, both reflecting that this was the very spot where they had stared at each other, first truly considering that Mrs Harris's death might be unnatural.

'You did well,' the Queen said.

'Shall we let them go on thinking that she was blackmailing Sholto, and that's what started everything?' Rozie asked.

'I think we should. It's unfair on her, I know. She didn't understand the power she had to bring Sholto down. However, it's easier that way. It keeps you out of it, and I don't want to complicate things for them unnecessarily.'

Rozie nodded. 'Ma'am. But what if DCI Strong realises Eric targeted me before I helped out Sir James with the spreadsheets?'

'I imagine he has realised,' the Queen said. 'But it would be hard for him to prove the cause. Easier, I think, for him not to probe too far. After all, the murders are solved and both murderers are dead.'

'Yes.' Rozie nodded again. She seemed very muted, and it occurred to the Queen that she must be thinking that she was personally responsible for all of this. Responsible, because she had alerted Eric Ferguson to danger by asking about a painting that went missing in 1986, and whose provenance she would diligently track. Eric had been right to fear that painting. It was the one mistake – the one act of reckless greed, without planning or thought for the consequences – that the Breakages Business had made. Rozie would have followed up with Cynthia Harris eventually. Even if the housekeeper didn't yet realise how much she knew, they would have unravelled the thread all the way back to Sholto and Sidney Smirke and poor Daniel Blake, as they eventually did. But Rozie was wrong to take on this burden.

'There was something else Sir Simon said that wasn't entirely accurate,' the Queen remarked. 'It got me thinking.'

'Oh, ma'am? What?'

'Do you remember, he mentioned Ferguson referring to a video in a message to Sholto?'

'I do,' Rozie said. 'When "things were hotting up".'

'Something struck me. It reminded me of a moment when I noticed Mr Ferguson, earlier this summer. He was monitoring a documentary team who were filming me when I sat for that bust.'

Rozie's gaze sharpened. 'Oh, really?'

'Yes. They were videoing me with Lavinia Hawthorne-Hopwood and I remember, quite distinctly, that I happened to remark that I'd seen a painting of mine in Portsmouth. It was around the time I asked you to look into it, but long before you would have talked to him.'

'I don't see how—'

'Oh come, Rozie. Ferguson was in the room at the time. It was *I* who alerted him to the problem, not you. It was probably then that he contacted Sholto Harvie.'

'But even so, ma'am, I—'

'You just did your job,' the Queen said with finality. 'I started this, however inadvertently, and I count myself very fortunate indeed that it ended without more bloodshed. Although, of course, I wish poor Mrs Harris hadn't been involved.'

'She wasn't the most pleasant person,' Rozie assured her.

The Queen could see the girl thought she was being sentimental about her old housekeeper, as so many had thought. But she wasn't. She let it go.

A week passed. All around them, the final preparations were being made for the Diplomatic Corps Reception. The Queen would soon be donning a white and silver evening gown and some of her sapphires, but in a quiet moment, she asked to be driven to St James's Palace for a brief appointment.

In the car, her thoughts were on Sholto Harvie, who had died of a self-administered overdose of pills in a squalid hotel in a Paris *banlieue* that didn't ask questions. How he would have hated his surroundings in those last days, she thought. He was a man who lived for glamour.

He had asked 'Lisa' for forgiveness, but he wouldn't be getting it. Cynthia Harris had come to London as a young woman bursting with ideas and ambition, and for his own sake, Sholto had ruined her. Not only her career, but her life, by placing her in the hands of a scheming, violent man. She had soldiered on, but lost the respect of all around her.

Bitter, Sir Simon had called her. *Vengeful*. Mrs Harris had not, in fact, been vengeful, except against herself. She had lived alone and died alone, and the Queen's heart went out to her.

She knew forgiveness wouldn't be forthcoming to Sholto, because she knew who 'Lisa' was. When he worked as the Queen's Deputy Surveyor of Pictures, Sholto used to call one 'Mona Lisa'. It could be short for Elisabetta, he told her . . . this expert on Leonardo, with his courtly ways. It was bumptious, bordering on rude, when it should have been 'Your Majesty', but he had the charm to get away with it. He must have thought charm could excuse any bad behaviour. He was wrong.

At the Royal Collection Trust, Neil Hudson accompanied her to a light-filled conservation studio. Here, the newly rediscovered Gentileschis, rescued from under Sholto's spare bed, were set up, side by side, on easels at eye level.

'Two muses, ma'am. It's a theme Artemisia addressed elsewhere. We're not certain, but that one holding the flute looks like Euterpe, goddess of music, and the one with the garland could be the goddess of dance, Terpsichore. We're trying to get the other two back from their current owners to join them. It may take a while. But these two would make a good centrepiece for a show we're thinking of doing about women artists. Wouldn't you agree?'

The Queen stood in front of these originals for a long time, remembering how quickly she had cast her eye over them before – so sure she would see them again soon, once they'd been cleaned. The copies had turned out much flatter and duller than expected. Now she knew why. These two, by contrast, were mesmerising. They were still grimy, but the faces shone out, each head thrown back at a challenging angle above an ample bosom or a half-turned shoulder. The eyes seemed to be posing a challenge: are you watching me or am I watching you? She loved their quiet subversiveness. They might be half-clothed goddesses, but in each of them she recognised a fellow soul: a woman who has more to think about than the act of being painted.

'They're delightful,' she said. 'Splendid. Didn't everyone do a marvellous job? It's good to have them back.'

Chapter 49

Another week went by. Rozie and her sister Fliss were up in Rozie's set of rooms in the attics, getting ready for the staff Christmas party. Not the formal one the royal family would soon attend, but the fancy-dress shindig, where plus-ones were invited, wine flowed faster than gossip, and the bacchanalian vibe was designed to match the Caravaggios on the walls.

The bedroom smelled of tobacco, rum and rebellion. Fliss, dressed in a purple jacket and tight paisley trousers, was putting the finishing touches to her eyeliner using a magnifying mirror on the bedside table. Rozie sat cross-legged in front of the wardrobe mirror, adding a blue edge to the glittery red flash that covered half her face.

'I wonder which hero Sir Simon will be going as,' Fliss mused.

'Guess,' Rozie said.

'Seriously, d'you think so? Which one?'

'Sean Connery, I imagine. Or Pierce Brosnan. He'll go for suave.'

'Is he totally up himself these days?'

'Actually, he's fairly subdued,' Rozie said. 'He's Mr Modest. They teach you that kind of thing at public school.

But everyone's wondering what kind of honour she's going to give him.'

'Ooh! Where do you go from "Sir"?' Fliss asked. 'Lord?'

'She's got loads of family medals up her sleeve that nobody's heard of. He'll probably go from KCVO to GCVO. It's a big deal.'

'OK, if you say so.'

'She's also given him and his wife the use of a cottage at Balmoral at Christmas so they can chillax.'

'Nice. By the way . . .' Fliss looked up from her finished make-up. 'You seem a lot better. You OK now?'

'Yeah, I am,' Rozie admitted. 'There are a few idiots here, but on the whole they're a good bunch. They work as hard as we did at the bank for a fraction of the money. They're proud of what they do. That whole . . . Gothic atmosphere seems to have vanished.'

'Amazing what a difference just one or two people can make,' Fliss said. 'You think something's endemic, but you get rid of a couple of sociopaths and . . . *ewey!*"

Rozie agreed. Those little folded notes had lit a flame of fury that still flared inside her from time to time. But they had been written to scare her off *because she was good at her job*, as much as because of the colour of her skin. She could go back to viewing the unthinking racism of men like Neil Hudson with pity. He would be mortified if he knew that his 'Nubian queen' compliment came with centuries of problematic objectification. He was an academic, though. He ought to know better. It often amazed her who did and who didn't. Sir Simon, despite his posh, white, public school, Establishment vibe, was always the perfect gentleman.

Fliss's thoughts were elsewhere by now. 'To think, you were heading to the house of a murderer when I called you in the car that night.'

'Yeah. And I was about to sleep on two stolen paintings.'

'And be given another one. By a *murderer*. I hope you're not keeping it. At least you escaped the dreaded Mark.'

'What d'you mean?' Rozie asked, looking round sharply.

'Whaaaat? I thought you knew. Jojo told me. It was the talk of the wedding.'

'What talk?'

'Mark was sleeping with Claire, no. You, know? Jojo's sister, whose boyfriend was on a business trip?'

'Um, no he wasn't.'

'He wa-as,' Fliss assured her. 'They got caught in flagrante by a guest who got the wrong room. He'd spent the evening chatting up one of the bridesmaids to throw everyone off the scent. It might have been you, but luckily you'd already gone.'

'Yeah . . .' Rozie said, shaking her head a little. Suddenly, she saw that stressful journey in the Mini in a totally new light. Sometimes bad decisions turned out to be very good ones. She studied her make-up in the mirror. The bolt of lightning was in perfect position. All she needed were her red boots. 'Huh. Lucky for me.'

'I never liked him,' Fliss went on. 'Sex on legs but . . . a total *Backpfeifengesicht*. Hey! Those boots look good on you. You should wear them more often.'

As they walked towards the Ballroom, among endless Wellingtons and Nelsons, Iron Men and Wonder Women heading in the same direction, they encountered Sir Simon in the Picture Gallery, accompanied by his wife. He sported a powdered wig, a cutaway red frock coat over parchment-coloured breeches and a white cravat. Lady Holcroft wore a wide silk court dress. James and one of his Bond girls they were not.

'I don't get it,' Rozie admitted. 'You'll have to tell me.'

'The Scarlet Pimpernel,' he grinned. 'It was my favourite book at prep school. I never miss a chance to dress up as Sir Percy. Rah is Marguerite St Just, my clever wife.'

'She was always one of my heroines,' Lady Holcroft said. 'Lucky we found each other, really.'

'And who's your hero?' Sir Simon asked, taking in Rozie's tinted red hair, catsuit and boots. 'Oh! Bowie! Of course. Aladdin Sane. Well done. And . . .?' He looked enquiringly at Fliss.

'Prince, dude. I'd have thought it was obvious.'

'Oh, I'm sure it is. Sorry. I'm more into rock than pop.'

'Funk, but OK. He just died, like Bowie, you know?' Fliss said with a sigh. 'April 21. It's been a tough year.'

'The Queen's birthday,' Sir Simon observed. 'It was a wonderful day for us in Windsor. But how tragic for funk. Well, I must say you do him justice. Shall we go in?'

The four of them linked arms and walked past the serried ranks of Rubens and Vermeer, Van Dyke and Canaletto. Looking around, Rozie hugged the knowledge to herself that she was now the proud owner of her own Cézanne. She wouldn't tell Fliss, but she had decided to keep her bequest. True, its last owner was a murderer and a thief, but he had come by this painting honestly at least. If Rozie didn't take it, it would only go to auction and be bought by someone who didn't love it as much as she did. She'd put it on her bedroom wall and take it down whenever her self-appointed moral compass came to visit. She still looked back fondly at that weekend in the Cotswolds. She shouldn't, but she did.

As they reached the raucous laughter and thudding bass of the Ballroom, the DJ announced the Stones and the room began to rock to 'Jumping Jack Flash'. She followed Sir Simon's bobbing wig towards the dance floor.

Chapter 50

The maids and dressers had already started packing for Sandringham. Everyone was looking forward to a quiet Christmas. They all felt they needed it after the year they'd had.

With a couple of days to go, the Private Office received a package with an MOD stamp on it, addressed to the Queen. Rozie was the one to open it. It contained an over-bright painting of the royal yacht *Britannia* surrounded by little sailing ships, and a very apologetic note from the Second Sea Lord, asking forgiveness for the delay.

She took it straight to the Queen in her study.

'I thought you might like to see this as soon as it arrived, ma'am.'

'Oh, goodness. Thank you, Rozie.'

Rozie, sensing herself dismissed, left the Boss to it.

The Queen stood at her desk, staring at the little painting for a while. Rozie would probably want to share this moment, after everything they had been through, but the Queen wanted to be alone.

They had changed the frame. It was no longer the original gilt one, but a plain wooden border, presumably applied by that bastard mandarin in Whitehall who had stolen it from her, to disguise its provenance. Resting her fingertips either side of it she bent down carefully, almost gingerly, and examined the canvas through her bifocals, starting at the top. The Second Sea Lord had mentioned 'restoration'. Indeed, the painting looked even brighter than she remembered it.

Would they be there? She hardly dared look.

She dragged her gaze first to the pennants waving between the masts, and then to the main deck. Her heart beat a little faster . . . But they *were* there. Those precious little flecks of oil paint, that had survived a theft and over fifty years.

What were they called? There was a name for them. She looked back at the handwritten message from the Second Sea Lord, which came attached to a typed note from the conservator. '. . . Relatively good condition. Unvarnished. Some light overpainting, assumed contemporary *pentimenti* by the artist . . .'

Pentimenti. That was it. It sounded like regret. A change of mind. The artist having a second go.

In fact, it had been Philip in a fury, about six months after the painting arrived.

'You know that ghastly thing by the Australian that we haven't worked out where to hang?'

'The *Britannia*?'

'Yes.'

'I rather like it.'

'I can't stand the bloody thing. Did you see, he has no understanding of wind? All the sails on the little craft go *that* way, see? So the wind must be coming in hard from the other side or it makes no sense. But the pennants on *Britannia* are drooping as if there's no wind at all. I don't know how you bear it.'

'I'm not a sailor. Or an artist. But you're both. Why don't you change them, if they bother you so much?'

'I think I just might.'

And so he had. A happy afternoon spent at his study desk, with oil paints spread around him and brushes in a variety of pots. He had worked on the pennants until he was happy with them at last. She noticed little difference, but she *had* picked up that while he was at it, he had also added three tiny splodges of white on the deck that some-how, from a distance, very cleverly looked as if they were someone waving.

'Is that me?'

'Of course it's you. Who else would it be?'

'How lovely.'

His face had softened entirely. 'You know, sometimes I go off fishing for the day, or whatever it is, and you're waiting for me on deck when I get back, with your sunglasses on and your camera out, waving frantically.'

'Hardly frantically.'

'You are. You look so pleased to see me then. I rather look forward to that sight of your arm windmilling at me.'

And she had dipped her head to meet his, which was still smeared with blue and white, and the kiss had been full of recent happy memories on tour.

She always thought of that moment, and the other moments it brought back, whenever she saw the 'ghastly little painting', with its little added flecks, which she would know at a hundred paces anywhere.

It didn't belong in Portsmouth – it belonged outside her bedroom, where she had arranged for it to be hung that day over fifty years ago. No doubt Philip would pass by and say, 'I never did understand what you see in that thing,' as he so often had in the years before it disappeared. He had forgotten, but he had put it there.

She saw herself. And the image of her sun-bronzed husband heading for her across the water, beaming. These were the memories that made the rest of it possible. What could be more precious than that?

Acknowledgements

Thank you, once again, to Queen Elizabeth II for remaining a constant source of inspiration, both literary and otherwise. And to the late Duke of Edinburgh for providing the Queen with a lifetime of support and encouragement, and these books with a favourite character.

Charlie Campbell continues to be the best agent in the business. I'm eternally grateful to Grainne Fox and the team at Fletcher & Company, Nicki Kennedy, Sam Edenborough and the team at ILA. I'm extremely lucky to have Ben Willis in the UK and David Highfill in the US as my editors. Their teams at Zaffre Books, William Morrow and HarperCollins have worked tirelessly to perfect and promote the series in the most challenging of times, so huge thanks to everyone who has pulled out all the stops.

For their generous friendship and help, thanks to Alice Young, Lucy Van Hove, Annie Maw, Michael Hallowes, Rupert Featherstone, Fran Lana, Oyinda Bamgbose, Lili Danniell, Abimbola Fashola, and those who prefer to remain anonymous. Any mistakes or deliberate deviations from fact in this story are entirely my own.

Thanks to the girls: the Place, the Sisterhood, the Masterminds and the Book Club, who are about so much more than reading good books together.

Thank you to my parents for a lifetime of stories, and to Emily, Sophie, Freddie and Tom, who still aren't really sure which royal family member is which, but make our family my favourite place to be. And to Alex, my strength and stay, for everything.

If you enjoyed *A Three Dog Problem*,
why not join the
S. J. BENNETT READERS' CLUB?

When you sign up you'll receive an exclusive short story
featuring the Queen, THE MYSTERY OF THE FABERGÉ
EGG – plus Royal Correspondence about the series and
access to exclusive material. To join, simply visit
bit.ly/SJBennett

Keep reading for a letter from the author . . .

Hello!

Thank you for picking up *A Three Dog Problem*.

I hope you have had the opportunity to read *The Windsor Knot* – the first account of the Queen's adventures as a detective in this series, though by no means her first outing as a secret sleuth, as later books will reveal. If you haven't, don't worry; I'd like to think you have a treat in store.

As I set out to write the series, my first thought was the wonderful array of settings for each book. Having described Her Majesty's life at Windsor Castle, my next stop was Buckingham Palace, surely? And so *A Three Dog Problem* was born. The title comes from physics and from Sir Arthur Conan Doyle. As you may know, the 'three-body problem' is a feature of classical mechanics. I'm joking – I had no idea, did you? But anyway, it is. More to the point, whenever Sherlock Holmes has a very difficult case to solve, he has to smoke three pipes to do it and it becomes a 'three pipe problem'. I loved this idea. And when the Queen has an exceptionally difficult case to consider, she needs to take three dogs for a walk in Buckingham Palace garden, hence 'a three dog problem'. In this case they are two dorgis and a corgi, because I'm afraid to say the Queen was down to her last corgi in the autumn of 2016, when the book is set.

What happened that autumn? These books set their mysteries among the real-life meetings and musings of a busy monarch. Surely, after her 90th birthday celebrations, I thought, she had a bit of quiet time? But no. It was the season of the fallout from the Brexit referendum, the

US presidential elections, and the launch of a major programme to stop the Palace from falling apart. Would the Queen and Rozie have time to solve a couple of murders in her own London home? Reader, you will have to dip into these pages to find out if they did.

If you would like to know more about the real-life inspirations for this book, along with snippets from my research about the Royal Family, then do visit bit.ly/SJBennett where you can sign up to receive Royal Correspondence about the series. It only takes a few moments to sign up, there are no catches or costs.

Bonnier Books UK will keep your data private and confidential, and it will never be passed on to a third party. We won't spam you with loads of emails, just get in touch now and again with news about my books, and you can unsubscribe any time you want.

And if you would like to get involved in a wider conversation about my books, please review *A Three Dog Problem* on Amazon, on Goodreads, on any other e-store, on your own blog and social media accounts, or talk about it with friends, family or reader groups!

Thank you again for reading this book, and I hope you enjoy the other books to come.

With best wishes,

S. J. Bennett

*Keep reading for an exclusive extract from the next
mystery in the Her Majesty The Queen
Investigates series . . .*

Murder Most Royal

Coming November 2022

Prologue

DECEMBER 2016

The girl on the beach emerged into the light and stared out across the mudflats at the horizon. She had been checking the hides at the end of the path to the wildlife reserve at Snettisham, to see how they had weathered the night's heavy storm. By day, they were home to birdwatchers who came from miles around to observe the geese and gulls and waders. By night, the huts were an occasional refuge from the cold sea breeze for beers and . . . more intimate activities. The last big storm surge had smashed up some of the hides and carried them into the lagoons beyond. This time, she mused, the little piggies at the Royal Society for the Protection of Birds had built their home out of wood, not straw. The wind had taken the door off the furthest structure and piled the inside with shingle, but that was all.

Back outside, she studied the skyline. One of the things she loved about this place was that here, at the edge of East Anglia, on the eastern-most coast of the United Kingdom, the coast stubbornly faced due west. It looked out onto the Wash, which formed a rectangular bite out of the coastline between Norfolk and Lincolnshire, where various rivers ran into the North Sea. No pale pink sunrise here. Instead, the sun had risen above the lagoons at her back. Ahead, a bank of cloud sat low and heavy, but the watery light gave the vast grey sky a pale gold glow that was mirrored in the mudflats, so that it was hard to tell where the earth ended and the air began.

Not far from the lagoons, a little further along the shore to her left, lay the marshy fringes of the Sandringham estate. Normally the Queen was there by now, with Christmas so close, but Ivy hadn't heard of her arrival yet, which was strange. The Queen, like the sunrise and the tides, was generally a reliable way of marking time.

She glanced upwards, where a trailing skein of pink-footed geese flew in arrowhead formation, home from the sea. Higher still, and closer, a hen harrier circled in the air. There was a brutal, brooding quality to Snettisham Beach. The concrete pathway at her feet, and the skeletal wooden structures jutting out into the mudflats beyond the shingle, were relics of her great-grandfather's war. Shingle mining for airbase runways had created the lagoons, where ducks and geese and waders now gathered in their thousands, filling the air with their hoots and honks and quacks. The gulls had deserted the land for decades, her father said, after the constant bombardment of artillery practice out to sea. Their return was a triumph of nature. And goodness knew, Nature needed Her little triumphs. She was up against so much.

Most of the birds themselves were out of sight, but they'd been busy. The vast mudflats ahead were the scene of a recent massacre, pitted with thousands upon thousands of footprints of all sizes, where goldeneyes and sandpipers had landed once the tide receded to feast on the creatures who lived in the sand. Suddenly, a black bundle of fur caught the girl's eye as it raced from right to left across the mud. She recognised it: a collie-cocker cross from a litter in the village last year who belonged to someone she didn't consider a friend. With no sign of its owner, the puppy sped towards the nearest wooden structure, its attention caught by something bobbing in the sky-coloured seawater that eddied around the nearest rotten post.

The storm had littered the area with all sorts of detritus, natural and man-made. Dead fish were dumped with plastic bottles and dense, bright tangles of fraying fishing nets. She thought of jellyfish. They washed up here too. The stupid young dog could easily try to eat one and get stung and poisoned in the process.

'Hey!' she shouted. The puppy ignored her. 'Come here!'

She began to run. Arms pumping, she hurtled across the scrubby band of lichen and samphire that led down to the shingle. Now she was on the mudflats too, the subterranean water seeping into each footprint left by her Doc Martens in the sand.

'Stop that, you idiot!'

The puppy was worrying at an amorphous, soggy shape. He turned to look at her just as she grabbed at his collar. She yanked him away.

The floating object was a plastic bag: an old supermarket one, stretched and torn, its handles knotted, with two pale tentacles poking through. Grabbing a stick that floated nearby, she used the tip to lift it out of the puppy's reach and looked nervously inside. Not a jellyfish, no: some other sea creature, pale and bloated, wrapped in seaweed. She intended to take the bag back with her for disposal later, but as she walked back towards the beach, the puppy straining against his collar at her feet, the contents slithered through a rip and plopped onto the damp, dark sand.

The girl assumed at first that it was a mutant, pale-coloured starfish, but on closer inspection, moving the seaweed aside with her stick, she realised it was something different. She marvelled for a moment at how almost-human it looked, with those tentacles like fingers at one end. Then she saw a glint of gold. Somehow one of the tentacles had got caught up in something metal, round and shiny. She peered closer and counted the baggy, waxy 'tentacles': one, two, three, four, five. The golden glint came from a ring on the little finger. The 'tentacles' had peeling human fingernails.

She dropped the broken bag and screamed fit to fill the sky.

Chapter One

The Queen felt absolutely dreadful in body and spirit. She regarded Sir Simon Holcroft's retreating back with a mixture of regret and hopeless fury, then retrieved a fresh handkerchief from the open handbag beside her study desk to wipe her streaming nose.

The doctor is adamant . . . A train journey is out of the question . . . The Duke should not be travelling at all . . .

If her headache had not been pounding quite so forcefully, she would have found the right words to persuade her Private Secretary of the simple fact that one always took the train. The journey from London to King's Lynn had been booked for months. The station master and his team would be expecting her in four and a half hours, and would have polished every bit of brass, swept every square inch of platform and no doubt had their uniforms dry cleaned to look their best for the occasion. One didn't throw all one's plans in the air over a sniffle. If no bones were broken, if no close family had recently died, one soldiered on.

But her headache *had* pounded. Her little speech had been marred by a severe bout of coughing. Philip had not been there to back her up because he was tucked up in bed, as he had been all yesterday. He had no doubt caught the infernal bug from one of the great-grandchildren at the pre-Christmas party they had recently thrown at Buckingham Palace for the wider family. 'Little petri dishes', he called them. It wasn't their fault, of course, but they inevitably caught everything going at nursery school and prep school, and passed it around like pudgy-cheeked biological weapons. Which young family should she blame? They had all seemed perfectly healthy at the time.

She picked up the telephone on her study desk and asked the switchboard to put her through to the Duke.

He was awake, but groggy.

'What? Speak up, woman! You sound as though you're at the bottom of a lake.'

'I *said* . . .' – she paused to blow her nose – 'that Simon says we must fly to Sandringham tomorrow instead of taking the train today.' She left out the bit where her Private Secretary had suggested Philip should remain at the Palace full stop.

'In the helicopter?' he barked.

'We can hardly use a 747.' Her head hurt and she was feeling tetchy.

'In the navy we were banned . . .' *wheeze* '. . . from flying with a cold. Bloody dangerous.'

'You won't be piloting the flight.'

'If it bursts my eardrums you can personally blame Simon from me. Bloody fool. Doesn't know what he's talking about.'

The Queen refrained from pointing out that Sir Simon was an ex-naval helicopter pilot. The GP who had advised him was renowned for his sound medical opinion. He had his reasons for counselling in favour of a quick journey by air instead of a long one by rail. Philip was ninety-five – hard to believe, but true. He shouldn't really be out of bed at all, with his raging temperature. Oh, what a year this had been, and what a fitting end to it. Despite her delightful birthday celebrations in the spring, she would be glad to see the back of 2016.

'The decision is made, I'm afraid. We'll fly tomorrow.'

She pretended she didn't hear Philip's wheezy in-breath before what would no doubt be a catalogue of complaints, and put the phone down. Christmas was fast approaching and she just wanted to be quietly tucked up in the familiar rural comfort of Sandringham, and to be able to focus on her paperwork without it swimming in front of her eyes.

For the last three months the Queen had played host to presidents and politicians. She had been a greeter of ambassadors, a pinner-on of medals, a patron of charities, mostly at Buckingham Palace, the place she thought of as the gilded office block on the roundabout. Now Sandringham drew her with its wide-open spaces and enfolding pines, its sea breezes, vast English skies and freewheeling birds. She had been dreaming of it for days.

The helicopter whisked the royal couple, blankets on their knees, past Cambridge, past the magnificent medieval towers of Ely Cathedral, the 'ship of the fens', and on, north-eastwards towards King's Lynn. Here at last was Norfolk, where farmland was patched with pine woods, with paddocks and flint cottages. Below them, briefly, was the shell-pink Regency villa at Abbotsgate, where a herd of deer ambled slowly across the lawn. Next came the stubbly, expansive fields of the Muncaster Estate, whose furthest reaches lay a mile or two from one of the Sandringham farms, and then at last the fields, dykes and villages of Sandringham itself.

She spotted a glint of seawater in the distant Wash and two minutes later Sandringham House appeared behind a ridge of pines, with its lakes and walled garden, and its sweeping lawn, amply big enough for the helicopter to land.

Sandringham *was* Christmas. Her father had spent it here, and his father before him, and his father before *him*. When the children were small it had been easier to go to Windsor for a while, but her own childhood Christmases were Norfolk ones.

The house was a Victorian architect's red-brick, beturreted idea of what a Jacobean house should be, and people who cared a lot about architecture were generally appalled by it, but the Queen didn't care. Over the years, the family had enlarged the surrounding estate to twenty thousand acres. She was a natural countrywoman and here she and Philip could quietly be farmers. Not the kind who mended fences in the lashing rain and were out lambing at dawn, true, but nevertheless the kind who cared about the land. Together, they looked after and loved it because it was a small part of the planet that was *theirs*. Here, in a corner of North Norfolk, they could actively participate in making the world a better place: for wildlife, for the consumers of their crops, for the people who worked the land, for the future.

It was a quiet legacy – one they didn't talk about in public (Charles's experience on that front explained why) – but one they cared about very much.

At the door, the housekeeper, Mrs Maddox, and her team were waiting to welcome them back. The interior smelled of woodsmoke from the fire that popped and crackled in the saloon, where the family would later gather for many of their activities together. Philip took himself straight off to bed, but the Queen had just enough appetite to do justice to a couple of freshly-made mince pies and a pot of Darjeeling in the light and airy drawing room, whose large bay windows over-looked the lawn. In one of the bays, a Christmas tree from the estate was already in place, its graceful branches partly decorated on a red and gold theme and ready to be completed when the rest of the family arrived tomorrow. Normally, she chose the tree herself, but this year there hadn't been time. A small price to pay for a cosy afternoon indoors, which she very much needed at the moment.

She had just finished talking to Mrs Maddox about the next few days' arrangements, when Rozie Oshodi, her effi-cient Assistant Private Secretary, appeared at the drawing-room door.

As Rozie curtsied, the Queen noticed she held a closed lap-top under her arm. 'Your Majesty, do you have a moment?'

'Is there a problem?'

'Not exactly, but there's something you ought to know about.'

'Oh dear.'

Rozie nodded. 'I'm afraid there's been a discovery.'

'Oh?'

'A hand was found yesterday morning, ma'am, washed up on Snettisham Beach.'

The Queen was startled. 'A human hand?'

'Yes, ma'am. It was washed up by a storm, wrapped in a plastic bag.'

'My goodness. No sense of where it came from?'

'Ocado, ma'am, since you ask. They deliver food from Waitrose.'

'I meant the hand.'

Rozie shook her head. 'Not yet. The police hope to identify the victim soon. One of the fingers was wearing a large gold ring, which may help.'

'So, a *woman's* hand?'

Rozie shook her head. 'A man's. It's a signet ring.'

'May I see?' the Queen asked. Terrible though the news was, she reflected with relief that the body part had been found on a reserve used by the RSPB – although strictly speaking the land between low and high tide belonged to the Crown Estate. This was not, to put it bluntly, her problem, except in the most technical sense. And just before Christmas, after a devil of a year, nor did she want it to be.

A footman removed the tea things and Rozie positioned the laptop on the table and opened it up. The screen lit up to reveal four images, received a few hours ago from the police. The Queen put on her bifocals and examined the grisly photographs. They had been taken against a white background in a brightly-lit forensic laboratory and showed what was unmistakably a male left hand and wrist with a pattern of fair hairs below the knuckles, the skin deadly white, bloated and wrinkled, but intact, except for a gaping slash across the palm. It looked, absolutely, like a gruesome theatre prop, or a model for a practical joke.

The Queen peered closely at the final image showing the little finger in closeup. Set tight into the ghostly flesh was the ring Rozie had mentioned: large for its type, with a reddish-black oval stone set in gold.

'They're working on the identification now, ma'am,' Rozie explained. 'It shouldn't take longer than a few days, despite the Christmas holiday. They think it may belong to a drug dealer. Two large holdalls containing drugs were found washed up on the beach as well. There's a theory the victim may have been tortured and the hand cut off as some sort of message, or for ransom. It was done with some violence, but there's no proof the owner is actually dead. They're casting the net widely. They –'

'I can save them the trouble,' the Queen said, looking up.

Rozie frowned. 'Ma'am?'

'They can draw in the net. This is the hand of Edward St Cyr.'

Rozie looked astonished. 'You *know* him? From this?'

In answer, the Queen pointed. 'Do you see that flat-topped middle finger? He cut off the tip doing some carpentry when he was a teenager. But it's the signet ring, of course . . . Bloodstone. Very large, as you say, and distinctive.' She peered at it again. It was a garish thing. She had never liked it. All the men in the St Cyr family wore one like it, but none of the others had lost the tip of their middle finger. Edward – Ned, as he was known – must have been about sixteen when he did it, just over half a century ago. She did a quick calculation. He had reached his three score years and ten, but nowadays one might expect to live another decade or two, at least. 'Poor Ned.'

'I take it he wasn't a local drug baron, ma'am,' Rozie ventured.

'No,' the Queen agreed. 'He was the grandson of a local *actual* baron. Not that that means he was a stranger to drugs of course. Quite the reverse, if anything – but latterly, Ned was very anti-drugs, I believe. Or *is*,' she corrected herself. It was troubling, this idea, as Rozie said, that he might not be dead – but he probably was, surely? And God knew what state he must be in if he wasn't. 'I hope the police get to the bottom of it very soon.'

'This will certainly speed them up.'

The Queen's blue eyes met Rozie's brown ones. 'We needn't say exactly who recognised the ring.'

'Absolutely, ma'am.' Rozie knew the drill by now: the Queen, categorically, did not solve, or even help solve crimes. She was merely an interested observer.

Rozie closed up the laptop and left the Boss in peace.